Gifted

Walter Strychowskyj

Copyright © 2025 by Walter Strychowskyj

All rights reserved. No part of this publication may be reproduced, distributed, or transmitted in any form or by any means, including photocopying, recording, or other electronic or mechanical methods, without the prior written permission of the publisher, except in the case of brief quotations embodied in critical reviews and certain other non-commercial uses permitted by copyright law.

This Certificate of Registration is issued pursuant to sections 49 and 53 of the Copyright Act. The copyright in the work was registered on the date of registration and as detailed herein.

Copyright Certificate of Registration Number: 1234365

Published by Book Writing Pioneer

Cover design by Book Writing Pioneer

ISBN: *XXX-X-XXXXXX-XX-X*

Table of Contents

About The Author

Walter Strychowskyj graduated from McMaster University with a degree in physical education. He with his wife bought several preconstruction condos for future rental income. They also bought several old condos to renovate and sell. During this time Walter was a cab driver until he retired. Walter's hobbies are reading novels. During the COVID lockdown, Walter had the opportunity to write his first novel.

Walter lives with his wife in Hamilton, Ontario, Canada.

Page Left Blank Intentionally

Chapter 1

Maria Kozak asked Danelo. "Are you ready? We have to be at the airport in an hour?" She, along with her parents, John Donna, and her childhood sweetheart, Danelo Klyn, was leaving their home. They lived in a small Ukrainian village in the Carpathian Mountains but now they were moving to New York City. The village mainly survived by farming, hunting, and fishing. Some of the villagers made pottery and painted pictures to sell to tourists. Meanwhile, the restaurants and pastry shops were highly sought after by the visitors. In the winter, the village would receive a lot of business from a nearby ski resort. The English language was taught in schools. Most of the villagers were fluent in speaking English because most of the tourists spoke English.

Cossack dancing was taught in schools. Many of the children joined dance ensembles from Lyviv to perform in concert halls throughout Europe. Maria's father was one of the many dance instructors in the village who taught children how to dance. The village had its own concert hall for tourists.

Maria's family loaded their luggage in a taxi and left for the city of Kalush. There, a bus would take them to the airport in the city of Lviv.

*   *   *

Maria's older brother, Ivan, and his wife, Lydia, lived in New York City. However, their son, Peter, stayed behind as he didn't want to live in New York. Michael Mills, a tourist, visited Ivan and Lydia's restaurant in the village. He owned a large restaurant corporation. Michael was so impressed with the food and service that he received that he offered them the job of opening and managing one of his finest restaurants in New York City. Michael provided them with a nice apartment located a block away from the restaurant that they would open and manage. The restaurant was located on Spencer's Way. Michael decided to call the restaurant Spencers Mill. It had a large banquet hall to hold 600 people to rent. The hall had a retractable wall to divide it into two smaller halls. Downstairs was a small hall that held 50 people to rent for meetings. Behind the restaurant was a wedding chapel where couples could get married and have their ceremony at the restaurant.

The restaurant was designed in a traditional style. The back wall had windows so customers could look out and see the forest. There were 20 round solid oak tables. Each table had six solid oak chairs. On one side of the restaurant stood a new hotel called Spencers. On the other side was a parquet - trees, flowers, and herbs beautifully landscaped it. It was a sanctuary for birds and butterflies. A driveway on the right side of the parquet leads to a locked gate with a sign that reads **"KEEP OUT, PRIVATE PROPERTY."** Beyond the street lies a forest and a ravine offering numerous hiking trails. In the forest where the private property stood was a small house hidden amongst the trees. A fence was built around the house to keep the hikers away. No one seemed to know who owned the house. Occasionally, a car would drive up to the gate and be allowed to enter. There was a lamp pole in front of the house.

Over the years, Spencers Mill became the most popular restaurant in the upscale community. Ivan and Lydia were able to move out of the apartment and move into their own beautiful house. It was a 2200 ft^2 two-story house with both floors and a basement having 9 ft ceilings, located on the street next to the parquet beside Spencers Mill. On the ground floor, there was a dining room on the left side of the front entrance. The right side had a garage, coat closet, and powder room. Behind the powder room was a den, where a door led to the backyard. On the left side, behind the dining room, was a huge kitchen and a huge family room. There was no wall between the huge kitchen and family room, just two pillars on each side of the wall. The upstairs area featured three bedrooms and a laundry room. The master bedroom boasted a private ensuite with both a shower and a tub. The backyard faced the forest with hiking trails that had a ravine. There was a good-sized storage shed and a large vegetable and flower garden.

Spencers Way ended in a court. There were only five identical homes in the court, two on one side where Ivan and Lydia lived and three on the other side. At the end of the court, there was a dense forest. A 200-foot-long tunnel road was cut into the forest, which led to a large open field where soccer and football were played. Parents would bring their chairs to watch their children play. There was room for 20 cars to park.

The apartment rent was still being paid because Maria and her family needed a place to live. Ivan and Lydia wanted them to come because they were family and naturopath doctors. Ivan and Lydia were not happy with the medical care that they were getting from their family doctor.

Maria was pregnant and wanted Danelo to come with her to New York. He had two older brothers, Pavlo and Gregory. They worked for the Russian KGB. Marie knew that they were nothing more than mafia-paid assassins. She gave Danelo a choice: come with her to New York and start a family or stay and join his brothers. Maria's mother taught her and Danelo to become naturopath doctors.

Ivan and Lydia met Maria's family at the airport. After a hugging session, Ivan and Lydia drove them to their new home. Stan Smith was the president of the New York School of Naturopath. He came from the same Ukrainian village as Maria's family. Since they were naturopaths already, Stan arranged for them to take the exam for certification. Maria's family was not required to enrol in the school. Everyone passed the exam with honours to become certified.

An empty storefront in a strip Plaza located across the street from Spencers Mill became the Kozak Naturopath Clinic. It didn't take long for the clinic to get busy with regular clients. Several of them became good friends with Marie and her parents.

Judy Grace was a judge, and her sisters Joan Grace and Christine Kelly were lawyers. Judy and Joan were both standing 5'

8" tall, weighed 125 pounds each, and often dressed similarly. Judy sported black wavy hair, while Joan's was brown and wavy. They both maintained their figures through exercise and diet. Christine, the blonde of the trio, stood tall at 6 ft and weighed 150 pounds. Like her sisters, she prioritized exercise and a healthy diet. Don Jordan, an FBI agent, matched Christine's height at 6 feet but was slender at 160 pounds. Despite Maria's desire for him to gain 20 pounds, Don did not exercise but watched his diet. Lastly, Henry Wilson, an elderly and frail man, stood at 5'8" and weighed 139 pounds. Despite his physical condition, Henry owned a multibillion-dollar conglomerate.

Joan Grace was divorced and lived with her infant daughter, Elizabeth, in a luxury townhouse complex nearby. Christine Kelly, her husband, and their infant son, Jeffrey, lived in the same townhouse complex as Joan. Judy lived in a condo apartment building located in the same townhouse complex. Her husband died of a heart attack last year. She had two sons in the military stationed somewhere overseas. She hardly ever knew their locations. Maria and her parents often had lunch with them at the Spencers Mill.

Don Jordan suffered severe pain in his right shoulder. The medication his doctor prescribed was costly and provided temporary relief. Marie was able to relieve his pain completely in three weeks with herbal teas and massages.

Henry Wilson had a weak heart and severe arthritis in his wrists. His doctor told him that there was nothing that they could do for him. Henry was a 60-year-old frail man. The medication his doctor prescribed made him feel like a zombie. Maria was able to relieve all the symptoms from the medication that Henry was taking. A good, healthy diet and herbal remedies made Henry feel alive again.

Michael Mills was also a client of Maria's. He was 85 years old and was happy that Ivan and Maria brought Maria's family to live in New York. He had enough of his doctor's prescribed medication and went to see Maria. She slowly got him off his medication with herbal teas. Maria gave him a diet plan to follow, and her father taught him how to meditate and exercise. As a result, Michael was sleeping much better and felt a lot more energetic. He decided to sell the Spencers Mill to Lydia and Ivan. They happily took out a mortgage to purchase it. There was no mortgage on their house. The bank used it for collateral.

Chapter 2

Marie gave birth to a son weighing 5 ½ pounds. She named him Tommy and took after his mother. Maria is 5'6" and petite. She weighed 115 pounds and was quite strong for her size. Danelo is 6'2" wide-framed and weighs 230 pounds of solid muscle.

Everyone was happy being a naturopath except Danelo; he was bored. Danelo was looking for action and to make big money. Jason, a client, noticed how disinterested Danelo was. He came to the clinic because he wanted to break his heroin addiction. He was also getting frail from not eating properly. Jason asked Danelo if he would be interested in making easy money distributing drugs using the naturopathic clinic as a front. Danelo shook his head," Jason, I would love to do it, but my family would not allow it. They are as honest as you can get."

"That's too bad; however, if you're still interested in the drug trade, let me know. I can introduce you to some people who could use you."

Danelo smiled and said," Jason, give me a phone number that I can call you?" Jason gave Danelo his number." I can tell by the look on your face that I will be hearing from you soon." said Jason.

Danelo discussed his plan to join Jason with Marie and his parents. He knew that they would want no part of the drug trade. That night, Danelo called Jason as he was expecting a call from him. Jason had an apartment ready for Danelo to rent. He was ready to learn the drug trade from Jason.

Jason had his assigned territory to distribute drugs. He bought drugs from his distributor. Then, he hired street kids to sell drugs to high schools and colleges. The street kids received 10% of the proceeds, whilst Jason got 90%. He hired goons to make sure that the street kids didn't steal from him. Jason mainly bought heroin and cocaine because they were the most profitable. He himself got hooked on heroin, which is why he went to the Kozak Naturopath Clinic. Jason was hoping to break his heroin addiction because he was getting low on cash flow to buy drugs from his distributor.

When Jason saw how Danelo was disinterested in the clinic, he offered him an opportunity to join him. A partner with cash flow would allow Jason to continue to buy drugs from his distributor. He was willing to share his profits as long as he had enough money to support his heroin addiction.

Danelo learned how easy it was to make money. He also knew that the big money was in being a distributor. He asked Jason, "What does it take to become a distributor?"

Jason reluctantly answered, "A distributor has to have tons of money, a source to buy tons of drugs for distribution, a territory to distribute the drugs, and loyal employees such as you and me to protect his territory."

Danelo started to get excited, "If a distributor wants to expand his business, what does he have to do?"

Jason said, "To do that, he must take over another distributor's territory. Let's say that the name of the distributor whose territory you want to take over is John. He and his family must be killed off. If John's drug source is not the same as yours, you must either kill the drug source or try to negotiate a business deal with him. If you refuse to negotiate, the drug source will try to kill you, and it's that simple."

Danelo really got excited, "It's that simple, thanks for telling me. Jason, if you want to become an employee of mine when I become a distributor, you must break your heroin addiction. Go see Maria at the clinic and do exactly what she tells you."

The next day, Danelo called his older brothers, Pavlo and Gregory, to explain to them his plan. They both agreed to come to New York to join him. He then asked Jason the name of his distributor, where he lived, whether he had a family, and if he had to use his source to buy drugs.

Jason said, "My distributor's name is Charles. He owns the laundry mat in the Plaza across from the Spencers hotel. I don't know where he lives, what his last name is, or if he has a family. I buy drugs from him at his laundry mat just like the other buyers do. You do have to buy drugs from Charles's source. They have enough resources to kill you if you don't deal with them."

Danelo asked, "How many buyers does Charles have?" Jason shrugged his shoulders, "He has about a dozen buyers. I don't know their names, but I have an idea who they are."

Danelo smiled, "Jason, you better kick your heroin addiction. Are you seeing Maria?"

Jason nodded yes. "Good. I have two brothers who live in Russia and have substantial resources. They are coming tomorrow; I want to introduce them to you. I also want you to find a place for them to live. Can you do that?"

Jason smiled, "There are two apartments available in this building on the same floor as your apartment. Your brothers can move in right away."

The next day, Danelo met his brothers at the airport. After a hugging session, he drove them to his apartment. Gregory was the older brother. He was much taller than Pavlo and were both in good physical health. They were trained in the Russian army. Jason prepared chicken, baked potatoes, and Caesar salad for them. Danelo introduced Jason to his brothers. After they finished their meal, Jason left while the three brothers started making plans.

Danelo explained to his brothers that Jason's distributor's name is Charles. "He does business from his laundromat located in the strip Plaza across from the Spencers hotel. We must find out where he lives and if he has family. When Charles is taken out, we are supposed to deal with his source. Jason tells me that they have a lot of resources and would be pissed off if we refuse to do business with them."

Pavlo smiled, "When the time comes, l will deal with his source. In the meantime, let's stake out Charles's laundry mat. We must find out where he lives and if he has any family."

The Klyn brothers found out that Charles lives alone in a luxury townhouse next to the strip Plaza. The time came for Jason to buy drugs from Charles and Pavlo, and his gun accompanied him. Jason had no idea that Pavlo was going to kill Charles. When they arrived at the laundromat, Jason smiled at Charles. Before Charles could ask Jason who was with him, he was shot in the head. Pavlo grabbed the bag of drugs that Jason was to buy and left, walking. Jason ran away as fast as he could.

Danelo took over Charles's laundromat business. He had Jason round up all the other buyers in Charles's territory. They were introduced to Danelo as their new distributor. The police suspected Danelo to be responsible for Charles's death; unfortunately, they had no evidence to arrest him.

Pavlo and Gregory provided the drugs for Danelo to distribute. They were ready to deal with Charles' drug source when the time came. Several days later, a motorcycle gang came to visit Danelo at his laundry mat. There were six of them. The leader wore a horned Viking helmet. He was massive, weighing well over 300 pounds, with tattoos covering his arms. A large, filthy red beard covered his face. He got off his bike and approached Danelo. The other gang members sat on their bikes and pointed guns at Danelo.

The leader, holding a baseball bat, said, "The name is Alvin, and who may you be?"

Danelo answered." My name is Danelo; please state your business."

Alvin shoved the end of his bat under Danelo's chin and shook his head, "Charles was not only a business partner but also a good friend. Killing him to take over his territory makes me very unhappy. To keep me from having your head blown off, you will be paying me double what Charles paid. Do you understand?"

Danelo nodded yes. "Good; your next payment for drugs is in two days. I expect full payment in cash." Alvin then got on his bike, and the gang rode off.

Pavlo and Gregory followed the gang to an old secluded mansion. It was surrounded by trees and weeds, which made it look uninhabitable. The mansion needed a new roof, and the wooden stairs and porch were starting to rot. The windows and doors needed to be replaced. There was a huge, decrepit barn behind the mansion.

The next night, three drones flew over the mansion and dropped several firebombs. The mansion lit up in flames. Pavlo and Gregory were watching the mansion burn. They made sure that anybody who tried to escape would be killed. Everyone in the mansion died in their beds. The police had no way of finding out who was responsible for the fire. However, they suspected that Danelo, the new distributor, was involved.

Chapter 3

Business was very good. The Klyn brothers wanted to expand to another territory. Before anything could be done, Pavlo and Gregory needed legal immigration status. Jason knew a lawyer who could provide that to anyone for a price.

Danelo looked at Gregory and said, "Once you get your legal immigration status, I think it would be a good idea for you to apply to the FBI. With your KGB credentials, you should have no problem getting hired." Gregory thought it was a good idea also. "Make sure you become the best FBI agent you could possibly be. There are opportunities for promotion."

When Gregory received his legal immigration status, he did apply to the FBI. He was hired almost immediately. Gregory thrived to do his best.

When Pavlo received his legal immigration status, Danelo wanted him to continue to be a paid assassin, just like he was in Russia. Danelo would hire Pavlo to kill anyone who stood in his way. Pavlo decided to recruit other assassins who worked for him in Russia. They were trained military snipers. Pavlo found them places to live in New York. The assassins were also provided with jobs in restaurants. This way, Pavlo could take on several contracts at once. As their leader, Pavlo would assign a contract to each assassin. Danelo kept Pavlo very busy.

It didn't take long for Danelo's drug business to flourish. The house next door to Ivan and Lydia's was for sale. Danelo bought it. He hired an interior decorator to furnish the house, which included a baby grand piano. All the rooms in the house were painted. Crown moulding and new baseboards were installed throughout the house. The appliances, washer, and dryer were replaced with top-of-the-line models. Danelo also had a huge basement finished with a furnished two-bedroom apartment. There was also enough room for a full-sized family gym, a sauna, and a whirlpool. The house had a large backyard facing the forest, just like Ivan and Lydia's.

Danelo insisted that Maria and Tommy move in with him. He also wanted Maria's parents to live in the basement. Marie and her parents were not happy, but they agreed to live with Danelo because he sponsored his mother to come to New York to look after Tommy. Maria had to take Tommy to her clinic to look after him during the day. Danelo's mother would sleep in one of the spare bedrooms.

The Kozak Naturopath Clinic was getting very busy. Danelo kept paying rent at the apartment where Maria and her parents lived. He knew that there would be other naturopaths from their village coming soon to help out at the clinic. They would need a place to live.

Maria was glad that Danelo had brought Ola, his mother, over to look after Tommy. Her parents were good friends with her. Marie and Danelo spent little time together. They rarely slept together. Danelo would come home late at night and sleep on the couch in the family room. Danelo and Maria were too busy to spend much time together. Occasionally, they had dinner at Spencers Mill. Maria didn't like what Danelo had become, but she did enjoy his company. He was very handsome and treated Marie with respect.

Ola not only took good care of Tommy but also was a good housekeeper and cook. She adored little Tommy. Ola had dinner ready for Maria and her parents when they got home from the clinic. Danelo came home late at night most of the time. Ola spent all of her free time with Maria's parents.

Chapter 4

Judy, Joan Grace, and Christine Kelly had appointments to see Maria. They wanted to know what she thought about taking statin drugs to reduce cholesterol levels. Their family doctors prescribed them.

Maria said, "In my opinion, statin drugs are a waste of money. Big pharmaceutical companies promote them to increase profits as much as possible. I have read in medical journals that the research that doctors rely on is flawed. Many studies are done in foreign countries. If they produce negative results, they will not be reported. The participants in these studies are usually healthy people in their mid-20s. This ensured that there would be very little, or if any, side effects from the drugs that were given. Big Pharma tells us that if we lower our cholesterol, we could significantly reduce our risk of having a heart attack or stroke. Cholesterol is a very important substance in our body. It helped to heal our daily oxidative damage. About 5% of cholesterol comes from our diet. The rest is produced in the liver while you sleep. If you want more information on statin drugs, I can give you some YouTube videos to watch."

Judy looked confused. "Then why does my doctor insist that I take these drugs?"

Marie answered, "Because doctors are influenced by big Pharma. The government receives billions of dollars in taxes from them. I believe that Big Pharma doesn't care about your health. All they care about is making as much money as possible. Every year, they pay out billions of dollars in out-of-court settlements and still make huge profits. However, some drugs that they develop are beneficial and lifesaving. A 40-minute brisk walk daily and a proper diet is all that is needed."

Joan couldn't believe what Marie had just said," Sounds like our doctors are nothing more than glorified drug dealers for big Pharma.

Maria held up some files and said," I have all your blood test results; none of you have anything to worry about. If you want, you can show your blood tests to your family doctor. Just keep watching your diet, take daily brisk walks, and drink lots of water and tea."

Chapter 5

Gregory did become a very good FBI agent. It didn't take long for him to get promoted. Gregory and Danelo decided to have monthly meetings in the den at Danelo's home. The den had a back door so they could come and go quickly unnoticed. Marie didn't like the idea of having their monthly meetings at the house, but she had no way of stopping them.

Maria's mother had an uneasy feeling and said, "Maria, make sure that you video record every meeting without their knowledge. Hide the video recordings in a safe place. They could be used to save lives in the future."

Maria hired a technician to install a hidden video camera in the den where Danelo and Gregory held their meetings. Every time someone entered the den, the video camera would automatically turn on. When someone left, it automatically turned off. Danelo and Gregory were the only people using the den. Marie was able to turn off the video camera to retrieve the filmed meetings. She downloaded the meetings on memory sticks and kept them in a safety deposit box at a bank that Danelo gave her.

Don Jordan started seeing Marie on a regular basis because of an acquired rash on his stomach and an ulcer. His regular doctor made him feel worse with prescription drugs. He said to Maria, "I know that you and your family are living with Danelo. He is bad news and will cause you lots of trouble. Please move out."

"Don, I have to stay with Danelo; there's no place for me to go. Danelo's mother is taking care of Tommy while I'm at the clinic. Danelo is very busy; I hardly ever see him."

Don shook his head, "Maria, as soon as you smell trouble when you are with Danelo, give me a call. You have my number."

Maria saw Danelo enough times to become pregnant again. Danelo was not happy. Marie knew that he was up to something that would cause trouble. Maria called Don to let him know that she was pregnant and that Danelo was planning to do something.

When Marie and her parents came home from the clinic, there was no dinner waiting for them. Tommy and Ola were not home. Danelo left a note on the kitchen table. It said, "Maria, I have decided to take Tommy with me. I will raise him myself with my mother's help. He will learn my business and eventually take it over. The child you are caring for now will be yours to raise on your own, without any influence from me. I'll make sure when Gregory and I have monthly meetings, you and your parents will not be home. I transferred the deed to our house to your name only. There'll be no more nights together; I'll be out of your life for good. Please don't try to find me."

Maria was shocked. She couldn't stop crying. Her mother gave her a sedative to calm her down. Maria was heartbroken, knowing that she would never see Tommy again. After Maria recovered from her shock, she called Don Jordan. She tearfully told him what Danelo did. Don told Maria that there was nothing that he could do.

Maria thanked Don. She decided not to tell him about the monthly meetings between Danelo and Gregory that were filmed without their knowledge at their house. Maria was afraid that Danelo would cause a lot of trouble. She dealt with knowing that she would never see Tommy again by being very busy at her clinic. She even put in extra hours in the evening.

Eight months later, Maria gave birth to a 9 lbs. 8 oz. baby boy. He definitely took after Danelo. She decided to call her son Wally. Danelo kept his word so far and stayed away.

Chapter 6

Gregory became a very resourceful FBI agent. He was promoted ahead of Don Jordan. Gregory became his boss. This made Don very unhappy. He was better qualified for the promotion than Gregory, but he didn't have the money that Gregory had.

Danelo would have the other distributor's territories staked out to find out their drug source. He and Gregory, at their monthly meetings, would decide which distributor's drug source the FBI would raid. Most of the drugs came in by boat. The FBI knew which boats to raid. Gregory made sure that Danelo's boats would never be raided.

Once a drug source's boat got raided by the FBI, Danelo would hire Pavlo to kill off the family that owned the drug territory. The family territory would belong to Danelo. His drug empire was expanding very quickly. The FBI seemed helpless to stop him. Don Jordan knew that Danelo and Gregory were brothers. It was obvious to him that they worked together. However, Don couldn't do anything to stop them. He had no evidence, and Gregory was his boss. Don also knew that Gregory had several FBI agents under his payroll.

Chapter 7

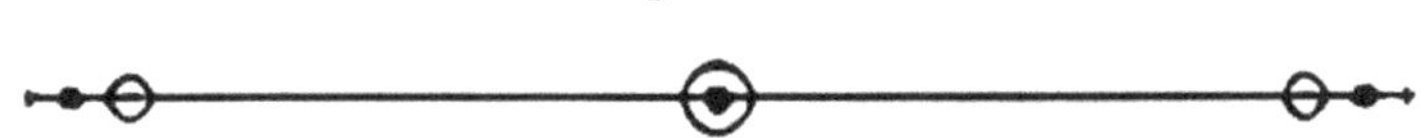

Danelo kept his word. He made no contact with Maria's family. Maria finally accepted the fact that she would probably never see Tommy or Danelo again. She continued with her naturopathic practice and concentrated on raising Wally. She received a lot of support from her parents, Ivan and Lydia.

Wally started to grow quickly and looked more like his father. At school, he was doing much better than the other children. Marie also noticed that his memory was much better than hers. She started to get worried. Maria took Wally downstairs to see her mother.

Wally's grandmother started watching him very closely. She looked for any indications of him being psychic. She said, "Maria, you are right; Wally is gifted just like Yuri." Many children were born with psychic abilities in the Ukrainian village. Yuri was the most gifted. He lived his entire life in the village, doing whatever he could to help the village prosper. Yuri was 110 years old when he died. Most of the psychic children stayed in the village. They used their psychic abilities to help the village prosper, just like Yuri.

Grandmother looked into Wally's eyes and said, "God has given you a gift that was meant to be a blessing, but it can also become a curse. Wally, you're only eight years old, and your abilities have not been fully developed. This may frighten you. Don't worry, Grandfather will teach you how to control your abilities. It is very important that you tell no one of your gift. There are many powerful people who would want to control you for personal gain. Your gift was meant to help people; please never abuse it."

Every morning before school, Grandfather will teach you how to dance and how to meditate. The dance will teach you to become a Cossack warrior so you can defend yourself. Meditation will let you relax and help you control your abilities. It is very important for you to stand in front of a mirror, look at yourself, and repeat the following prayer at least three times a day."

"I love myself, and I believe in myself because I was created by God, who never made anything badly; his creations are wonderful, so I am wonderful; divine perfection is within me. I love life, and I love people; I have the ability to do things well, I am happy, I am grateful, I treat myself with respect, I am successful, and nothing can keep me from obtaining my goals. As a child of God, I believe in myself, and all is well."

Donna said to Maria," As Wally gets older, his eyes will become more like a computer. Everything he sees will be scanned in his memory, just like an unlimited database. He will have the ability to scan other people's memories into his memory and read their minds just by touching them. Wally will have the ability to retrieve any information he wants from his unlimited memory bank."

"Wally, you have the ability to score 100% on your tests and exams in school. Make a few errors deliberately so no one will suspect that you have such a gift."

"Maria, keep Wally busy, have him take singing and piano lessons. Wally should also take yoga lessons. This will help him to meditate. When he gets older, teach him to become a naturopath. If he wants, send him to culinary school. Ivan and Lydia would love to have Wally working as a chef at the Spencers Mill. Most importantly, keep Wally away from Danelo!"

Maria said, "Don't worry, mother. I haven't seen or heard from Danelo in 8 ½ years. He's keeping his promise to stay away."

Over the years Wally enjoyed taking voice and piano lessons. He excelled in both. Wally was told that he could train to be an opera singer or concert pianist. He wasn't interested in having a career singing or playing the piano professionally. However, he did enjoy singing and playing the piano at the end of every month at church. The concerts that he performed raised money for the church.

Maria also wanted Wally to be kept busy, to keep him away from his friends. One of his best friends is Louis. He is a scrawny little guy. Louis was only 5' 6" tall and weighed only 125 pounds. He wore a baseball cap and was always smiling. Louis lived in a small house with his father in a nearby neighbourhood that had a high crime rate. He is a very fast runner. Only Wally could outrun him in a race in the neighbourhood. His father is a hired torch. He is hired to burn down buildings.

Maria didn't like any of Wally's girlfriends either. They used too much profanity and drugs. However, they came from rich, respectable families. Maria didn't care. Maria didn't like any of Wally's friends.

Marie asked Wally, "Why are you still friends with Louis? His father will probably teach him how to burn down buildings. Louis also hangs out with street gangs. Why do you hang out with Clarence and Harvey? They're nothing more than big bullies?"

Wally smiled, "I know, Mother; Louis is okay. He only comes over to play chess. His father taught him how to play. None of his friends want to play chess with him, except me. Playing chess with Louis keeps him out of trouble. Louis will never beat me because I could read his mind and memorize moves from the great chess masters that I studied. I stay away from Clarence and Harvey as much as I can. They are always trying to get me to take drugs. I always refuse and run away. I could beat the crap out of them if I wanted to. However, grandfather taught me never to use violence unless it was absolutely necessary."

Maria was not very happy. She shook her head. "Wally, next time that I see Clarence or Harvey, I'm going to call the police. Make sure Louis takes a bath before he comes over to play chess with you."

Marie also wanted to keep Wally away from Joan, Judy Grace and Christine Kelly. They adored Wally and wanted him to become a lawyer. A lawyer was one of the last things Maria wanted Wally to become.

When Wally turned 16, Maria arranged for him to take the naturopathic certification exam without enrolling in the naturopathic school. Wally became the youngest person ever to get certified. It was easy for Wally because he never forgets. He deliberately made several errors. Wally had no problems obtaining his driver's license.

On weekends, Wally went to culinary school. On his 18th birthday, Wally graduated from culinary school. Wally started to work at the Spencers Mill on weekends and occasionally during the week. He excelled as a chef in the Spencers Mill kitchen. Ivan and Lydia were very disappointed when Wally told them that he didn't want to become a full-time chef.

Marie asked Wally, "If you don't want to become a full-time chef or naturopath, why not become an opera singer or a concert pianist? You still have the opportunity to choose either one."

Wally said, "Mother, I enjoy singing and playing the piano, but I don't want to make a career in either. I will work part-time as a naturopath and chef until I finish college, then I'll decide what I want to do."

Marie was disappointed with Wally's decision. To keep him busy, she let Wally have two regular clients. Henry Wilson, a multibillionaire. He was a 78-year-old frail man with a weak heart. Henry was very fond of Wally. The other client was Don Jordan, the FBI agent. He kept an eye on Wally to make sure that he didn't join his father's drug Empire.

Chapter 8

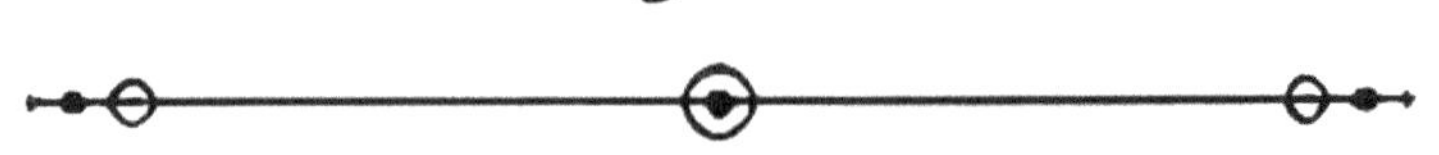

When Wally finished college, Marie asked him what he was planning to do. Wally said to his mother," I applied and got accepted to go to Harvard Law School. I want to become a lawyer."

Maria was shocked; she thought it was one of the worst careers Wally could choose. She shook her head, "We will discuss your decision with your grandmother."

At the end of the day, Marie and Wally went downstairs to see Grandmother. She asked Wally, "Do you say your prayer in front of a mirror at least three times a day? Do you practice the dance and meditations the way grandfather taught you? Do you practice your yoga?" Wally nodded yes. Grandmother was pleased.

Grandmother said to Maria," You don't have to worry. Some lawyers sincerely want to help people. I'm sure Wally will become a very good lawyer."

Maria shook her head and said to Grandmother, "If Wally wants to go to law school, he'll have to find a way to pay for his education. I will not help him, and I forbid you to help him!"

Wally could not afford to go to law school. As a last resort, he went to see Danelo. Wally found out where he lived by reading Don Jordan's mind. Danelo was surprised to see Wally. He gave Wally a big hug. "I am very happy to see you; what brings you here?" Wally took a deep breath and said, "I've been accepted to go to Harvard Law School. Mother doesn't want me to go. She will not help me."

Danelo took a good look at Wally and smiled, "Maria took real good care of you. Tommy, come here and meet your little brother." Wally was 6'2" tall and weighed 220 pounds of solid muscle, just like Danelo. Tommy was 5'8" and weighed 140 pounds. He looked a little malnourished, just like Maria.

"Tommy, your little brother has been accepted to go to Harvard Law School. Mother will not allow him to go. What should I do?"

Tommy took a good look at Wally and said, "He is also your son. You should help him." Danelo gave Wally another big hug," Wally, you are going to Harvard Law School. I promised your mother that I would stay out of her life. Please don't tell her that I helped you. I'll set up a scholarship fund for you to use. Good luck, and make me proud even if I never see again."

Maria wanted to know where Wally got the money to go to Harvard Law School. Wally told her that when he applied to Harvard Law School, he also applied for a scholarship. Marie asked Wally why he didn't tell her about the scholarship. Wally told his mother that he forgot to tell her and found out only today that he had received it. Maria told Wally not to forget that she was still his mother and loved him. She also reminded him not to abuse his gift.

Chapter 9

Wally left home for Harvard Law School in a brand-new BMW that Danelo bought for him. Wally told his mother that the BMW was a rental paid for by the scholarship fund. When Wally arrived, someone was waiting for him to escort him to his room at student housing. Wally's roommate was already settled and introduced himself. He said," I am Jeffrey Kelly; you are lucky to have me as your roommate."

Jeffrey was Wally's height but was much heavier and wider. He was built like an offensive lineman. If Jeffery wanted to, he could have played in the NFL. Wally shook his hand. He thought that Jeffrey was an arrogant, pompous fool. Jeffrey thought that he was the smartest student in all of Harvard. He will be shocked when Wally proves him wrong. Wally said, "I am Wally Kozak. Time will tell if it's lucky to have you as a roommate."

During classes, Jeffrey was always the first one to raise his hand to answer questions. When writing tests or exams, Wally always scored the highest in the class, followed by Jeffrey. This made Jeffrey very unhappy. When Wally and Jeffrey returned to their room after an exam, Jeffrey started to scream profanities at Wally. He then threw a punch at Wally's face. He missed and put a hole in the wall. Jeffrey was screaming in pain.

Poor Jeffrey had no way of knowing that Wally had access to his notes just by reading his mind. All he had to do was touch Jeffery and all the teachers in his classes. Wally left for the campus coffee shop. He figured an hour would be long enough for Jeffrey to calm down. If Wally wanted to, he could have broken every bone in Jeffrey's body, courtesy of his grandfather's training. Wally still practised the dance and meditations that his grandfather taught him. Every day, at least three times a day, Wally would look in the mirror and recite the prayer his grandmother taught him. He also did yoga every day and lifted weights three times a week at the school's gym.

Wally went back to his room. He found Jeffrey sitting in a chair, sulking. Wally looked at him and said, "If you have that hole in the wall repaired during the weekend, I will not report you and forget what happened today." Wally then picked up some books and headed for the library. Jeffrey said nothing as he watched Wally leave.

At the end of the first semester of the first year, Wally had the highest score in class, followed by Jeffrey. In his mind, Jeffrey believed that he was the top student. He was convinced that Wally was cheating but couldn't prove it. Wally drove home to spend Christmas with his mother and grandparents.

At the end of the second semester, Wally again had the highest score in class, followed by Jeffery. In his mind, Jeffery still believed that he was the top student. However, he couldn't prove that Wally was cheating.

Chapter 10

Wally packed his belongings and drove home for the summer. He is ready to help at his mother's clinic during the week. On weekends, he worked as a chef at the Spencers Mill.

Wally's first client was Henry Wilson. Wally went to his examination room to see Henry. He looked at Wally and said, "You have grown a lot since the last time I saw you. I missed you very much. Maria says that you made the Dean's Honour List at the top of your class. I have a job waiting for you when you graduate."

Wally hugged Henry, "If you want to see me graduate, you better get rid of your gold-digging wives." Henry smiled, "I know that these young ladies are after my money. I don't mind giving them money. They know that the marriage will last only about three years. I enjoy their company. They are happy to leave me. The prenuptial agreements I give them are quite generous."

Wally said, "Henry, you may enjoy their company, but your heart doesn't. You will not enjoy their company if you are lying in bed. It's in a nursing home."

Henry smiled at Wally and said, "You and your mother are the reason I'm not in a nursing home. If I stayed with my regular doctor, I would have died long ago. Wally, I have no family and need tax deductions for the IRS. I get a better tax return by paying off my wives than I would if I gave the same amount to charity."

Wally shook his head, "Okay, Henry, just remember that you are a 78-year-old frail man with a weak heart and severe arthritis in both your wrists. I'll see you next week if you're still alive."

Maria sent Wally another client. Wally looked at him and said, "Clarence, is that you?" Clarence Leon and Harvey Katz were neighbourhood bullies when Wally was growing up. Wally thought

Clarence would have overdosed on drugs or spent the rest of his life in prison. Clarence grew up to be a huge black man with large white teeth. When they were young, Clarence and Harvey used to beat up the neighbourhood kids, except Wally. He was too quick and fast to be caught. The training that Wally received from his grandfather gave him the ability to beat up the bullies if he wanted to. Wally's grandfather taught him never to use violence unless it was absolutely necessary.

Wally asked, "Clarence, how come you're not dead or in prison?" Clarence smiled and said, "When I was 15, me and Harvey got arrested for robbing a liquor store. We were given a choice: join the Salvation Army or go to prison. I chose the Salvation Army, and Harvey chose prison. Joining the Salvation Army saved my life. Wally, your mother told me that you are going to Harvard Law School. She also told me that you made the Dean's honour list at the top of the class, congratulations." Clarence then gave Wally a goodbye hug.

Don Jordan was waiting for Wally in the next room. He said, "Wally, if you decide to quit law school, you have a job waiting for you with the FBI. Wally smiled at Don and said, "That's not going to happen; you know that my uncle Gregory, your boss, is dirty. He's been trying to recruit me ever since I finished college."

Don replied, "I know, but big trouble is coming. The Chinese drug triad is coming. They want to take over Danelo's territory. If Danelo gets involved in a drug war with the Chinese, he will be killed."

Wally said to Don, "I don't consider Danelo my father. He left my mother before I was born. I only met him once in my life when I asked for financial help to go to law school. I don't really care what happens to him. How is your ulcer behaving?"

The next day, Wally received a registered letter from Danelo. He wrote, "Dear son, big trouble is brewing. If anything happens to me, call your uncle Pavlo. He will protect you. I set up a bank account for you to use to pay for his services. The enclosed debit card will give you access to $3,000,000 that you will need. I wrote down Pavlo's number on the debit card. I heard that you made the Dean's Honour List at the top of the class. Congratulations, you make me proud. Maria brought you up way better than I could. Good luck, son. I love you."

After Wally read the letter, he put it in the safety deposit box where the memory sticks of Danelo and Gregory's meetings were kept. He also made copies of those meetings in case something happened to them. He had no intention of showing the letter to his mother.

Chapter 11

Danelo and Gregory met at Maria's house for their monthly meeting. Gregory said, "The Lee family just opened their software business in the old warehouse down the street from us. That is just the front for their drug business. My FBI sources tell me that they have way more resources and manpower than we do. We cannot compete with them. We have to negotiate a business deal."

Danelo replied, "They may outgun us, but we have Pavlo. All we have to do is find out who they are and have Pavlo wipe them out before they could get established."

Gregory shook his head in disgust, "Danelo, if that's what you want to do, keep me out of it. I don't want to get involved in any drug wars that we can't win. This meeting is over."

Wally finished helping his mother at her clinic. That night, he had to go over to Spencers Mill to help out in the kitchen. Uncle Ivan was happy to see Wally. He said, "Our regular chef had to leave. His wife had just given birth to a baby boy. We have a large birthday party to cater to."

Wally was ready to help. When the birthday party was over, Uncle Ivan wanted Wally to help him with washing the dishes. Wally smiled at him and said, "It's getting late now; I need to go home and get some sleep. Tomorrow morning, I'm leaving for law school." Uncle Ivan was not happy. "Wally, you are always making excuses for not helping." Wally replied, "I was hired to be a chef, not a dishwasher. Wally ran out before Uncle Ivan could say another word. The next early morning, Wally loaded up his car and drove off to law school.

Chapter 12

Pavlo was sitting in his chair at home, devastated. The Chinese drug triad hired him personally to kill Danelo and his family. He could not refuse them. They had far more resources than Danelo. They didn't need him. The Chinese triad knew that he and Danelo were brothers. They wanted to see if he would take their contract. Pavlo knew that if he refused, Chinese assassins would be hired to kill Danelo and his family, himself included. If he did take on the contract, he would not be killed and would take over Danelo's drug territory. He had a week to complete the contract.

Pavlo had a birthday coming in two days. He made a reservation for a room at the Spencers Mill to celebrate his birthday. He invited Danelo, Gregory, Maria, and a few close friends. Pavlo rented a Rolls-Royce to pick up Danelo and Maria. He was wearing a pair of white gloves while driving.

It was Saturday night. Wally was flown in from law school. He was to sing and play the piano at Pavlo's birthday party. Wally decided to sing songs by Frank Sinatra, Billy Joel, and Tony Bennet. Aunt Lydia prepared potato dumplings, spicy cabbage, bean salad, and prime rib, and for dessert, cheesecake wafers covered in dark chocolate served with coffee or tea. Champagne and liquor flowed freely. Wally received a standing ovation for his performance. Tommy came to Wally to congratulate him on his performance. Everyone had a good time at Pavlo's birthday party. He had no trouble blowing out 58 candles. He didn't want any birthday gifts and asked his guest not to bring any.

When the party was over, Pavlo, Danelo, and Maria got into the Rolls-Royce. Pavlo was wearing white gloves. He did not drive Danelo and Maria home. He drove them into the forest tunnel, the entrance leading to the open field. At night, it was pitch dark. Danelo and Maria were worried. Danelo shouted, "Pavlo, what are you doing!"

Pavlo stopped the Rolls-Royce in the middle of the tunnel. He took out a flashlight and a gun from the glove compartment and got out. Pavlo said with tears in his eyes, "I love you." He then shot Danelo and Marie in the head. Pavlo walked out of the tunnel and hailed a cab to get home.

The next day, the police showed up at the crime scene. They knew that this was a mafia hit. Unfortunately, there was nothing they could do. There were no witnesses to talk to, no fingerprints or other evidence. The rented Rolls-Royce was paid in cash by a young man. He received a phone call. A voice told him to drive the Rolls-Royce to a nearby shopping mall, park it, and leave. There was $500 left in the glove compartment for his payment. No one noticed Pavlo getting into the Rolls-Royce and driving away.

Sunday morning, Pavlo made a phone call, "I just killed Danelo and Maria. I want to hire Tommy, Danelo's son, to kill the rest of the family. If he does, will you let him live?" A voice replied, "If he does do it, his father's drug territory will be his."

Pavlo drove off to see Tommy. He was still in bed. Pavlo slapped him in the face, "Get up, Tommy, you have a job to do. The Chinese Triad hired me to kill Danelo and his family. I have just killed Danelo and Maria. You must kill the rest of his family. That means you have to kill Danelo's mother, Wally, the grandparents, Aunt Lydia and Uncle Ivan. Do this, and the Chinese triad will let you live and take over Danelo's territory; if you refuse, you die." Tommy got dressed and grabbed his gun. He drove off to see Wally before he left for law school.

Wally was in shock when he heard that his mother and Danelo were killed. His grandparents came over to see him. Grandmother hugged Wally and said, "Your mother knew that seeing Danelo was dangerous. She made the choice of seeing him and paid the consequences. Remember, the choice she made allowed you to be born. Wally, continue to say your daily prayer as much as you can each day, keep practising your Cossack dance, and meditate.

Meditate throughout the day. God will give you strength to cope with your loss. Now pack up your things and get ready to fly back to law school." The grandparents left for their clinic

A few minutes later, Tommy showed up. He gave Wally a big hug. Wally grabbed Tommy's gun and kneed him in the groin. Tommy didn't know that Wally was reading his mind. Wally looked into Tommy's eyes and said one word, "Why!"

Tommy closed his eyes and said, "The Chinese triad hired Pavlo to kill Danelo and his family. He killed Danelo and our mother. Pavlo hired me to kill the rest of the family. If I did this, I would be allowed to live and take over Danelo's territory. If you kill me, Pavlo or someone else will finish the job."

Wally started to tremble and said, "Tommy, I don't want to kill you. Remind Pavlo that mother never married Danelo. He left her before I was born. She raised me by herself. Our grandparents, Uncle Ivan and Aunt Lydia, had nothing to do with Danelo's drug business. They lived in New York many years before Danelo and his brothers came to New York. I promise you, Tommy, that I won't interfere with your life if you promise me that you won't interfere with my life. Is it a deal?"

Tommy said, "If I'm still alive tomorrow, it is a deal; if the Chinese triad lets me live, you live." Tommy gave Wally a big hug and left.

Pavlo made a call to the Chinese triad. He explained to them what happened when Tommy tried to kill Wally. They allowed Tommy and the rest of the family to live. Tommy took over Danelo's territory. Uncle Gregory was on the Chinese triad payroll. Danelo's mother made arrangements to fly back to the Ukrainian Village with Danelo's body to bury him. Maria's funeral was in New York. Wally's grandparents made the funeral arrangements. Wally was surprised to see so many people at his mother's funeral. The Kozak Naturopathic Clinic stayed in business. The Spencers Mill and Maria's clinic received a lot of business from the Chinese triad.

Wally was puzzled and confused. He called Uncle Pavlo and said one word to him, "Why?" Pavlo replied, "The Chinese triad is much more powerful than Danelo. They offered him a partnership. Danelo refused. The Chinese triad hired me to kill Danelo and his family personally. I had no choice but to refuse, and somebody else would be hired to kill Danelo and his family, including me. I have good news: the Chinese triad allowed Tommy to live so he could take over Danelo's drug territory. That means that you and the rest of the family will be allowed to live as long as you keep your end of the bargain." Wally didn't say a word. He hung up the phone and went to see Uncle Gregory.

Wally walked straight into Uncle Gregory's office unannounced. He said to him, "Uncle Gregory, if you knew what was happening, why did you not try to stop it?"

A surprised Uncle Gregory said, "There was nothing I could do to stop it. If I tried, Pavlo or somebody else would be hired to kill me. I told him not to get involved in a drug war with the Chinese triad. They are too powerful. He wouldn't listen and suffered the consequences. It's very hard to take down the Chinese triad. They own legitimate businesses that hire thousands of people. They also contribute millions of dollars to charity. If a Chinese family gets charged and convicted of drug trafficking or human trafficking, thousands of people would lose their jobs, and charities would lose millions of dollars in donations. They also own a lot of property in New York."

Wally asked Uncle Gregory, "Why did you get involved in the drug trade?" Uncle Gregory answered, "Why not get involved? Drugs are in high demand, making the drug trade a very lucrative business." Wally couldn't believe what Uncle Gregory was saying, "It's also very dangerous business. Most people who are involved don't live very long."

Uncle Gregory smiled and said, "Wally, we're not here, on earth for a long time. You might as well have a good time and not worry about when it's time for us to go. Better to die happy and young than miserable and old."

Wally smiled back at Uncle Gregory and said, "It is possible to live over a hundred years and live a happy, prosperous life."

Uncle Gregory kept smiling and said, "Wally, I wish you over 100 years of happy life. I have to leave now. Do you want to join the FBI?" Wally left, saying to Uncle Gregory, "I can't join the FBI. If I did, I would be interfering in Tommy's life."

Wally went home to pack his things for law school. He now understood why grandmother insisted that his mother videotape Danelo and Gregory's meetings every month. He had 10 years of meetings downloaded on memory sticks. He was glad that he made copies. Wally knew that Tommy would eventually interfere with his life. Grandfather was ready to drive Wally to the airport.

Chapter 13

Wally arrived at his campus apartment. He was introduced to a new roommate. His name was John Connor, and Wally found that he had no interest in becoming a lawyer. He wasn't planning to study for any tests or exams. John managed to score high enough to barely pass his first year. His parents insisted that he go to law school. They wanted him to become a lawyer so he could join the family law firm.

Jeffrey decided to have as little contact as possible with Wally. He honestly believed that Wally was cheating but couldn't prove it. This made Jeffrey very bitter because he was always the head of the class until he met Wally.

Wally didn't need to steal Jeffrey's notes. All Wally had to do was touch the teachers who prepared the tests, assignments, and exams. Wally knew the questions and answers before he wrote any tests, exams, or assignments. Wally would never forget the answers, either.

Wally became very popular with other students, especially the girls. He would help other students with their studies. Michael Cook was very grateful for Wally's help. Without Wally's help, Michael would have difficulty graduating. Michael was extremely shy. He spent most of his free time training for the 2000-metre race. Michael joined the school's track and field team to avoid contact with girls. Wally taught Michael how to pray and meditate to help him.

Most of the girls that Wally helped were more interested in his body than his brain. He grew up to be 6'2" tall. He was 230 pounds of solid muscle and had dark hair, blue eyes, and a wonderful smile. Wally could choose any girl he wanted.

Gloria, one of the girls Wally dated, proposed marriage. She was gorgeous and came from a wealthy family. Gloria was 5' 10" tall, had long wavy dark hair, and weighed 120 pounds. Wally spent a lot of time being her personal trainer at the school's gym. The problem was that she drank too much alcohol and smoked cigarettes and weed. Gloria also enjoyed snorting cocaine at school parties. These were bad habits that she picked up from her parents. Wally tried to help her by getting her to say the prayer that was taught to him by his grandmother and meditate. Gloria was not interested in prayer or meditation; she was having too much fun partying.

Wally did enjoy dancing with the girls at parties, but he refused to indulge in drugs and alcohol. Jeffrey was also popular with some of the girls because he did enjoy dancing, drugs, and alcohol. Jeffrey always tried to pick a fight with Wally because he wanted Gloria. She didn't want to have anything to do with Jeffrey because he had a foul mouth and a bad temper. At the end of the second year, Wally made the Dean's honour list at the head of the class again. Jeffrey came in second. He still believed that Wally was cheating.

Chapter 14

Wally packed his belongings and drove home for the summer. His grandparents were waiting for him. The naturopathic clinic was getting much busier. They needed help since Wally was at law school. Grandmother sponsored a family from the Ukrainian Village to come to New York to help them. The family members were all naturopaths. It was a good thing that Danelo kept paying rent on the apartment where Wally's grandparents used to live.

Grandmother said to Wally, "Henry Wilson is sitting in the next room waiting to see you." Wally went inside to see Henry. He gave him a hug and said, "I see that you're still alive, Henry. Do you still have a gold digger living with you?"

Henry smiled and said, "I just got rid of one, and a new one is coming in next week. She'll be the last one." Wally smiled at Henry, "You are a year older, and your heart is not getting better. You don't need any more gold diggers."

Henry laughed and said, "I know your grandmother prescribed no touching; keep at least 10 feet away and just look. Please come and see me before you go back to school." Wally promised Henry that he would.

Wally had another client, Don Jordan, waiting for him. He was surprised to see Wally alive. "Why do you think I should be dead?" asked Wally. Don answered in disbelief," When the triad takes over drug territory, they kill off the entire family to make sure that there is no possibility of revenge. You, your grandparents, uncle, and aunt should be dead."

Wally smiled and said, "I guess that we are not considered part of Danelo's family. Why Tommy and his grandmother are still alive?" Don answered," The Chinese triad allowed Danelo's mother to fly back to Ukraine with Danelo's body to bury him. There is no way that she can pose a threat to them. My guess is that the Chinese offered Tommy Danelo's territory if he killed him. Wally, your mother was collateral damage. She was in the wrong place at the wrong time. I have to go now, and your grandmother is taking really good care of me."

Chapter 15

Wally was having lunch at home. He heard a knock on the front door. It was Louis holding a chessboard. He said, "Wally, it's been a long time since we played chess. It's time for revenge. I joined a chess club and played every day." Wally said, "Louis, you're just in time for lunch. Have a seat."

Wally and Louis enjoyed pizza and perogies for lunch. After lunch, they began playing chess. Wally always knew Louis's chess moves just by reading his mind. Wally always countered with moves that he learned from chess masters. They played three games. Wally won all three games quite easily. Louie couldn't believe that he lost all three games. He said to Wally, "You could become a great chess master."

Wally replied, "Louis, I'm not interested in being a chess master. I want to be a successful lawyer." Louis was disappointed when he left. Wally cleaned the dishes and headed for the Spencers Mill. Aunt Lydia and Uncle Ivan were waiting for him; they had a large party to cater to.

Summer vacation went by quickly. Wally enjoyed a quiet, uneventful vacation. He was glad that it was time to get ready for his third year of law school. Wally packed up his things and loaded his car; he said his goodbyes and drove off.

When Wally arrived at his campus apartment, he found no roommate. His roommate decided to drop out of law school. He paid rent for the entire year. The school does not give refunds, so Wally had the room all to himself. This made Wally very happy. Gloria was also very happy. She slept more in his bed than her own. Wally enjoyed her company but not her addictions. She refused to go to rehab.

At the end of the third year, Wally was again on the Dean's honours list and was the head of the class. Jeffrey came in second. Wally packed up his belongings and drove home. His grandparents were waiting for him. When Wally arrived home, his grandparents introduced the Ukrainian family to their village. Grandmother happily said," Wally, this is Natalie and John Lyschuk, their daughters Oksana and Olenka. They are going to help us at our naturopathic clinic."

Wally shook hands with them and said, "Please to meet you. I am sure you will all enjoy living in New York." Natalie and John were 45 years old. Oksana was 22 years old, and Olenka was 20 years old. The entire family were naturopaths. They would have no problem passing the certification exam. Oksana and Olenka had boyfriends back home. If they decided to live in New York City, they would sponsor their boyfriends, who were also naturopaths, to come live with them. If they didn't want to stay in New York, they would return home. Wally was confident that the entire family would stay in New York. They will be too busy to leave.

Wally spent most of the summer helping the Lyschuk family get settled. On weekends, Wally spent his time at Spencers Mill. In his spare time, he would let Louis come over to play chess. While playing chess, Wally asked him," Louis, is your father teaching you how to burn down buildings?" He didn't want to admit it but said, "My father did teach me how to burn down buildings. He said I'm very good at burning buildings. Wally, I am not interested in my father's business. I want to become a chess master. Wally, you could easily become a chess master if you want to. There is serious money to be won."

Wally smiled at Louis and said, "I'm not interested in becoming a chess master; I'm too busy studying law. I only play chess because I enjoy beating you all the time."

Louis said to Wally, "You're the only person that beats me in chess all the time. Come to the chess club. You could win lots of money."

Wally shook his head and said, "Louis, I'm not interested and too busy. It's time for you to leave." When Louis left, Wally said his prayer in front of the mirror, practised the dance, and meditated before going to bed. The summer went by quickly. The Lyschuk family settled in New York nicely. They were ready to make New York their new home. Oksana and Olenka will sponsor their boyfriends to live with them. Wally packed his things, said his goodbyes, and drove off to law school. When he arrived, Wally was happy to find out that he still didn't have a roommate. Gloria was also happy.

Chapter 16

Wally continued to excel. George Shaw, the Dean, called Wally into his office. He offered Wally a chair. He said to Wally, "Jeffrey Kelly is accusing you of cheating. You always have the highest mark in class. That is very unusual. Can you explain yourself?"

Wally said to the Dean, "Jeffrey is very jealous of me because he never gets the highest mark in class. He was a roommate of mine and always tried to pick a fight with me. Jeffrey put a hole in the wall, trying to punch me in the face. I didn't report him because I didn't want to have any trouble."

The Dean asked Wally. "How do you manage to get the highest mark in class consistently?" Wally smiled and answered, "Sir, I have a very good memory. I record all my lectures. I study and edit them at the end of each class. Before each test or exam, I spent many hours going over my notes and recordings."

George said to Wally, "I'm going to give you an oral test to see how good your memory is." The Dean gave Wally 100 questions to answer. He would have answered all the questions correctly but decided to answer only 93 questions correctly. The Dean was amazed. He said, "Wally, you do have a remarkable memory. You proved to me that you're not a cheater. "

George Shaw wrote Wally a letter of recommendation. He also suggested a law firm that Wally should apply after graduation.

Final exams were three weeks away. Wally already knew the answers to the exam questions. He was looking forward to a career in law. Gloria took Wally out to dinner. They ordered lasagna and Caesar salad. She was annoyed, "Wally, how could you celebrate your good fortune by drinking pomegranate juice?"

Wally smiled and said, "Gloria, I'm not allowed to drink alcohol. Remember who is driving you home." Gloria shook her head and said, "Okay, Wally, as soon as we graduate, we rent a hotel room, get drunk, no drugs, and have sex all night. Wally smiled, "Sounds like a good plan to me." After dinner, Wally drove Gloria to her apartment.

When Wally got to his apartment, he found Louis waiting for him. Wally was not happy and said, "Louis, how did you get into my apartment!"

Louis replied, "Wally, I'm in big trouble. I borrowed $500 from a loan shark. I need $5,000 to pay it back by next week. If I don't, the loan shark will hire his goons to beat me to death."

Wally shook his head and said, "Louis, you fool, I don't have that kind of money. There's nothing I can do to help you."

Louis gritted his teeth and said, "Wally, there is this girl I know. Her name is Kathy. She is scheduled for tomorrow night to write an entrance exam for Harvard Law School. She needs 90% to pass the exam. Kathy is willing to pay $5,000 for anyone to write her exam, provided that her score is 90% or better. Wally, you are smart enough to score 90%. You could write her exam. Kathy has a friend, Richard, scheduled to write the same exam. He decided not to take the exam. Wally, you can take his place. No identification is required. Only attendance is taken. When Richard's name is called, you put your hand up. You write the exam and put Kathy's name on it. Kathy will put Richard's name on her exam. It's that simple."

Wally couldn't believe what he was about to do. He said to Louis, "I must be out of my mind, but I will write her exam for your sake." Louis gave Wally a big hug and said goodbye.

The next evening, Wally met Kathy. She was a good, looking tall brunette. Kathy said to Wally, "Louis promised me that you would have no problem scoring 90% on the test for me." Wally told Kathy not to worry. "I wrote that same exam before, and I remember most of the questions."

They went to the classroom together to write the exam. Wally raised his hand when Richard's name was called. Wally could not understand why no identification was required to write these exams. Wally scored 94% for Kathy. She scored only 60% for Richard. She gave Wally $5,000, who gave it to a very happy Louis.

Unfortunately, Wally was recognized in class by someone who knew him. The school found out that Kathy didn't write her exam. She was expelled. Kathy was also the Dean's daughter. When the school found out that Kathy was George Shaw's daughter, he was asked to hand in his resignation three weeks before his retirement. George was furious when Kathy told him that it was Wally Kozak who wrote her exam. He checked Wally's financial status and found out that Danelo Klyn paid for his education. He was shocked.

George Shaw called Wally into his office. He said, "Wally, I find it hard to believe that you wrote Kathy's exam for $5,000. I would never have guessed that you would do such a thing for money. Why did you do it!"

Wally replied, "I did it because a friend of mine needed $5,000 to pay back a loan to a loan shark. If he didn't pay it back within a week, my friend would have been beaten to death.

George Shaw asked, "Wally, did you receive money from Danelo Klyn to pay for your education?"

Wally replied," Sir, Danelo Klyn was my biological father. My mother never married him. She raised me all by herself. He left her before I was born. I couldn't afford to go to law school, so I went to see him. He agreed to pay for my education. That was the only time that I ever saw him."

George Shaw shook his head and said," Wally, you didn't know that Kathy was my daughter. When the school found out who she was, I was asked to resign three weeks before my retirement. I just lost my pension."

"I'm sorry, sir, but I couldn't let my friend be beaten to death," Wally said remorsefully.

George angrily said, "Wally, you should not have written the exam for Kathy. Your friend should have known better, and I'm not going to allow you to write the final exams. You will be expelled for racketeering. I'm sure the president will agree with me when I tell him that your father was Danelo Klyn. You ruined my life, and I'm going to ruin yours!"

Two days later, Wally went to his tribunal. Art Jenkins, the president, gave Wally a lecture on why there was no place like him at Harvard Law School. When Art finished, Wally was escorted off campus by security. Art did not give Wally an opportunity to defend himself. He packed up his belongings, got into his car, and drove home. He didn't tell his grandparents that Louis got him expelled from law school.

Chapter 17

Wally googled the Columbia Correspondence School of Law. He called the president of the school. Wally asked him if he could only write the final exams. Wally explained to the president that he already completed law school except for writing the final exams. "When my parents were killed, I had to go home and make funeral arrangements and missed writing the final exams. I don't want to wait until next year to write them." Said Wally

The president said," Before I let you write the final exams, you will have to pay for each of the four years of law school. The government will loan you the required $200,000. You will have four years to pay it back before the government will start charging you interest."

Wally decided to take out the loan. He applied for a loan on the Internet. When Wally started to write the exams, he noticed that the questions were the same ones that Harvard Law School had, only given in a different order. He scored 97.8%.

The president couldn't believe that it was possible to score such a high mark. He believed that Wally cheated but couldn't prove it. Wally graduated from law school.

Wally made an appointment for a job interview at the Samantha Franklin Law firm, the one that George Shaw suggested. He still had the letter of recommendation that he received from George. On his transcript, Wally taped the Harvard Law School logo over the Columbia Law School logo.

Wally arrived for his interview. Samantha Franklin's office was on the top floor of a high office tower. At his interview, Wally was introduced to Thomas Moore. He was a tall, slender, good-looking man in his 40s. Wally could tell that he watched his diet and exercises. Thomas read Wally's letter of recommendation from the Dean and looked at his transcript. Thomas then shook Wally's hand and said, "Congratulations, Mr. Kozak, you are hired." Wally thanked Thomas and told him that he was looking forward to working for this law firm.

Thomas took Wally to meet Samantha Franklin. She was a tall, slender, good-looking black woman in her 50s. Wally didn't need to read her mind to know that she didn't like young white boys. Wally reminded Samantha of a young white boy that has caused her trouble. Everyone else in the office that Wally met was nice to him.

Donna, the receptionist, was a tall, well-figured 40-year-old brunette. Wally found her very attractive. He could tell that she was in love with Thomas. Wally read Thomas's mind and found out that when he was 22, he was engaged to a girl who died in a car accident on their wedding day. He did love Donna but was hesitant to get married.

Lawrence Smith was a chubby 45-year-old lawyer. He was Wally's height. Lawrence was a cat person who loved ballet. His brother was the ticket manager for the New York City Ballet. Lawrence gets free tickets that he could scalp. Lawrence lives in a huge house that he inherited from his parents. He looks after four cats. The money he receives, he donates to the Cat Rescue House Association. Wally liked him.

Jonathan Quick, a senior partner with the law firm, was tall and slim with curly black hair. He had a black curly beard. Jonathan offered Wally to be his mentor. Wally didn't trust him.

Christine Bell, another lawyer, was a beautiful blonde who enjoyed flirting with the male staff. Wally did not like her and didn't plan on playing any of her games.

Patricia Conrad was another beautiful blonde. She was a career girl who was not interested in any relationships. She got hired a week before Wally. He was disappointed that Patricia had turned down his dinner invitation. Cindy O'Rilley, a paralegal working in the office, was studying to go to law school. She was 5'8" tall, had a slender body, and had black wavy hair. Cindy was dating Michael Cook. He was one of Wally's best friends at law school. He got hired the same day as Patricia. Michael did his best to avoid Samantha as much as possible.

When Cindy was introduced to Wally, she immediately asked him for a date. She was very demanding and beautiful. Wally didn't want to have a relationship with her. However, he did take her to the Spencers Mill for dinner.

Chapter 18

Linda Parker was a 72-year-old healthy woman. She owned Parker Mining Company. Her company just bought a diamond mine in South Africa. It was located on the outskirts of Kimberly. Linda ran her company from her office in New York City. Her nephew, Alex, was in Kimberly looking after their diamond mine. Linda, at her age, decided that it was time to leave the fieldwork to somebody much younger. Her shareholders are very happy.

Osgoode Law Firm represented Linda's company in South Africa. Conrad Wells was the lawyer who handled all the legal issues involved with the diamond mine. Everything was going well until Alex met up with some sheep farmers. Linda's company needed their farmland to continue to mine diamonds. Alex offered to buy their farms. He offered three times more than the farms were worth. The sheep farmers refused to sell their farms. Alex called Conrad, "What am I going to do? The farmers refused to sell?"

Conrad answered, "I know where you can hire thugs to kill off the farmers for a mere $100,000. Once the farmers are gone, the government will auction their farms to the highest bidder.

Alex shook his head, "Linda will never agree to do it. She is against violence. Linda would rather give up the diamond mind than have anyone killed."

Conrad smiled, "Then don't tell her and go ahead with it; just say the word, and I will arrange for it. What she doesn't know won't hurt her."

The next day, Alex went to see Conrad. He wrote out a cheque for $100,000 to Conrad Wells. He took the cheque and said," Alex, in three days, your company will own the farms."

Conrad Wells had a childhood friend. They played soccer together. His friend, Elroy Biggs, played on several international soccer teams. He retired a very rich man. Injuries ended Conrad's soccer career. Elroy's brother, Claude, was too fat and lazy to play soccer. He became a leader of a motorcycle gang. They were hired killers as well as drug dealers. Conrad deposited $100,000 into Elroy's bank account so he could hire Claude to kill the sheep farmers. Elroy Biggs lived in New York. He paid Claude to kill the farmers. Claude had the farmers killed, and the Parker Mining Company bought the farms.

No one was aware that some of the farmers had families working for the government. The government knew that Parker Mining Company was responsible for killing the farmers, but they couldn't prove it. They blamed Linda Parker for the killings because she owned the mining company. They knew that her mining company needed the sheep farmer's land to continue to mine diamonds. Extradition procedures were filed with the US government to have Linda Parker brought to Kimberly to face murder charges.

The media found out about the sheep farmer killings, and the Parker mining company shares plummeted. It was a good time for a takeover. The shareholders voted in favour to sell the company to Baxter Mining. They put in the highest bid and best offer. Linda Parker lost her company. However, her shares were worth over $14,000,000 she was not unhappy.

Samantha Franklin's law firm was hired to defend Linda Parker. Thomas Moore was assigned to be her defence lawyer. He called Wally into his office," I need you to research the Parker mining company. Find out all the people who were involved with the company and the diamond mine as soon as possible."

Richard Kiley was hired by the South African government to have Linda Parker extradited. Richard did not want Linda Parker extradited. He wanted her to spend time in prison for murder in the United States. He wanted to settle out of court. Richard asked the defence to have Linda spend 3 to 5 years for murder in prison to avoid extradition.

Thomas Moore refused Richard's offer. He wanted Linda to spend no time in prison because she was innocent of any wrongdoing and she was an elderly lady. Linda had no idea that her company needed the farms. Thomas was ready for court. He was impressed with Wally's research skills. Wally's speed reading and photographic memory made him a very good researcher.

Conrad Wells and Alex Parker flew to New York City from Kimberly to testify on Linda's behalf. When Wally shook hands with them, he found out that it was Conrad who advised Alex to hire assassins to kill the sheep farmers. Conrad also convinced Alex not to tell Linda because he knew that she would not allow the sheep farmers to be killed. Wally knew that Conrad's friend Elroy Biggs would hire his brother Claude to kill the sheep farmers.

When Wally shook Alex's hand, he found out that he had embezzled more than $5,000,000 over several years from his aunt. Linda Parker's $14,000,000 from the sale of her shares was deposited in Alex's personal bank account. Wally added all this information to his research.

Thomas said to Wally," Your research just saved Linda Parker from doing time in prison." Thomas didn't care how Wally got his results as long as he got them legitimately.

Chapter 19

Wally took his research documents over to Donna's desk. She took his documents and filed them. He said to her." I could tell by the look on your face that you were in love with Thomas. He said to her that Thomas loves you. Why are the two of you not married?"

Donna shook her head" I don't know, we have been engaged for several years. Thomas keeps making excuses to postpone our wedding date."

Wally said to Donna," Did you know when Thomas was 22 years old, he was engaged to be married? His fiancée was killed in an automobile accident on their wedding day."

Donna was surprised to hear what Wally just said to her," Thomas never told me about her. How do you know?" Wally smiled," I'm a very good snoop. I like to see people happy. It's obvious that you and Thomas are not happy. Since Thomas seems to be afraid of weddings, maybe the two of you should elope."

Donna looked puzzled and said to Wally," How am I going to get Thomas to elope with me if he doesn't want to get married?"

Wally just smiled at Donna and said," The two of you can get married in his office. I'll bring a priest to marry you and Thomas in his office. You can decide later if you want a wedding."

Donna nervously said," Wally, how do you know that Thomas will agree to marry me in his office when he keeps postponing our wedding date?"

Wally looked into Donna's eyes and said," I know Thomas will marry you because he loves you. He's just afraid of having a wedding because of what happened to him when he was engaged.

Make sure that you have your wedding ring with you when the two of you are ready to elope. I'll bring a marriage certificate with me."

Two days later, Wally made an appointment for a priest to come to Thomas's office. Thomas had no idea what Wally was planning for him. Wally had the wedding ring that Thomas bought for Donna and a marriage certificate ready. Wally, Donna, and the priest entered Thomas's office. Wally locked the office front door and said to Thomas," No one leaves this room until you and Donna are married."

Thomas saw the look on Donna's face. He really did love her. The priest performed the marriage ceremony. Thomas was happy that it was over, but he was not ready to announce that he and Donna were married. Wally agreed to keep the marriage a secret.

The next day, Wally approached Donna and asked her. "Are you and Thomas going on a honeymoon? Where are the two of you going to live?"

Donna was excited and said, "I'm moving into Thomas's condo apartment. He lives in a large three-bedroom penthouse facing a forest. We'll have a beautiful view of the forest from our balcony. Thomas made reservations for a honeymoon suite in Niagara Falls."

Wally smiled and asked Donna, "How long are you and Thomas will keep your marriage a secret? Everyone in the office will start noticing how you and Thomas are a lot closer together?"

Donna gave Wally a big hug," I don't know, and I don't care. I'll let Thomas decide when he wants to announce our marriage. Knowing him, he'll probably never want to tell anybody."

Chapter 20

Samantha called Wally to come to her office. "Wally, I have a friend, Jane Smith. She has a son in college. His name is Darrell. He is a star quarterback who had an affair with a teacher who got pregnant. Sarah Jones, the pregnant teacher, agreed to marry him if he quit school and got a job to support a family. Darrell just quit school. His mother got a court order to stop the wedding. Darrell hired a lawyer to defend him against his mother in court. Wally, you are going to be Jane Smith's lawyer. Your butt is on the line, so don't screw up."

Wally said, "Don't worry, Samantha, I will not let you down." Wally knew that Samantha really wanted him to screw up to give her a reason to fire him.

Jane Smith was a tall, slender, handsome black woman. Her husband was away on business. Wally and Jane arrived at the pretrial. Wally was introduced to Sarah Jones, Gail Morris, Darrell's lawyer, and Darrell. Sarah Jones was a 30-year-old attractive white girl who was mentally unstable. Darrell was an immature, confused 18-year-old that Sarah took advantage of.

Gail North approached the bench. She motioned to Judge Judy Grace to have the court order against Darrell dropped. She said, "Your Honour, Darrell is 18 years old. He is legally an adult and has a legal right to make his own decisions without his parent's consent if he chooses."

Wally didn't object; he called Darrell to take the stand. He asked Darrell, "Did you just quit school so you could find a job to support a family." Darrell answered, "Yes."

Next question Wally asked. Did you find a job? Darrell answered, "Not yet."

Wally asked, "Have you prepared yourself for a job interview?"

Darrell answered, "Not yet."

Wally asked, "Why not?"

Darrell answered, "I haven't figured out what to do yet."

Wally looked at Darrell and said, "To give you some idea of what you need to do, let's have a mock job interview in court. I'll be the human resource manager of Acme Widget Company. You will come to see me for a job."

Darrell was furious and said, "That's the stupidest idea that I ever heard. I won't do it, and you can't make me do it!"

Judge Judy looked at Darrell and said to him, "Mr. Kozak can't make you do it, but I can. You will do it because I think it's a great idea."

Wally stood in front of Darrell, holding a clipboard, and started the interview. He said, "Darrell Smith, my name is John Turner. According to your resume, you just quit school so you could find a job to get married and raise a family."

Darrell replied, "That's right, sir."

John asked Darrell, "What position are you applying for?" Darrell hesitated and said, "Any position with your company will do."

Next question John asked was, "What do you have to offer?" Darrell hesitated again and said," I am a very hard worker, and I learn very fast."

John looked at Darrell and said, "My advice for you, young man, is to go back to school to finish your education. When you do, google Acme Widget Company. Find out all you can about us and the positions that are available. Then, choose the ones that you feel you are qualified for and then decide how much of a salary you feel that you are worth. When you do your research and are ready, come see me." Darrell was furious. He told Wally that no employer would say that to him.

"You are right, Darrell, because no employer will give you a job with your qualifications unless it's a minimum wage paying job," smiled Wally.

Darrell pouted, "You're crazy!"

Judge Judy banged her gavel on her desk and said, "Darrell, you may think he is crazy, but Mr. Kozak is giving you good solid advice that you should take!"

Wally then motioned to have Darrell's parents have custody of him. He also motioned that Sarah Jones be sent to social services for counselling. Judge Judy granted both motions.

Darrell asked, "What's going to happen to the baby?"

Wally replied, "Once the baby is born, social services will decide what is best."

Darrell said to his mother, "I just quit school. The college will never take me back. There's nothing I can do."

Wally said to Darrell," You can ask your lawyer to act on your behalf. I'm sure she can persuade the college to take you back."

"What if she turns me down?" Asked Darrell.

Wally replied, "She might turn you down, but you won't know unless you ask her. If she says no, you ask me to act on your behalf, and I will say yes."

"Why are you doing this?" Asked Darrell. Wally was getting really annoyed, "Because I don't want to see anyone squander a golden opportunity to get an education. Even if that person is an ungrateful, spoiled brat like you!"

Darrell became very angry. He threw a punch at Wally's face. He missed and fell down. Wally looked down on Darrell. Wally said to him. "You have no idea how lucky you are to have parents that have the means to pay for your education. You have no idea how it feels to have to pay back a $200,000 student loan like I do. Now get up and ask your lawyer for help right now. If you don't do it, I will press criminal charges against you for attempted assault with intent to cause bodily harm. You will have a criminal record and possible jail time!"

Darrell got up from the floor and walked over to Gail North. With tears in his eyes, he begged her to help him. Darrell did not want to have anything to do with Wally. He was relieved when Gail agreed to help him.

Jane Smith was so happy that she ran over to Wally to give him a big hug. She said, "How can I ever repay you, Mr. Kozak!"

Wally took a deep breath and said, "You really don't have to repay me; however, if you want to make a contribution to help pay down my student loan, I will be very grateful."

Jane Smith took out a cheque book from her purse to write out a cheque for Wally. The cheque was for $50,000. Wally couldn't believe it and said to Jane, "This is way too much!"

Jane smiled, "No, it's not; you deserve every penny. Samantha will be proud of you when I tell her what a wonderful job you did." Wally didn't want to tell Jane that Samantha will probably be pissed off because she will not have a good reason to fire him.

Judge Judy smiled at Wally, "Congratulations, Wally, you behaved admirably. Samantha called me. She said that you are an arrogant, self-centred jerk and would probably behave like a jackass in court."

Wally smiled and said, "When I first met Samantha, I got the impression that she thought of me as a jackass. Samantha was expecting me to screw up so she could have a good reason to fire me because Thomas likes me, and she doesn't want to upset Thomas.."

Judge Judy laughed, "Wally, I'll call Samantha and give her the bad news. I have a feeling that she will have a difficult time trying to get rid of you." Wally Thanked Judge Judy for the compliment and left. Judge Judy thought that Wally looked familiar but couldn't place him.

Chapter 21

Cindy O'Rilley enjoyed watching college basketball. She took Wally to see a college basketball game. Cindy personally knew the home team coach and took Wally to see him after the game. Wally shook hands with John Thompson, the coach. Wally found out that he was under a lot of stress. Several of the star players were charged with rape. The college arranged to have out-of-court settlements for most of them. He also found out that some of these star players did not attend classes. Their tests and exams were written for them. Most of the star players could not read or write beyond grade 3 level and yet graduated with honours.

Many employers would hire these students over students who earned their education. Employers waste a lot of time and money trying to train them. This was allowed because college basketball generated hundreds of millions of dollars through television.

Wally remembered a blog that he read. The author wrote that the New York City College Basketball Association should be commended. They provide free education to underprivileged students by offering them basketball scholarships. Wally thanked Cindy for introducing the coach to him while driving her home.

Wally decided to write his own blog. He wrote that some of these star players should graduate with a separate degree. Wally suggested the degree should be in Stupideologyy. That way, employees could decide if they wanted to hire these star basketball graduates to promote their company and hire student graduates who earned their education to work for them.

The next day, Cindy walked into Wally's office to remind him of their date to watch college basketball tonight. She told him not to be late because it was a very important game. Wally went home, said his prayers, danced, meditated, and then prepared dinner.

Grandmother called Wally to ask him to help at the clinic. Wally called Cindy to tell her that he had to cancel the basketball game tonight. Cindy was not happy and let him know how she felt.

The next morning, Wally went to see Cindy to apologize. Cindy was not in her office. Donna told Wally that she saw Cindy going to the library. Wally went there to look for her. He found Cindy and Michael lying on the floor in the back room. They were naked and having sex. This made Wally furious. He took a video of them with his phone to show Samantha. When Wally calmed down, he decided not to show the video to Samantha. Wally liked Michael, and Samantha would've fired him and Cindy if she had seen the video. That would ruin their careers. Wally knew that his relationship with Cindy was not going to last. He doubted that Michael's relationship with Cindy would last much longer either.

A week later, after Wally had written his blog about college basketball star players, the New York College Basketball Association filed a lawsuit against Wally and Samantha Franklin's law firm for writing his discriminatory blog. Samantha was furious," Wally, you fool, what have you done!"

Wally told Samantha not to worry. The lawsuit will be dropped when he gets a chance to defend himself. Samantha, still furious, said, "Wally, good luck! If you lose, you're fired. Don't expect any help from me!" Wally was not worried. Samantha will not be firing Wally anytime soon.

Wally was prepared to go to court. He gathered statistical information from the last 10 years. During that time, the colleges had paid out over $3,000,000 for 30 out-of-court settlements for rape and domestic violence to keep star players out of prison. There were also over 1,000 drug violations covered up. The more championships a school won, the more money it generated. Wally knew that the New York College Basketball Association would not want the media to get hold of this information.

Wally appeared in court by himself. The New York College Basketball Association hired Elizabeth Grace as their legal counsel. Elizabeth was very beautiful. She was 5'8" tall and weighed 120 pounds, all muscle, had long wavy red hair and a beautiful smile. When Wally saw her, his heart started to throb. He finally found the girl that he wanted to marry. She sat beside Gordon Johnson, the president of the basketball association.

Elizabeth gave her testimony. She said that Wally Kozak tried to discredit the New York College Basketball Association by writing a racial slur in his blog. The New York College Basketball Association has high standards with an excellent reputation.

Wally gave testimony in his defence. "I have a friend whose company builds roads, sewers, and bridges. He told me that in certain neighbourhoods that he has to go into to do a job, the police have to escort his crew and equipment. The police have to patrol the neighbourhood while the crew is working. At the end of the day, the police escort the crew out of the neighbourhood. Most of the people who live in these neighbourhoods are more interested in guns, drugs, alcohol, and sex than food and water. The high school students play mostly basketball or football. Their dream is to play in the NBA or NFL so they can get rich. Many of the students that the colleges recruit come from these neighbourhoods."

Wally saw the disturbed look on Gordon's face and continued, "That is why there are so many problems. In the last 10 years, the colleges who recruited students from these neighbourhoods to play basketball paid out over $3,000,000 for 30 out-of-court settlements for rape and domestic violence to keep star players out of prison. They also covered up over 1,000 student drug violations."

"The colleges don't care about the student's education. They only care about how they perform on the basketball court. Some of these students don't attend classes. The colleges have someone write their tests and exams for them. They graduate with honours, and yet they can barely read or write".

Elizabeth said to Wally," To implement such a separate curriculum for these students would take too much time and money. It's not practical".

Wally smiled and said," It would take very little time and money. Just write down on a piece of paper Stupiditeology. You can have Joy of being stupid, Art of being stupid, Stupid 101, etc. The college would hire a guy who is big and strong to take attendance in case any students do show up. He would not be required to prepare lectures. Grades would be based on students not attending classes. The more "classes they miss, the better grades they receive."

Elizabeth could not believe what Wally just said. She thought his idea was the most stupid idea that she had ever heard. Gordon Johnson looked at Wally and said," I agree with Elizabeth; I think it is a stupid idea, but I agree with you that something must be done. However, the New York College Basketball Association will not go for it. There's too much money at stake. If you agree not to publish your findings on the out-of-court settlements and drug coverups, all charges against you will be dropped."

Wally smiled and said, "I will agree if the New York College Basketball Association pays me $50,000 for my legal costs." Gordon Johnson happily agreed to pay Wally's legal costs.

Wally asked Gordon," Is it true that you give $50,000 bonuses to some of the students if they can consistently do a 3-foot vertical jump?" Gordon answered," We do if a college wants to recruit a student badly enough. The money that the students receive is put in a trust. They have no access to this money until they graduate. If they don't graduate, they will not be entitled to the money."

"Wally got excited," How much money will you give me if I can do a 4-foot vertical jump three consecutive times?" Gordon said, "Mr. Kozak, I don't think that is possible. If you can do it, I will write you a cheque for $100,000."

Wally knew that he could do it. He jumps that high every time he practices his Cossack dance. Wally asked Judge Judy permission to attempt his jumps in court. She reluctantly permitted him. Gordon conveniently had a tape measure. He measured 4 feet from the floor. Wally successfully made his jumps. Gordon was amazed and congratulated Wally. He wrote out a cheque for $100,000 to Wally Kozak. He said, "Wally, it's too bad that you are too old to be recruited." Elizabeth was stunned, and she couldn't believe what she just saw.

Wally gave Elizabeth a big smile and asked her out for a dinner date. She told him to get lost and left. Wally was disappointed. He asked Judge Judy, "What's her problem? Why doesn't she like me?"

Judge Judy smiled at Wally and said, "Elizabeth probably does like you. The problem is that she is engaged to be married."

Wally was heartbroken and said to Judge Judy, "That's too bad. Do you know who the lucky guy is?" Elizabeth is engaged to Jeffrey Kelly," said Judge Judy. Wally was in shock, "What! That lazy, fat slob. He has a foul mouth and a violent temper. She can't possibly love him!"

Judge Judy said, "Elizabeth and Jeffrey are childhood friends. Their families arranged for their wedding years ago. After the wedding, the parents plan to start their own law firm."

Wally shook his head and said, "Jeffrey will abuse Elizabeth both verbally and physically. She will divorce him."

Judge Judy looked at Wally with a concerned look, "Elizabeth grew up knowing Jeffrey. She knows how to handle him. Jeffery will not hurt Elizabeth. She has a black belt in karate. Elizabeth is not interested in having a loving relationship. She is only interested in a business relationship. Wally, you had better take my advice and keep your nose out of their affairs."

Wally had no intention of taking Judge Judy's advice. He doesn't know how he will get Elizabeth to break off her engagement with Jeffrey. All he knows is that an opportunity will present itself, and he will be ready. Wally went back to his office.

Donna asked Wally how his day in court went. He told her that he won and received $50,000 for legal costs. He also told her that he received $100,000 for jumping four times vertically three consecutive times. "The president of the New York College Basketball Association couldn't believe that I could do it." Donna gave Wally a big hug. Wally asked Donna, "I noticed a rooftop running track outside Samantha's office window. Who uses it?"

"Donna smiled," A sporting goods company has an office in this building. Their running club uses it every early morning and late evening. You're welcome to run on it in the afternoons every day if you want." Wally thanked Donna. He was planning to have daily runs on the rooftop track in the afternoons.

Chapter 22

Samantha was surprised at how Wally successfully defended himself in court. She still wanted to get rid of him. Samantha decided to check his Harvard Law School graduation class. She was furious when she found out that Wally hadn't graduated. Wally was called into her office. Samantha screamed at him," You never went to Harvard Law School! That letter you received from the Dean had to be a forgery!"

Wally tried to calm her down and said," Samantha, I did go to Harvard Law School. Let me explain."

Samantha screamed again, "There is no possible explanation. You weaselled your way into my law firm. You're nothing more than a despicable, sneaky, conniving snake. I bet you don't even have a license to practice law. Wally, you are fired!"

Wally screamed back at Samantha, calling her an ungrateful, stubborn, foolish bitch. Thomas stepped into her office. He heard everything. When Samantha calmed down, Thomas managed to persuade her to let Wally stay until the end of the week so that he could be with him in court. Samantha left her office, slamming the door on her way out.

Thomas asked Wally if he had a valid license to practice law in New York City. Wally nodded yes. Thomas smiled and said," Good, once we kicked Richard Kiley's butt in court, I will write you a letter of recommendation. You show this letter to any law firm in New York and tell them that you got fired because you called Samantha an ungrateful, foolish, stubborn bitch; you will be hired on the spot." Wally thanked Thomas. Samantha listened to the conversation that Wally had with Thomas.

Wally drove home to get his gym bag. It was lunchtime, and he wanted to run on the rooftop track. The office building had a gym. Wally started running; he noticed Samantha was in her office watching him. He decided to have some fun with her. When Wally finished his run, he stopped in front of Samantha's window. Wally took off his T-shirt to show off his muscular physique. Then, he started doing floor exercises. Wally saw Samantha. Her mouth was wide open, and she began to breathe heavily. When Wally finished, he waved goodbye to her and headed for the shower.

The next day, Wally again ran on the track and did his floor exercises in front of Samantha's window. Before he could head for the shower, Samantha called Wally into her office. She had a proposition for him.

She said to Wally, "Give me one night of sexual bliss with you, and I will offer you a senior partnership in my law firm."

Wally asked her, "Why, and what else do you want?"

Samantha answered, "I may be getting old, but I'm not dead yet. All I want you to do is to come to my apartment tomorrow night."

Wally didn't trust Samantha. He knew she was up to something. He couldn't get near enough to touch her to find out what she was planning to do because he was sweating and wearing his gym shorts. He decided to turn down her offer. Samantha told Wally that if he didn't accept her offer, he would be immediately fired, and there would be no letter of recommendation from Thomas.

The next night, Wally went over to Samantha's apartment. He took off his clothes and laid down on his back on the bed. Samantha handcuffed his ankles and wrists to the bedpost. She put on a black leather negligee'. She held a whip in her right hand and a chain in her left hand. Wally immediately closed his eyes and started to breathe deeply and slowly. Samantha skilfully snapped the tip of the whip against Wally's ears several times. She then wrapped the chain around his neck and jumped on top of his chest. Wally experienced a most terrifying and humiliating night.

In the morning, Samantha removed the handcuffs from Wally's ankles and wrists.

She said to him, "Wally, you realize that the senior partnership will cost you $500,000." Wally answered, "I know, but six months is enough time for me to raise the money."

Samantha happily said, "That six months to raise the money is not law. It is a policy. As the owner of my law firm, I can change policies whenever I want. Wally, I believe that you can raise $500,000 in six months. That is why I am giving you until 6:00 tomorrow night to raise the money. If you fail to raise the money in time, you will be fired, and there will be no letter of recommendation from Thomas."

Samantha was waving goodbye to Wally as she was leaving. Wally went to the washroom to shower. Wally then got dressed and drove home. He took out the deed to his house and went to see Richard Kiley.

Thomas introduced Richard Kiley to Wally at a meeting last week. Wally was able to read his mind. He found out that Richard and Samantha had a mutual hatred for each other. It started way back in law school. They both graduated from Harvard Law School in the same year and in the same class. They competed with each other. Richard ended up with a higher grade than Samantha. This made her very bitter. They also competed against each other in court. Richard and Samantha argued all the time in court, upsetting the judge.

Richard was a tall, slender man, weighed 165 pounds, had black hair, and was handsome. He was divorced. He was too busy to have much contact with his two grown daughters.

Samantha was also divorced. Her husband left her penniless when she became pregnant. She gave birth in prison. She had to give up her baby boy for adoption. Samantha was charged and convicted of drug trafficking and prostitution. She served three years in prison, where she earned a college degree. When she got out of prison, Samantha applied to the Harvard Law School as an underprivileged minority. She was chosen because of the high grades that she received in the College prison.

Richard's office was on the top floor of a tall office tower three blocks from Wally's home. Wally asked the receptionist if he could see Richard regarding an urgent matter. Richard agreed to see him. He asked Wally to sit down. Wally said to Richard, "I need $500,000 by 6 o'clock tonight. Samantha offered me a senior partnership. If I don't raise the money in time, Samantha will fire me. I can pay you back with interest in six months. The deed to my house is sufficient collateral."

Wally went on to explain what happened. He told Richard that he had a fight with Samantha. She called him a despicable, sneaky, conniving snake, and he called her an ungrateful, stubborn, foolish bitch. When Wally got to the part where Samantha tied his ankles and wrists to the bedpost and tortured him with a whip and chain while wearing a black leather negligee', Richard picked up the phone and called Samantha.

He said, "Samantha, I understand that you offered a young man a senior partnership." Samantha grunted," How do you know that I did?"

Richard smiled and said," I have the young man sitting in my office in front of me. He wants me to loan him $500,000." Samantha screamed into the phone," Richard, don't you dare give that despicable, sneaky, conniving snake a loan!"

Richard laughed, "Samantha, you are an ungrateful, stubborn, foolish bitch. I'm going to do you a favour and give the young man the loan. I'll have the money transferred to your business account by noon." Before Samantha could say another word, Richard hung up.

Wally thanked Richard for the loan and said, "You don't have to worry about me paying you back the loan on time. I have no intention of losing my house." Richard smiled at Wally, "It was a pleasure meeting you. I'm confident that you will pay back the loan in time." Wally liked Richard. He had a lot more compassion for people than Samantha.

Samantha was waiting for Wally in his office. She had a big smile on her face and said to him, "I have decided on another policy. You will participate in a mock trial. I will be the judge, and you will be the prosecutor. Thomas will be the defence lawyer. Cindy will be that defendant. If you win, you will stay. If you lose, I will return the $500,000 to Richard and you will be fired with no letter of recommendation from Thomas. Here is your file, go home; the mock trial will be on Thursday morning. That will give you three days to prepare. You are not allowed to use any of the office resources." Wally took the court file and left. Samantha was certain that Wally would lose in the mock trial and that she would finally be rid of him.

Wally took his file and went to see Judge Judy Grace. Wally waited a half-hour before he was allowed to see her. Wally explained to her that he had an argument with Samantha. She called him a despicable sneaky conniving snake, and he called her an ungrateful, stubborn, foolish bitch. Thomas heard the argument and persuaded Samantha to wait a week to decide if she wanted to fire Wally. Samantha decided that he would participate in a mock trial. She would be the judge, and Wally would be the prosecutor. If he wins, he stays; if he loses, he's fired. Wally told Judge Judy that he has three days to prepare for the mock trial at home. He is not allowed to use any of the office resources, and he needs help.

Judge Judy shook her head, "Wally, it looks like Samantha really wants to get rid of you. I don't like her, and Thomas seems to like you. I will let you have access to the court library. Let me know if you have any questions."

Wally thanked Judge Judy and went to the library. Using his photographic memory, Wally quickly found everything that he wanted to prepare for the mock trial. Wally knew that the mock trial was actually a real trial that Thomas successfully defended.

Angela Stone was on trial for the murder of Judge Gerald Childress. He was stabbed to death with a sharp knife. A drop of the judge's blood was found on Angela's shoe at the time of his death. Angela claimed that she had no motive to kill Judge Gerald

Childress. She never met him. Angela said that the blood from the judge was planted on her shoe by the real killer to incriminate her.

Wally called Don Jordan. He explained his problem and asked him to find out if Angela's family had any history with Judge Gerald Childress. Wally found out that Angela was divorced. Her ex-husband, George Saunders, received custody of their son Jamie. He was 18 years old when Jamie was charged and convicted of first-degree murder. Judge Gerald Childress sentenced Jamie to 20 years in prison with no parole until 15 years. Thomas didn't know that Jamie Saunders was Angela's son. Wally sent this information along with a disclosure form to Thomas.

Judge Gerald Childress had lunch behind the courthouse on a picnic table every day. There was a garden park behind the courthouse. That was where he had his lunch when the weather was nice. This was public knowledge.

Wally concluded that Angela had the motive and opportunity to kill Judge Childress. Two days later, Wally had Judge Judy go over his notes. Judge Judy was impressed, "Wally, I can see why Thomas is fond of you. You have excellent research skills. There are just a few minor things that need to be changed; otherwise, you're good to go." Wally made the necessary changes and thanked Judge Judy for her help.

Wally arrived Thursday morning for the mock trial. The jury was made up of office staff. Samantha was confident. She thought that Wally had absolutely no chance of winning.

The mock trial commenced. Thomas called Cindy to the stand. He asked her, "Did you personally know Judge Gerald Childress?"

Cindy answered, "I did not know him, and I never met him."

Thomas asked, "Do you have any reason to want to have Judge Gerald Childress killed?"

Cindy answered, "No." Thomas had no more questions for Cindy.

Wally approached the stand and asked Cindy, "Are you divorced?"

Cindy nodded yes. "Did your ex-husband receive custody of your son?"

Cindy nodded yes. "Is his name Jamie Saunders?" Cindy nodded yes.

"Does he live with his father? Angela said yes. Wally asked, "Do you love your son?" Cindy nodded yes.

Wally then asked, "Was Jamie charged and convicted of first-degree murder?" Cindy nodded yes. Wally asked, "Did Judge Gerald Childress sentence Jamie to 20 years in prison with no parole for 15 years? Angela nodded yes.

Wally said to Angela, "You do have the motive and opportunity to kill Judge Childress. Witnesses saw you walk behind the courthouse at the same time as the judge. It is common knowledge that the judge has lunch behind the courthouse every day when it's nice outside."

Angela said, "I saw a bunny rabbit run behind the courthouse and went looking for him so I could take a picture of him. I was not aware that the judge was having lunch."

Wally asked Cindy," How do you explain the drop of the judge's blood found on your shoe?"

Angela answered," The real killer placed the drop of the judge's blood on my shoe to incriminate me. He did it without my knowledge."

Wally had no more questions. Angela stepped down after deliberation from both sides. The jury found Angela guilty as charged. Samantha was shocked when Wally won. Thomas was very happy. He wanted Wally to stay. Cindy, the defendant, was not happy. She wanted Wally to lose because he dumped her without any explanation.

Wally took a picture of Samantha's face with his phone and did a victory dance with Donna. She was also happy that Wally won.

Samantha called Wally into her office. She told Wally that his name would not be put on the senior partnership wall. She also asked Wally not to tell anyone that he was a senior partner. Wally agreed. He did not want to upset Samantha more than he already did.

Judge Judy Grace was sitting in her office. She googled on her computer Samantha Franklin Law firm. She looked at all the employees listed. Wally's name was not on the list. Judge Judy was disappointed. She assumed that Wally lost the mock trial and got fired. She was hoping that he would win because he had a very good chance of winning.

Later in the afternoon, Judge Judy received a beautiful gift basket. In it, there was a loaf of sourdough bread, prosciutto, mustard, several kinds of cheeses, organic chocolate, organic blueberry jam, almond butter, and a bottle of fine brandy. The gift basket was from Wally. He wrote a thank you card saying that without her help, he would have lost the mock trial. Judge Judy was confused. How could Wally win the mock trial and not have his name on the employee list? She checked to see if Wally had a valid license to practice law in New York City. Judge Judy found out that he did. This became more confusing. Next time Wally shows up in her courtroom, he will have some explaining to do.

Chapter 23

Monday morning, Thomas and Wally arrived in court for Linda's pretrial. Conrad Wells and Alex Parker were waiting for them. Richard Kiley showed up five minutes later. He said, "This is your last chance to accept the settlement. It was Linda Parker's company. That makes her responsible for the death of those farmers."

Thomas cleared his throat and said, "Linda Parker is not responsible for the death of those sheep farmers; Conrad Wells is. He talked Alex into giving him $100,000 so he could hire Claude Biggs to kill the sheep farmers. Conrad also convinced Alex not to tell Linda. He knew that Linda would not allow the killings to happen. Linda did not know that her company needed the farmland. She didn't know that Claude Biggs was hired to kill the sheep farmers. Linda had no control over what happened. Linda was forced to sell her company. That should be enough punishment for what happened."

Richard Kiley turned to face Conrad Wells and Alex and said to them, "You better get yourselves a good lawyer. There will be extradition proceedings against both of you to face murder charges back home." Thomas and Wally left the courtroom, leaving a bewildered Conrad and Alex behind.

Samantha's law firm was retained to represent Conrad. She chose Wally to be his lawyer. Samantha told him if he screwed up, he would be asked to resign his partnership. Wally knew that Samantha was still trying to get rid of him. He was not worried. Thanks to his psychic abilities, Wally had enough information to save Conrad's butt.

The day before the pretrial, Wally said to Conrad, "If you want me to save your butt, make sure that your friend Elroy Biggs and

Alex Parker show up at the pretrial. I know that Elroy is living in New York. It's up to you to make sure that he comes."

Wally called Don Jordan. He wanted Don to be with him at Conrad's pretrial. Wally told Don that all he had to do was sit and listen. He explained to Don that he intends to get one scumbag to pay off his $500,000 loan, and another scumbag will go to prison for murder. Don agreed to come. He liked Wally and was grateful for the medical care that he received from Wally's grandparents.

The next morning, Wally and Don arrived in court for the pretrial. Conrad, Elroy, and Alex were waiting for him. Wally introduced Don Jordan to them. When the pretrial commenced, Wally started by saying,

"The South African government does not want Conrad. They want Elroy Biggs and Alex Parker. Alex provided the money for Elroy to hire his brother Claude to kill the sheep farmers. I have extradition papers to sign for each of them. Once signed by me, Don Jordan will arrest them. They will become guests of the FBI until the extradition papers get processed." Elroy and Alex were shocked.

Wally faced Elroy and said to him, "You can avoid extradition. All you have to do is make two e-money transfers to these emails—one for $550,000 and another for $50,000. If you do this, I will tear up your extradition paper. Don will give you five minutes before he comes after you."

Elroy didn't say a word. He took out his phone to make the e-money transfers. The $550,000 went to Richard Kiley's bank account to pay for Wally's loan plus interest. The $50,000 went to Wally's bank account. Wally tore up the extradition paper, and Elroy disappeared. When five minutes elapsed, Don Jordan got up and left.

Wally turned to face Alex and said, "The extradition paper that I tore up was for Elroy. This one's for you. Once I sign it, the FBI will put a freeze on your bank account. I know that over $14,000,000 was deposited in your bank account from the sale of Linda's company. That money belongs to Linda. Our accountants audited your assets. There were several large deposits made into your bank account for several years. It was estimated that you had embezzled over $5,000,000 in the last five years.

In order for you to avoid extradition to South Africa, I want you to make three e-money transfers. One for $20,000,000 to Linda's bank account. Another one for $1,000,000 to Richard Kiley's bank account and the last $1,000,000 to Samantha Franklin's bank account. Then, I want you to sign this confession that I have prepared for you. We will ask the court for a 3 to 5-year jail sentence. The accountants estimated that there will still be $3,000,000 in your bank account when you get out."

Alex didn't say a word and took the confession from Wally. He signed it without reading and then made the e-money transfers. Alex quietly got up and left. Alex did not want to be extradited. Conrad got up and went after Alex. Wally collected his paperwork and started to leave. Richard shouted, "Hold on, Wally, you have a lot of explaining to do. Those extradition papers are phony. How did you get access to my bank account!"

Wally smiled at Richard, "You and I know that those extradition papers are phoney, but Elroy and Alex didn't. You could have said something to stop the bluff. Richard, I do not have access to your bank account, but the FBI does. I was given a temporary code that allows me only to deposit money into your bank account and Linda's. I have no idea how much money you have in your bank account. The FBI did an audit on Alex's assets at my request, and Conrad told me that Elroy Biggs was very rich."

Richard was still very furious, "Wally, that's no excuse for breaking the law. I could bring criminal charges against you!" Wally smiled and knew that Richard would not bring criminal charges against him. He would have to explain the $1,550,000 that was deposited into his bank account.

Richard's face turned red, "Wally, Samantha was right. You are a despicable, sneaky, conniving snake." Wally, still smiling, said," Richard, you sat in your chair for half an hour and did absolutely nothing while $1,550,000 was deposited in your bank account, thanks to me. You should be very happy; I know I would, and Richard, please return the deed to my house." Wally then reminded Richard to inform the South African government that Linda Parker was innocent. Her nephew Alex was guilty and will be spending time in prison for murder.

Chapter 24

S amantha was waiting in Wally's office for him. When Wally arrived, Samantha said, "Conrad called me. He told me that you did an extremely wonderful job defending him. To show his appreciation, he made dinner reservations for our office staff at the Spencers Mill tomorrow night."

Wally was not happy and said to Samantha, "My uncle Ivan called me a few minutes ago. I promised him that I would help him in the kitchen for a catering event tomorrow night. He didn't tell me what the occasion was for."

Samantha was surprised, "Wally, I didn't know that Ivan was your uncle. He is a good friend and never told me that he had a nephew."

Wally said, "Before law school, I was a chef at the Spencers Mill; I probably prepared some meals for you."

Samantha asked Wally, "How old were you when you started to work for your uncle?"

Wally answered, "I became a certified chef at 18. That's when I started to work at the Spencers Mill. I sometimes sang and played the piano to entertain the customers. My uncle was very upset when I told him that I didn't want to become a full-time chef. He thought I made a big mistake."

Samantha shook her head and said, "I agree with your uncle that you made a big mistake. Wally, you are a very talented chef, and I enjoyed listening to you sing and play the piano. I knew you looked familiar. I just couldn't place you. Wally, you're wasting your talents working at a law firm."

Wally asked Samantha if she still wanted to get rid of him. Samantha said, "More than ever. You don't belong here. You belong at the Spencers Mill helping your uncle Ivan." Wally had no intention of leaving. He enjoyed being a lawyer more than being a chef.

Conrad Wells reserved a room for 25 people. Wally and Aunt Lydia showed up four hours before the dinner party. As a head chef, Wally had to prepare everything in advance. He prepared prime rib, scalloped potatoes, bean salad, and Caesar salad. For dessert, Aunt Lydia prepared various pastries. Uncle Ivan was on the floor meeting with the guests. Everyone from the office came except Wally. Samantha was the only person who knew why he didn't show up. She wasn't going to tell anyone. Uncle Ivan said that Wally would have enough time to entertain the staff. Lawrence was allowed to bring one of his cats. He wanted to bring his cat because he knew that prime rib was on the menu.

The meal that Wally and Aunt Lydia prepared was exactly what Conrad wanted on the menu. Everyone enjoyed the meal. When Wally finished preparing dinner, he changed into his tuxedo. He was ready to entertain the guests. Wally played the piano and sang songs by Billy Joel, Elton John, and Frank Sinatra while the guests were being served. When Wally finished, he received a standing ovation.

At the end of the night, Uncle Ivan wanted Wally to help wash the dishes. He politely declined. Wally knew that Uncle Ivan wouldn't make a scene with so many people around.

Thomas and Donna entered Wally's office. They asked him if he could prepare an anniversary dinner at their apartment. They had a piano, so they wanted Wally to play the piano and sing. It was their first wedding anniversary. Wally agreed to do it, but he had Thomas and Donna promise not to tell anyone. If word got around, everyone in the office would ask Wally to prepare dinner for them.

The menu that Wally prepared for them had large potato dumplings, pork back ribs, spicy cabbage, bean salad, and Caesar salad. For dessert, cheesecake wafers were covered in dark chocolate. Brandy was served just before dessert. Wally sang romantic love songs on the piano. Donna and Thomas were very pleased.

Chapter 25

Jonathan Quick resigned from the law firm without giving an explanation. He gave up his partnership. Christine Bell was fired without notice. She was very upset. Christine decided to sue Samantha for wrongful dismissal.

Wally read their minds. He found out that Jonathan was drawing company funds without authorization. He embezzled just over $60,000 to buy expensive jewellery for Christine Bell. Jonathan was having an affair with her. He offered to resign if Samantha wouldn't press criminal charges against him. Samantha agreed to avoid bad publicity.

Wally also found out that Betty, Jonathan's wife, was dying from breast cancer. Her doctor, Eric Clydesdale, told her that she had about a year to live. When Jonathan found out, he immediately took out a million-dollar insurance policy, naming him as the beneficiary. He made sure that the insurance company would not know about Betty dying from breast cancer. He gave them Betty's forged health records. Six months later, Jonathan had another doctor examine Betty. Dr. Carl Smith concluded that Betty had terminal breast cancer. He estimated that Betty had about six months to live. Jonathan filed a claim with the insurance company.

Wally went to Steve's Jewelry Store, where Jonathan bought the jewellery for Christine. Wally told the manager what he wanted and why. He received a list of all the items that Jonathan bought at the jewellery store.

Christine Bell's court date was scheduled for two weeks. She chose Elizabeth Kelly, her best friend, as her lawyer. Samantha chose Thomas Moore to defend her. She decided not to attend court.

Wally asked Thomas if he could defend Samantha. Thomas agreed to let Wally defend Samantha since she would not be in court. Thomas knew that Wally was more interested in Elizabeth Kelly than Christine Bell's lawsuit. However, Thomas had complete confidence in Wally to defend Samantha successfully.

Chapter 26

Sally Jones, a college student, filed criminal charges against Will Johnson. She claimed that he assaulted and raped her at her apartment. Will's father was a billionaire; he owned the Johnson Robotics Company. According to Sally, Will was drunk when he barged into her apartment and raped her.

Will claimed that he had consensual sex with Sally. He filed a countersuit claiming that Sally was a racist. He said that Sally called him a stupid, ugly ni**er because he refused to have a relationship with her. Will hired his father's lawyer, Harry O'Reilly.

Sally hired Samantha Franklin. Samantha chose Wally to defend her. Sally arrived at Wally's office for her appointment.

Wally asked her what happened on the day that she claimed that Will Johnson raped you. She began to explain, "Will approached me when I was in a bar. He insisted that I go to his place with him for some fun. I refused to go with him. He persisted, and I got annoyed and ran out of the bar. Will found out where I lived and barged into my apartment. He was drunk and raped me." Wally asked Sally if she called him a stupid, ugly ni**ger. She said that she didn't call him that. Wally told Sally not to worry; Will was going to pay for what he did to her.

Wally knew of Will's reputation. He was a playboy interested in partying and casinos. The day before court, Wally went to the casino looking for Will. When Wally saw him, he deliberately bumped into him. Wally read his mind and found out that Will's father had paid several millions of dollars in out-of-court settlements over the years to keep Will out of prison because he wanted to avoid bad publicity. The shareholders of his company would not be happy if they knew that Will was a rapist.

Wally was able to type out the police reports from Will's rape cases just by reading his mind. The police report provided evidence to use against Will. Wally didn't want to use the police reports unless it was absolutely necessary.

Wally decided to prove to the court that Will was ugly. That was why Sally Jones didn't want to have sex with him when he frightened Sally by attacking her. For evidence, Wally provided a fabricated ugly survey using social media. Will was rated on the ugly scale from 1 to 10. Wally made sure that Will received a nine on the ugly scale. He also rated Will's lawyer, Harry O'Rilley. He got a three on the ugly scale.

The next day, Wally was ready for court. Samantha warned Wally that Harry was a very experienced and good lawyer. He represented Will many times in court. "If Harry offers a settlement, take it. He will make a fool out of you in court if you refuse to settle." Wally had no intentions of settling. He intends to win.

Judge Judy was ready to start court proceedings. Harry did not have Will take the witness stand. Harry testified that Will and Sally had consensual sex. She enjoyed having sex with Will so much that she wanted to start a relationship with him. When Will told Sally that he was not interested in having a relationship with her, she got upset; that is why she called Will a stupid, ugly ni**er. That proved that she was a racist.

Wally did not have Sally take the stand. Wally testified that Will was drunk and barged into Sally's apartment and forced her to have sex. She became frightened but did not call him a stupid, ugly ni**er. This proves that Sally is not a racist. Wally said, "For my evidence, I have done an ugly survey using social media. On a scale of 1 to 10, Will received a nine. This proves that Will is very ugly. Harry, his lawyer, received a three. I make a motion that the court award Sally Jones $100,000 in punitive damages and $50,000 in legal costs."

Harry got up and immediately accused Wally of being crazy. He approached the bench and said, "Your Honour, this survey has absolutely no bearing on this case. If Wally Kozak believes it has, he lost his mind!"

Judge Judy agreed with Harry. She asked Wally to explain why this ugly survey had a bearing on this case. Wally held up a file and said, "Your Honour, I have police reports on Will Johnson with me. It shows a history of dangerous sexually deviant behaviour. His father spent millions of dollars in out-of-court settlements over the years to keep Will from going to prison. If you don't grant my motion. I'll use these police reports as evidence against Will Johnson."

Judge Judy asked Wally where he got those police reports. Wally said, "Your Honour, I went to a police station and asked someone for a copy of Will Johnson's police reports. I told that person that I wanted to use the police reports as evidence against Will Johnson in court. That person was happy to give me a copy. I will not tell you the name of that person for obvious reasons.

Judy asked Wally to let her see the police reports. Wally gave her the police reports. She started to read them. After she finished reading, she handed them back to Wally. Judge Judy granted Wally's motion. She advised Harry not to waste time and money on an appeal. Sally Jones ran up to Wally and gave him a big hug before she left.

Will approached Wally and asked him, "What are you going to do with those police reports?" Wally smiled and said, "These police reports are my property. I can do whatever I want with them. If you want to buy them from me, it'll cost you $50,000."

Will was shocked and said, "Are you blackmailing me!"

Wally smiled and replied, "If you were in my shoes, you would be asking for a hell of a lot more money." Will laughed and took out his chequebook to write out a cheque for $50,000 to Wally Kozak. Wally took the cheque and handed him the police reports.

He then asked Will, "If you want to buy the ugly survey from me, it'll cost you another $50,000. If you don't buy it, I will post it on social media." Will had a lot of friends who would make fun of him for a long time if they saw his ugly survey.

Will started to laugh again and wrote out another cheque for $50,000 to Wally Kozak, and he said, "I like you, Wally, but I would love to have five minutes alone with you, so I can beat the crap out of you." Will was much taller and more muscular than Wally. However, he was no match against Wally in a fight because Wally is a Cossack warrior.

Wally smiled at Will and said, "That can be arranged for another $50,000." Will smiled back at Wally with his big, beautiful white teeth and wrote out another cheque for $50,000 to Wally Kozak. Wally approached Judge Judy to ask permission to use one of the interview rooms for five minutes. He told her that he had a Master's in martial arts. Wally said to Judge Judy, "Will won't hurt me, and I will be gentle with him. Harry can be the timekeeper."

Judge Judy didn't know why, but she gave Wally permission to fight Will in one of the interview rooms. Harry started the time on his watch. Will immediately threw a punch at Wally's head. He missed. Wally grabbed his nose and started to squeeze it. Will screamed in pain. Wally let go of his nose. Will attempted to kick Wally in the chest. He missed; Wally grabbed his foot. Will fell down on his back. Wally grabbed Will's other foot and raised his legs to expose his butt. Wally whacked Will's butt real hard.

Will screamed in pain and said, "Are you some kind of ninja!"

Wally nodded yes." You never told me.! Wally answered, "You never asked me if I was."

Will pulled out a jackknife, opened the blade, and lunged at Wally. He missed him. Wally was furious; he quickly disarmed Will and threw him against the wall. Harry announced," Times up."

Wally grabbed Will by the throat and said, "You tried to assault me with the intent to cause bodily harm. An out-of-court settlement to keep you out of prison will cost you $100,000." Without saying a word, Will wrote out a cheque for $100,000 to Wally. Harry gave

Will his police reports and ugly survey. He walked away, shaking his head. Wally received four cheques from Will for $250,000.

Harry was very impressed and congratulated Wally. With a big smile, Wally told Harry that he could have his ugly scale survey for a favour.

Harry looked concerned, "What kind of favour?" Wally kept smiling, "Just a simple little favour." Harry said," You could ask your simple little favour at lunchtime in my office." Harry left. He was not happy.

Judge Judy looked concerned, "Wally, don't mess around with Harry. He can cause you a lot of trouble. Please let me know the favour that you're going to ask him."

Wally explained, "Elizabeth Kelly works for Harry's Law firm. In a week, she will represent Christine Bell in court. Christine is suing Samantha Franklin for wrongful dismissal. Samantha will not be present at her trial. She doesn't know that I will be her defence lawyer. I want Harry to tell Elizabeth that she must go out with me on a dinner date if she loses in court. I will buy Harry dinner at Spencers Mill if Elizabeth agrees to go on a dinner date with me."

Judge Judy said," Wally, you know that Harry cannot legally force Elizabeth to go out with you on a dinner date. Elizabeth is my niece, and I know she can be very stubborn. She will refuse to go on a dinner date with you, even if she loses. Wally, don't stick your nose where it doesn't belong. Elizabeth's mother, Jeffery, and his parents also worked for Harry's Law firm. They will cause you a lot of problems if you interfere."

Wally replied, "I'm not worried; Harry knows that Jeffrey is wrong for Elizabeth. I have a plan B if Elizabeth refuses to go out with me." Wally then said goodbye to Judge Judy.

Judge Judy was really concerned. She forgot to ask Wally why he is not listed as an employee at Samantha's law firm. It doesn't matter; she will have another opportunity to ask him in a week's time.

Wally arrived at Harry's office in time for lunch. On his way, he picked up a deluxe pizza from Spencers Mill. Wally never met anyone who didn't like Aunt Lydia's pizzas. Aunt Lydia uses organic whole wheat flour for the pizza crust. Homemade sauce is made from organic tomatoes. She even makes her own cheese.

Wally explained his favour to Harry, "I want you to tell Elizabeth to go out on the dinner date with me if she loses in court. I will buy you dinner at Spencers Mill if she agrees to go."

Wally continued, "I know that Elizabeth is engaged to Jeffrey Kelly. There is no way that she could possibly love him."

Harry agreed to do Wally's favour but reminded him there are no legal grounds to fire Elizabeth if she refuses to go on a dinner date with him. Wally told Harry that he knew and had a plan B if she refused to go out with him.

Harry mentioned to Wally that he has a daughter, Cindy, who is working in Samantha's law firm. "She is a paralegal studying to go to law school."

Wally told Harry that he used to go out with Cindy. He explained to him why he broke off with her. Wally did not show the video of Cindy and Michael having sex to Harry.

On the day of court, Wally was prepared. He made sure that Jonathan Quick was in court. When court commenced, Elizabeth had Christine Bell take the witness stand to give testimony. She stated that Samantha Franklin fired her without warning or any explanation. Therefore, Samantha fired her without just cause. Christine Bell stepped down.

Wally called Jonathan Quick to the witness stand. Wally asked Jonathan, "Did you have an affair with Christine Bell?" He said yes. "Did you embezzle just over $60,000 from Samantha Franklin to buy jewelry for Christine Bell?" Jonathan said yes. "I have a list of jewelry you bought from Steve's Jewelry Store. Please examine the list for errors." Jonathan looked at the list and stated that there were no errors.

Wally then asked Jonathan," During your affair with Christine Bell, was your wife Betty dying from terminal breast cancer?" Jonathan said yes. Wally had no more questions for Jonathan. He called Christine Bell to the stand.

Wally asked Christine," Did you have an affair with Jonathan Quick?" Christine said yes. She admitted to receiving expensive jewellery from Jonathan and knew that his wife Betty was dying from terminal cancer. Christine denied that she knew Jonathan bought her expensive jewellery with stolen money.

Wally said to Christine, "You admitted to having an affair with Jonathan. You admit that you knew that his wife Betty was dying from terminal breast cancer, and you admit to receiving expensive jewellery from Jonathan. Tell me, Christine, do you believe that Samantha had just cause to fire you?"

Christine closed her eyes, took a deep breath, and said yes. She then stepped down and went straight to Elizabeth and said to her, "We are no longer friends; get someone else to be your maid of honour at your wedding!"

Wally reminded Christine that she had to return all the jewellery given to her by Jonathan to Samantha since it had been bought with stolen money. Wally gave her a list of all the jewellery that was given to her. She took the list and stuck out her tongue at Wally as she was leaving. Wally laughed. He will ask Samantha to donate the jewellery to the Salvation Army.

Wally called Jonathan Quick back to the stand. He said to him, "I know that Samantha agreed not to bring charges against you when you resigned. I also know that she did not free you from making restitution. The million dollars from the insurance company that you will be receiving will suffice."

Jonathan shouted at Wally, "If you think that I am going to hand over $1,000,000 to Samantha, you are crazy!" Wally smiled and said, "Jonathan, I'll make a deal with you. I have with me a transfer form. If you sign it, the insurance money will be transferred to Samantha Franklin's bank account. I want you to read it carefully.

If you decide to sign it, you will give me the $50,000 that you have in your bank account. If you decide not to sign it, I will give you $50,000. Do you agree with my proposition?" Jonathan smiled and said that it would be a pleasure to take Wally's money.

Wally made a motion for a 15-minute recess so he could talk to Jonathan privately. The motion was granted. Wally and Jonathan went into one of the interview rooms. Wally gave the form to Jonathan to read. Wally then said, "I know that on January 15, your family doctor, Eric Clydesdale, diagnosed Betty, your wife, with terminal breast cancer. He estimated that Betty had a year to live. On January 16, you took out a million-dollar insurance policy on Betty, naming you as a benefactor. On May 20, you had another doctor, Carl Smith, examine Betty. He also diagnosed Betty with terminal breast cancer. He estimated that Betty would have six months to live. The next day, you filed a claim with the insurance company."

Wally told Jonathan he got all this information from Betty before she died. She also mentioned that he had just over $50,000 in his bank account. "Betty wanted you to rot in hell. She instructed me to report you to the insurance company. I will not report you if you sign the transfer form and give me $50,000.

Jonathan was shocked and said, "Wally, I thought we were friends." Wally replied, "Jonathan, we are friends. Thanks to me, you are not going to lose your license to practice law; you will not have a criminal record or spend time in prison."

Jonathan signed the transfer form and wrote out a cheque for $50,000 to Wally Kozak. Jonathan and Wally left the interview room just in time for court to resume. Jonathan left the court dejected. Wally informed the court of their settlement.

Wally went to see Elizabeth, "I kicked your butt. You have to go out on a dinner date with me."

Elizabeth angrily said, "No way, Harry has no legal grounds to fire me. I will not go out with you on a dinner date."

Wally made a motion to hold Elizabeth in contempt of court. Judge Judy asked Wally why she should grant him his motion. Wally said, "If you don't grant me my motion, I will sue Elizabeth for breach of contract. I may not have any legal grounds, but I'm sure I can find enough legal trivial nonsense to last a whole year in court." Judge Judy granted Wally's motion because she doesn't like Jeffery and wants Elizabeth to go on a dinner date with Wally.

Judge Judy said to Elizabeth, "I'm not going to waste my time listening to trivial nonsense in my court for a whole year. Your choice: go with Wally on a dinner date or spend the night in jail."

Elizabeth shook her head, "Aunt Judy, there is no way that Wally's lawsuit will last a whole year!" Judge Judy said to Elizabeth, "You don't know Wally like I do. He could probably come up with enough legal trivial nonsense to last two years."

Wally told Elizabeth to get dressed up because he wanted to take her to the Spencers Mill. Elizabeth refused to go there. She wanted Wally to take her to McDonald's. Wally said to Elizabeth, "Going to McDonald's is not a dinner date; it's an insult. Just because Jeffrey likes to take you there doesn't mean I will. We'll go somewhere else nice. You don't have to dress up. Be ready to go out for 7:00 tomorrow night."

Elizabeth ran out of the courtroom. Judge Judy asked Wally to stay. She said, "Wally, you sent me a beautiful gift basket. The card said that without my help, you would not have won the mock trial. I googled Samantha Franklin Law; your name was not listed as an employee. Please explain to me how you could win the mock trial, be an employee of the Franklin Law firm, and not have your name listed as an employee?"

Wally closed his eyes, held his breath, and slowly told Judge Judy to Google Samantha Franklin Law's senior partners. She did and was shocked to see his name listed as a senior partner. She said to Wally, "Samantha is a very tough and ruthless lady. What did you do to her, blackmail or threaten her life somehow?"

Wally had to explain everything to Judge Judy about how Samantha forced him to be her sex slave for a night at her apartment. He also told Judge Judy that he got a loan from Richard Kiley using his deed to his house as collateral. The mock trial judge, Judy, knew about the situation except for the senior partnership position. Wally took out his phone to show Judge Judy the look on Samantha's face when he won the mock trial.

Judge Judy laughed, "Wally, Samantha is right, you are a despicable, sneaky, conniving snake, and you are right; Samantha is an ungrateful, stubborn, foolish bitch. You deserve each other. Now tell me how much money you have saved to pay back Richard's loan?"

Wally told Judge Judy that the loan was paid off. Wally mentioned how he managed to weasel $600,000 from a rich scumbag. "Richard got $550,000, and I got $50,000."

Judge Judy laughed again, "Wally, you never cease to amaze me. Just remember your dinner date with Elizabeth is for only one night. She is determined to marry Jeffrey. Please don't cause any trouble."

Wally told Judge Judy not to worry. He will treat Elizabeth with love and respect. "If she still wants to marry Jeffrey after our dinner date, I will not interfere." Wally left the courtroom smiling. He believes that he can persuade Elizabeth to break off her engagement with Jeffery.

Judge Judy called Joan, Elizabeth's mother, to let her know that Elizabeth has a dinner date with Wally Kozak tomorrow night. Joan was not happy. When Elizabeth got home, Joan asked her why she had let Aunt Judy arrange for her to have a dinner date with Wally Kozak.

Elizabeth said, "Mother, Wally made a motion in court to hold me in contempt of court if I refused to go with him on a dinner date. Wally said that he would sue me for breach of contract. Wally said that he could find enough legal trivia to last a year in court. Aunt Judy didn't want to get involved in a trivial lawsuit, so she granted

Wally's motion. I agreed to go out with Wally because I didn't want to spend a night in jail."

Joan was furious and said, "Elizabeth, you should have refused to go out with Wally. His lawsuit would have been dismissed before it got to court, and I would have made sure that you wouldn't spend a night in jail!"

Elizabeth got upset and said, "Mother, Wally wanted to take me to the Spencers Mill. I turned his invitation down. I have been asking Jeffrey to take them there for years. He goes there every year with his parents and never invites me. I don't know where Wally's taking me, but I'm sure it will be so much better than McDonald's or IHOP!"

Joan reminded Elizabeth that she was engaged to Jeffrey and told her not to let Wally cause any trouble.

Judge Judy made another call to Richard Kiley. She told Richard that her niece, Elizabeth, was going out on a dinner date with Wally Kozak. She asked him, "Richard, please tell me what you know about Wally Kozak?"

Richard said," Wally can be an arrogant S.O.B. He is very smart. If you take him lightly in court, he'll make a fool out of you. I know from personal experience. Don't worry; Wally will treat Elizabeth with love and respect. He cares for people. Once you get to know him, you will like him."

Judge Judy asked Richard if he had loaned Wally $500,000. Richard told her he did and that Wally had paid back the loan within a month with interest. Judge Judy then asked Richard why he gave Wally the loan and how he paid it back.

Richard laughed, "I gave Wally the loan because I wanted to piss off Samantha. She offered Wally a senior partnership in exchange for all-night sex. If Wally refused, he would have been fired. Samantha tied Wally's wrists and ankles to the bed posts and tortured him all night with a whip and chain while wearing a black leather negligee. She gave Wally only 12 hours to raise $500,000. That is why he came to see me.

Judge Judy laughed and said, "Richard, Wally came to see me because Samantha forced him into participating in a mock trial. If he wins, he stays. If he loses, Samantha fires him and returns your $500,000. Samantha gave him three days to prepare for the mock trial. He wasn't allowed to use any of the office resources. Wally came to me for help. I let him use the court library. Wally won the mock trial, and Samantha was royally pissed off." Richard was happy to hear that Samantha couldn't get rid of Wally.

Richard told Judy that Wally paid him back by scamming $600,000 from a rich scumbag, $550,000 for him and $50,000 for Wally. Judge Judy laughed and told Richard that Wally also made a fool out of Harry O'Reilly. She explained to Richard what Wally did at the trial.

Richard laughed," How did the old bulldog feel when Wally humiliated him?"

Judge Judy told Richard that Harry was impressed with Wally and that they had become friends. Richard thanked Judge Judy for calling him.

Chapter 27

Wally went to see Aunt Lydia. He told her he had a dinner date tomorrow night with Elizabeth Grace. He told her that he wanted to prepare dinner at her house because she would not come to his house. Aunt Lydia asked Wally if he was very serious about having a relationship with this girl. Wally told Aunt Lydia that she was the girl he wanted to marry. "The problem is that Elizabeth is engaged to be married to Jeffrey Kelly."

Aunt Lydia was shocked, "I don't like that boy. He is an arrogant, foul-mouthed fool, just like his father. How did you manage to get a date with her?"

Wally smiled and said," Elizabeth is Judge Judy's niece. She likes me and doesn't like Jeffrey. I was able to have her arrange a dinner date with Elizabeth and me.?" Aunt Lydia told Wally to be on his best behaviour.

Early the next morning, Wally said his prayer, practised his dance, and meditated. He then went next door to see Aunt Lydia. She was waiting for him. Uncle Ivan was asleep. She wanted to know what Wally planned for dinner. Wally told her that dinner would have large potato dumplings, pork back ribs, bean salad, broccoli salad, spicy cooked cabbage and for dessert, a cheesecake wafers covered in dark chocolate served with coffee or tea. A shot of brandy will be served before dessert. Aunt Lydia asked Wally to prepare four servings because she and Uncle Ivan would be hungry after working all night at the restaurant.

Wally spent all morning preparing dinner. He placed the potato dumplings in the oven and programmed it to start cooking at 5 PM. The salads that he made were put in the refrigerator. The cabbage and pork back ribs were placed in another oven and programmed to start cooking at 6 PM. Aunt Lydia made the cheesecake wafers last night because it was Wally's favourite dessert.

When dinner preparations were completed, Wally left for his office. Harry O'Rilley called him. He wanted to congratulate Wally on getting a dinner date with Elizabeth. He asked Wally how he managed to get Elizabeth to accept his dinner invitation. "She is very stubborn and committed to marrying Jeffrey." Wally laughed and told Harry that he should ask Judge Judy. She is the person who arranged the dinner date for him.

A minute later, Jeffrey barged into Wally's office. He was furious and told him not to go out with Elizabeth tonight. He shouted, "Wally, she belongs to me!" Wally smiled and asked Jeffrey, "What are you going to do if I do go out with Elizabeth?" Jeffrey knew better. He was not going to threaten Wally in any way. Jeffrey said nothing and left Wally's office.

Soon, it was time to pick up Elizabeth. Aunt Lydia was at home waiting for them. She was anxious to meet Elizabeth. Uncle Ivan had to leave for the Spencers Mill. Wally arrived with Elizabeth. When Aunt Lydia was introduced to Elizabeth, she said to Wally, "Elizabeth is a very beautiful girl."

Aunt Lydia then put both of her hands on Elizabeth's cheeks and looked straight into her eyes. She said," Wally, you finally found the right girl. Please don't do anything stupid to upset her." Aunt Lydia mentioned to Elizabeth that Wally is a wonderful chef. "He worked for us at the Spencers Mill." She also mentioned that Wally spent all morning preparing dinner.

Aunt Lydia turned to face Wally, "When you finish dinner, don't worry about doing the dishes. Just play some nice music on the stereo and dance with Elizabeth. When you finish dancing, take her over to the piano and play something soothing like Brahms's Lullaby. When Elizabeth is relaxed, play and sing that love ballad by Gordon Lightfoot called Beautiful. Sing it with emotion, and Elizabeth will fall in love with you. Now I have to leave. Ivan is waiting for me. Have a wonderful time."

As soon as Aunt Lydia left, Elizabeth said to Wally, "I'm not hungry, and I don't have anything to say to you. Please take me home." Elizabeth was frightened. She did not want to fall in love with Wally.

Wally got very upset and said, "I spent all morning preparing this dinner. You're not going home; sit down and have dinner with me!"

Elizabeth sat down. She refused to eat or talk. Wally was not happy. He placed a morsel of potato dumpling on a fork, then grabbed one of Elizabeth's fingers and twisted it. When she screamed out in pain, Wally shoved the potato dumplings in her mouth. He put his hand underneath Elizabeth's chin to close her mouth to make sure that she could not spit out the potato dumpling. Once Elizabeth tasted the potato dumpling, she decided she was hungry and started eating dinner. Every time Wally said something to her, Elizabeth stuck out her tongue at Wally and said nothing.

When they finished dinner, Wally picked up a flask of brandy and two large brandy snifters. He poured an ounce of brandy into a brandy snifter for Elizabeth. She thought that the brandy was wine. Elizabeth didn't know that brandy has 40% alcohol. She grabbed the flask from Wally and poured the entire flask into her brandy snifter. She then guzzled the brandy down as fast as she could. Elizabeth thought Wally was mad at her and decided to be cheap with the wine.

Wally was really upset and said, "Congratulations, Elizabeth, you just down 12 ounces of brandy. You are wasted."

Elizabeth smiled at Wally, took another serving of food, and started eating without saying a word. Wally was shocked, "Elizabeth, do you realize you are eating Uncle Ivan's breakfast."

Elizabeth stuck out her tongue at Wally and kept eating without saying a word. Wally watched Elizabeth eat. He couldn't believe that she was capable of eating so much food. When Elizabeth finished her plate, Wally asked her if she was going to eat Aunt

Lydia's breakfast. Elizabeth smiled, stuck out her tongue at Wally, and started to eat Aunt Lydia's breakfast without saying a word.

When Elizabeth finished eating, Wally asked her if she was ready for dessert. Elizabeth, smiling, nodded yes. Wally brought out a plate of cheesecake wafers covered in dark chocolate. There were eight wafers, two for each person. Wally watched Elizabeth eat all eight cheesecake wafers and drink a pot of coffee.

When Elizabeth finished her dessert, Wally was ready to take her home. Elizabeth was not ready to go home. She reminded Wally that Aunt Lydia had told her to put on some nice music so they could dance. Wally became really annoyed, "Elizabeth, you are too drunk to dance; you can barely walk!"

Elizabeth smiled at Wally and slurred, "If you don't put on some nice music so we can dance, I'll scream bloody rape for the entire neighbourhood to hear!"

Wally put on some nice music on the stereo. Elizabeth tried to dance but was unable to. She kept on getting dizzy and falling down. Wally was ready to drive Elizabeth home. She was not ready to go home. Wally had to play Brahms's Lullaby on the piano for her. When Wally finished, Elizabeth insisted he play that romantic love ballad by Gordon Lightfoot called Beautiful. Elizabeth told Wally that if she didn't fall in love with him after he sang the love ballad, she would scream bloody rape.

Wally reluctantly started to sing the love ballad for Elizabeth. He was playing the piano and singing with emotion. After he finished singing the song, Elizabeth grabbed Wally's cheeks with her hands and kissed him in the mouth with all her might. She then dragged Wally into the bedroom. Elizabeth started to unbutton Wally's shirt. He grabbed her wrists to stop her. Elizabeth stomped on Wally's toes real hard. When Wally let go of her wrists, she whacked him in the chest. The wind was knocked out of him momentarily; he could not breathe. Wally helplessly watched Elizabeth undress him until he was completely naked. Elizabeth whacked Wally in the chest again. She then pushed Wally onto the bed. Wally watched Elizabeth undress.

When Elizabeth became completely naked, she jumped on Wally's face. Wally was suffocating because Elizabeth's pussy was covering his nose and mouth. Wally panicked and somehow managed to throw Elizabeth off his face. She landed on her butt. Elizabeth immediately got up from the floor and jumped on Wally's stomach. Wally stared helplessly as Elizabeth did whatever she wanted.

When Elizabeth finished her sex romp on Wally, she laid down on top of him and fell asleep. Wally also fell asleep. Two hours later, Elizabeth started releasing loud, disgusting, smelly farts. Wally almost puked. Elizabeth got up and headed for the washroom. Wally got up and headed for another washroom to take a shower. When Wally finished his shower, he got dressed and was ready to take Elizabeth home. Elizabeth was gone. She plugged the toilet with her poop. Elizabeth got dressed and left before Wally finished his shower.

Elizabeth took a cab home. When she got home, she saw her mother waiting. Elizabeth told her mother not to worry. Nothing happened. She and Wally fell asleep drinking wine while listening to music. Elizabeth also told her mother that she would not be seeing Wally anymore. Elizabeth's mother was happy and went to sleep. Elizabeth went to take a shower.

Aunt Lydia and Uncle Ivan pulled into the driveway. Wally was still in the house. He opened the back window and jumped out before he was seen. Wally got into his car and drove to a nearby hotel. He didn't want to face Uncle Ivan alone. Aunt Lydia is a forgiving person, but Uncle Ivan is not. He would freak out.

When Aunt Lydia and Uncle Ivan entered the house, they heard Wally driving away. Uncle Ivan screamed, "What is that awful smell? What happened here?"

Aunt Lydia told Uncle Ivan that someone plugged the toilet with poop. The smell must be coming from the poop. Uncle Ivan saw the bed and cried out, "Wally and his girlfriend were sleeping in our bed. I'm going to kill him!"

Aunt Lydia told Uncle Ivan to calm down and said, "Wally is a good boy. Give him a chance to explain what happened."

Uncle Ivan did calm down and said, "No matter what explanation Wally gives, he is responsible for our toilet being plugged with poop. He will be paying the plumber to unplug our toilet." Aunt Lydia smiled at Uncle Ivan, and they both entered the guest bedroom. Uncle Ivan opened the window to let the smell out.

Chapter 28

It was 9:00 am when Wally checked out of the hotel. He drove straight to the courthouse to see Judge Judy. She was waiting for him. Judge Judy wanted to know how the dinner date went with Elizabeth. Wally told her that Elizabeth was a disgusting pig, and he explained, "Elizabeth didn't want to go to the Spencers Mill with me, so I decided to prepare dinner for us at my aunt and uncle's home. They own the Spencers Mill. I used to be a chef there."

Wally introduced Elizabeth to aunt Lydia. He told her that Elizabeth was engaged to Jeffrey Kelly. Aunt Lydia was shocked that any girl would want to marry Jeffrey. Wally prepared four servings of food. Two servings were for his aunt and uncle's breakfast when they got home. Wally told Judge Judy what aunt Lydia said to Elizabeth when she put her hands-on Elizabeth's cheeks. Elizabeth became frightened. Elizabeth decided that she was not hungry and wanted to go home. Wally wasn't ready to take Elizabeth home because he spent all morning preparing dinner. He shoved a morsel of food into Elizabeth's mouth. She decided that she was hungry. She ate without saying a word. Every time Wally said something to her, she stuck out her tongue at him.

The real trouble started when she thought the flask of brandy was wine. Elizabeth poured the entire flask into a brandy snifter and guzzled it down as fast as she could. Brandy was 40% alcohol. Judge Judy didn't believe Wally. He told her that she received a bottle of brandy in her gift basket. Judge Judy opened her desk drawer and took out the bottle of brandy. The label said 40% alcohol.

Wally continued saying that Elizabeth ate his aunt and uncle's breakfast and all the cheesecake wafers and drank a pot of coffee. There were eight cheesecake wafers, two for each person. Wally told Judge Judy how Elizabeth almost suffocated him with her dandruff-infested pussy. How Elizabeth laid on top of Wally and released loud, smelly, disgusting farts. Then she plugged the toilet with poop. Elizabeth snuck out of the house while Wally was taking a shower.

Judy had a hard time believing Wally. She picked up the phone and called Elizabeth. She said, "I heard you had a wonderful time with Wally last night." Elizabeth told aunt Judy that it was aunt Lydia's fault. She wanted her to fall in love with Wally.

Judge Judy said, "That is no excuse for your bad behaviour. Was it Aunt Lydia's fault that you guzzled down a flask of brandy? It has 40% alcohol; you were only supposed to receive an ounce."

Elizabeth was very embarrassed and said, "Aunt Judy, I thought the brandy was wine, and Wally was being cheap because I refused to talk to him."

Elizabeth admitted to everything that Wally said that she did but refused to admit that she had a dandruff-infested pussy.

Wally said to Judge Judy, "I made dinner reservations for Elizabeth and myself at the Spencers Mill tonight. Uncle Ivan is not a forgiving person. He will not freak out in front of a room full of people when I tell him what happened at our dinner date last night. Tell Elizabeth that she must dress up for dinner."

Elizabeth heard what Wally said and told aunt Judy that Jeffrey would not allow it. Judge Judy laughed and said, "Elizabeth, since when did you ever ask Jeffrey for permission to do anything? Tell Jeffrey that you are going out to dinner with Wally at the Spencers Mill. Tell him that you are going because he's too cheap to take you. Put on that beautiful red dress that you just bought, and have a good time."

Elizabeth said, "Aunt Judy, I can't go; I need to have my hair done. My hairdresser will charge me double to do my hair without an appointment."

Wally told Elizabeth that he'd pay for her hairdresser if she wore that beautiful red dress that she just bought. Elizabeth said to Wally, "My hairdresser is located in the strip Plaza across the street from the Spencers Mill. Pick me up at 6:30 tonight. Be ready to pay a fortune to have my hair done."

Wally thanked Judge Judy and left for his office. He was looking forward to having dinner with Elizabeth. Judge Judy called the Spencers Mill to talk to Lydia. She said, "I did not know that Wally Kozak was your nephew." Lydia replied," I didn't know that you knew Wally."

Judge Judy told Lydia she knew Wally quite well because he was in her courtroom many times. "I knew that Wally looked familiar but couldn't place him." She told Lydia everything that had happened the previous night and that she was mostly responsible. Judge Judy said, "Didn't Wally tell you that Elizabeth is stubborn and engaged to Jeffrey Kelly?"

Lydia took a deep breath and said, "Elizabeth cannot marry Jeffrey. He is a horrible boy. That is why I tried to encourage Elizabeth to fall in love with Wally."

Judge Judy replied, "Lydia, you frightened Elizabeth. She did not want to fall in love with Wally. That is why she behaved so badly."

Lydia shook her head and said, "I can't believe Elizabeth could eat so much food. The brandy must have increased her appetite. It's no wonder that she stunk up our house with smelly farts. She ate a lot of spicy cabbage. The amount of food she ate produced a lot of poop. Wally will be receiving a bill from the plumber for $350."

Judy laughed and said, "Lydia, Wally made reservations tonight. He is bringing Elizabeth. Wally doesn't want to face uncle Ivan alone when he explains what happened last night. I want to be there. Can you reserve a table for three beside Wally's table? Joan and Christine will be coming with me. I want to make sure that they'll be no trouble."

Lydia smiled and said, "Judy, thanks for telling me what happened last night. I'll reserve a table for you and tell Ivan what happened. How did Wally convince Elizabeth to go with him?"

Judge Judy laughed, "I talked Elizabeth into going with Wally. She had never been to the Spencers Mill and always wanted to go there. Jeffery is too cheap to take her." Aunt Lydia laughed and said goodbye.

Judge Judy called Joan and Christine to tell them why Elizabeth was going out with Wally for dinner at the Spencers Mill. She also told them to make sure that Jeffery doesn't cause trouble. They were not happy with Judge Judy for allowing Wally to interfere with Elizabeth's life. Judge Judy said," I reserved a table for us next to Wally's to make sure that there is no trouble."

Aunt Lydia told uncle Ivan what happened last night. She said, "It was my fault, not Wally's, that Elizabeth behaved so badly. Ivan, Elizabeth is such a nice girl, and she is just right for Wally. It's too bad that she is engaged to marry that horrible boy. Jeffrey will make Elizabeth's life miserable."

Uncle Ivan smiled and said, "Maybe we can help Wally get Elizabeth to call off her engagement to Jeffrey." Aunt Lydia shook her head, "I don't think we can. Elizabeth is stubborn and determined to marry Jeffrey." Uncle Ivan, still smiling, said, "We'll see."

Wally left his office to pick up Elizabeth at her hairdresser. She was waiting for him. Wally took a good look at Elizabeth and said, "Wow! Elizabeth, you are very beautiful!" Wally then gave Elizabeth a kiss, and she gave him a slap in the chest.

Wally was annoyed and said, "Elizabeth, that is no way to behave. I agreed to pay your hairdresser and take you to the Spencers Mill for dinner. I deserve more than just a kiss."

Sally, Elizabeth's hairdresser, was watching, shaking her head, "Elizabeth, Wally is right. He deserves a lot more than just a kiss. What is wrong with you? Wally is a gorgeous hunk, and Jeffrey is a disgusting pig! Wally, you are not going to pay for Elizabeth's hair. She's going to pay for it. It's not your responsibility. Call me if she misbehaves during dinner. If she does, I will dump her as a regular customer."

Elizabeth was shocked. She didn't say a word and gave her credit card to Sally. Wally took her hand, and they left for Spencers Mill to have dinner. When they arrived, Judge Judy, Joan, and Christine were already at their table waiting for them. Wally and Elizabeth were not happy to see them. Uncle Ivan approached Wally's table and said, "It's nice to see you, Wally." Uncle Ivan faced Elizabeth, "You must be the naughty little girl that caused all that trouble last night."

Uncle Ivan smiled at Wally and said, "Elizabeth is a very beautiful girl. I can see why you have forgiven her for causing all that trouble last night and invited her for dinner. She must be very fond of you because she agreed to come. Now tell me, Wally, where are you planning to take her on your next date?"

Wally became annoyed, "Why do you want to know where I'm taking her, uncle Ivan?"

Uncle Ivan replied, "I want to make sure that you take her out somewhere nice, not somewhere stupid. If you don't tell me where you are going to take her, you and her will be washing dishes after dinner."

Wally asked Elizabeth if she would like to see the ballet. Elizabeth nodded yes. Wally took out his phone and called Lawrence. He said, "Can you get me two tickets to the ballet for tomorrow night? I have a hot date who would love to go."

Lawrence replied, "Wally, I could probably get you the tickets, but they will be very expensive." Wally replied, "Lawrence, I don't care how much they cost; just get me the best seats you can."

Lawrence happily said, "Wally, I will have the tickets reserved in your name at the box office. Pick them up a half-hour before the ballet starts." Wally thanked Lawrence.

Uncle Ivan was smiling, "That is very nice of you to take Elizabeth to the ballet. Wally, when you get to the ballet, say as little as possible. I don't want you to say something stupid to upset her. Hold Elizabeth's hand gently but firmly. If you start to get excited, take several deep breaths. That will calm you down; after all, you are a big, strong boy. You wouldn't want to crush Elizabeth's delicate little hand."

Wally was getting annoyed, "Uncle Ivan, get lost!" Uncle Ivan smiled at Elizabeth and said, "Elizabeth, how many times did you tell Wally to get lost before you decided to go out with him?" Elizabeth shook her head and told Ivan that she did not know, but it was lots.

Uncle Ivan kept smiling, "I thought so. Wally, take Elizabeth over to the piano and have her sit beside you. Then sing a romantic love song." Wally replied, "I'm sure Elizabeth would rather hear some Van Morrison songs instead." Wally was not in a romantic mood.

Uncle Ivan was still smiling and said, "We can move the piano into the kitchen. Wally, you can sing Van Morrison songs all night while Elizabeth washes dishes."

Wally walked Elizabeth over to the piano. She sat beside him. Since Elizabeth was wearing a red dress, Wally decided to sing Lady in Red. When he finished singing the song, Wally received a standing ovation from the customers.

Judge Judy told Jean, "Elizabeth would have jumped Wally last night even if she was sober." Uncle Ivan was very pleased, "Wally, that was wonderful. You have time to sing another love song for Elizabeth."

Wally chose to sing a song called You and I. It was a sweet little love song that Elizabeth enjoyed. Judge Judy nudged Joan, "Do you still want Elizabeth to marry Jeffrey." Joan and Christine gave Judge Judy a dirty look. They said nothing.

Uncle Ivan was really happy, "Wally, you have time to sing one more song for Elizabeth before dinner is served. Wally chose one of his favourite love songs called Nobody Can Love You Quite Like I Do. When Wally finished singing the song, Elizabeth got up and ran to the washroom. Judge Judy got up and ran after her.

Judge Judy asked Elizabeth, "What's the matter with you?" A red-faced Elizabeth replied, "I peed my panties! That's what's the matter. Wally set me up. I'll kill him!"

Judge Judy said to Elizabeth, "Wally's innocent. You can blame me. I called aunt Lydia and told her what happened last night. Wally had no way of knowing that uncle Ivan was going to play Cupid. Now, hold up your dress while I pull down your panties." Elizabeth held up her dress, and Aunt Judy pulled down her panties. She said, "Elizabeth, Wally was right; your pussy is infested with dandruff."

Elizabeth screamed, "Aunt Judy, don't start on me; just dry me off!" Aunt Judy wiped Elizabeth dry. Then she pulled out a diaper from her purse. Elizabeth was embarrassed but took the diaper and put it on. She said, "I want to go home now, aunt Judy. Please drive me home."

Aunt Judy said to Elizabeth, "You will go back to the table and have your dinner with Wally. He will drive your home." Elizabeth went back to her table. She did not feel like talking. Wally was not in a talking mood either. They quietly ate their dinner. Aunt Lydia prepared prime rib, scallop potatoes, steamed vegetables, and Caesar salad.

Judge Judy smiled and said to Joan, "Doesn't Wally sing like an angel?" Joan rudely replied, "After tonight, the angel better keep away from Elizabeth."

Uncle Ivan approached Wally's table and said, "Dinner is on the house. However, this $350 plumbing bill is not. It's the cost to unplug our toilet with poop. Please pay the cashier on your way out."

Judge Judy got up and walked over to Wally's table and told him to give her the plumbing bill. Wally thanked Judge Judy and gave her the plumbing bill. He walked out with Elizabeth. He drove directly to his house. Wally said to Elizabeth, "This is where I live. There is a piano in my living room. It's only 9:30. Would you like me to sing some Van Morrison songs for you?"

Against her better judgment, Elizabeth said yes. She was surprised that Wally lived in such a beautiful house. She was also surprised how the inside of the house was beautifully decorated. Elizabeth sat in a lazy boy chair beside the piano. Wally started to sing Brown Eyed Girl. Elizabeth enjoyed singing the chorus with Wally. He sang several other Van Morrison songs. Elizabeth was enjoying all the songs that Wally sang. She lost track of time. It was 2:30 in the morning. Wally decided that it was time to take Elizabeth home. She was very tired and didn't want to go home. Wally allowed her to stay if she promised not to stomp on his toes or whack him in the chest. Elizabeth promised.

Wally decided to sing one more song called Loving You is Easy. When Wally finished singing the song, he stood up. Elizabeth jumped Wally and wrapped her legs around his waist. He carried her to the bedroom. Elizabeth went to the washroom to take off her clothes. She didn't want Wally to see the diaper that she was wearing. Wally knew that Elizabeth was wearing a diaper. When she came out, Wally was lying in bed naked. Elizabeth slipped into the bed next to him. Wally reminded Elizabeth that she had to go to the ballet with him tomorrow night. She told Wally that she was not going. Wally said to Elizabeth, "You have to go to the ballet with me tonight. Lawrence will be very upset. He can cause me a lot of trouble. Uncle Ivan will have us wash dishes all night."

Elizabeth replied, "Wally, that is not my problem. There is no way that I'm going to the ballet with you. Your uncle Ivan has no legal grounds to force us to wash dishes. Jeffrey will be very upset if I go to the ballet with you."

Wally smiled and whispered in Elizabeth's ear, "I will tell Sally that you have been a naughty girl. That means you will be looking for another hairdresser." Elizabeth was shocked that Wally would turn to blackmail. She had no choice.

Elizabeth took a deep breath, smiled and said, "Alright, Wally, I will go to the ballet with you if you promise me when you pick me up, you will say as little as possible. I don't want you to say something stupid to upset me. At the ballet, take a firm but gentle hold of my hand. Wally, if you start to get excited, take several deep breaths. This will calm you down. After all, you are a big, strong boy and would not want to crush my delicate little hand."

Wally whispered in Elizabeth's ear, "I promise, and you must promise me that you will be on your best behaviour, you naughty little girl." Elizabeth, giggling, said, "I promise to behave."

Wally and Elizabeth lay quietly and fell asleep. Joan was very worried. It was 4 o'clock in the morning, and Elizabeth was not home. She called a sleepy Aunt Lydia to let her know that Wally didn't bring Elizabeth home. Aunt Lydia told Joan not to worry. "Elizabeth is having such a good time with Wally that she lost track of time. Don't worry. Wally will bring Elizabeth home safely." Joan was still upset. She told aunt Lydia that she would hold her responsible if Wally didn't bring Elizabeth safely home soon.

It was early in the morning when Wally woke up. He opened a dresser drawer and took out a package of a brand-new pair of panties. Wally woke up Elizabeth and told her that he had no use for these panties. They belonged to his mother. Elizabeth thanked Wally and took the panties. She got out of bed to put her clothes on. Wally got out of bed. He got dressed and prepared breakfast. Elizabeth enjoyed hot cereal with blueberries and maple syrup with toast and coffee.

Joan waited all night for Elizabeth to come home. Wally dropped off Elizabeth and drove off to his office. Joan was furious, "Elizabeth, you have a lot of explaining to do. I waited all night for you. Why didn't you call me!"

Elizabeth smiled, "Wally showed me his home. He lives in a beautiful house. He invited me inside. In the living room stood a beautiful baby grand piano. Wally asked me to stay so he could play and sing Van Morrison songs. I stayed because I am a huge Van Morrison fan. Wally has such a wonderful singing voice. He sang and played the piano beautifully. I was having such a wonderful time, but I lost track of time. I was getting tired, so I asked Wally if I could spend the night with him."

Joan was not happy, "Elizabeth, did you forget that you are engaged to marry Jeffrey?"

Elizabeth smiled and said, "Mother, Jeffrey is a complete, cheap bore. I wanted to have some excitement in my life. Wally took me to the Spencers Mill. I had a good time. Tonight, he is taking me to the ballet. Unlike Jeffrey, Wally did not ask Lawrence how much the tickets cost. He told him to get the best seats available."

Joan shouted at Elizabeth, "You can't go to the ballet with Wally tonight. Jeffrey will not allow it!" Elizabeth calmly said, "Since when do I need permission from Jeffrey? If he wasn't so cheap to take me to the ballet, I wouldn't be going with Wally. Don't worry, Mother; the only reason that he is taking me to the ballet is that he doesn't want to upset Lawrence. It's not my fault that uncle Ivan played Cupid last night. He would've made us wash dishes all night if Wally wasn't going to take me to the ballet."

Joan calmed down and said, "Elizabeth, I can't blame you for wanting to go to the ballet with Wally. Just remember that you are going to marry Jeffrey. Please stay away from Wally after tonight." Joan hugged Elizabeth and went to bed. Early the next morning, Joan called Christine to let her know what had happened. Christine was not happy.

Chapter 29

Wally entered his office; he saw Patricia waiting for him. She heard he had a dinner date with Elizabeth at the Spencers Mill. Wally knew that Patricia was not going to leave unless he told her what happened. He told Patricia that he had invited Elizabeth for dinner at the Spencers Mill.

"She accepted my dinner invitation because Jeffery is too cheap to take her there. I wasn't expecting uncle Ivan to play Cupid. Now I have to take Elizabeth to the ballet. Jeffrey will want to kill me if I do take her. Lawrence will be very upset if I don't take her."

Patricia started to laugh, "Wally, have a wonderful time at the ballet. Please let me know how it went."

Elizabeth told Jeffrey that she was going to the ballet with Wally because he was too cheap to take her. Jeffrey was furious and said, "Elizabeth, you can't go to the ballet with Wally. He is a Casanova and only wants to get between your legs!"

Elizabeth calmly said to Jeffrey, "I have been asking you to take me to the ballet for years. You keep telling me that tickets are too hard to get and too expensive. Wally is not a Casanova. He is a perfect gentleman. I'm going to the ballet with Wally, and there is nothing you can do to stop me."

Jeffrey ran out of his office to see his father. He told him that Elizabeth was going to the ballet with Wally tonight. Jeffrey's father said to him, "Jeffrey when Wally drives Elizabeth home from the ballet, be there waiting for him. As soon as Elizabeth walks into the house, beat the crap out of Wally. That'll send a message to him to stay away from Elizabeth."

Jeffrey thanked his father for his advice and went to see Wally. He barged into his office. Jeffrey poked his finger into Wally's chest and said, "Wally, you better not take Elizabeth to the ballet. If you do, you will be very sorry!"

Jeffrey left before Wally could say a word. Wally was able to read his mind. He knew that Jeffrey was planning to beat the crap out of him after he took Elizabeth home from the ballet. Wally was capable of breaking every bone in Jeffrey's body. However, Wally would allow Jeffrey to beat him up. Wally will be video recording the beating he gets from Jeffrey on his phone.

That night, Wally drove Elizabeth to the ballet. She was wearing the same beautiful red dress that she wore at the Spencers Mill. Wally kept his promise by saying very little. Two tickets were waiting for him at the box office.

Lawrence was already sitting in a seat next to Elizabeth. Lawrence took a good look at Elizabeth and said, "Wally, when you said that you had a hot date, you weren't kidding. She is gorgeous!" Wally introduced Elizabeth to Lawrence and told him that he would pay for the tickets tomorrow.

Lawrence said, "Wally, there is no rush to pay for the tickets. Consider them a wedding gift when you get engaged to Elizabeth. Now relax and enjoy the ballet."

Wally took a firm but gentle hold of Elizabeth's hand. He spent more time looking at Elizabeth then watching the ballet. He didn't need to breathe heavily. Reading her mind, Wally knew that Elizabeth did not love Jeffrey. She could barely tolerate him. Wally couldn't understand why Elizabeth made a commitment to marry Jeffrey.

At the end of the ballet, Wally thanked Lawrence for getting the tickets. He was happy that Elizabeth enjoyed the ballet. As Wally was driving Elizabeth home, she asked him, "Wally, why didn't you tell Lawrence that I was engaged?"

Wally replied, "I didn't want to spoil the evening. I will tell Lawrence tomorrow morning."

When Wally arrived at Elizabeth's home, he saw Jeffrey hiding behind an evergreen on the front lawn. Wally took out his phone, ready to video record the beating that he was about to receive from Jeffrey. Elizabeth walked into the house and saw Joan waiting for her. Elizabeth smiled and told her mother that she didn't have to worry. "Wally promised to leave me alone to marry Jeffrey. Wally was a perfect gentleman. The ballet was wonderful." Joan gave Elizabeth a big hug and went to bed without saying a word.

Wally's back was facing Jeffrey. He kicked Wally in the back and smiled, "I told you to stay away from Elizabeth. That cock sucking bitch belongs to me!" Jeffrey kicked Wally in the stomach and punched him in the face several times. Jeffrey grabbed Wally by his shirt collar and threw him into a wet flower bed.

Jeffrey stepped on Wally's chest and said, "This is just a warning. You come near Elizabeth again; I'll make sure that you end up in the hospital!" Jeffery left Wally lying in the flower bed.

Wally got up and went to his car. Wally's face was swollen, and had two black eyes. Wally was smiling. He video-recorded everything that Jeffrey did and said to him. Wally also read Jeffrey's mind. He found out that the engagement ring that Elizabeth got from him was bought at a pawn shop for $500. Wally also discovered that Jeffrey went with his father every Friday afternoon for a massage. They not only received a massage but also received sex from the girls who were giving the massage. Wally wondered why Jeffrey was so cheap. He spent all his money on sex every Friday afternoon and couldn't afford to take Elizabeth anywhere nice.

Wally also found out that Jeffrey's parents agreed to pay off Elizabeth's entire $200,000 government student loan as soon as she and Jeffrey got married. Now, Wally knew the main reason that Elizabeth had agreed to marry Jeffrey.

Wally opened the trunk of his car and took out a blanket. He used it to cover the front seat. Wally's suit was wet and covered with soil. He drove home. Wally took off his clothes, showered, and put on a robe. He put his dirty suit in a plastic bag and placed it in the trunk of his car. Wally went to bed.

Chapter 30

The next morning, Wally said his prayer, did his dance and meditated. Wally had a raisin muffin and tea for breakfast. He then drove to Steve's Jewelry Store to buy an engagement ring for Elizabeth. The saleslady showed Wally an expensive ring that he liked. She said to Wally, "This ring is priced at $21,000. If you buy it right now, I will let you have it for $18,000."

Wally took out his credit card to buy the ring. The saleslady placed the ring in a box. She gave it to Wally and wished him good luck. The saleslady didn't ask what happened to Wally's face.

Wally got into his car and drove to the courthouse to see Judge Judy. He got to see her right away. Wally entered her office wearing sunglasses. He held a bag of dirty clothes in his left hand and his phone in his right hand.

Judge Judy was shocked and asked him, "Wally, what happened to your face!" Wally took off his sunglasses. He then took out his dirty suit to show to Judge Judy and then played the video recording of the beating he got from Jeffrey. He told Judge Judy that he let Jeffrey beat him up. "I could have broken every bone in his body if I wanted to. There's no way that Elizabeth will marry Jeffrey now."

Wally told Judge Judy that Jeffrey bought Elizabeth's engagement ring for $500 at a pawn shop. He also told her that every Friday afternoon, he and his father pay for sex at a massage parlour. He also told her that Jeffrey's parents agreed to pay Elizabeth's $200,000 government student loan as soon as they got married.

Wally smiled and asked Judge Judy to show the video recording to Jeffrey's parents. He gave her a copy of the video recording on a memory stick. Judge Judy said, "Wally, go to Jonathan's Clothier and get the most expensive tailor-made suit for yourself. I'll make sure that Jeffrey's mother will pay for it."

Wally took out the engagement ring that he got for Elizabeth to show Judge Judy. She took a good look at the ring and said, "Wally, this is a very beautiful, expensive ring, but I don't think Elizabeth is prepared to accept your marriage proposal."

Wally smiled and said, "I know Elizabeth may not be ready. When I see her, I will remove the cheap trinket from her finger that Jeffrey gave her and put on the ring that I bought for her. When Elizabeth is watching the video recording, I will tell her where Jeffrey bought her engagement ring and how much he paid for it, and that he pays for sex every Friday afternoon at the massage parlour. If she accepts my marriage proposal, I will pay off her entire government student loan once we are married. I will tell Elizabeth to think about my marriage proposal while she is wearing my engagement ring for the rest of the week. Every day this week, I will bring her lunch and let her watch the video recording. I also will bring Harry lunch. He'll keep Jeffrey busy to keep him away from us."

Judge Judy was very surprised and said, "Wally, you never cease to amaze me. I wish you all the luck." Wally thanked Judge Judy and left for his office.

Patricia was anxiously waiting for Wally in his office. She was shocked when she saw his face. Wally told Patricia everything that happened to him. He even showed her the video recording of Jeffrey beating him up and told her of his plans to marry Elizabeth. Patricia stared at the ring that Wally had bought for Elizabeth.

Patricia said, "Wally, I think you have a great plan. But what happens if Elizabeth foolishly turns you down."

Wally said, smiling, "I'm going to remove my engagement ring from Elizabeth's finger and put it on your finger."

Patricia took a deep breath and said, "Wally, I hope that Elizabeth turns out to be a fool. If you give me that ring, there is no way that I will give it back!"

Wally went home to prepare lunch for Elizabeth and Harry. He decided on pierogies and pizza. Wally packed his lunch and drove off to see Elizabeth. He showed Harry his two black eyes, his muddied suit, and the video recording. Harry was more than happy to keep Jeffrey away from Wally and Elizabeth when he saw what Wally had brought for lunch. Wally walked into Elizabeth's office with lunch. He took off his sunglasses and showed her his muddied suit.

Wally said," Jeffrey jumped me as soon as you got into the house. I want to show you a video recording of Jeffrey beating me up."

Elizabeth was shocked to hear what Jeffrey called her and what he did to Wally. Wally told Elizabeth that Jeffrey bought her engagement ring for $500 at a pawn shop. Wally also told her that Jeffrey and his father go to a massage parlour to pay for sex every Friday afternoon. Wally then took hold of Elizabeth's ring finger and removed Jeffrey's cheap trinket. He put the engagement ring that he bought on her finger.

Wally looked into Elizabeth's eyes and said, "Elizabeth, if you marry me, I will pay off your entire $200,000 government student loan as soon as we get married." Elizabeth said nothing. She just kept staring at the engagement ring that Wally bought her. Wally left a copy of the video on a memory stick for Elizabeth.

Wally kissed Elizabeth and said to her, "You don't have to make a decision right away. Keep the ring on your finger till the end of the week. I will be bringing you lunch each day. At the end of the week, you can decide to keep the ring and marry me or give back the ring."

Elizabeth was speechless; she kept staring at her ring finger. Wally brought out the lunch. They quietly had lunch. When he finished lunch, Wally got up to leave and sang, How Sweet it is to be Loved by You.

Elizabeth went to see Harry. He told her to ditch Jeffrey and marry Wally. Elizabeth left Harry's office and drove to Steve's

Jewelry Store. The saleslady told Elizabeth that the ring she wore cost \$21,000. She couldn't believe Wally would spend so much money to buy her an engagement ring. Elizabeth left for the office to see her mother.

Elizabeth barged into her mother's office. She told her what Jeffrey had done and showed her the video recording that Wally had taken. She then held up her hand to show the engagement ring that Wally had bought her.

"Mother, this ring cost \$21,000, and the ring that Jeffrey bought cost \$500, which he bought at a pawn shop. Jeffrey told me that it was a valuable family heirloom. Wally also told me that every Friday afternoon, Jeffrey pays to have sex at a massage parlour. Wally said that he would pay off my entire government student loan once we get married."

Elizabeth told Joan what Wally had planned for her. "Mother, do you still want me to marry Jeffrey?"

Joan gave Elizabeth a big hug and said to her, "Elizabeth, you have to decide for yourself. Ask Aunt Judy; she knows Wally quite well and likes him. Elizabeth, if you decide to marry Wally, you have my blessing."

Elizabeth took a deep breath and, with a worried look, said, "Mother, I definitely will not marry Jeffrey. My problem is that I don't know if I'm ready to marry anyone at this time." Elizabeth gave Joan a big hug and left.

Joan called Christine, Jeffrey's mother, "Christine, did you know what Jeffrey did to Wally after he drove Elizabeth home from the ballet?"

Christine grumbled, "Judy gave me a video recording that Wally made. She told me to expect a bill from Jonathan's Clothier. Wally wants a new suit. She also told me what Wally is planning to do. Joan, Elizabeth's and Jeffery's wedding will be in 10 weeks. It's too late to cancel."

Joan shook her head and said, "Christine, you didn't see the engagement ring that Wally bought Elizabeth. It cost him \$21,000.

Jeffrey paid $500 for his ring at a pawn shop. You don't expect Elizabeth to marry Jeffrey after what he did and called her. I told Elizabeth if she decided to marry Wally, she would have my blessing."

Christine was not happy and she slammed down the phone.

Wally explained to everyone in the office that he got beat up by a jealous boyfriend. He didn't tell who it was or what he was planning to do. No one knew except Patricia. She promised Wally that she wouldn't tell anyone. Wally went home to prepare lunch for Elizabeth and Harry. He prepared a spinach salad containing various nuts and seeds. He added tomatoes, red peppers, and mushrooms. Wally also made lasagna using Aunt Lydia's recipe. He prepared lunch for six people. Wally was ready to leave.

A pot of coffee was brewing in Harry's office. He was anxiously waiting for lunch. Wally showed up to deliver Harry's lunch. Wally then walked into Elizabeth's office with their lunch. He told Elizabeth that if she didn't feel like talking about that, it was okay because he understood. Elizabeth was smacking her lips; she was hungry. Elizabeth quietly ate her lunch. Wally didn't care if Elizabeth didn't want to talk. He was just happy to see Elizabeth wearing his engagement ring. When Elizabeth finished lunch, she gave Wally a big kiss.

Wally gathered the dishes and went to see Harry. He said to Wally, "I want to hire you to prepare daily lunches. Are you interested?"

Wally answered, "Harry if you want gourmet lunches prepared daily, talk to my aunt Lydia at the Spencers Mill."

Patricia went to see her best friend, Stephanie. She breeds Yorkies. Patricia said to her, "Stephanie, I know someone who wants to buy your two Yorkie teacups."

Stephanie shook her head, "I always screen potential buyers before I let them purchase a Yorkie."

"Stephanie, my friend Wally wants to convince his sweetheart to marry him. That is why he wants to buy them. He works in the same office as I do. He will take very good care of the puppies. I personally will make sure that they will not be abused," begged Patricia.

Stephanie took a deep breath and said, "Alright, I don't know why, but I will allow Wally to buy my two little Yorkies. If I find out that they are abused in any way, we are no longer friends." Patricia gave Stephanie a big hug and told her not to worry. The Yorkies will be treated with love and respect. Patricia would have loved to buy those little Yorkies herself but couldn't afford them.

Chapter 31

Clarence from the Salvation Army was waiting for Wally in his office. Wally could see that Clarence was worried. Clarence said, "Wally, Harvey Katz came to see me last month. He wanted me to join him in robbing banks. I'm telling you this because he is the one who has been robbing all those banks last month. The police are unable to catch him. I told Harvey that I wouldn't join him because I found God. He is crazy, and I know that he will cause me trouble."

Wally asked him," Clarence, what do you want me to do?" Clarence replied, "Harvey's mother knows where he is. She won't tell me, but she might tell you because she likes you. Please go visit her."

Wally told Clarence it had been many years since he saw her, but he would pay her a visit this afternoon. Clarence thanked Wally and left. Wally started to catch up on his paperwork. It was 10:00 AM when Wally decided to pay Harvey Katz's mother a visit.

He found Harvey's mother outside the house, watering her flowers. She looked up and saw Wally. She ran to him to give him a big hug. Wally read her mind and knew where Harvey Katz was hiding. Mrs. Katz invited Wally inside the house for tea. Wally said he was in the neighbourhood and saw her watering her plants. He let her know that he was a lawyer working for a law firm. Wally asked how Harvey was doing. Mrs. Katz told Wally that she hadn't seen Harvey in years. She doesn't know what he's doing. Wally finished his tea, said goodbye to Mrs. Katz, and drove back home to prepare lunch.

Wally called Don Jordan and told him that his friend Clarence said that Harvey Katz was the one who was robbing all those banks last month. Wally said that he went to visit his mother.

"Harvey was one of the neighbourhood bullies when I was growing up. His mother used to hide me from Harvey. She told me that Harvey is staying at the Sandy Cove trailer park." Don was grateful for Wally's tip. He told him that he knew where the Sandy Cove trailer park was and would send agents over there immediately.

For lunch, Wally prepared chicken lentil soup. He used all organic ingredients. He also made cabbage rolls. Fresh cabbage was used, never frozen. Wally already had breaded chicken breasts that he prepared the night before. Wally packed his lunch and drove to see Elizabeth. Catherine Kelly was waiting for Wally in Harry's office. She was not happy. Harry was not happy.

As soon as Wally showed up, Catherine screamed at him, "Wally, you are wasting your time and money. Elizabeth will never marry you. She is committed to marrying Jeffrey. The wedding is set. It's too late to cancel. Elizabeth is using you. Stop bringing her lunch and take back the ring you bought her!"

Wally ignored her. He didn't say a word. Wally put Harry's lunch on his desk and went to see Elizabeth. Catherine looked at Harry. He shrugged his shoulders and began eating his lunch. Catherine was frustrated and ran out of the office.

Elizabeth was rubbing her hands and licking her lips. She was interested in eating, not talking. Wally didn't care because Elizabeth was still wearing his engagement ring. When lunch was finished, Elizabeth thanked Wally and gave him a big kiss. Wally gathered the dishes and went to see Harry.

Harry said to Wally, "I'm so glad that you ignored Catherine. You just avoided a big scene. Catherine has a mean temper and a big mouth. What's for lunch tomorrow?" Wally picked up the dishes and said, "Harry, you will find out tomorrow."

Patricia was waiting for Wally in his office. She had a big surprise for him. When Wally arrived, Patricia told him to close his eyes and hold out his hands. Wally closed his eyes and held out his hands. Patricia placed a cute little Yorkie puppy in each of his hands. Wally opened his eyes and saw two little furballs looking at him.

Patricia said, "Wally, these are teacup Yorkies. They will not weigh more than 3 pounds each. Stephanie, my friend, breeds them. The Yorkies are sisters, and Stephanie doesn't want to separate them. You'll have to buy both of them." Wally looked confused and asked Patricia why he should buy them.

Patricia said, "Wally, because they are chick magnets. Get Elizabeth to take them home. She will fall in love with them and will never give them back. The one in your right hand is called Leo, short for Leona, and the one in your left hand is called Cleo, short for Cleopatra. You are lucky that I was able to talk to Stephanie to let you buy them. Not everyone can buy them. Stephanie's buyers are screened."

Wally looked bewildered. He shook his head and said, "Okay, Patricia, I'll take your word for it. How much do they cost?" Patricia handed Wally the bill. He was shocked to see that each Yorkie pup cost $3,000.

Patricia was getting annoyed, "Wally, if you could afford to pay $21,000 for an engagement ring, you could afford to pay $6000 for two Yorkie teacup puppies. Many people would pay double just to have one. If you really love Elizabeth, you should be excited to buy these two little Yorkies."

Wally took out his chequebook and asked Patricia to whom the cheque should be made out. He wrote the cheque and gave it to Patricia. She thanked Wally for the cheque and told him to buy some doggie food. Elizabeth will need to feed them. Patricia put the Yorkies in a basket and told Wally she would keep them for him until he was ready to go home.

At the end of the day, Wally went to see Patricia to pick up Cleo and Leo. She handed Wally the basket of the two yorkies and told him that he must take great care of them. "Stephanie is very particular to who she sells Yorkies to, especially if they are teacups,"

Wally told Patricia to tell Stephanie that Cleo and Leo will be happy and healthy.

Wally took Cleo and Leo home. He decided to prepare homemade doggie food. He used the same ingredients to make the food that baby goats were fed at the Ukrainian village. Wally thought that if this food was good for baby goats, it should be good for baby Yorkies. After Wally fed Cleo and Leo, he let them loose in the backyard for half an hour. Wally then brought them inside and placed them in a basket. Cleo and Leo shortly fell asleep.

Early the next morning, Wally let Cleo and Leo lose out in the backyard to relieve themselves. He grabbed a plastic bag to pick up their poop. The poop looked like little raisins. Wally brought them back into the house to be fed. Cleo and Leo were allowed to roam around the house while Wally prepared lunch for Harry and Elizabeth. He decided to make bean salad and head cheese. The recipe for headcheese called for pork. Wally decided to use turkey instead. He also made six cheesecake wafers covered in dark chocolate—two for Harry and four for Elizabeth. When Wally finished preparing lunch, he received a call from Don Jordan.

Don said, "Wally, thanks to your tip, we found Harry Katz and his partner at the Sandy Cove trailer park. We also found most of the stolen money." Wally told Don that he was happy to help. He packed his lunch, grabbed the basket of Yorkies, and headed to see Elizabeth.

Harry was surprised to see Wally carrying a basket of Yorkies. He said, "Wally, I hope those fur balls are not our lunch."

Wally laughed and said, "Harry, don't worry, these doggies are chick magnets, not lunch. If Elizabeth takes them home, she will fall in love with them. This one is called Leo, and the other one is called Cleo. Elizabeth will have to marry me if she wants to keep them."

Harry was relieved and asked what was for lunch. Wally took out Harry's lunch and said." Harry, I'll leave the puppies with you. After lunch, take them over to Elizabeth. Tell her that I bought them at a pet store on my way here and forgot to take them home with me.

Ask Elizabeth to take them home because you don't want to leave them alone in the office with the janitor. Tell her that she can bring them back tomorrow."

Harry smiled and said, "Wally, are you going to invite me to your wedding?" Wally smiled back and said, "Harry, I will if you agree to be my master of ceremony." Harry told Wally he would be honoured to be his master of ceremony.

Wally went to see Elizabeth. Wally didn't care if she didn't want to talk. She was still wearing his engagement ring. When Elizabeth finished her lunch, she thanked Wally and gave him a big kiss. He gathered the dishes and went to see Harry.

Wally left smiling. Harry went to see Elizabeth to show her the puppies. Elizabeth was surprised to see the puppies. Harry said, "Wally bought them at the pet store on his way to bring us lunch. He forgot to take them home with him. This one is Cleo, and the other one is Leo. Please take them home with you. You can bring them back tomorrow. I don't want to leave these puppies alone in the office with the janitor."

Elizabeth didn't say a word. She took the basket of Yorkies and the food that Wally prepared for them. Cleo and Leo were asleep. When Elizabeth arrived home, the Yorkies woke up. She fed them and then let them run loose in the backyard. Elizabeth stayed with them, waiting for her mother to get home.

When Joan arrived and saw the puppies, she shook her head and said, "Elizabeth, Wally, just set you up. If you don't bring back those puppies to the office tomorrow morning, you will become Wally's wife." Elizabeth smiled while rubbing their tummies and said, "Mother, I don't believe Wally would stoop so low. He bought these puppies because he fell in love with them."

Joan laughed and said, "Elizabeth, don't be naïve. Wally deliberately bought those puppies so you could fall in love with them. What about that engagement ring you are wearing? You will have to return the ring as well as those puppies if you refuse to marry

Wally. Remember, he promised to pay off your entire government student loan if you marry him."

Elizabeth shrugged her shoulders and said, "I don't know what I will do, Mother. I'll find out tomorrow." Joan didn't say a word; she just shook her head and went upstairs to change clothes.

Early the next morning, Wally got up. He was excited. Today was the day that Elizabeth would make her decision. Wally was assured that once Elizabeth took Cleo and Leo home, there would be no way that she would return them. Wally also knew that Elizabeth wanted to keep the engagement ring. Wally decided that he would prepare a feast for lunch. He was going to have prime rib, scallop potatoes with steamed vegetables, and Caesar salad. For dessert, Wally chose to make Maple Walnut cake.

Harry was also excited. Elizabeth didn't bring Cleo and Leo with her. When Wally walked into his office, Harry's eyes lit up when he saw the prime rib. He told Wally that Elizabeth didn't bring Cleo and Leo with her.

Wally walked into Elizabeth's office. Her eyes lit up when she saw the prime rib. Wally decided to have lunch before he asked for Elizabeth's decision. Wally let Elizabeth eat his piece of cake. When he finished lunch, Wally asked Elizabeth, "Where are Cleo and Leo, and are you going to keep the engagement ring that you are wearing?"

Elizabeth looked out the window and said, "Wally, I'm not ready to marry you. I'll pay for the ring and the puppies." Wally just smiled and said, "Elizabeth, where will you get $26,000? You have to pay back your $200,000 government student loan, and Harry just fired you. Marry me, and I will pay off your entire student loan. You also get to keep the engagement ring and Cleo and Leo."

Elizabeth was shocked, and she stormed out of her office to see Harry. Wally followed her. She screamed at Harry, "Wally told me that you just fired me!" Wally told Harry that Elizabeth didn't want to marry him and didn't want to return the engagement ring and the puppies.

Harry just smiled and said, "Elizabeth, you are fired. You have no choice but to marry Wally." Elizabeth was speechless. Wally took her by the hand and said, "It's time to meet Samantha. Harry, please tell Jeffrey that he will not marry Elizabeth."

Wally arrived at Samantha's law firm with Elizabeth. When Donna found out that they were engaged, she gave Wally and Elizabeth a big hug. Wally and Elizabeth went to see Thomas. He was very surprised. He shook Wally's hand and said, "Wally, congratulations on finding such a nice girl to marry. You need a good wife to keep you out of trouble."

Wally thanked Thomas and went to see Lawrence. He showed Elizabeth's engagement ring to him. Lawrence said, "Wally, it's about time you got engaged to her. What took you so long?"

Wally said to Lawrence, "I had to convince Elizabeth to break off her engagement to Jeffrey Kelly."

Lawrence took a good look at Elizabeth's engagement ring and said to her, "Elizabeth, I'm glad that you had enough sense to break off your engagement with Jeffrey. You're much better off marrying Wally. He may sometimes drive you up the wall, but he will always treat you with love and respect."

Wally thanked Lawrence and went to see Patricia. She gave Wally and Elizabeth a big hug. Patricia said to Elizabeth, "I know that we dislike each other, but I'm still happy for you and Wally."

It was time to see Samantha. Wally and Elizabeth walked into her office. Wally said to Samantha, "I want you to meet our newest recruit." Wally then lifted Elizabeth's hand to show Samantha the engagement ring.

Samantha was very surprised. She grabbed Wally's arm, shoved him out of her office, and closed the door. She faced Elizabeth and said, "You are supposed to marry Jeffrey Kelly; what happened? What did Wally do? Did he threaten your life or blackmail you in any way?"

Elizabeth shook her head and explained to Samantha what Wally did. Elizabeth mentioned the lawsuit that Christine Bell had against Samantha for wrongful dismissal. She represented Christine, and Wally represented Samantha.

Elizabeth told Samantha how Wally made a motion in court to have her held in contempt of court because she refused to go out on a dinner date with him. Wally not only won but had Jonathan transfer the million dollars he would receive from the insurance company to Samantha Franklin Law's bank account. Jonathan even wrote out a cheque to Wally for $50,000.

Samantha was surprised. She called accounting and found out that the million dollars from the insurance company had been deposited into the law firm's bank account. Elizabeth mentioned that Wally wanted to take her to the Spencers Mill. When she refused, he took her to Aunt Lydia's house. He spent the entire morning preparing four servings of food. "Two servings for us and two for Aunt Lydia and Uncle Ivan for breakfast."

Elizabeth also mentioned how Aunt Lydia wanted her to fall in love with Wally. How she got drunk on brandy, thinking it was wine, and caused a lot of trouble. She ate three servings of food, raped Wally, almost suffocated him with her pussy, stunk up the house with her farts, and plugged the toilet with her poop.

Elizabeth mentioned what happened at the Spencers Mill to Samantha. "I didn't expect that Ivan would play Cupid and make us go on a date. Wally took me to the ballet. This made Jeffrey very angry." Elizabeth then showed Samantha the video recording Wally made of Jeffrey giving him a beating.

Elizabeth held her hand and said, "Samantha, Wally gave me this engagement ring. It cost him $21,000. Jeffrey paid $500 for his, which he bought at a pawn shop. Jeffery also went to a massage parlor to pay for sex every Friday afternoon. Wally gave me until the end of this week to keep the ring or give it back. He brought us a delicious lunch every day. Wally also bought two Yorkie teacup puppies. He tricked me into taking them home. I fell in love with them and want to keep them."

Samantha couldn't believe it and said, "Elizabeth you lucky girl. I have been trying to get a Yorkie teacup puppy for years. You get to have two. You must show them to me. How did Harry feel about you leaving his office?"

Elizabeth just shook her head and said, "Harry fired me when I refused to marry Wally. I was dragged here by Wally so he could introduce me as his fiancée."

Samantha laughed and said, "Wally needs a wife to keep him out of trouble. You are the perfect wife for him. I know that you won't take any crap from him. He must love you; otherwise, he would not have spent $21,000 on an engagement ring and bought you two Yorkie teacup puppies."

Elizabeth was curious and asked Samantha, "Aunt Judy tells me that Wally is a senior partner at your law firm. I didn't see his name on the wall." Samantha took a deep breath, ground her teeth, and said, "Elizabeth, Wally is a senior partner."

Elizabeth started to smile and said, "Samantha, if you want me to marry Wally. You better tell me how Wally managed to get you to give him a senior partnership. Did he threaten your life or blackmail you in any way?"

Samantha had no choice but to tell Elizabeth everything that had happened. She told her what she did to try to get rid of Wally and what he did to keep her from firing him. Samantha wanted to fire Wally because he hadn't graduated from Harvard Law School.

Elizabeth started to laugh, "Samantha, I feel much better now that I know that Wally also made a fool of you. You and Wally deserve each other."

Samantha started to get worried, "Elizabeth, you better promise me that you will not tell anyone what I just told you." Elizabeth stopped laughing and promised Samantha that she wouldn't tell anyone.

Elizabeth said, "Samantha, I have a problem. Christine Bell was to be my maid of honour. When she lost her lawsuit against you, she told me to get another maid of honour. We are no longer friends. Who is going to be my maid of honour on such short notice?"

Samantha smiled at Elizabeth, "I will be honoured to be your maid of honour. Who else will be in the wedding party?"

Elizabeth shrugged her shoulders, "I don't know, and I don't care. I'll let Wally choose the rest of the wedding party."

Samantha called Wally back into the office and told him she would be the maid of honour. Elizabeth wanted him to choose the rest of the wedding party. Wally was surprised and pleased.

Jeffrey suddenly barged into the office. He started to scream at Wally, "You will never marry Elizabeth. She belongs to me!" He then lunged at Wally. Before Jeffrey could reach him, Wally shoved a chair in front of him. Jeffrey fell down. As he was getting up, security arrived. They handcuffed Jeffrey and escorted him out of the building.

Samantha was glad to see Jeffrey leave. She asked Elizabeth, "When is the wedding day, and where is it going to be held?" Elizabeth replied, "Samantha, I guess it will be in eight weeks on August 28. That's the date that I was supposed to marry Jeffrey."

Wally's eyes lit up. He said, "The wedding will be held at the Spencers Mill. They have a wedding chapel there. We can get married there as well as have our wedding."

Samantha was happy. She said, "Elizabeth, everything is settled. It is time for you to show me your Yorkie teacup puppies." Elizabeth and Samantha left for Elizabeth's home so that Samantha could see Cleo and Leo.

Chapter 32

Gregory Klyn showed up for his early morning appointment with Col. Donald Chandler. The Col. shook Gregory's hand and escorted him to his lab. He said, "Agent Klyn, the military has developed drugs to give our soldiers superhuman abilities. This is Zac Brown. He is one of our soldiers."

Gregory was looking at a small little man smiling at him. Gregory couldn't believe that he was looking at a soldier with superhuman abilities.

Col. Chandler said to Gregory, "Our drugs work better on small, young, healthy men. Don't let his size fool you. Zac is 100 times stronger than the average man. He can run 100 times faster than the average man. He can smell and see in the dark better than any animal. He can also heal from injury 100 times faster than any human."

Zach Brown ran circles around Gregory with blinding speed. He then picked up a 500-pound barbell with one hand and held it above his head for several minutes.

Col. Chandler told Gregory that they had just started to recruit soldiers. "Zac is the first complete super soldier. In two weeks, another soldier will be completely transformed. The transformation takes approximately four months to complete. The soldiers spend their time in a transparent tank. They sleep in a drug solution that allows them to breathe. The government allows us to recruit only people with criminal records."

Agent Klyn, the military wants to recruit your nephews, Tommy and Wally. You are required to charge and convict them of drug trafficking. After their convictions, we will offer them the opportunity to become a super soldier or spend the rest of their lives in prison. I'm sure they will want to become a super soldier."

Gregory didn't want his nephews to become super soldiers but knew he had no choice. If he refused Col. Chandler's request, Zac Brown would be very happy to make Gregory unhappy.

Chapter 33

Wally went to his office to do some paperwork. He received a phone call. It was Tommy. He said, "Wally, I need your help. The police arrested me for drug trafficking. I'm in jail."

Wally replied, "Tommy, I can't help you. You are my brother. That is a conflict of interest. The court will not allow me to represent you. Doesn't your Chinese boss have lawyers to help you? Do you want me to recommend someone to you?"

Tommy replied," Wally, my boss has lots of lawyers, but will not help me because it'll hurt his reputation as an outstanding citizen in the community. Don't worry, Wally, I'll find someone on my own."

Wally decided to call Harry, "Jeffrey attacked me in Samantha's office. She and Elizabeth were there. Security showed up before he could cause trouble. He is to appear in court next week. Please tell Christine that if she wants to keep Jeffrey out of jail, he must pay the bar bill for our wedding. It is being held at the Spencers Mill. They have a wedding chapel there." Harry told Wally it would be a pleasure to tell Christine what Jeffrey did. He also said that he was looking forward to his wedding.

Harry went to see Christine. He told her what Jeffrey did. He also told her that Jeffrey must pay the bar bill at Wally's wedding to stay out of jail. Christine stormed out of her office to see Jeffrey. He wasn't in his office. She sat down and waited for him.

Jeffrey arrived a few minutes later. Christine got up and started to scream at him. "Harry just told me what you did. Wally wants you to pay the bar bill at his wedding if you want to stay out of jail. I'm not going to pay the bar bill for you. I have already received a bill of $ 8,000 from Jonathan Clothier. Wally had a tailor-made suit made to replace the suit that you ruined when you beat the crap out of him. What were you thinking!"

Jeffrey cleared his throat and said, "Father told me to beat up Wally to scare him so he would stay away from Elizabeth."

Catherine took out her phone and showed Jeffrey the video recording that Wally had made of Jeffrey beating the crap out of him. "Do you think Elizabeth still wants to marry you after what you called her and did?" Jeffrey watched the video recording. He was shocked.

Christine told Jeffrey," I already paid for Wally's tailor-made suit. You are going to pay his bar bill. Ask your good-for-nothing father to help you if you can find him. He's probably in bed with some young floozy."

Christine ran out of Jeffrey's office, and FBI agent Gregory Klyn walked in. He showed his credentials to Jeffrey and said, "I know that Wally Kozak caused you a lot of trouble. Do you want to return his favour?"

Jeffrey started to smile, "FBI agent Gregory Klyn, what do I have to do?"

Gregory smiled at Jeffrey and said, "Wally's father was Danelo Klyn. He paid for Wally's education. Wally was expelled from Harvard Law School for racketeering. A girl paid Wally $5,000 to write her entrance exam to Harvard Law School. The school found out that he wrote the exam for the Dean's daughter. That is why he didn't graduate."

Jeffrey was very happy to hear what happened to Wally and said, "I always wondered why I didn't see Wally at graduation. I was the head of the class on the Dean's honour list. What do you want me to do?"

Gregory said, "Wally is extremely smart. He has eluded us for years. We cannot arrest him without crucial evidence. Jeffrey, all you have to do is citizen arrest against Wally for racketeering. Just sign this form. You will not be required to give testimony or be at the trial."

Jeffrey took out a pen to sign the form. He smiled and said, "I'll be at Wally's trial. I want to see him fry!" Jeffrey knew that Wally was very clever and smart enough to be cleared of racketeering. However, his reputation will be severely damaged. Samantha will probably fire him, and Elizabeth will break off her engagement. Jeffrey believes that she is still willing to marry him.

Chapter 34

Wally went to see Donna. He wanted her to be a bridesmaid at his wedding. Donna excitedly accepted. She told Wally that Thomas would be happy to be an usher. Next, Wally went to see Patricia and asked her to be a bridesmaid. She wanted to know who her usher would be. Wally told her that Michael Cook would be her usher.

Patricia was uncomfortable and said," Wally, Michael doesn't like me. He won't agree to be my usher." Wally smiled at Patricia and said to her, "Patricia, you are a beautiful girl, and Michael is my friend. Trust me, he will be happy to be your usher."

Patricia was not convinced that Michael would agree to be her usher, but she did agree to be a bridesmaid. Patricia also didn't know why Wally asked her to be a bridesmaid because Elizabeth didn't like her.

Wally went to see Jonathan Quick. He wanted him to be an usher at his wedding. Jonathan had no idea why Wally would want him to be an usher.

He said, "Wally, I will be happy to be an usher at your wedding if Christine Bell agrees to be my bridesmaid." Christine did agree to be Elizabeth's bridesmaid. She was no longer angry at Elizabeth and still considered her a friend. The last person Wally went to see was Richard Kiley.

Wally entered his office with a big smile. Richard was happy to see him and said, "Wally, it's nice to see you. What can I do for you?" Wally told Richard that he had just gotten engaged to Elizabeth Kelly. The wedding was in eight weeks. Richard was happy to hear the news. He congratulated Wally and said, "I'm glad you are going to marry Elizabeth. Jeffrey, that foul-mouth jerk, never deserved her."

Wally told Richard that Elizabeth asked Samantha to be the maid of honour. Samantha said yes. Wally took a deep breath and said, "Richard, I want you to be the best man at my wedding."

Richard started to laugh so hard that he fell off his chair. When he got control of himself, Richard got up, apologized to Wally, and said, "Wally, I will be more than happy to be your best man."

Wally thanked Richard and said to him, "Richard, pray that at the end of the wedding, when Elizabeth throws her bouquet over his shoulders, Samantha doesn't catch it. If she does, Richard, you will get a box of whips and chains for a wedding gift." Richard fell off his chair laughing; Wally said goodbye.

Wally decided that it was time to pay a visit to Harry Wilson. It had been a while since he had seen him. Harry lived in a huge, old, luxurious mansion nearby. The furniture was over 100 years old but was in immaculate condition. A security fence surrounded the mansion. It had so many rooms that Henry didn't know some existed. The mansion was surrounded by an acre of trees, plants, and flowers. Security let Wally in.

Wally walked into Henry's office, gave him a big hug, and said, "Henry, I'm getting married in eight weeks. I hope you are still alive to come to my wedding." Wally showed Henry a photograph of Elizabeth.

He took a good look and said to Wally, "If I would have met her, I would have asked her to marry me. Wally, she is very beautiful, and I can hardly wait to meet her." Wally reminded Henry that he has a very weak heart.

Henry happily replied, "Wally, don't worry about me. Your grandmother's taking very good care of me. I'm so happy to hear that you're getting married. Let's celebrate with some fine brandy and dark Belgian chocolates."

Wally asked Harry where his gold-digging wife was. He told Wally that she was out shopping. When it was time for Wally to leave, he promised Henry that he would visit him again soon before his wedding.

Elizabeth and Samantha arrived at Elizabeth's home. Samantha was anxious to see Elizabeth's puppies. When she saw them, she picked up the puppies and said, "Elizabeth, they are so adorable. I was trying to get one for years, and you have two. You are a lucky girl. How did Wally manage to get them?"

Elizabeth told Samantha that she had no idea how Wally got them. "The one on the left is Cleo, short for Cleopatra, and the one on the right is Leo, short for Leona." Samantha and Elizabeth played with Cleo and Leo. Samantha scratched their ears and rubbed their tummies. After an hour, it was time for Samantha to leave. Elizabeth stayed home with Cleo and Leo, waiting for her mother.

Joan arrived home. She wanted to know what had happened that day. Harry didn't say anything to her. Elizabeth told her that Harry fired her when she refused to marry Wally. Elizabeth decided to marry Wally because he agreed to pay off her entire government student loan. She also got to keep the engagement ring, Cleo and Leo.

Elizabeth said to Joan, "Wally then dragged me over to see Samantha. Christine Bell was mad at me and refused to be my maid of honour. Samantha said that she would be honoured to be my maid of honour. Wally wants to have the wedding at the Spencers Mill. They have a wedding chapel there. The wedding date is still August 28."

Joan got excited and gave Elizabeth a big hug saying, "Jeffrey never loved you. Wally definitely does. I'm very happy for you. I will have to send our guests new wedding invitations. Now, start packing. Wally is waiting."

Joan helped Elizabeth pack. She dragged Elizabeth's suitcase to her car, and Elizabeth carried Cleo and Leo in the basket. She drove off to see Wally. When she arrived, Elizabeth got out of the car, holding Cleo and Leo in her right hand, and dragged a huge suitcase in her left hand. Elizabeth knocked on Wally's door. He answered the door. Elizabeth was very nervous and said, "Wally, my mother threw me out of the house. I have no place to go."

Wally invited her into the house. He took Elizabeth's suitcase. She held onto Cleo and Leo. Wally went to the kitchen cupboard to grab a plate.

He said," I was about to have dinner. Are you hungry?" Elizabeth was tired and hungry. She was enjoying the beet soup, spicy cabbage, and pierogies. During dinner, the phone rang. It was Louis. He told Wally that Tommy asked your friend Harry to be his lawyer, but Harry refused. "Tommy doesn't take no for an answer. He hired a couple of goons to put him away. They just left."

Wally thanked Louis and said to Elizabeth. "Harry is in big trouble; he needs my help. I have to go. I'll explain everything when I get back!"

Wally got into his car and called Harry, "You shouldn't have refused to be Tommy's lawyer. He sent a couple of goons to kill you. Have your family grab your car and drive away somewhere safe. You wait for me. The goons are on their way." Wally pulled into Harry's driveway. He got into Wally's car just in time. The goons showed up. Wally drove away, and they followed him. Wally told Harry, "I'm going to play chicken with these goons. I'll drive through the forest tunnel leading to the football field. When I reach the end, I'll stop the car, and you jump out."

The goons followed Wally into the tunnel. At the end of the tunnel, Wally stopped the car, Harry jumped out. Wally turned the car to face the tunnel. Wally put the car in drive, stepped on the accelerator, and jumped out. Wally's car went on a head-on collision with the goon's car. The collision killed them, and both cars burst into flames.

Wally took out his phone and called Don Jordan. He and another agent showed up shortly. The agent handcuffed both Wally and Harry. Don read them their rights. Wally screamed. "Don, I can explain everything!"

Don replied, "Wally, you can explain to me everything in jail."

Wally and Harry kept quiet as Don drove them to the county jail. When Wally and Harry were safely in jail, Don removed the handcuffs. He said, "Wally, now you can explain what happened."

Wally explained that Harry refused to be Tommy's lawyer. Tommy sent a couple of goons to kill Harry. "I had to save his life."

Don shook his head angrily, "Wally, you fool, don't you think other goons will be hired to kill Harry? They will also come after you for interfering!"

Wally calmly said, "Don, not if I hire an assassin to kill off the entire Chinese family that Tommy worked for." Don was still angry, "Wally, you don't have that kind of money to hire an assassin, and where are you going to find an assassin?"

Wally smiled and said, "Don, my uncle Pavlo was Danelo's hired assassin. I have his number. You have access to enough money for me to hire him."

Don looked at Wally and said to him, "Wally, give me one good reason for me to release enough money to save your butts?"

Wally looked back at Don and said, "Don, you know my uncle Gregory, your boss, is dirty. I have undisputed evidence to prove it."

Don thought for a few seconds and said, "Wally, show me the evidence, and I will think about it."

Wally became angry and screamed, "Don, you have known me since I was a baby. If you can't trust me, who can you trust? Now make an e-money transfer for $2,000,000 to my bank account!"

Don couldn't believe what he was about to do. He made the e-money transfer to Wally's bank account. As soon as Wally received the funds, he called his uncle Pavlo.

Uncle Pavlo said, "Wally, it's nice to hear from you. Danelo told me that I should be expecting a call from you anytime soon. I assume that this is not a social call. Do you have enough money to hire me?"

Wally replied, "I wouldn't be calling you if I didn't. You know what I want you to do. Kill off the entire family that Tommy worked for, including Tommy." Uncle Pavlo told Wally to make an e-money transfer to an email he was about to receive. The family and Tommy will be gone within 24 hours. Wally made the e-money transfer to Uncle Pavlo's bank account. He thanked Wally for the business.

Wally took a memory stick off his keychain and gave it to Don. Wally told Don that Gregory and Danelo had monthly meetings at his mother's house. "My mother and sometimes I video-recorded every meeting without their knowledge."

Don plugged the memory stick into his phone. While he was watching, Wally took off a key from his keychain. "This key is for a safety deposit box. In it, you will find 10 years of such meetings on memory sticks. I am willing to testify that I was involved in video recording some of the meetings."

Don thanked Wally for the key and memory stick. Wally didn't tell Don that he made copies of the meetings on a different memory. He also didn't tell Don that Danelo gave him access to enough money to hire Uncle Pavlo.

Don had some bad news for Wally. He said to him, "Wally, I can get you out of the car crash investigation, but you still have to stay in jail. Jeffrey Kelly made a citizen's arrest against you for racketeering. The prosecutor convinced the court to refuse you bail. I can't help you. This is out of my jurisdiction. You will have to rely on your friend Harry to get you out of this mess. I'll leave you alone with him."

As soon as Don left, a prison guard walked in carrying Cleo, Leo, and an engagement ring. He said, "A young lady brought these puppies and this ring. She said that they belonged to Wally Kozak. What should I do with them?" Harry told the guard to leave them with him and that he'd take the puppies and the ring home with him later. Wally knew that Jeffery called Elizabeth.

Wally started to explain everything to Harry. He told Harry that he had only met Danelo once when he asked for financial support to go to Harvard Law School. Danelo left his mother before he was born. At school, Wally always scored the highest mark. Jeffrey was bitter because he could never score higher than Wally.

Three weeks before the final exams to graduate, Louis, a childhood friend, came to see him. He needed $5,000 to pay off a loan shark. If he didn't pay it within a week, he would be beaten to death. Louis wanted Wally to write an entrance exam to Harvard Law School for a girl he knew. She would pay $5,000 if she scored 90% or higher. Wally wrote her exam and scored 93%. The girl gave Wally $5,000, and Louis's life was spared.

The girl was the Dean's daughter; she was expelled, and the Dean was asked to resign three weeks before his retirement. The Dean was very upset when he learned that Wally wrote his daughter's exam. The Dean thought he was going to lose his pension and blamed Wally. He convinced the president of the school to expel Wally for racketeering. At his tribunal, the president did not allow Wally to defend himself.

Wally paid $200,000 to the president of the Columbia Correspondence School of Law so he could write the final exam without taking their courses. Wally scored 97.8%. Wally then taped over the school's logo with the Harvard Law School logo on his transcript. At his interview, Thomas Moore hired Wally after he saw his transcript and read the Dean's letter of recommendation.

Everything was going along just fine until Samantha got nosy and looked up his Harvard graduating class. She was furious when she found out that Wally didn't graduate. She didn't give Wally an opportunity to explain. Thomas convinced Samantha not to fire Wally until the end of the week. He wanted Wally to be in court with him. Wally told Harry that Samantha called him a despicable, sneaky, conniving snake. Wally called Samantha an ungrateful, stubborn, foolish bitch.

Wally continued to explain how Samantha forced him to be her sex slave for a night by offering him a senior partnership. Samantha gave Wally only 12 hours to raise $500,000 to pay for the senior partnership. Wally went to see Richard Kiley for a loan. He used the deed to his house for collateral. After Wally explained to Richard why he needed the loan. Richard happily gave Wally the loan.

Samantha was not happy. She decided to force Wally into participating in a mock trial. If Wally wins, he stays. If he loses, the loan is returned to Richard, and he is fired. Wally was sent home to prepare for the trial. He was not allowed to use any of the law firm's resources. Judge Judy was kind enough to let Wally use the court library and help him. With her help, Wally won the mock trial, making Samantha very unhappy because she couldn't get rid of Wally and had to make him a senior partner.

Wally also mentioned to Harry that his friend Louis was the person who called him to let him know that the goons were coming after him. Louis was also the friend who needed the $5,000 to pay off his loan to the loan shark. Wally looked at Harry and said, "Harry, if I didn't save Louis's life. You would be dead."

"Harry, now that you know that my father was the biggest drug dealer in New York, that I am a cheat, a liar, a thief, a prostitute, and a killer, would you still want me as a son-in-law?"

Harry looked straight into Wally's eyes and said, "Wally, when I look at you, I don't see any of those things that you said about yourself. I see a very intelligent, resourceful young man who cares for people. Any man would be proud of having you for a son-in-law or son. Don't worry, Wally, I'll get you out of this mess."

Don Jordan showed up to let Harry out. He wanted to know why Wally hadn't come up with this evidence sooner. Wally smiled and said, "Don, I promised Tommy that I wouldn't interfere with his life if he didn't interfere with my life. That's why the Chinese triad let Tommy and my family live. When Tommy hired goons to kill Harry, he interfered with my life. Harry is a good friend and will be the master of ceremony at my wedding."

The next morning, Harry read the newspaper. The front-page story read that Wally Kozak was involved in a fatal car accident. His car collided with another car. The two people who were killed were known drug dealers by the police. Wally was not injured and disappeared. His father was Danelo Klyn. Harry was shocked. Don Jordan promised to keep Wally out of trouble. This story will give Wally lots of trouble.

Harry called the FBI and asked to speak to Don Jordan, "Don, you promised to keep Wally out of trouble!" Don replied, "Gregory Klyn, my boss, leaked the story to the newspaper. He also had Jeffrey file a citizen's arrest against Wally for racketeering. Gregory has been trying for years to recruit Wally. He wants Wally to be convicted so he can offer Wally a job with the FBI in order to stay out of prison."

Another front-page story mentioned that George Lee and his family were shot dead at their home by a sniper. George, his two daughters, his wife, his brother, and his parents were having dinner when they were killed. At the bottom of the front page there was a story about Tommy Klyn. He was found dead in his jail cell. Tommy was strangled to death.

Harry went to see Samantha Franklin. He found her in her office reading the newspaper. Harry grabbed the newspaper away from her and said, "Wally's innocent; he needs our help!"

Samantha was shocked and said to Harry, "Wally deserves to rot in prison. I knew that there was something suspicious about him. I would never have hired him if I knew that his father was Danelo Klyn."

Harry started to smile and said, "Samantha wasn't your father, a drug-dealing pimp who died in prison. Didn't your mother and brother overdose on heroin? I know that you spent three years in prison for drug trafficking and prostitution. I also know that Harvard Law School chose you to be their underprivileged minority token student."

Harry continued to explain how Wally was expelled from Harvard Law School three weeks before the final exams. He had to pay $200,000 to the Columbia Correspondence School of Law president so he could write their final exams without taking their courses.

Harry looked into Samantha's eyes and said, "Wally told me that you forced him to be your sex slave for a night. You tortured Wally all night and then tried to get rid of him by giving him only 12 hours to raise $500,000 to pay for a senior partnership. When Richard Kiley gave him the loan, you tried to get rid of him again by forcing him to participate in a mock trial. You couldn't get rid of Wally because he won the mock trial. Samantha, you are pissed off because Wally, a young white boy, outsmarted you. Now tell me, if Wally deserves to go to prison, do you deserve to keep all the money he generated for your law firm!"

Samantha was shocked. She just realized that Harry was right. She said to Harry, "Wally is right. I am an ungrateful, stubborn, foolish bitch. We have to help him!"

Harry said to Samantha, "Tomorrow morning, we are going to visit Wally. You can apologize to him. Then we are going to pay a visit to George Shaw, our old friend."

It was lunchtime and Harry wished that Wally was preparing lunch.

Chapter 35

Don Jordan drove straight to the bank where Wally kept the safety deposit box. He spent an hour watching the videos of Danelo and Gregory's meetings. Don decided to leave the memory sticks in the safety deposit box. He also placed a memory stick that Wally had given him into the safety deposit box. It was a lot safer to leave the memory sticks in the bank than to leave them at the FBI's office. He knew that Gregory had some FBI agents under his personal payroll. The video recordings and Wally's testimony would be enough evidence to convict Gregory of drug trafficking. With Gregory in prison, Don would get promoted.

Don arranged to have a court order to have Gregory Klyn arrested and charged with drug trafficking. When Gregory was charged and arrested for drug trafficking, he managed to get bail. The FBI suspended him indefinitely, and a court order put him under house arrest. Gregory's arrest was kept from the media as a matter of FBI pride.

In court, Don Jordan arranged for Gregory and his lawyers to watch the video recordings of the monthly meetings. Gregory and his lawyers signed a disclosure form saying that they saw the video recording. Wally was given a disclosure form to sign saying that his mother, Maria Kozak never made copies of the video recording. Wally was never asked if he made copies of the recordings, which he had.

Gregory was very surprised that Maria had video-recorded his monthly meetings with Danelo. He knew that those video recordings showed enough evidence to have him convicted of drug trafficking. He also knew which bank Maria's safety deposit box was kept. Danelo gave it to her and made the monthly payments until his death. Wally took over the payments and ownership. Gregory also knew Danelo would leave the memory sticks in the safety deposit box because Don knew that Gregory had FBI agents under his personal payroll.

Gregory paid a crooked judge for a search warrant so he could hire one of his FBI agents to search Maria's safety deposit box. The next day, FBI agent Sam Fox showed up at the bank five minutes before closing. He made sure that everyone left. Sam showed the warrant to the bank manager. The bank manager escorted Sam to an examining room and then brought Maria's safety deposit box. Agent Sam watched some of the videos on his phone for a few minutes. Then he took all the memory sticks and put them in his pocket.

The bank manager returned the safety deposit box. Sam then pushed the bank manager against the wall, shoved a gun under his chin, and said, "You're not to tell anyone what happened today." He then shoved an envelope containing $10,000 into the bank manager's pocket. The bank manager promised that he would tell no one and ran away. The bank manager knew that when he received the envelope, he would be on the triad's payroll.

No one would know that the video recordings would be missing from Maria's safety deposit box until the court date. Gregory knew that without those video recordings, all charges against him would be dropped. He would then have Don Jordan killed.

Chapter 36

Harry and Samantha paid Wally a visit. Bail for him was denied. Samantha took his hand, looked straight into his eyes, and said, "Wally, I'm so ashamed of myself. You are right; I am an ungrateful, stubborn, foolish bitch. Can you ever forgive me!"

Wally smiled and said, Samantha, "I forgave you when I did my victory dance at the mock trial." Samantha was relieved and thanked him.

Harry asked Wally if he saw the front page of the newspaper. Wally told him that the prison guard showed him the newspaper this morning.

Harry said, "Wally, we need to have Don Jordan testify at your trial next week." Wally replied, "Harry, Don will testify; he promised to keep me out of trouble."

Harry and Samantha said goodbye to Wally. They told him that they were going to see George Shaw. Harry and Samantha didn't say a word until they arrived at George Shaw's home. They saw him; he was outside his home, watering his plants. Harry waved to him and said, "Good morning, Mr. Shaw. We came to ask you about Wally Kozak."

George Shaw got very upset, "I don't want to talk about him." Samantha asked him, "George, why did you have Wally expelled three weeks before the final exams?"

George shook his head and said, "Wally was paid $5,000 by my daughter to write her entrance exam to Harvard Law School. The school found out that she cheated, expelled her, and asked me to resign three weeks before I retired. I thought I was going to lose my pension and blamed Wally."

Harry asked," George, did Wally tell you why he wrote your daughter's entrance exam?" George replied, "Wally did, but it didn't matter. I thought I was going to lose my pension, so I decided to ruin his career."

Samantha asked, "George, do you still feel that Wally is to blame for losing your pension?" George closed his eyes, took a deep breath, and said," When I resigned, the school still gave me my full pension. I should never have expelled him. Wally was a wonderful student. That is why I wrote him a recommendation letter and suggested that he apply to your law firm. I lost a lot of sleep knowing that I ruined Wally's career."

Samantha happily said to George," Wally's career was not ruined. He paid $200,000 to the president of the Columbia Correspondence School of Law to write the final exams without taking their courses. He graduated with 97.8%. Wally was hired because of the letter you gave him and his assumed Howard Law School transcript. When I found out what he did, I was furious and ready to fire him. Then I realized that Wally was special. I had to offer him a senior partnership. If I didn't, some other law firm would."

George felt relieved and said, "Samantha, you made me very happy. I knew that Wally was special and would be very successful. Thank you for coming here to tell me."

Harry looked at George, who was very happy, and said to him, "Wally is in big trouble. Jeffrey Kelly filed a citizen's arrest against Wally for racketeering. Jeffrey's fiancé, Elizabeth Grace, broke off her engagement with him so she could marry Wally. He is sitting in jail facing racketeering charges. We need you to testify at his trial next week."

George got angry and said, "I never did like Jeffrey. I will definitely testify at Wally's trial!" Harry also mentioned to George that they needed Art Jenkins to testify at Wally's trial. "Do you think he will testify?"

George grabbed his jacket and hat and said, "Art will testify when I tell him what I did. Let's go visit him now. He lives nearby." George called Art, telling him that they were coming to see him. Art was sitting on his veranda waiting for them. George told Art the reason for their meeting. Everything that happened to Wally was explained to Art. George also mentioned that Wally only met Danelo once when he asked for financial support to attend law school. His mother raised him by herself. "Danelo left her before Wally was born."

Samantha asked Art. "We need you to testify at Wally's trial next week, will you?" Art got up and shook his head and said, "Damn right, I will be there to testify. If I hadn't been such a stubborn old fool and given Wally a chance to defend himself, we would not have this meeting. I would have forgiven Wally because he wanted to save his friend's life!"

Wally's trial was in three days. The court finally allowed bail for him. Samantha paid for it. She told Wally to go home and help his grandparents and his aunt and uncle. He didn't need to do anything.

Harry said to Wally, "You better stop by my house to pick up your puppies. It's a good thing that Cindy is not home; she wants to keep them. Come to my office, and I will give you Elizabeth's engagement ring."

Wally didn't argue. He said goodbye. Wally stopped by Harry's office to pick up his engagement ring. He then stopped by Harry's home to pick up Cleo and Leo. Wally decided not to call Elizabeth until after his trial. He planned to spend a lot of time playing with Cleo and Leo.

Chapter 37

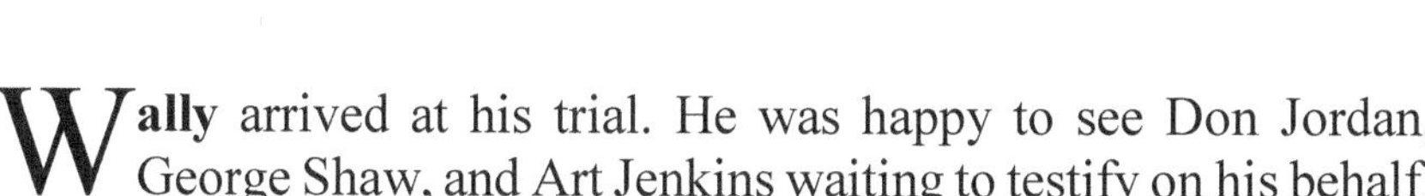

Wally arrived at his trial. He was happy to see Don Jordan, George Shaw, and Art Jenkins waiting to testify on his behalf. He wasn't happy to see Uncle Gregory staring at him. Wally also saw Jeffrey, his mother, his father, Joan, and Judge Judy. He didn't expect to see Elizabeth.

The prosecutor called Wally to the stand. He asked Wally, "Was Danelo Klyn your father?" Wally said yes. "When you attended Harvard Law School, did you get paid $5,000 to write an entrance exam for the Dean's daughter and was expelled for racketeering before the final exams to graduate?" Wally said yes. The prosecutor had no more questions for Wally. He called Don Jordan to the stand.

The prosecutor asked, "Are you aware that Wally Kozak was involved in a fatal car crash?" The two passengers that were in the other car were killed in the head-on collision. They were known drug dealers by the police. Wally was not injured."

Don replied, "Wally's car was involved, not Wally. The crash is still being investigated." The prosecutor asked Don, "Why did your boss, Gregory Klyn, leak this information to the newspaper?"

Don answered, "Gregory has been trying to recruit Wally for years. He's the one who asked Jeffrey Kelly to file a citizen's arrest against Wally. I believe that Gregory wants Wally to be convicted as charged. He would then offer Wally a job with the FBI to keep him out of prison. The prosecutor asked Don, "Do you believe that Wally Kozak is a law-abiding citizen?" Don answered yes. The prosecutor had no more questions for Don.

He called Gregory Klyn to the stand. He asked Gregory, "Did you ask Jeffrey Kelly to file a citizen's arrest against Wally Kozak?" Gregory said yes."If Wally Kozak gets convicted, are you going to offer him a job with the FBI so he can avoid prison?" Gregory shrugged his shoulders and said, "Maybe." The prosecutor had no more questions for Gregory.

Harry called Wally to take the stand. He asked him, "Did you get paid $5,000 to write the Dean's daughter's entrance exam to Harvard Law School? If you did, why?"

Wally answered, "My friend Louis needed $5,000 to pay back a loan shark. If he didn't pay it back soon, the loan shark would have his goons beat him to death. I did it to save his life."

Next question Harry asked, "Why did the Dean have you expelled before the final exams?"

Wally answered, "When the school found out that the Dean's daughter cheated, she was expelled, and he was asked to resign three weeks before his retirement. The Dean thought he was going to lose his pension and blamed me. He had me expelled so that I couldn't graduate. Art Jenkins, the president, expelled me without giving me a chance to defend myself at my tribunal."

Harry had no more questions for Wally. He asked George Shaw to take the stand.

He asked George, "Did you lose your pension when you resigned?"

George answered. "No, I didn't, I received my full pension."

Harry asked George, "Do you regret having Wally expelled three weeks before the final exams so that he couldn't graduate?"

George replied, "Yes, I do. Wally was a wonderful student. That is why I wrote a letter of recommendation for him. I had a lot of sleepless nights." Harry had no more questions for George. He called Art Jenkins to the stand.

He asked, "Mr. Jenkins, did you allow Wally Kozak to defend himself at his tribunal, and if you didn't, why not?"

Art replied, "I didn't give Wally Kozak a chance to defend himself because I was a stubborn old fool. I assumed he was guilty and greedy for money. If Wally was allowed to defend himself, I would not be sitting in court today."

Harry asked Art Jenkins if he was going to make restitutions for Wally Kozak. Art Jenkins replied, "I definitely will. I have a cheque for Wally from the Columbia Correspondence School of Law for $220,000. Harvard Law School has a cheque for $2,000,000 for an out-of-court settlement if Wally agrees to settle. I also have a diploma from the Harvard Law School with Wally's name on it. Every year, the school sells its final exams to correspondence schools. The exam that Wally wrote was the same one that he would have written if he hadn't been expelled. His 97.8% is the highest score. That makes him the head of the class on the Dean's honour list. Jeffrey Kelly was ahead of the class. He will be sharing second place with Denise Campbell."

The prosecutor approached the bench and said, "Your Honour, I heard enough. I don't want to waste any more of the court's time. I make a motion for all charges against Wally Kozak to be dropped." The motion was granted.

George Shaw and Art Jenkins approached Wally to congratulate him. Wally accepted the $2,000,000 settlement and the $220,000 cheque from Columbia Correspondence School of Law. Wally was happy and relieved to graduate from Harvard Law School finally. Art Jenkins shook Wally's hand and said, "Can you ever forgive us for what we had done to you?"

Wally was smiling and said, "I not only will forgive you and George but I'll invite you to our wedding, providing there is one. Elizabeth Grace returned her engagement ring when I got arrested."

Art happily said, "Wally, don't worry, I know Elizabeth, she is a fine girl. You two make a wonderful couple. I'll talk to her."

Joan approached Wally to congratulate him. She said, "Wally, make sure you have the engagement ring with you. Elizabeth will be coming to see you today."

Christine and Jeffrey Kelly also came to congratulate Wally. Jeffrey was very upset. He told Wally that he wished he never met him.

Judge Judy ran over to Wally to give him a big hug. "Wally, I'm so happy for you. I can hardly wait to be at your wedding." After everyone left the courthouse, Wally went home.

Louis was also very happy that Wally was found not guilty. Wally was the only true friend that Louis had. He didn't feel comfortable to go over and congratulate Wally. He sat in the back row to make sure Wally wouldn't see him.

Colonel Donald Chandler and Zac Brown also sat in the back row. They were not happy. Zac shook his head and said, "I guess we won't be recruiting Wally."

The Colonel smiled. "Don't worry, Zac, we will be recruiting Wally eventually. I have some favours to call in. Be patient; we may have to wait a few years before we can recruit him. It's too bad that Wally had Tommy killed. When it is time to recruit him, he will still be young and strong enough to withstand the transformation. We still have several other people to recruit."

Chapter 38

Cleo and Leo were home to greet Wally. They were hungry. Wally fed them and chased them out to the backyard. Wally was hungry and didn't want to have any distractions while preparing dinner. Wally made a lot of perogies, a pizza, and a large salad. Elizabeth is coming, and Wally knows that she has a huge appetite.

When Elizabeth arrived, she immediately asked Wally where Cleo and Leo were. Then she ran out to the backyard. Wally called Elizabeth for dinner. She brought Cleo and Leo in. Elizabeth said, "I missed Cleo and Leo very much." Wally was a little hurt and said, "Elizabeth, did you miss me at all?" She told Wally she did not miss him as much as she missed Cleo and Leo.

Wally was annoyed and said, "Elizabeth, maybe I should feed you doggie food for dinner if you prefer to be with Cleo and Leo."

Elizabeth smiled and said, "Wally, the only reason I am here is that my mother threw me out of her house. I have no job, and Samantha will not hire me unless I marry you. "

Wally couldn't believe what Elizabeth was saying. "Are you telling me you love Cleo and Leo and not me?"

Elizabeth looked at Wally and said, "Wally, you are a handsome and wonderful person. My problem is that I'm not ready to marry anyone at this time."

Wally was really annoyed and told Elizabeth if she was not ready to marry him, she would never be ready to marry anyone. "I don't think you want to become an old maid; now, let's eat."

After dinner, Wally took Elizabeth by the hand and went downstairs to meet his grandparents. They just got home. Wally said, "Grandfather, Grandmother, I want you to meet my fiancé, Elizabeth Grace."

Grandmother ran to give Elizabeth a big hug and said, "Wally, it's about time that you introduced us to her. Aunt Lydia told us that you were about to be engaged to a nice, beautiful girl."

Grandmother, still hugging Elizabeth, said. "Welcome to our family. Wally will take good care of you, but if he gets too mischievous, come see me, and I'll straighten him out."

Grandfather also gave Elizabeth a big hug and welcomed her to the family. Just then, Cleo and Leo ran down the stairs. Grandmother picked them up and said, "Elizabeth, your little doggies are adorable.

Elizabeth said to Grandmother, "Wally bought them for me. The puppy in your left hand is Cleo, and the puppy in your right hand is Leo."

Wally laughed, saying, "Cleo and Leo are my chick magnets." Grandmother thanked Wally and Elizabeth for their visit. She and her grandfather had to go back to their clinic.

Wally helped Elizabeth to unpack. He noticed that she had a bag full of prescription drugs. Wally couldn't believe that a doctor would prescribe such drugs to a healthy person. He threw the bag of prescription drugs into the garbage disposal.

Wally looked at a shocked Elizabeth and said to her, "No more toxic poison for you. From now on, I will take care of all your healthcare needs. I did work for my mother at her naturopath clinic. I am still a certified naturopath. I will also be your personal trainer, nutritionist, and yoga teacher. We'll plant a vegetable garden in the backyard together and raise a family. Elizabeth, you are sweating. Let me take your temperature to see if you have a fever."

Elizabeth ran out of the house. She got into her car and drove to her mother's house. Elizabeth ran to her mother for a big hug. Joan, Christine Kelly, and Judy were having tea. They asked Elizabeth what happened. Elizabeth, crying, said," Mother, I can't marry Wally. He is planning some terrible things for me!"

Joan, still hugging Elizabeth, said, "If Wally is such a terrible person, you will not have to marry him. Now tell me what terrible things Wally has planned for you?"

Elizabeth stopped crying and dried her tears. She said, "Wally threw all my meds in the garbage disposal. He said that from now on, he will be taking care of all my healthcare needs. Wally said that he is a naturopath and worked for his mother at her clinic. He also wants to be my personal trainer nutritionist and teach me yoga. He expects me to help him with gardening. Worst of all, Wally wants children. Jeffrey and I decided not to have children. I want to be under my doctor's care, not Wally's. I'm not interested in a personal trainer, nutritionist, or yoga. The thought of gardening makes me sick. I'm a career girl; I don't have time for Wally!"

Elizabeth couldn't believe what just happened. Joan, Aunt Judy, and Christine Kelly fell to the floor, laughing their heads off. When they finally got control of themselves, Joan gave Elizabeth a hug and said, "Elizabeth, if you found an old lamp, rubbed it, and a genie came out to offer you a wish, and you wished for the perfect husband, the genie would give you Wally. We knew Wally's mother; she was a dear friend of ours. We were heartbroken when she was killed. Do you know how much health care costs? Wally will take care of your health care needs much better than your family doctor. People pay a lot of money for personal trainers, nutritionists, and yoga teachers. You are getting it all for free. Gardening is very relaxing, especially doing it with Wally. Most of all, I want grandchildren."

Catherine placed her hands on Elizabeth's cheeks and said, "Elizabeth, Jeffrey doesn't deserve to have you. He's a pompous jerk, and you are a fool if you refuse to marry Wally."

Joan dragged Elizabeth into her car and drove off to Wally's house. Judy and Christine followed them. When they arrived, Joan held onto Elizabeth's hand and said to Wally, "Elizabeth doesn't want to marry you."

Wally just smiled and said, "If Elizabeth does not marry me, she will have to return the engagement ring, she will never see Cleo and Leo again, and I will not pay off her government student loan. She won't have a job because Samantha will not hire her unless she marries me."

Elizabeth took her phone and googled naturopaths in New York City. She said, "Mother, Wally is a fraud; he is not listed as a naturopath in New York City." Wally gave Elizabeth a kiss and told her to Google the Board of Directors for the Society of Naturopath Doctors in New York City. Elizabeth did and was surprised to see Wally's name listed as a member.

Wally took a thermometer and said, "Elizabeth, it's time to take your temperature. I want to make sure that you don't have a fever." Elizabeth was not going to cooperate. She closed her mouth and ducked when Wally tried to insert the thermometer into her mouth.

Wally became annoyed and said, "Elizabeth, we can do this the easy way or the hard way; it's your choice." Elizabeth kept her mouth closed. Wally grabbed her by the waist, turned her upside down, lifted her skirt, pulled down her panties, and stuck the thermometer in her butt. He held onto Elizabeth while she was screaming.

After a minute, Wally took out the thermometer and told Elizabeth she had no fever. Elizabeth pulled up her panties and skirt, "Wally, you just assaulted me. I'm going to bring assault charges against you. I have three witnesses."

The three witnesses were laughing. Joan said to Elizabeth, "We didn't see any assault. All we saw was Wally taking your temperature. Elizabeth, if you don't marry Wally, you'll have to find a place to live on your own. I will not let you live with me. What is wrong with you? You have been very bitchy lately!"

Wally smiled and said, "Elizabeth is not only bitchy, but she eats like a horse. That can only mean that she is pregnant."

Joan, Judy, and Christine were very happy to hear the news. They kissed Elizabeth goodbye. They left an unhappy Elizabeth behind. Wally put on a kettle to make tea. When they finished their tea, Wally asked Elizabeth if she wanted to walk Cleo and Leo with him into the trails. She quietly went with Wally. When they returned, Wally decided to go to bed early. Elizabeth stayed up all night playing with Cleo and Leo.

Wally got up early the next morning. Elizabeth was still asleep. Wally quietly said his prayer, danced and meditated. Then he showered and drove off to the office. Elizabeth, Cleo, and Leo were asleep.

Chapter 39

Wally decided to have breakfast at a diner before he got to his office. It was located in the Plaza across the street from the hotel. Just as he ordered breakfast, Wally saw Gloria walking in. She looked a little malnourished but still beautiful. Gloria didn't look too happy. When Gloria saw Wally, she ran to him to give him a big hug. "Wally's, it's been a long time since I saw you. What happened to you? I didn't see you at the graduation. I read about you and the newspaper."

Wally, smiling, said, "Gloria, I couldn't be at the graduation because my parents were killed. I had to go home to make funeral arrangements. Remember Jeffrey Kelly? He filed a citizen's arrest for racketeering against me when he found out that my father was Danelo Klyn. I never knew my father. My mother raised me on her own. Thanks to a lot of support from friends, all charges against me were dropped. I'm working for Samantha Franklin's law firm. What have you been doing?"

Gloria sadly said, "Wally, since graduation, I have been working for Donald Stone's law firm. I fell in love with his son Donnie. We were married. Six months later, he divorced me because of my alcohol and drug addiction. Right now, I'm spending time in rehab. I have no choice but to go if I want to keep my job."

Wally told Gloria that he was getting married in four weeks. He asked Gloria to do him a favour. "Elizabeth, my fiancé is getting cold feet and doesn't want to marry me. I want to introduce her to you. I'll ask Elizabeth if she is ready to marry me. If she says no, I will tell her to take off her engagement ring and give it to you. Then I'll ask her to pack her belongings and leave." Wally knows that there is no way that Elizabeth will give back her engagement ring.

Gloria began smiling and said, "Wally, if Elizabeth refuses to marry you, I'll keep the engagement ring."

Wally brought Gloria home to meet Elizabeth. Gloria looked at Wally's House and said, "Wally, I didn't know that you are such a successful lawyer." They went inside the house. Gloria was surprised at how beautifully Wally's house was furnished.

Wally introduced Gloria to Elizabeth and said, "Elizabeth, are you ready to marry me? Elizabeth said no." Wally was really upset and said, "Elizabeth, take off your engagement ring and give it to Gloria; pack up your belongings and leave right now!"

Elizabeth was shocked. She started to cry and ran into the washroom. Gloria held Wally back. She said, "Wally, stay here. I'll go bring her out. Elizabeth is adorable; she definitely loves you. Getting married can be stressful and frightening. I know from personal experience."

Glory went into the washroom to talk to Elizabeth. Wally walked over to the piano. He played and sang one of Elizabeth's favourite love songs, the Look of Love. When Wally finished singing the song, Elizabeth ran out of the washroom, jumped on his lap, and gave him a big kiss.

Gloria screamed, "Wally, why didn't you sing me romantic love songs when we were going out together!"

Wally replied, "Gloria, I did sing you romantic love songs. The problem was that you were always wasted on drugs and alcohol when I sang to you."

Gloria put her hands on her cheeks. "Oh my gosh, I do remember. If I wasn't such a stupid fool, I would be wearing Elizabeth's engagement ring!"

Wally asked Gloria a favour. He wanted her to take Elizabeth to Celine's bridal shop and help her choose a wedding dress. Wally opened an account there. He told Elizabeth to charge the wedding dress to his account.

Gloria took Elizabeth by the hand and dragged her out of the house. "Let's go, sweetheart. I'll make sure that you choose the most beautiful and expensive wedding dress in the shop."

Wally was happy to see them leave. Wally called Samantha to remind her that as a maid of honour, she is responsible for choosing the bridesmaid's dresses. Wally also called Richard Kiley to remind him that the best man was responsible for booking an appointment for the ushers to be measured for the tuxedos. Wally didn't tell Samantha that he chose Richard to be the best man.

Wally had to feed Cleo and Leo because they started yapping. Wally fed them and then took them out for a walk in the forest trails. He took them to a trail that passed the house located behind the parquet. The one that no one knew who owned it. The sign that says keep out private property. When they reached the house, Cleo and Leo started to bark continuously. Wally picked them up and carried them back home. Sidney Dinkledorf was inside the house. He looked outside the window and saw Wally carrying Leo and Cleo home.

Wally was not going to take Cleo and Leo anywhere near that house again. When he got home, he decided to take a nap in the lounge on the chair in the back patio. Cleo and Leo jumped on Wally's stomach. All three of them fell asleep.

Gloria and Elizabeth arrived at Celine's bridal shop. The first thing that Gloria said to the saleslady was, "Show us the most expensive wedding dresses that your store carries."

Elizabeth spent all afternoon trying on beautiful wedding dresses. With the help of Gloria and the saleslady, Elizabeth chose a wedding dress that cost $12,000. She told the saleslady to charge the wedding dress to Wally's account. The saleslady said, "Elizabeth, it'll be my pleasure to charge it to Wally's account. Come back a week before your wedding for a proper fitting."

Gloria and Elizabeth were excited. While driving Elizabeth home, Gloria said, "Oh, I would love to see the expression on Wally's face when he receives the bill for the wedding dress."

Elizabeth laughed and said," I could take a picture of Wally's face and email it to you."

Gloria laughed and said, "Elizabeth, please do. I would blow up his face at my friend's photo studio, issue 1,000 prints, and sell them on Amazon."

Elizabeth stopped laughing and said, "Gloria, Wally paid $21,000 for my engagement ring. He said that he would pay off my entire $200,000 government student loan. I don't think paying $12,000 for my wedding dress will upset him."

Gloria pulled over onto the shoulder and stopped the car. "I didn't know Wally was so rich. Now I know why you ran into the washroom. You didn't want to give me your engagement ring. Let's have a look at it." Gloria started to cry when she saw Elizabeth's engagement ring. Gloria dried her eyes and drove Elizabeth home. When they arrived home, Elizabeth invited Gloria to come in for tea.

They found Wally, Cleo, and Leo asleep in the lounge chair. Elizabeth decided to let them sleep. Gloria asked Elizabeth where she could get such adorable puppies. Elizabeth told Gloria that Wally had bought them for her. She better ask him where he got them.

Wally, Cleo, and Leo woke up just in time for tea. Cleo and Leo received doggie treats. Wally gave Gloria the name of the breeder from whom he bought the puppies. He did not tell her how much they cost and how difficult it is to get one. When they finished tea, Gloria gave Wally and Elizabeth a goodbye hug.

Wally and Elizabeth walked quietly with Cleo and Leo in the forest. Elizabeth suddenly got the urge to have a poop. Wally gave her a napkin. Elizabeth took the napkin and walked over between two trees to do her business. Cleo and Leo were happily exploring the trails.

Wally took out his phone to take a picture of Elizabeth pooping. While Elizabeth was still crouching, Wally said to her," Smile." She turned her head to see Wally taking a picture of her. He immediately saved the picture. Elizabeth screamed, "Wally, you idiot!"

When Elizabeth was done, she grabbed Wally's phone and deleted her picture. Elizabeth quickly walked home. Wally followed with Cleo and Leo. Elizabeth took a shower, then grabbed the book and went to bed.

Wally sat in a chair in the kitchen. He looked at Elizabeth's picture of her taking a poop. A photography magazine had a contest for amateur photographers. The picture that was judged the most unusual wins a $10,000 first prize. The look on Elizabeth's face while she was pooping was very unusual, and could have a chance of winning the first prize. Without Elizabeth's knowledge, Wally entered her picture. The title for the picture that he chose was Nature Calls. Wally then grabbed a book and joined Elizabeth in bed.

Chapter 40

Wally woke up at 6 o'clock in the morning. It was Saturday morning, and it was time to go to the Spencer Valley outdoor farmer's market. Elizabeth was still sleeping. Wally let her sleep. When Cleo and Leo get hungry, they will wake her up. Elizabeth still might be mad at Wally.

While Wally was looking at some organic tomatoes at the market, he noticed a man staring at him. The man was bald, wore sunglasses, and had his mouth tightly closed. He was very tall and wore dark clothes. This man gave Wally the creeps. He took a picture of this man. The creepy man disappeared. A few minutes later, Wally saw the creepy man. Wally started to walk towards him. Before Wally could get close enough to touch him, the creepy man disappeared into the market crowd.

Wally emailed the picture of the creepy man to Don Jordan and immediately called him. Wally told Don that the creepy man was following him. Don looked at the picture that Wally just sent him. Don recognized the man immediately. He was worried.

Don said, "Wally, the man's name is Doug Johnson. He was a police officer in Detroit three years ago. The police suspected him of being a serial killer. He was charged but never convicted. Don Johnson left the police force three years ago. Police lost track of him. It looks to me like he will start killing again. Don't worry, Wally. I'll have agents watching your family around the clock until Doug is found."

Wally thanked Doug and went home. He did not tell Elizabeth what happened at the farmers market. Elizabeth would be stressed out to find out that a serial killer is after him. When he got home, Wally fed Cleo and Leo, then chased them into the backyard. For breakfast, Wally prepared bacon, eggs, home fries, toast, and coffee.

Wally and Elizabeth spent the weekend playing with Cleo and Leo. They visited Wally's grandparent's clinic. Grandmother confirmed that Elizabeth was pregnant. Elizabeth was worried; she had never planned to be a mother. Monday morning, Wally drove Elizabeth to her family doctor. She wanted a second opinion to make sure that she was pregnant. Wally dropped Elizabeth at her doctor's and drove to his office.

Samantha was waiting for Wally in his office. She wanted to show Elizabeth her new office. Wally told Samantha that Elizabeth was pregnant and was at her doctor's. He'll pick her up later.

Samantha wanted to ask Wally something. Wally didn't need to read her mind to know what she was about to ask. Wally held his breath and closed his eyes because Samantha was about to ask Wally who was the best man. Wally told her that it was Richard Kiley. Samantha couldn't believe what Wally just said." Are you out of your mind, Wally? How could you!"

Wally, grinning, said, "There was nobody else to ask on such short notice. Harry is the master of ceremony. Donna is a bridesmaid. She would not allow Thomas to be the best man. Just consider this as me getting even with you for torturing me all night at your apartment. Richard was more than happy to be my best man."

Samantha was still upset, "Wally, Richard was happy to be your best man because he wanted to piss me off." Samantha left Wally's office. Wally left to pick up Elizabeth. He was early. Wally decided to go to the cafeteria to buy tea and a blueberry bran muffin for Elizabeth. She was not happy when her doctor confirmed that she was pregnant. Wally quietly drove her back to the office.

Samantha gave Elizabeth a big hug and congratulated her for being pregnant. She showed Elizabeth her office. Elizabeth was impressed. This office was much larger than the one that she had with Harry. It was a lot nicely decorated. Elizabeth was very happy with her new office and gave Samantha a big thank-you hug. At the end of the day, Wally drove Elizabeth home. All week, there was no sign of Doug Johnson.

Next Saturday morning, Wally left for the farmer's market. Elizabeth was not an early riser. He let her sleep because she was pregnant. At the farmer's market, Wally saw Doug Johnson. He took out his phone to call Don Jordan to let him know. Don told Wally to go into the forest behind the Pavilion. An agent was waiting for him. Don didn't want any innocent bystanders involved.

Wally slowly started to walk towards the forest. When he entered the forest, Wally found a man lying on the ground. Wally assumed that he was dead and the agent that he was supposed to meet. When he approached the dead agent, Doug Johnson stepped out from behind the tree. He had a large knife in his hand and was ready to attack Wally. Doug lunged at Wally. Being a Cossack warrior, Wally was prepared for him. Wally easily took hold of Doug's wrist and removed his knife from his hand.

Don Johnson was surprised at how easily Wally disarmed him. He knew that he was no match for Wally. Doug ran out of the forest into the farmer's market. Wally lost sight of him in the crowd. It didn't matter. Wally was able to read Doug's mind and found out everything about him. Wally knew all the six people, four girls and two boys, that Doug killed, their names, and where he had buried them. Wally also knew where Doug was hiding. Wally had to think of an appropriate lie to tell Don.

When Don showed up, Wally told him that Doug killed the agent and then jumped him. Wally said, "Don, when I saw the agent lying on the ground, Doug jumped me. He held a knife against my throat. He started to brag about how he outsmarted the police. He told me the names of the people he killed and where he buried them. Doug even told me where he was hiding. I then stomped on his toes; he dropped the knife and ran into the farmer's market."

Wally gave all the information to Don. He told him that Doug was staying with his mother at her home. Wally gave the address of Doug Johnson's mother. The coroner showed up to look after the dead agent. Nobody at the farmer's market knew what happened. The death of the agent would be kept from the media.

Don Jordan had Doug's mother's house staked out. He wanted to make sure Doug's mother left the house, leaving Doug all alone. Around noon, Doug's mother left the house. That's when several agents wearing bulletproof vests approached the house. One of the agents knocked on the front door. Another agent ran to the back of the house. He was ready to break down the back door if necessary.

Doug answered the door. The agent identified himself and said, "Doug Johnson, you are under arrest for murder; come on out with your hands up!" Doug slammed the door. The other agent broke down the back door. He had his gun pointing at Doug's chest. He told Doug to get on his knees and put his hands up. Doug took out a gun hidden in a flower pot. Before he had a chance to use it, the agent shot Doug in the head.

Don called Wally the next day. He told Wally what happened. Don said to Wally that the bodies that Doug buried were being recovered and sent to their families. He also mentioned that there was a $50,000 reward for helping the FBI to catch Doug.

Wally told Doug to give the money to his friend Clarence Leonard. "He works for the Salvation Army; they need the money a lot more than I do," Don told Wally that he was getting a $50,000 tax receipt.

Wally asked Don if he could find out who owns the house in the forest behind the parquet. He told Don that Cleo and Leo started barking like crazy whenever they went near it.

Don knew that the house was owned by the military. He called his friend Col. Alexander Bung and asked him what the military was doing in that little house. Col. Alexander Bung asked Don who wanted to know. He told the colonel that a friend of his, Wally Kozak, lived in the house beside the parquet. "His dogs bark like crazy whenever they go near the house." The colonel told Don that what the military does in that house was classified.

Col. Bung did a background check on Wally Kozak. He knew that Wally's father was Danelo Klyn. He wanted to recruit Wally. Col. Bung assumed that Wally was a criminal. The government only allowed the colonel to recruit convicted criminals for his experiments. The colonel believed that Wally was a criminal. He knew that criminal charges were dropped against him for racketeering. He still planned to recruit Wally.

Col. Bung said, "Sidney, we are going to recruit Wally Kozak eventually. Unfortunately, we may have to wait a few years because we are committed to choosing recruits for this year. Some of the recruits become unpredictable. It is better that we find out what the problem is before we recruit Wally." Sydney Dinkledorf will be very excited to have Wally for his experiments. All their recruits were lacking in intelligence. This made them not very suitable for the military's purpose. Sidney wanted someone who was very intelligent, like Wally.

Later that day, Don called Wally. He told him that the house behind the parquet belonged to the military. What they do there is classified. Wally thanked Don for this information.

Chapter 41

Rhonda Jones walked into Henry Wilson's office. She wore white gloves. Rhonda carried a gun in her left hand and a dagger in her right hand. She placed the dagger on Henry's desk. He looked up at Rhonda and said, "Sweetheart, what is the meaning of this?"

Rhonda smiled and said, "I received your divorce papers this morning. Do you think that you can get rid of me as easily as you did with your other wives?"

Henry nervously said, "Rhonda, you knew our marriage was going to last only a short time. You're getting a generous divorce settlement. What is your problem?"

Rhonda kept on smiling and said, "Henry, the problem is that I enjoy living here. I want to keep on living here after you die."

Henry became really upset and said, "Rhonda, you cannot stay here. The Board of Directors will not allow you to take over my company!"

Rhonda stopped smiling and said, "Henry, I don't care about your Board of Directors. I have other plans. Stand up, Henry, and pick up the dagger!" Henry grabbed his cane, stood up, and picked up the dagger. Rhonda said," Henry, it is time for you to die!" Rhonda shoved her gun against Henry's chest and pulled the trigger. He was dead before he reached the floor.

Rhonda grabbed the dagger and managed to make several self-inflicted wounds. She called 911 before she passed out. The ambulance arrived and put Rhonda on life support. At the hospital, Rhonda was diagnosed with serious but not life-threatening knife wounds. After spending a week in the hospital, Rhonda was released.

The police thoroughly investigated the death of Henry Wilson. They decided that there was enough evidence to charge Rhonda with murder. She was not happy. Rhonda was convinced that she would have gotten away with murder. She hired Henry's lawyer, Richard Kiley, to defend her. The Board of Directors had to find another lawyer. Richard Kiley recommended Wally Kozak to them.

George Anderson, the president of the Board of Directors, met Wally. He was very nervous because Wally was so young and inexperienced. George instructed Wally to offer Rhonda Jones $500,000,000 for a civil out-of-court settlement.

Wally was shocked, "Mr. Anderson, are you crazy! Do you want Rhonda to get away with murder with all that money!"

George Anderson replied, "We don't care; we don't want to take a chance of her winning in criminal court and taking over Henry's company. Richard Kiley is a very good lawyer." Wally replied, "Mr. Anderson, I am also a very good lawyer. That is why Richard recommended me." George Anderson didn't care how good a lawyer Wally was. He insisted that Wally offer the out-of-court settlement to Rhonda.

Wally met Rhonda and Richard in court. Wally presented the $500,000,000 civil out-of-court settlement to Rhonda. Richard did his best to convince Rhonda to take the settlement. Rhonda stubbornly refused. She was convinced that she was going to win in criminal court and take over Henry's company. Wally shook hands with Richard and Rhonda. He called Rhonda a fool for not taking the settlement.

Wally read her mind. He learned that Rhonda had a black belt in karate and was a bodybuilder for many years. She was 6 feet tall and weighed 160 pounds of solid muscle. Wally also found out that Rhonda spent three years in prison for drug trafficking. There was no way that a jury would find her not guilty.

Wally called George Anderson and said, "I have good news. Rhonda Jones turned down your offer to settle. She will be spending the rest of her life in prison. I won't need you in court.

George was very upset and said, "I'm very worried; you're so young and inexperienced. "Wally was getting annoyed, "Mr. Anderson, you need to chill out. Take a month-long vacation at some health resort."

George Anderson was really upset. He slammed the phone down. Wally started to prepare for court. There is no way that Rhonda was going to get away with murder. Henry Wilson was a good friend. He was also Wally's client at the Kozak Naturopath Clinic. Wally had his medical records. He downloaded Henry's medical records onto a memory stick.

Wally went to see Uncle Ivan at the Spencers Mill. When he arrived, Wally took a pizza box and placed a freshly made deluxe pizza in it. Then he taped the memory stick on the bottom back of the pizza box. Wally went to find Uncle Ivan. He found him in his office.

Wally smiled. "Uncle Ivan, I need a favour from you. Please deliver this pizza to Richard Kiley. You know where his office is. Give Richard this pizza and have him sign this form. It's a disclosure form that proves that he received the evidence that I will use against his client. I taped the evidence on the back bottom of the pizza box. Don't tell him where the evidence is unless Richard asks where it is."

Uncle Ivan was confused. "Wally, why do you want me to do this?" Wally handed the pizza box to Uncle Ivan and said, "Rhonda Jones killed our friend Henry Wilson. She is claiming self-defence. If Rhonda is successful at her criminal court trial, she will get control of Henry's company. If Richard signs a disclosure and doesn't ask where the evidence is, she will spend the rest of her life in prison. If Richard sees the evidence, Rhonda will receive $500,000,000 in an out-of-court settlement in civil court and will get away with murder if she wins in criminal court."

Uncle Ivan wasn't happy with delivering the pizza to Richard, but he did it because Wally was doing the right thing. Uncle Ivan arrived at Richard's office. Richard told the receptionist to send him in. Richard was happy to see him. Uncle Ivan placed the pizza box on Richard's desk and said, "Wally wanted me to deliver this pizza to you. He also wanted you to sign this form."

Richard took the form, read it, and signed it," Thank Wally for the pizza for me. I'm glad you came. It is lunchtime, and I was planning to have pizza at your restaurant."

Uncle Ivan smiled and said goodbye. Wally was waiting to hear from him. He was happy to hear that Richard Kiley signed the disclosure and didn't ask where the evidence was.

Two weeks later, Wally arrived at the courthouse for the trial. When the trial commenced, Richard Kiley called Rhonda Jones to the stand. Richard asked her what happened on the day that Henry Wilson was shot and killed.

Rhonda testified that Henry was mostly a kind and gentle man. She also mentioned that there were days when Henry was very cruel and demanding. She said, "Henry wanted to have sex that day. When I refused, Henry became angry and attacked me with his dagger. Henry stabbed me several times. That is when I took out my gun and was able to shoot him in the chest." Richard mentioned to the court that Henry's fingerprints were found on the dagger that he used to stab Rhonda.

Wally approached Rhonda and asked her," You lived with Henry for nearly 3 years. Why did you purchase a gun two days before you shot Henry? His home was well secured?"

Rhonda answered," I decided to buy the gun for protection when I go out shopping or visit friends." Wally asked Rhonda, Did Henry file for divorce, and is that the reason why you shot him?

Rhonda answered," Henry was very moody. He was in a bad mood when he filed for divorce. The next day, he was in a good mood and told me that he wasn't going to divorce me."

Wally said to Rhonda, "You are 6 feet tall, 160 pounds of solid muscle, and have a black belt in karate. Henry Wilson was an 80-year-old frail man. He was 5'8" tall, weighed 130 pounds, and walked with a cane. His medical records show that Henry had a very weak heart and severe arthritis in both his wrists." Richard Kiley immediately objected. He approached the bench and said the prosecutor never disclosed Henry Wilson's medical records to the defence.

Wally approached the bench and said, "Your Honour, I have a disclosure form signed by the defence saying they received the medical records." Richard argued." Your Honour, when I signed that disclosure, all I received was a pizza, nothing else!" Wally answered, Your Honour, I put Henry's medical records on a memory stick. I taped the memory stick on the bottom back of the pizza box. Why didn't the defence ask the delivery boy or call me to find out where the evidence was? Why didn't the defence file a court order to release Henry Wilson's medical records."

The judge looked at Richard and said, "The prosecutor is right; you should have filed a court order to have those records released. Since you did receive the evidence and signed the disclosure form, I will allow them as evidence."

Wally asked Rhonda, "How can a six-foot woman weighing 160 pounds with a black belt in karate be terrified of Henry Wilson? He was a frail 80-year-old man who walked with a cane. He also has a very weak heart and arthritis in both his wrists?"

Rhonda answered, "You were not there; you have no idea how vicious Henry can be!" Wally mentioned that the coroner concluded that knife wounds were made by a person who is left-handed, while Henry was right-handed. Rhonda said," Just because Henry was right-handed doesn't mean that he couldn't attack me with his left hand."

Wally said, "The doctor's report says that your wounds were very deep and could have been fatal. How could Henry inflict such wounds with arthritis in both wrists?"

Rhonda answered, "Henry's arthritis was controlled by prescription drugs. You can't know what Henry is capable of doing just by looking at him!" Wally said, "Rhonda if he terrified you so much, why didn't you accept the $500,000,000 civil out-of-court settlement the Board of Directors offered you?"

Rhonda answered, "I turned down the offer because I truly loved Henry and wanted to be his wife." Wally replied, "Rhonda, you purchased a gun two days before you killed Henry. You wanted to get control of Henry's company. It's worth over $6 billion. You walked into his office and forced him to pick up the dagger you placed on his desk. Then you shoved your gun against his chest and shot him. Henry was too weak to inflict the wounds that you received. However, a young, big, strong woman like yourself is capable of inflicting such deep wounds. Henry's weak heart would not allow him to have sex. You did not love Henry! You wanted his company!"

It took the jury only 15 minutes to find Rhonda Jones guilty of first-degree murder. Richard Kiley approached Wally, but he was not happy. He said, "Wally, what you did was very unethical. I'm very disappointed in you."

Wally smiled at Richard and said," Henry was a dear family friend. He was also your friend. Richard, you knew that Henry had a weak heart and arthritis in both his wrists. You didn't need to get his medical records. You could've told Rhonda what you knew, and she would've taken the out-of-court settlement in civil court and possibly got away with murder."

Richard said," Wally, I'm glad that Rhonda was convicted, but I still don't like what you did. Now tell me, how did you know that Rhonda had a black belt in karate? She never told me?" Wally mischievously said, "Richard, do you know what a private detective is?"

The next morning, George Anderson came to visit Wally. He met Samantha in Wally's office. He told her how pleased he was with Wally. Samantha happily left. George shook Wally's hand and said, "I have some great news for you. Henry Wilson appointed me as his power of attorney. He willed his shares in his company to you. The shares are incorporated as a separate company. The Board of Directors will be running Henry's company. All the dividends produced by your shares will be deposited in your personal bank account. Those shares are worth over $1 billion. You will receive approximately $100,000,000 in dividends every year. Henry also willed his personal house to you. You could afford to move in and live there if you want, or you can sell it for $8,000,000. I have a buyer ready to buy it from you. Congratulations, Wally, you just became a very rich man."

Wally thanked George for delivering such great news and told him to sell Harry's mansion. Before George could leave, Wally said," It's almost lunchtime. I reserved a room at the Spencers Mill for the office staff to celebrate Henry's passing. George, you are welcome to come." Wally will tell Elizabeth that he inherited Henry's mansion and had it sold. He decided not to tell her that he also inherited Henry's shares in his company.

The piano was moved into the reserved room. Wally played the piano and sang songs while everyone was waiting for lunch to be served. Richard was invited to come. He forgot what Wally did at Rhonda's trial. Wally played Brahms's Lullaby and then sang some of Henry's favourite Frank Sinatra songs. Aunt Lydia served Henry's favourite meal. There were turkey meatballs, lasagna, bean salad, broccoli salad, and pierogies. For dessert, fine brandy and dark Belgian chocolates.

Chapter 42

Gregory Klyn got up early in the morning. He was looking forward to his trial. Gregory could hardly wait to see the look on Don Jordan's face when he found out that the memory sticks showing the meetings between him and Danelo were missing from the safety deposit box.

Don Jordan called Wally. "The memory sticks are missing from Maria's safety deposit box. Gregory found out where they were. We are screwed!"

Wally calmly said," Don, don't worry. I knew that Gregory would have the memory sticks removed. That is why I made a copy of those videos before I gave you the key to my mother's safety deposit box."

Don was still worried. "Wally, didn't you just sign a disclosure saying that no copies of the video recordings were made?"

Wally replied, "I signed a disclosure saying that my mother Maria never made copies. No one asked me if I made any copies," Don Jordan was relieved. He told Wally that he should join the FBI. Wally told Don that he would meet him in the courthouse.

At Gregory's trial, the court allowed the memory sticks showing the meetings between him and Danelo to be used as evidence. It didn't take long for the jury to find Gregory Klyn guilty as charged. Gregory didn't bother to waste money and time on an appeal.

Wally went to see Gregory before he officially started his prison term. He was sentenced to 20 years. Wally knew that his uncle didn't want to see him. Wally said," Uncle Gregory, I want to let you know I never broke my promise to Tommy. He broke his promise when he hired goons to kill Harry O'Rilley. He is a dear friend. I chose him to be my master of ceremony at my wedding."

Uncle Gregory was facing the wall. He said to Wally, "It doesn't matter what you did or why you did it. I'm still a dead man, so why are you telling me this?"

Wally calmly replied, "Uncle Gregory, if you go to prison, you will be beaten to death within a week. Don Jordan can put you in the witness protection program if you provide everything you know about the Chinese drug trade. "

Uncle Gregory shook his head and said, "Wally, it wouldn't make any difference. The Chinese triad would eventually find me and have me killed."

Wally smiled." Uncle Gregory, your choice: get beaten to death in prison within a week, or live several months and get shot in the head by your brother Pavlo. I want you to live long enough to be at my wedding in three weeks."

Uncle Gregory looked at Wally and said," Wally, why are you doing this for me? You know I am in the drug business." Wally told Uncle Gregory that he is family and wants him to be at his wedding.

Uncle Gregory started to cry." Wally, I would love to be at your wedding. Please call Don Jordan. Tell him I am ready to enter the witness protection program."

Chapter 43

Wally was excited. He and Elizabeth Grace will be married within a week. Elizabeth was living with him. That night, while lying in bed with Elizabeth, Wally noticed a small lump on her breast. He opened a dresser drawer and took out a very small surgical instrument. Wally cut a sample from the lump on Elizabeth's breasts. She was not happy. Wally ignored her displeasure.

Wally went downstairs to see Grandmother. He was worried. He asked his grandmother to analyze the sample he took from Elizabeth's breast. Grandmother told Wally she would have it analyzed by tomorrow afternoon and told him to go to bed.

The sample that Wally took from Elizabeth's breast showed that she has breast cancer. Elizabeth was shocked when Wally told her. Elizabeth ran out of the house to see her family doctor for a second opinion. Her doctor checked the medical analysis of Elizabeth's breast and confirmed that she did have breast cancer.

He told Elizabeth that she needed a mastectomy and had to go through several sessions of chemotherapy. Elizabeth ran out of her doctor's office crying. She went to see her mother to tell her the terrible news.

Joan gave Elizabeth a big hug. "Elizabeth, don't worry. Wally still loves you. He will take good care of you; let's go see him."

When Wally heard what Elizabeth's doctor recommended for treatment, he became very angry." "Elizabeth, you are not going to have a mastectomy or any chemotherapy. The cancer hasn't spread. We can contain it. Let's go see Grandmother right now!"

Grandmother looked at a frightened Elizabeth and a worried Joan. "Wally, on your honeymoon, you and Elizabeth should visit our Ukrainian village. Both of you can stay at your cousin Peter's home. Uncle Ivan will let him know that you and Elizabeth are coming. The village doctor, Bernie, will know the best way to treat Elizabeth's cancer. I'll give Elizabeth some herbal teas to help control her cancer for now. Please don't tell anyone that Elizabeth has cancer. You don't want to spoil the wedding. Don't worry. We will be praying for Elizabeth's good health."

Joan and Elizabeth thanked the grandmother. Wally hugged Elizabeth and said," Grandmother said not to worry. She knows best. I'm sure we will have a wonderful time on our honeymoon."

Elizabeth said nothing. Wally told her to stay home, relax, and prepare for the wedding. He kissed Elizabeth goodbye and left for his office.

Lawrence was waiting for Wally in his office. He was holding a little orange kitten. As soon as Wally walked in, Lawrence said, "Her name is Purdy; she's Jenny's sister. Purdy needs a good home. Consider Purdy as another wedding gift." Lawrence then placed Purdy on Wally's desk and quickly ran out of the office.

Wally looked at Purdy and said to her, "Welcome to our family, Purdy. I'm sure you will become good friends with Cleo and Leo."

Wally sat down to do some paperwork, leaving Purdy to roam around the office. When he was finished, Wally found Donna giving Purdy a dish of milk. Donna looked up at Wally and said," Wally, is this adorable little kitten yours?" Wally told Donna that her name was Purdy. "She is a wedding gift from Lawrence. Hopefully, she will get along with Cleo and Leo." Donna asked Wally if she could get a picture of the three of them together.

Wally picked up Purdy and said while leaving," I will get you a picture of them together if they cooperate to pose for the picture." Wally and Purdy drove home.

When Elizabeth saw Wally holding a kitten, she screamed, "Wally, I hate cats, get rid of it!" Wally shook his head and said, "I can't; her name is Purdy. She is a wedding gift from Lawrence."

Wally held Purdy up to Elizabeth's face and said, "Elizabeth, look straight into Purdy's eyes and say I hate you."

Elizabeth looked into Purdy's eyes and said, "Wally, you take care of Purdy, and I will take care of Cleo and Leo." Wally put Purdy down. He waited for Cleo Leo to show up. Wally was pleased to see that Cleo and Leo took nicely to Purdy. He took a picture of the three of them together for Donna.

The phone rang. It was Jeffrey. "Wally, I heard that Elizabeth has breast cancer. Are you still planning to marry her? I'm happy that you took Elizabeth away from me. I wouldn't want to marry damaged goods."

Wally was furious!" Jeffrey, be prepared to receive a large bar bill for our wedding. I don't consider Elizabeth damaged goods, and I do love her!"

Jeffrey said," Wally, I'm not worried about the bar bill. My father agreed to pay for it. I'm sure I'll be enjoying myself at your wedding. Don't worry, I won't tell anyone that Elizabeth has breast cancer." Wally hung up the phone. He couldn't believe how heartless Jeffrey could be.

On his wedding day, Wally was looking forward to seeing Elizabeth wearing her wedding dress. Everyone at the wedding party was waiting at the wedding chapel. Many of the guests were surprised to see Samantha and Richard as a maid of honour and best man. The ushers looked handsome in their tuxedos. The bridesmaids wore beautiful long pink gowns covered with red roses.

The music started to play the wedding march as Wally and Elizabeth walked down the aisle. The photographer started to take pictures. When the priest announced that Wally and Elizabeth were husband and wife, a lot of pictures were taken of them by the guests. The priest led Wally and Elizabeth inside the restaurant to the head of the table.

Louis was hiding behind a tree. He took several pictures of Wally and Elizabeth. Louis was happy that Wally was married to such a beautiful girl. He understood why Wally didn't invite him to his wedding.

Harry O'Rilley, the master of ceremonies, gave his speech. When he finished his speech, other speeches followed. Wally was the last person to give a speech. He thanked his family for their support and mentioned how happy he was to have Elizabeth as his wife. When Wally finished his speech, Uncle Ivan began serving dinner. The menu began with beet soup, followed by prime rib and scallop potatoes with bean salad, broccoli salad, and coleslaw. For dessert, Aunt Lydia prepared various pastries served with coffee or tea. Each table had two bottles of wine, one red and one white.

During dinner, Uncle Gregory walked over to Wally's and Elizabeth's table. He said," Wally, you never met your uncle Pavlo. You didn't have a chance to meet him at his birthday party. He is sitting at the table behind you. Would you like to go over and see him for a few minutes?"

Elizabeth was busy talking to Samantha. Wally got up and headed for Uncle Pavlo's table. Don Jordan was sitting with him. Uncle Pavlo gave Wally a big hug. "Wally, I'm so happy for you. Your bride is very beautiful. Sit down and have a drink with us." Wally shook hands with Don Jordan and sat down between his two uncles.

Wally smiled and said, "Uncle Gregory, do you realize that Uncle Pavlo will eventually be hired to put a bullet into your head?" Uncle Gregory told Wally he would rather have Pavlo do it than someone else. He told Wally that he was not afraid to die.

Wally smiled and faced Uncle Pavlo. "Does it bother you that you will eventually have to kill your own brother?"

Pavlo smiled and said, "Not as much as when I had to kill Danelo and your mother. Uncle Gregory knows that his time to die is coming soon. He wants to make the most of the little time he has left."

Wally, still smiling, said to his uncles," Elizabeth is pregnant; I would like to see Uncle Gregory live long enough to see the birth of our child." Wally then got up and left to go back to his table. He told Uncle Pavlo that he hoped never to use his services again.

The band started to play. Almost everyone started to dance. Wally was smiling when he saw Richard and Samantha dancing. Uncle Ivan asked Wally to sing a few songs with the band. He sang songs by Al Martino, Tom Jones, and Marty Robbins. When Wally finished singing, the band started to play polkas.

It was time for Elizabeth to throw her bouquet of flowers over her shoulder. Patricia was the lucky girl who caught it. Wally and Elizabeth left for home. They had to get up early the next morning to get to the airport to go on their honeymoon. Grandmother and grandfather had already packed everything for them. Elizabeth had such a good time at her wedding that she forgot that she had breast cancer.

Chapter 44

The next morning, Wally and Elizabeth got up, showered and dressed. Grandmother had hot porridge with blueberries and maple syrup waiting for them. Wally and Elizabeth kissed Grandmother goodbye. They took their luggage into their car. Grandfather drove them to the airport. Wally and Elizabeth had an eight-hour flight. During the flight, they slept most of the time. When the plane landed at the airport in the city of Lviv, it didn't take long to find Wally's cousin Peter. He looked a lot like his father. After a hugging session, everyone got into a taxi to get to the village.

When they arrived, Peter introduced Wally and Elizabeth to his family and friends. Peter and his wife Irene owned a restaurant that belonged to Uncle Ivan and Aunt Lydia. They had two children, Taras and Oksana. Taras was nine years old. He had blond hair and well-developed muscles for a boy his age. Oksana was seven years old. She also had blond hair and well-developed muscle for a girl her age. Both children plan to join the Ukrainian dance ensemble. They perform in concert halls throughout Europe. Peter has a brother. He was 12 years older. His name was Yuri. He was a major in the Ukrainian army. The last time Peter saw him was 10 years ago.

Wally and Elizabeth were shown to their room. Peter told them to shower and take a nap while Irene prepared dinner. There was no indoor plumbing. They had to go shower behind the house in a shower stall. After their shower, Elizabeth and Wally lay down for their nap. When they woke up, Elizabeth looked around and said to Wally," I feel like I am in Sherwood Forest waiting for Robin Hood."

Wally smiled. "Elizabeth, my parents came from a simple lifestyle. This village hasn't changed much in the last 200 years. However, people do have cell phones and television."

Dinner was ready. The bread was baked in stone ovens. Elizabeth pigged out on the bread. The huge salad had several kinds of nuts and seeds in it. Sauerkraut had grated apples and carrots. Elizabeth ate the baked chicken. It was the best she ever tasted.

After dinner, Peter told Elizabeth to get a good night's sleep. "Bernie, our doctor will be waiting to see Elizabeth early in the morning. Don't worry, he'll make her healthy."

Before going to bed, Wally and Elizabeth took a walk through the village. There was a trail in the forest leading to a lake where villagers were fishing. Wally and Elizabeth entered the trail. They sat on a large rock to watch some of the villagers and fish. Wally received a large fish from one of the villagers to take back to Peter. Wally and Elizabeth walked back to the village. Wally gave the fish to Peter. He and Elizabeth went to bed.

Elizabeth and Wally were awakened by a rooster. Irene announced that breakfast is ready. Elizabeth had never eaten such delicious fish before. After breakfast, Wally and Elizabeth went to see Bernie. His office was a short walk away.

Wally gave Bernie, Elizabeth's medical file. Bernie gave Elizabeth a thorough examination. Wally waited in his office for over an hour. When he finished, Bernie smiled, "Wally, Elizabeth does have breast cancer but don't worry, the cancer hasn't spread, and she can be cured." He told Elizabeth to relax. To help her, Bernie wanted to hypnotize Elizabeth to forget that she had cancer. To learn how to hypnotize people, Wally was allowed to put his hand on Bernie's forehead while he hypnotized Elizabeth. Bernie told Wally that the villagers would pray for Elizabeth's recovery.

Bernie said, "Wally, it's very important to keep Elizabeth as active as possible. This will keep the cancer from spreading quickly. Make sure that she eats a lot. I have some prepared herbal remedies for Elizabeth to take daily. The cancer should disappear within three weeks." Wally thanked Bernie and left with Elizabeth. He told Peter what Bernie prescribed.

Peter called Taras and Oksana. "Wally, they will keep Elizabeth very busy. You could help in repairing some roofs. We had some severe rainstorms that damaged a lot of roofs."

Elizabeth bent down to shake hands with Taras and Oksana. Something hit her in the butt. She fell down. When Elizabeth looked up, she saw a goat staring at her. Tara and Oksana were laughing. Oksana said," His name is Zychok. Never bend down when he is around." Elizabeth got up. She was now laughing.

Taras was holding a wooden stake with a sharp tip. He said," This is where our garden will be. The ground is still soft from the rain. I will be digging a long trench. Elizabeth, you will be dropping seeds one inch apart in the trench. Oksana will cover the trench with soil. We will do three rows. In the first row, we will plant carrots, the second row will have beets, and the third row will have garlic. When we finish, each of us will water a row with a water bucket. When we finish, we will do another three rows. This will keep us busy until dinner."

Elizabeth didn't say a word. She began dropping seeds in the trench. Wally has to explain to Elizabeth why she has to do gardening on their honeymoon.

After dinner, Wally explained to Elizabeth that gardening was a way for us to pay for our accommodations. Tomorrow morning, after breakfast, they will go sightseeing in the big city. Later in the evening, they will attend a concert. The village dance ensemble and orchestra will perform.

The next morning, Wally and Elizabeth took a taxi to Lyviv. It was nearly lunch when they arrived. They went to a restaurant for lunch. A tour guide approached Wally and Elizabeth to offer his services. Wally decided to hire him. The tour guide took them through many churches and museums. Wally and Elizabeth learned a lot about Ukrainian culture. At the end of the tour, Wally paid the tour guide with a generous tip.

There was still time to have dinner before the concert. Elizabeth and Wally went to have dinner. They had fish and salad. After dinner, they headed for the concert hall. When they arrived, the orchestra started to play some classical music. Fifteen minutes later, the Cossack dancers came on stage. Elizabeth was amazed to see their colourful costumes. She couldn't believe how high the dancers could jump and twirl in circles. Elizabeth said to Wally," I wish I could dance like those Cossack girls."

At the end of the concert, Wally and Elizabeth rode back to the village in a taxi. It was late, and everyone was asleep. They walked quietly to their room. The next morning, during breakfast, Wally asked Peter if Elizabeth could have dancing lessons during her stay. Peter smiled." Taras and Oksana will be happy to give Elizabeth dancing lessons. She can start this afternoon while you help with the roof repairs."

Wally said, "Peter, I want to make Elizabeth dancing more meaningful. I'll hypnotize her into believing that she is a Cossack dancing girl who just recovered from injuries and is ready to start dancing again. After I finish with the roof repairs, I can be her dancing partner. My grandfather taught me how to dance."

Peter smiled. "Wally, that is an excellent idea. Elizabeth will be so active and enjoying herself that her cancer will be completely gone."

Taras and Oksana came to see Elizabeth. Oksana said," Before we start your dancing lessons, we have to feed the pigs and clean out the pig hut. Put on some boots; it rained last night."

Elizabeth was not happy. She put on her boots. Oksana handed Elizabeth a bucket of pig feed. They all walked over to the pig hut. Oksana pointed to a trough. She told Elizabeth to pour the feed into the trough and then come and help them clean the pig hut.

Taras used a fire hose to hose down the floor in the pig hut. Elizabeth and Oksana used squeegee brooms to push all the filth off the floor and into a trough sloped to the ground. They then washed the walls using scrub brushes. When they finished cleaning the pig hut, everyone walked out. Oksana pointed to a huge mud puddle and said," Elizabeth, come over here and look."

Elizabeth went over to the mud puddle. She bent down to look. Zychok came running and head-butted her. She fell into the mud puddle. Taras and Oksana were laughing out of control. Elizabeth decided to get even. She grabbed them by the wrists and pulled them into the mud puddle. All three of them started a mud fight, laughing.

When they got out of the mud puddle, Wally was waiting for them, holding a fire hose. Elizabeth, Taras, and Oksana were laughing while Wally was hosing them down. When he finished, Elizabeth asked Wally if she was going to get into trouble for being in a mud fight with Taras and Oksana. Wally asked Elizabeth if she enjoyed the mud fight. Elizabeth told Wally that she had had a blast. Wally smiled." Elizabeth, we are on our honeymoon, and we are supposed to have fun. Now get ready for lunch."

Wally gave Elizabeth some herbal tea to drink. The tea relaxed her. Wally then hypnotized Elizabeth into believing that she was a Cossack dancer who recovered from injury. After lunch, Elizabeth was ready to see Taras and Oksana. They had her meditate to get her in the right frame of mind. Elizabeth gave her full cooperation. She wanted to dance as soon as possible. Elizabeth was happy to have Wally as her dancing partner.

When Wally started to dance with Elizabeth, he was very impressed with how she progressed in such a short period of time. At the end of the third week, Elizabeth was ready to perform with the dance ensemble. A beautiful costume was given to Elizabeth and Wally. He was looking forward to dancing with Elizabeth. Elizabeth and Wally got on the bus with the dance ensemble. The orchestra got on a separate bus. Several hours later, the buses arrived at the concert hall. Wally and Elizabeth were ready to perform with the dance ensemble. They blended nicely with the dancers. They performed in the back row. At the end of their performance, the dance ensemble received a standing ovation.

Wally led Elizabeth into an empty room and hypnotized her to become his wife again. She was still able to remember dancing with

Wally in the concert. Elizabeth told Wally that she remembered dancing with him at the concert but couldn't remember how she actually danced. Wally smiled." Elizabeth, it doesn't matter if you don't remember how you danced. It was a pleasure dancing with you. That is all that matters." Elizabeth then screamed, "Wally, my knees and ankles are in incredible pain!"

Wally put his arm around Elizabeth's waist and said," It takes years of dancing to develop enough muscle to avoid pain. Elizabeth, you started dancing lessons three weeks ago. Your knees and ankles were not ready for dancing."

Wally, Elizabeth, and the dance ensemble got on the bus to get back to the village. No one said too much; everyone was very tired. When the bus arrived at the village, Wally and Elizabeth went straight to bed. In the morning, Elizabeth bathed in warm water and Epsom salt to soothe her painful knees and ankles before the appointment to see Bernie. She can't remember why she has to see him.

Irene had breakfast ready. She prepared bacon and eggs with fresh buttered homemade bread served with tea. It was the best bacon that Elizabeth ever tasted. She also enjoyed the buttered bread. After breakfast, Wally and Elizabeth went to see Bernie. He was waiting for them. Bernie hypnotized Elizabeth so she could remember that she had breast cancer when she arrived at the village. Bernie examined Elizabeth; he took a blood sample and removed the lump on Elizabeth's breast. An hour later, Bernie smiled and said," Good news, Elizabeth, you are cancer-free."

Elizabeth was surprised; she couldn't believe it. "My family doctor told me that there was no cure for my breast cancer. He said that I must have a mastectomy and several sessions of chemotherapy. My doctor believes that all naturopaths are quacks."

Bernie smiled. "When you get back home, Elizabeth, have your family doctor examine you. Then ask him if he still believes that all naturopaths are quacks."

Still confused, Elizabeth thanked Bernie. It was lunchtime. Elizabeth enjoyed eating perogies, salad, and homemade bread.

After lunch, they went back to their room to pack their belongings. Tomorrow afternoon, they were to leave the village for home. Wally then took Elizabeth to see Peter's garden.

Wally smiled. "Elizabeth, look how beautiful everything is growing in the garden. You helped plant this garden. Do you still think gardening is disgusting?" Elizabeth told Wally that when the time comes to plant his garden, she'll decide if gardening is disgusting. She may not have time to help him plant a garden when she becomes a mother. Wally and Elizabeth went back to their room to sleep.

Taras and Oksana entered Wally's and Elizabeth's room to give them a big goodbye hug. Irene walked in carrying the dancing costumes that Wally and Elizabeth wore during the concert. Elizabeth was surprised; she had never expected to receive such a beautiful gift. Irene gave Wally a memory stick that had a video recording of the concert in which he and Elizabeth danced with the dancing ensemble. Elizabeth was really surprised and gave Irene a big hug. She was looking forward to seeing the video recording.

Wally and Elizabeth got dressed and headed for the breakfast table. They enjoyed hot porridge with blueberries and maple syrup and freshly baked bread. After breakfast, Wally took out an envelope containing $5,000. He thanked Peter for his hospitality and slipped the envelope into Peter's pocket. Wally and Elizabeth then went to say goodbye to the villagers. A taxi was waiting for them to take them to the airport.

Chapter 45

Once airborne, Elizabeth gave Wally a big kiss. "Thank you for choosing your village for our honeymoon. I had a wonderful time, and I know why you chose to go there. However, I'm not convinced that Bernie cured me of breast cancer. I want my family doctor to confirm that I am cancer-free."

The plane landed, and Wally and Elizabeth got off. They saw Joan and aunt Judy waiting for them. Joan came running to Elizabeth to give her a big hug. She looked at Elizabeth and said, "Elizabeth, I've never seen you look so healthy!"

Aunt Judy was also happy to see a healthy-looking Elizabeth. Wally mentioned that Elizabeth was not convinced that she was cancer-free. She wanted confirmation from her family doctor. Wally reminded Elizabeth that she was also pregnant. Joan and aunt Judy jumped for joy. Elizabeth was not happy. Wally and Elizabeth sat quietly in the back of Joan's car, waiting to get home. When they arrived home, Wally and Elizabeth were too tired to unpack. They went straight to bed. Grandfather was walking Cleo and Leo in the forest trails. Joan and aunt Judy happily drove home.

In the morning, Wally and Elizabeth showered and got dressed. Cleo and Leo were downstairs sleeping with Wally's grandparents. Wally drove off to his office. Elizabeth drove to see her family doctor. He was anxiously waiting for her. Elizabeth was carefully examined for cancer. Elizabeth wanted to know if she still had breast cancer.

Her doctor said, "Elizabeth, I won't know if you still have cancer until I get the test results. They won't be ready until this afternoon." Elizabeth told her doctor she had lots of time and wanted to wait for her test results in his office. The receptionist brought

Elizabeth a muffin and coffee. Elizabeth waited three hours for her test results.

Elizabeth's doctor walked in smiling. "Elizabeth, great news, you are cancer-free; you no longer have high blood pressure, high blood sugar, or high cholesterol; congratulations, you are still pregnant. I guess not all naturopaths are quacks. You're lucky to have Wally for a husband."

Elizabeth was happy to be cancer-free but not happy that she was pregnant. Elizabeth thanked her doctor and said goodbye. She decided to drive home. Grandmother was waiting for her. When Elizabeth arrived home, she saw her grandmother and ran to her for a hug.

Elizabeth said to grandmother, "I'm pregnant. When I was engaged to Jeffrey, we agreed not to have children. I'm scared, grandmother."

Grandmother smiled at Elizabeth and said, "Elizabeth, it is natural for every woman to feel scared at first when they find out they are pregnant. Don't worry; you will have plenty of support from Wally, me, my Grandfather, and your mother, Aunt Judy, your aunt Lydia, and Uncle Ivan. You will be a wonderful mother." Grandfather showed up to give Elizabeth a big hug. "Elizabeth, we are so happy for you and Wally. If you have any problems, please come see us."

Elizabeth dried her tears. She went upstairs to look for Cleo and Leo. She found them and Purdy waiting for her at the top of the stairs. Elizabeth fed them and let them loose in the backyard. She then went to see what Wally had in the refrigerator. Inside, Elizabeth was happy to find homemade lentil soup and head cheese made with turkey, not pork.

When Elizabeth finished eating, she went to the backyard to see Cleo and Leo. Purdy was nowhere to be found. She rubbed Cleo and Leo's tummies. She then took them for a walk on the forest trails.

When Wally arrived at his office, everyone from the wedding party was waiting for him. They all wanted to know how the honeymoon was. Wally told them everything that happened. He did not tell them that Elizabeth had breast cancer. Wally told him that Elizabeth was pregnant at home. Wally also mentioned their performance with the dance ensemble during a concert. He said, "Our performance with the dance ensemble was video recorded. Everyone who wants a copy of the video recording will get one."

Patricia stood up and announced that she and Michael were engaged. The wedding will be on June 28th of next year at Spencers Mill. Michael wanted Wally to be the best man, and she wanted Elizabeth to be the maid of honour.

Wally congratulated Patricia and Michael. He said to Michael that he would be happy to be the best man and told Patricia that Elizabeth would be delighted to be the maid of honour. By that time, Elizabeth would be a mother.

Wally decided to go home early. He found Elizabeth sleeping on the sofa. Cleo and Leo were sleeping on the floor beside her. Wally quietly headed for the refrigerator. He should have known that it would be empty. Elizabeth was pregnant and had a huge appetite.

Wally called Spencers Mill to order a pizza for take-out and left. Aunt Lydia and uncle Ivan were waiting for him. Wally told them everything that happened during the honeymoon. He brought a copy of the concert on a memory stick of them dancing with the dance ensemble. Aunt Lydia and uncle Ivan gave Wally a big hug. Uncle Ivan gave Wally two pizzas. He knew that Elizabeth would be hungry and would want one. Uncle Ivan told Wally that he and Aunt Lydia were looking forward to watching the concert. Wally thanked uncle Ivan for the pizzas and said goodbye.

When he got home, Elizabeth was eyeing the pizzas that Wally was holding. Elizabeth asked Wally which pizza was hers. Wally let Elizabeth choose. She chose the one with the most toppings. Wally only ate half his pizza. Elizabeth devoured her pizza and finished Wally's half.

Chapter 46

Wally and Elizabeth went for a walk in the forest trails early in the morning. Cleo and Leo were running ahead of them. Wally held Elizabeth's hand and asked her if she was ready for motherhood. Elizabeth asked Wally if he was ready for fatherhood. Wally smiled." We will soon find out if we are ready to become parents when the time comes."

Wally and Elizabeth continued walking. Wally mentioned to Elizabeth that Patricia and Michael are engaged. "Their wedding is on June 28th of next year. Michael wants me to be his best man. Patricia wants you to be the maid of honour."

Elizabeth was confused. "Wally, why would Patricia want me to be her maid of honour? She hates me." Wally replied, "Elizabeth, maybe she doesn't hate you. Be prepared to be her maid of honour."

After their walk with Cleo and Leo, Wally went to get the mail. There was a cheque for $10,000 from the photography magazine. A picture of Elizabeth pooping was on the cover of the magazine. Her picture was the winner of the amateur photography contest. Wally shoved the cheque into his pant pocket and then threw the magazine in the blue box. Wally did not want Elizabeth to see the magazine. He would be in big trouble if she saw it.

Cleo and Leo managed to tip the blue box on its side. Cleo put the magazine in her mouth and ran to the front door. Elizabeth saw Cleo with the magazine in her mouth and took it from her. Elizabeth was shocked to see the magazine cover. She screamed! "Wally, how could you!"

Elizabeth ran out of the house to see her grandmother at her clinic. Wally followed her. Elizabeth showed the cover of the magazine to grandmother and grandfather. Elizabeth was very upset and said,

"Wally took this picture of me. He saved it before I deleted it. Wally entered the picture in an amateur photography contest without telling me and won. How can I trust him? What should I do?"

Grandfather grabbed Wally by the arm and said, "Wally, what got into you? You shouldn't have taken the picture of Elizabeth pooping. She is very upset!"

Wally shrugged his shoulders and said, "I really like the picture of her pooping. I saved it for personal viewing. She was not supposed to know that I saved the picture. I don't know why I entered her picture in the amateur photography contest. I would have never guessed in a million years that her picture would have won the contest."

Grandmother was not happy that Wally took a picture of Elizabeth pooping; she said, "One of our clients is a psychiatrist and a marriage counselor. His name is Dr. Reggie Neale. He is a good friend of ours. I'm going to call him to make an appointment for you and Elizabeth to see him."

Elizabeth became really upset. "Wally, see what you did! Our grandparents think we are nuts. I'm going to stay with my mother until we see the nut doctor. Then I will decide if I want to stay with you!"

Elizabeth ran home, got into her car, and drove to see her mother. Wally went home to look for Cleo and Leo. He found them sleeping on the backyard patio. Wally woke Cleo and said, "Cleo, you are a bad doggie. Why did you take the magazine out of the blue box? Because of you, Elizabeth went to stay with her mother. She is so mad at me that we may never see her again!"

Cleo put her chin on Wally's foot and started to wimper. Wally said, "Cleo, everything will be alright. Elizabeth will forgive me and come back because she loves you and Leo too much. Let's go for a nice walk."

Elizabeth arrived at her mother's home. She showed Joan the magazine. "Wally humiliated me. Without my knowledge, he took this picture of me and entered it in an amateur photography contest. It won first prize. I showed this magazine to my grandmother. She thinks we're both nuts and made an appointment for us to see a psychiatrist. I'm staying with you until we see the psychiatrist, and then I'll decide what to do!"

Joan hugged Elizabeth. "Sweetheart, you are overreacting. Wally loves you. He did a stupid thing to upset you. Remember, Wally is a man, and all men sometimes do stupid things to upset their wives. Elizabeth, go back to Wally and forgive him."

Elizabeth was still upset. "Mother, I am staying here until Wally and I see the psychiatrist." The phone rang. It was Wally's grandmother. She told Joan that Wally's and Elizabeth's appointment to see the psychiatrist is for 7 o'clock tomorrow morning. Wally will pick Elizabeth up at 6:30 in the morning.

Elizabeth looked at Joan. "Mother, promise me that you won't tell anyone that Wally and I have an appointment to see a psychiatrist," Joan told Elizabeth that the only person she would tell was Aunt Judy. "She will be very upset if I don't tell her."

Elizabeth went to her old room. Joan hugged Elizabeth goodbye and left to go to the office. Elizabeth decided to stay, and she didn't want to face Wally at the office. Elizabeth went to the refrigerator. She was disappointed to find out she was in it. Elizabeth forgot that her mother was a terrible cook. She was spoiled with Wally's cooking.

Elizabeth drove to Spencers Mill to see aunt Lydia. Uncle Ivan led Elizabeth to the kitchen, where Aunt Lydia was about to have lunch. She invited Elizabeth to join her. Aunt Lydia told Elizabeth that grandmother told her what a stupid thing Wally did to upset her. "Sometimes men do things or say stupid things without thinking. Most men are like that. Uncle Ivan is no different from Wally."

Aunt Lydia then placed a plate full of food for Elizabeth. She really enjoyed the shish kebab sticks, cabbage rolls, and Caesar salad. Elizabeth thanked aunt Lydia for a wonderful lunch and said goodbye.

It was 6:30 in the morning when Wally showed up for Elizabeth. She got into Wally's car, and they drove off to their 7 o'clock appointment to see Dr. Reggie Neale. On the way, they didn't say a word to each other.

The receptionist led Wally and Elizabeth into Dr. Reggie's office. He showed up two minutes later. Dr. Reggie was 6'5" tall, slender, weighed 230 pounds, baldheaded, wore glasses, and had a large smiling face. He reminded Wally of a basketball player. Dr. Reggie said good morning and shook hands with Wally and Elizabeth.

Dr. Reggie looked at Elizabeth and said, "Elizabeth, according to your grandmother, you have been married only eight weeks and are already thinking of going for a divorce." Elizabeth said yes because she couldn't trust Wally.

Dr. Reggie got out his pen and notebook. "Elizabeth, before we start, I want to ask you some questions. Did Wally ever abuse you physically or verbally? Do you have any financial problems? Do you have any problems having sex? Do you like the house you live in?" Elizabeth answered no to all the questions except for the last one. She said yes.

Dr. Reggie put down his pen, looked at Wally, and asked him, "Wally, could you please tell me why Elizabeth would want a divorce?"

Wally smiled at Elizabeth and said, "I took all her prescribed medications and threw them in the garbage disposal. I'm still a certified naturopath, and I told Elizabeth that I would take care of all her health care needs."

Dr. Reggie interrupted. "Your grandmother told me that Maria was your mother. She was a dear friend of mine. I was heartbroken when she was killed."

Wally continued. "Elizabeth thinks all naturopaths are quacks. Elizabeth was diagnosed with breast cancer. Her family doctor recommended a mastectomy and several sessions of chemotherapy. Thanks to me, Elizabeth did not have a mastectomy or chemotherapy. She is also cancer-free." Dr. Reggie looked at Elizabeth and asked her if Wally was telling the truth. Elizabeth nodded yes.

Wally said that Elizabeth was sweating. "I wanted to take her temperature to see if she had a fever. Elizabeth refused to open her mouth, so I stuck the thermometer in her butt. I want to be Elizabeth's personal trainer and nutritionist. We have a fully equipped gym in our basement. I also want to be her yoga instructor. Elizabeth has no interest in any of those things. I want Elizabeth to help me plant a garden in our backyard. She finds gardening disgusting. When we got married, I paid off her entire $200,000 government student loan. She doesn't want to become a mother, and yet she is pregnant."

Wally showed the photography magazine to Dr. Reggie. "I entered Elizabeth's picture in an amateur photography contest and won the $10,000 first prize."

Dr. Reggie smiled at Elizabeth's picture. "Wally, your grandmother told me that you are a certified chef."

Wally replied, "I still work occasionally at Spencers Mill. My aunt and uncle own it. Elizabeth loves the meals that I prepare for her."

Dr. Reggie shook his head and asked Wally, "Did Elizabeth ever abuse you physically or verbally?" Wally smiled and described to Dr. Reggie how Elizabeth got drunk on brandy and nearly suffocated him with her dandruff-infested pussy.

Elizabeth screamed! "I do not have a dandruff-infested pussy. It was Wally's fault; he got me drunk!" Wally screamed back! "Elizabeth, you got yourself drunk. I tried to keep you from getting drunk. Elizabeth, you did have dandruff on your pussy!"

Dr. Reggie heard enough of their bickering and shouted! "Elizabeth, it doesn't matter if you had dandruff on your pussy. Did you almost suffocate Wally with your pussy!" Elizabeth admitted that she did.

Dr. Reggie looked into Elizabeth's eyes in disgust, "Let me tell you something, young lady. If you found an old lamp, rubbed it, and a genie came out to offer you a wish, and you wished for the perfect husband, you would be wasting your wish because the genie would give you the same husband that you have now." Elizabeth couldn't believe what Dr. Reggie just said.

Dr. Reggie continued to say, "Elizabeth, you have a handsome husband who knows how to take care of you. There are no financial problems. There are no problems having sex. You are going to be a mother. You live in an upscale neighbourhood. Wally prepares gourmet meals for you. What else could you ask for?" Elizabeth said nothing. She just sat quietly, sulking.

Dr. Reggie was really annoyed. "Elizabeth, you are nuts for wanting a divorce. If you go through with the divorce, I will send you to the nut house, and I have the authority to send you there. Now get out here and stop wasting my time!"

Wally got up and thanked Dr. Reggie for his time. He led a very unhappy Elizabeth out of Dr. Reggie's office. On their way home, Wally started to sing How Sweet it is to be Loved by You. Elizabeth screamed! "Shut up!" Wally kept quiet the rest of the way home.

When they arrived home, Jean and Judy were waiting for them. Elizabeth ran into the bedroom and locked the door. Joan, ask Wally what happened. Wally said, "Dr. Reggie Neale told Elizabeth that she is nuts if she wants a divorce. He also told her that if she filed for divorce, he would send Elizabeth to the nut house and that he has the authority to send her there."

 Judy turned to Joan and said, "Don't worry, Elizabeth will get over it. Wally will take good care of her."

Wally went over to the piano to sing one of Elizabeth's favourite love songs, The Look of Love. When Wally finished singing the song, Elizabeth unlocked the bedroom door and ran out of the house. Joan shouted! "Where are you going, Elizabeth?"

She shouted back!" I'm going to see Grandmother alone at her clinic!" Judy told Joan to let Elizabeth go. She loved Wally's grandmother. She'll know what to do with Elizabeth.

Grandmother was very busy. Elizabeth had to wait two hours before she could see her. Elizabeth was in tears. She said to his grandmother, "What is wrong with me? Dr. Reggie said that I was nuts for considering a divorce. He said that she would send me to the nut house if I went through with the divorce and that he has the authority to send me there!"

Grandmother smiled and gave Elizabeth a hug. "Don't worry, Elizabeth, you are not nuts. You are overwhelmed and stressed out because you planned for years to marry Jeffrey and have a career with him. Both plans were abruptly changed for the better. The sudden change is too much for you to handle all at once. Let Wally take care of you, and you will feel much better very soon. Yoga will help you to relax."

Grandfather walked in, holding a large bag of dark chocolate-covered almonds. Elizabeth dried her eyes and smiled. She was glad that she went to see Wally's grandparents. They knew how to make her feel better. Elizabeth started to eat some chocolate-covered almonds. Grandmother gave Elizabeth a cup of herbal tea to calm her down. She thanked her grandparents for the chocolate-covered almonds and tea. Elizabeth then gave them a goodbye hug and cheerfully left to go home.

Wally, Joan, and Aunt Judy were sitting at the kitchen table, having tea and cheesecake wafers covered in dark chocolate, waiting for Elizabeth. Wally smiled at Elizabeth." Aunt Lydia brought a tray full of cheesecake wafers; you better join us before they are all gone."

Elizabeth's eyes lit up as Wally handed her a plateful of cheesecake wafers. Wally watched how Elizabeth was wolfing them down. He said to her," Elizabeth, tomorrow morning, I'm going to show you some exercises and yoga. If you don't want to get up early in the morning, you can do them later in the day at home or at the gym in our office building. If you want, you could do some of the exercises that you did when you took karate." Elizabeth stopped doing karate when she started law school.

Elizabeth didn't say a word; she kept eating cheesecake wafers. Joan looked at Elizabeth; she had a mouthful of cheesecake wafers. "Elizabeth, you better behave and cooperate with Wally tomorrow morning. If you don't, you'll be in big trouble." Aunt Judy asked Wally to call her when Elizabeth finished her exercise program. She wanted to know how Elizabeth behaved. Elizabeth sat quietly, eating the last cheesecake wafers. Joan and aunt Judy thanked Wally and said goodbye.

Wally woke up Elizabeth early in the morning. She didn't want to get out of bed. Wally threatened to call Elizabeth's mother if she didn't get out of bed. Elizabeth jumped out of bed. Wally gave Elizabeth some floor exercises to do for 15 minutes. He showed her how to use the exercise machines for 20 minutes. And had her do yoga for 25 minutes. Elizabeth was not happy, but she did cooperate because she didn't want Wally to call her mother. Wally wanted Elizabeth to pray with him, but she was not interested.

Wally was smiling. He told Elizabeth that she did very well for the first time. He told her that it'd become much easier as she continued to do the exercises. "When grandfather does his exercises at home, you can join him if you want. I'm going to call aunt Judy and tell her how well you did." Elizabeth grunted at Wally and headed for the shower. Wally fed Cleo and Leo and took them out for a walk in the forest trails. Wally had a hot bowl of oatmeal with blueberries and maple syrup, waiting for Elizabeth.

After breakfast, Elizabeth and Wally drove to the office. He told Elizabeth once she learns how to do the exercises and yoga properly, she will be able to do them on her own. Wally wants Elizabeth to give birth to a strong and healthy baby.

Elizabeth didn't say a word. She was still stressed out. She brought the photo magazine to show Samantha. Wally had a lot of work to catch up on and help Elizabeth with hers. With Wally's photographic memory, it wouldn't take long. He knew exactly where to look to find the information that he needed.

Chapter 47

Samantha was waiting for Elizabeth in her office. She had tea and a pumpkin-spiced muffin for her. When Elizabeth walked in, Samantha gave her a hug. "I haven't had a chance to see you since you got back from your honeymoon. How was it, and did Wally behave? I want a copy of that video of you and Wally performing with the dance ensemble."

Elizabeth sat down, holding the photography magazine. She said, "I had a wonderful time on our honeymoon, and Wally was on his best behaviour until we got home."

Elizabeth told Samantha everything they did during their honeymoon. She mentioned that it was not a good idea to bend down when Zychok, the goat, was around. Then she handed Samantha the magazine and told her what Wally did. Samantha looked at the front cover and laughed. "Elizabeth, you look so adorable in this picture. It's no wonder that Wally won first prize. You should be pleased."

Elizabeth was annoyed. "Samantha, would you be pleased if Wally took a picture of you pooping in the woods and entered it in the amateur photography contest?"

Samantha laughed again. "Elizabeth, I am not as adorable as you. My picture would not have won first prize in the contest. Can I keep this magazine.?" Elizabeth let Samantha keep the magazine.

Wally just finished his research for the day. It was nearly lunch time. Wally decided to go home to feed Cleo and Leo and take them for their walk in the forest trails. He also wanted to bring lunch for Elizabeth. When Wally arrived home, he fed Cleo and Leo and then took them for a walk in the forest trails. After the walk, he went to the refrigerator to take out some perogies and Caesar salad that aunt

Lydia prepared. The perogies had a potato and cheddar cheese filling because it was Elizabeth's favourite.

Wally drove back to the office. When he entered Elizabeth's office, he saw her about to eat a submarine sandwich. Wally immediately grabbed Elizabeth's sandwich and threw it in the garbage. "Elizabeth, I will not allow you to eat processed crap. You are pregnant, remember!"

Elizabeth was furious until Wally showed her the perogies and Caesar salad. She smacked her lips and gave Wally a big kiss, and then chased him out of her office so she could enjoy her lunch. At the end of the day, Wally and Elizabeth drove home.

Chapter 48

Wally went to pick up the mail. There was an entry form for the annual purebred dog show. Wally was smiling. "Elizabeth, we are going to enter Cleo and Leo at the annual pure-breed dog show. The entry form we received in the mail is for two dogs."

Elizabeth shouted! "Wally, are you crazy? Cleo and Leo are too tiny to be entered in the dog show. We would be a laughing stock if we entered them!"

Wally gave Elizabeth a kiss. "We received this entry form, and Cleo and Leo are pure-breed Yorkie teacup puppies." Elizabeth was not happy. "Wally, if you want to make a fool of yourself, go right ahead and enter them in the contest. I want no part of it!"

Wally took out his pen and started to fill out the entry form. He said, "Elizabeth, if the organizers of the dog show thought that if Cleo and Leo had been entered in the dog show, it would have been stupid, they would not have sent us an entry form. I'm sure Cleo and Leo would enjoy being in the dog show." Wally looked at Elizabeth and told her that she did not have to attend the dog show with him if she felt uncomfortable. He'll find someone else to come with him.

Elizabeth said nothing and went upstairs to bed. She was planning to see Samantha tomorrow morning. During breakfast, Elizabeth did not want to talk about the dog show.

Elizabeth entered Samantha's office. She said, "Samantha, Wally wants to enter Cleo and Leo in a pure-breed dog show. I told Wally if he entered them, I would not go with him. Cleo and Leo are so tiny. How could they possibly compete with the other larger dogs?" Elizabeth handed the entry form to Samantha.

Samantha looked at the entry form and said, "Elizabeth, if you don't want to go to the dog show with Wally, I would be more than happy to take your place."

Elizabeth couldn't believe that Samantha would want to go to the dog show with Wally. She took the entry form and left Samantha's office without saying a word. She went to see Wally. Elizabeth gave the entry form to Wally and said, "I have decided to go with you if you enter Cleo and Leo in the dog show." Wally gave Elizabeth a big kiss. He was happy and told her that they would have a great time at the dog show.

The day before the dog show, Wally had Cleo and Leo groomed. The groomer said, "Cleo and Leo are so adorable; I am looking forward to seeing them at the dog show."

Samantha, Joan, aunt Judy, Wally's grandparents, Aunt Lydia, and Uncle Ivan were also looking forward to seeing Cleo and Leo at the dog show.

Patricia found out that Wally had entered Cleo and Leo in the dog show. She and her friend Stephanie plan to show up and watch Cleo and Leo. Stephanie was the breeder from whom Wally bought Cleo and Leo. She wanted to see if Cleo and Leo were healthy and happy.

Cleo and Leo were excited. They were each given a number. When their numbers were called, Wally and Cleo, as well as Elizabeth and Leo, were judged on obedience. They were rated on a scale of 1 to 10 based on how well they behaved. Wally and Cleo received a 10. A nervous Elizabeth and Leo received an 8. Cleo and Leo both received tens for grooming and posture.

Cleo and Leo were anxiously waiting to run the obstacle course. Everyone in attendance was excited to see them run. Elizabeth was not excited. Cleo and Leo were so tiny they could not possibly compete with the much larger dogs. When their turn came up, Cleo and Leo happily started to run the obstacle.

The judges took Cleo and Leo's size into consideration when scoring. They each scored eight while running the obstacle course.

Cleo and Leo didn't win any ribbons but received a standing ovation from the audience. One of the judges approached Wally and asked him if he was going to enter Cleo and Leo in next year's dog show. Elizabeth snapped at the judge. "Certainly not!"

The judge gave Elizabeth a nasty look. "Your dogs brought a lot of excitement to the show. Thanks to you and your husband, the dog show will have a separate category for pure-breed teacups next year!"

Patricia and Stephanie approached Wally. Stephanie hugged Wally and told him that she was very pleased with how he treated Cleo and Leo. She said to Wally. "When Cleo and Leo are gone to doggie heaven, I'll have another two teacup puppies waiting for you."

Wally thanked Patricia and Stephanie and left with an unhappy Elizabeth. Wally was disappointed at Elizabeth's behaviour. "Elizabeth, what is wrong with you? Cleo and Leo had a wonderful time. I had a wonderful time." Elizabeth shrugged her shoulders. "I don't know; I guess I don't like dog shows."

Samantha caught up with Wally and said, "Wally, I'm so glad you entered Cleo and Leo in the dog show. They were so much fun to watch." Wally pointed to Elizabeth and said, "Tell that to her."

Samantha looked at Elizabeth, frowning. "Wally, ignore that sourpuss." Samantha then took a picture of Cleo and Leo and said, "I'm going to blow this picture up, frame it, and hang it up in my office."

Wally picked up Cleo and Leo and took them to his car. Elizabeth followed. They drove quietly home. Joan, Aunt Judy, and Wally's grandparents were waiting for them. Joan gave Elizabeth a big hug. "I'm so happy you entered Cleo and Leo in the dog show. We had a wonderful time."

Elizabeth growled. "Mother, Wally entered Cleo and Leo in the dog show. I didn't have a wonderful time." Joan was surprised at Elizabeth's attitude. "Elizabeth, what is wrong with you? Don't you love Cleo and Leo? They had a wonderful time."

Wally smiled with delight. "I think I know what is wrong with Elizabeth. Lately, Elizabeth has been very bitchy, and eating an enormous amount of food. It could only mean that Elizabeth is going to have twins!"

Elizabeth screamed! "Wally, stop saying such stupid things. You are making me upset!" Grandmother placed her ear on Elizabeth's tummy and listened.

"Elizabeth, I believe Wally is right. You are going to have twins, congratulations." Elizabeth was shocked. She never wanted to have children. Now, she finds out that she will have twins.

Joan's eyes lit up. "That is great news. Let's go to Spencers Mill to celebrate." Wally called aunt Lydia to tell her the news and to reserve a table for him. Everyone was happy except Elizabeth. She went to the bedroom, sulking. Wally prepared tea for everyone. He gave Cleo and Leo some doggie snacks. Wally then cleaned out Purdy's letterbox and placed some cat food beside her bed. Wally spent little time with Purdy. She is either outside roaming the neighbourhood or downstairs with his grandparents.

When everyone finished their tea, they and an unhappy Elizabeth left for the Spencers Mill. Uncle Ivan had their table ready. Aunt Lydia prepared pizza, pasta, and Caesar salad. She ran to Elizabeth to give her a big hug. Uncle Ivan brought out some bottles of wine. Everyone had a good time. Elizabeth enjoyed the food, but she was not happy.

Chapter 49

The next morning, Elizabeth called her family doctor to make an appointment. At breakfast, she said nothing. Wally left for the office without her. Elizabeth decided to stay at home until her afternoon doctor's appointment. She went to sit on the back patio. Purdy showed up and jumped on her lap. Elizabeth rubbed Purdy's tummy and said, "Purdy, you have the best life. You have no worries, and Wally takes good care of you."

Cleo and Leo came running. Elizabeth fed them and then took them for a walk on the trails. At noon, Elizabeth drove off to see her family doctor. He was waiting for her. The doctor said to Elizabeth, "Wally told you that you are going to have twins; let's find out if he is right."

Elizabeth was given an ultrasound. An hour later, her doctor came into her room. He was smiling,

"Congratulations, Elizabeth, Wally was right. You are going to have twins." Elizabeth was not happy. She left without saying a word. Elizabeth called Samantha to see if she was busy.

Elizabeth sat down and said, "Samantha I just found out I will be having twins. Jeffery and I planned not to have any children. Why am I so miserable?" Samantha smiled at Elizabeth. "Don't worry; the shock of knowing you will have twins will soon wear off." Elizabeth looked at Samantha. "How would you know? Did you ever give birth?"

Samantha closed her eyes, took a deep breath, and said, "Elizabeth, you have no idea how lucky you are to be married to Wally. I was married once to an abusive husband. When he found out that I was pregnant, he disappeared with all our money. I became a homeless drug dealer and prostitute. Eventually, I was arrested, charged, and convicted. My baby boy was born in prison. I had to give him up for adoption. It took me a long time to get over the burden of knowing that you will never see your child again." Elizabeth stared at Samantha in dismay. "What did you do to cope?"

Samantha quietly said," I spent three years in prison to get a college degree. When I got out of prison, I applied for a scholarship to Harvard Law School. The school chose me as one of their underprivileged token minorities. That's how I graduated from Harvard Law School."

Elizabeth started to cry. She gave Samantha a big hug." Samantha, thank you for sharing your story with me. I feel so much better now."

Chapter 50

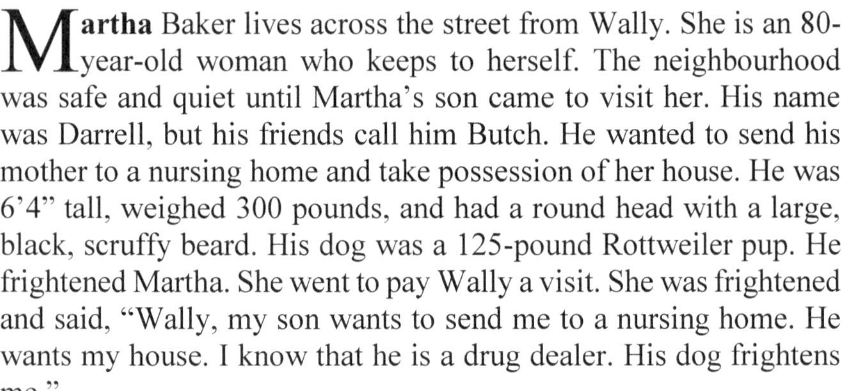

Martha Baker lives across the street from Wally. She is an 80-year-old woman who keeps to herself. The neighbourhood was safe and quiet until Martha's son came to visit her. His name was Darrell, but his friends call him Butch. He wanted to send his mother to a nursing home and take possession of her house. He was 6'4" tall, weighed 300 pounds, and had a round head with a large, black, scruffy beard. His dog was a 125-pound Rottweiler pup. He frightened Martha. She went to pay Wally a visit. She was frightened and said, "Wally, my son wants to send me to a nursing home. He wants my house. I know that he is a drug dealer. His dog frightens me."

Wally calmed Martha down. "Don't worry, I will deal with your son. Do you have a place to stay?" Martha told Wally she would visit her sister, who lives in Pompano Beach, Florida, for a month. She leaves tomorrow morning. Wally said, "That's good; by the time you get home, your son and his dog will be gone." Martha thanked Wally and went back home to pack.

Elizabeth was downstairs visiting his grandmother. Wally took Cleo and Leo for a walk on the forest trails. They were not on a leash. Wally came across Butch and his dog. Cleo and Leo ran towards his dog. He ran away, and Cleo and Leo ran after him. Wally started to laugh.

Butch screamed! "Call off your dogs!" Wally kept on laughing and said, "It's not my fault that your dog is a spineless wimp." Butch took out a knife and attacked Wally. He was no match for Wally. He received a kick in the chest and fell to the ground. Wally removed the knife from Butch's hand. He also removed a gun from Butch's pant pocket. He told Butch that he was not allowed to carry such weapons in this neighbourhood. Wally kept the knife and gun and left Butch lying on the ground. Wally then called Cleo Leo to come home.

Wally read Butch's mind. He was a known drug dealer from San Francisco. His dog's name was Baron. Butch was wanted by the police for suspicion of murder in San Francisco. Wally also found out that Butch was planning to set up a lab in his mother's basement to produce street drugs for distribution.

Wally called Don Jordan and said, "I had a fight with a new neighbour. I relieved him of his knife and gun. Can you check them out for fingerprints?" Don showed up at Wally's home 15 minutes later. Wally gave Butch's gun and knife to Don. He thanked Wally and left.

An hour later, Don called. He confirmed what Wally already knew. He said, "Wally, your neighbour, is a known drug dealer from San Francisco. He is wanted by the police on suspicion of murder."

Wally told Don that his mother said to him that her son plans to set up a lab in the basement of her house to produce street drugs for distribution. Don told Wally that FBI agents would stake out his mother's home. "When he is ready to distribute drugs, he will be arrested."

Wally was served with a summons to appear in court. He couldn't believe that Butch was so stupid. He claimed that Cleo and Leo were evil, vicious dogs and that they had been terrorizing his defenceless puppy. Wally showed Butch's lawsuit to Elizabeth. When she read it, she started to laugh, "Butch's brain must be fried from taking too many drugs. I'm going to show this lawsuit to Samantha. When Samantha read the lawsuit, she laughed." I want to be at Wally's trial. I need a good laugh."

On the day of his trial, Wally picked up Cleo and Leo. He placed them in a basket. They were going to be his evidence. Wally and Elizabeth drove off to the courthouse. Samantha was already in court waiting for the trial.

Court proceedings began. Charles Dyson, Butch's lawyer, called Wally to the stand. He asked Wally if he had two dogs called

Cleo and Leo. Wally said yes. Charles then asked Wally, "Did your dogs chase Baron Butch's defenceless puppy?" Wally said yes. Charles had no more questions for Wally.

Wally stepped down and approached the bench. He said, "Your Honour, I'm making a motion to have all charges against me dropped. Mr. Butch Fletcher has absolutely no grounds for his lawsuit."

The judge asked Wally if he had evidence to support his motion. Wally said yes. The judge asked Wally to produce his evidence. Elizabeth approached the bench carrying Leo and Cleo in a basket. Wally put the basket on the judge's desk.

Wally said to the judge, "Your Honour, this is Cleo and Leo. They are Yorkie teacups, each weighing 3 pounds. Mr. Butch Fletcher claims that they are evil, vicious dogs. His defenceless little puppy is a 125-pound Rottweiler."

Cleo and Leo started to lick the judge's face. Wally smiled, "Be careful, your honour; they may lick you to death."

Elizabeth picked them up and put them back in the basket. The judge called Butch Fletcher and Charles Dyson to the bench. The judge looked straight at Butch. "Mr. Fletcher, are these two dogs the ones you claim are evil and vicious?" Butch replied," Yes, Your Honour."

The judge then faced Charles Dyson and said, "Mr. Dyson, do you have anything to say on behalf of your client?"

Charles Dyson replied, "No, Your Honour."

The judge hit his desk with a gavel and said, "Motion is granted, court is adjourned."

Butch screamed! "Your Honour, you can't allow Wally's dogs to terrorize my puppy!" The judge became annoyed at Butch's outburst. "Mr. Fletcher, one more word out of you, and I will hold you in contempt of court. If you think that I believe that Wally's dogs are evil and vicious, you are crazy!"

Charles Dyson grabbed Butch's arm, and they quietly left the courtroom. Everyone else left laughing. Samantha walked over to Wally to congratulate him.

Butch had no idea that the FBI was staking out his mother's house. Soon Butch brought in equipment that he needed to produce street drugs. He then hired a chemist. The FBI was filming Butch's drug operation. They were ready to barge in with the search warrant.

Agent Dugan knocked on the front door when the FBI had enough evidence on the video camera. Several agents were behind him. When Butch opened the door, Agent Dugan identified himself. Before Butch could close the door, the other agents grabbed him. They handcuffed Butch and read him his rights. Agent Dugan went downstairs to the basement. He found several large containers of street drugs ready for distribution. The chemist tried to run away. The other agents caught him, handcuffed him, and read him his rights.

Don Jordan called Wally to let him know that the FBI had arrested Butch and his chemist. "They have enough evidence to charge and convict Butch and the chemist of drug trafficking."

Wally asked Don, "What will happen to Baron, Butch's dog?" Don told Wally that Baron would be taken to the ASPCA. Wally didn't want Baron to go to the ASPCA. He told Don to bring Baron to him. Wally will find a good home for them. Ten minutes later, an agent brought Baron to Wally.

Elizabeth was shocked when she saw Baron. "Wally, are you crazy? Why did you bring that dog into our home!" Wally smiled and told Elizabeth to calm down." Elizabeth, this is Baron, Butch's dog. Tomorrow is Lawrence's birthday. Baron is going to be his birthday present. "Elizabeth shook her head and told Wally that Lawrence is a cat person. He won't take Baron."

Wally smiled. "Elizabeth, Lawrence gave us a kitten that we didn't want. We are going to give him this puppy that he doesn't want." Wally then took Baron downstairs to his grandparents. He didn't want Cleo and Leo frightening Baron.

Wally said, "Grandmother, Grandfather, you have a visitor." Grandmother saw Wally with Baron. She was delighted to see him. "Wally, where did you get such a beautiful dog?"

Wally smiled. "His name is Baron. He belonged to Butch, the person who caused trouble in our neighbourhood. Butch was arrested today for drug trafficking. Baron needs a home. Tomorrow morning, I'm going to take Baron to see Lawrence. He is a friend of mine. It's Lawrence's birthday tomorrow." Grandmother started to scratch Baron's head, "Wally, I'm sure Lawrence would love to have Baron. How could he not want such a beautiful dog?" Wally smiled and said good night to Baron.

Wally snuck into Lawrence's office with Baron. As soon as Lawrence showed up, "Wally shouted! Happy birthday, Lawrence!" Baron ran up to Lawrence. He stood on his hind legs and placed his front paws on Lawrence's chest. Lawrence shouted!" Wally, I am a cat person, and I hate dogs!"

Wally laughed. "Lawrence hold Baron's paws and look straight into his eyes. Say to him, "I hate you." Lawrence looked into Baron's eyes and couldn't say I hate you. "Wally, my cats don't like dogs." Wally looked at a very unhappy Baron. "Lawrence, if you don't take Baron. I will have to give him to the ASPCA. They will put him down; do you want that to happen to Baron? Just take him home for a week. At the end of the week, I'll take Baron away if you don't want to keep him."

Lawrence looked at Baron and said, "I'll take him for a week as long as he gets along with my cats. Promise me that you will take Baron back if I decide not to keep him." Wally thanked Lawrence and gave him a week's supply of home-made dog food." I know that once you get to know Baron, you'll want to keep him."

Three days later, Wally went to see Lawrence. He wanted to know how Baron was getting along with Lawrence's cats. To Wally's surprise Baron and the cats got along nicely. Lawrence was shaking his head and said, "Wally, I would've never guessed that my cats would get along with Baron. They hate dogs." Wally laughed. "Lawrence, you better hold on to Baron if you don't want to upset your cats." Wally gave Lawrence some doggie treats to give to Baron and said goodbye. Elizabeth asked Wally if Lawrence was going to keep Baron.

Wally smiled. "Elizabeth, I will know in a couple of days. It looks to me that Lawrence will be keeping Baron. Lawrence lives alone in a large house. There's a lot of room for Baron and the cats. They all got along."

Chapter 51

Wally and Elizabeth finished their paperwork and then left for home. Elizabeth took Cleo and Leo for a walk on the trails. Wally prepared dinner. He prepared lentil soup, roast beef, coleslaw, and Caesar salad.

Wally had a question that he couldn't answer. This question bothered him. Only a woman would be able to answer his question. During dinner, he asked Elizabeth, "Tell me, there are a lot of girls with extremely long fingernails working in our building. When they go to the washroom to have a poop, how do they wipe their butt?"

Elizabeth screamed! "Wally, you just spoiled a nice dinner by asking me such a stupid question!" She ran downstairs to see Grandmother. Wally's grandparents were relaxing and having tea. Elizabeth said to Grandmother, "Wally got me upset by asking me a stupid question. He asked me how girls who have extremely long fingernails wipe their butt after having a poop!"

Grandfather was intrigued. "You know, Elizabeth, I think Wally asked a very good question. I often thought about it myself."

Elizabeth screamed! "Grandfather, what is the matter with you? Have you lost your mind!" Grandmother took Elizabeth by the hand. "Elizabeth men sometimes asked their wives stupid questions to get them upset. It's in their DNA. I know from personal experience. Now sit down and take some deep breaths." Purdy walked in; she jumped on Elizabeth's lap. She rubbed Purdy's tummy. Purdy's purring calmed Elizabeth down.

Elizabeth was at home preparing for court. She was happy to have Wally help her. After breakfast, Elizabeth put on a trench coat. Wally asked her why she was wearing a trench coat because it was not that cold outside. Elizabeth replied, "Wally, it's still pretty windy outside. My tummy is starting to get big. I want to cover it up."

It was time to drive Elizabeth to the courthouse. When Wally and Elizabeth arrived, Elizabeth got out of the car. It was a good thing that Wally was watching Elizabeth walk towards the courthouse. A tall, young black man approached Elizabeth.

He said to her, "Hey, pretty mama, let's have some fun." Elizabeth ignored him and kept on walking. The young man shouted! "Pretty mama, don't ignore me. I want to have some fun!"

Wally knew what was going to happen. He called 911, got out of his car, and ran towards Elizabeth. She started to run away from the young man. He ran after her. The young man caught up to Elizabeth and grabbed her arm. She slapped him in the face. The young man became angry. He grabbed Elizabeth by the hair and threw her down to the ground. A lot of people were watching, but no one came to help.

When the young man saw Wally running towards him, he took out a knife. Wally grabbed the young man by the throat. It was a good thing that the police arrived. Wally let go of the young man's throat. They handcuffed the young man and read him his rights. The police then interviewed people who saw what happened. When they finished, they drove off with the young man in their custody.

Wally drove Elizabeth to the Kozak Naturopath Clinic. He called his grandmother to tell her what happened. Grandmother was waiting for them. She examined Elizabeth. Luckily, Elizabeth had only a few minor scrapes. Wally left Elizabeth at the clinic so his grandmother could look after her. Wally kissed Elizabeth goodbye and left for his office. When he got to the office, Wally closed the door and pulled down the window blinds. Wally then lit a candle, sat cross-legged on the floor, and began to meditate. He didn't tell anyone in the office what happened to Elizabeth. At the end of the day, it was time to pick up Elizabeth. He drove to his grandmother's clinic. Elizabeth greeted Wally with a hug.

The young man who attacked Elizabeth was a college graduate. He received a basketball scholarship. His name is Jeremy White. He is expected to be picked first overall in the upcoming NBA draft. Nike just signed him to an $8,000,000 contract.

Jeremy White sat down with his lawyer, Carl Smith. He asked him, "How much money is it going to take to pay her off?" Carl looked at Jeremy, shaking his head. "Jeremy, you tried to rape Elizabeth Kozak, a pregnant woman. What were you thinking? She and her husband don't want your money. They want revenge. I personally know Wally Kozak. He'll make your life a living hell. I hate to be in your shoes."

During breakfast, Elizabeth asked Wally, "Are you going to send Jeremy to prison?" Wally grinned. "Jeremy belongs in prison. I found out from Don that he raped six other girls before he tried to rape you. Three of the girls settled out of court. The college paid for Jeremy's settlement. The other three girls were too scared to press charges against him. I have other plans for Jeremy. I called the judge and he allowed me to give Jeremy an alternative to prison."

Wally took out a box from the kitchen drawer. He opened it. Elizabeth saw a light bulb, a can of chili, a spoon, and a miniature flashlight. She was curious and asked Wally, "What are you going to do with that box?" Wally smiled. "Elizabeth, you will find out at the pretrial tomorrow."

Wally and Elizabeth arrived at the pretrial. Jeremy White and Carl Smith were waiting for them. Wally shook hands with Carl. He said," Wally, my client is offering $4,000,000 to settle out of court.

Wally declined the offer. He looked at Jeremy and said, "We want Jeremy to donate the entire $8,000,000 that he will receive from Nike to the Salvation Army. When Jeremy signs his three-year rookie contract with an NBA team, he must be put on probation for the length of the contract. Jeremy is not allowed to have any sex, drugs, or alcohol during his probation. He must have counseling daily. The first time Jeremy is caught breaking probation rules, he is fined $100,000; the second time he is caught, he is fined $1,000,000. The third time he is caught, he is fined $3,000,000. The fourth time

Jeremy gets caught, he is suspended for life. The Salvation Army will be carefully watching him."

Jeremy got up and started to scream at Wally! "If you think that I'm going to give my money away to the Salvation Army, you are crazy!" Carl got up. He placed his hands on Jeremy's shoulders. "Be quiet and sit down!" Carl asked Wally if Jeremy had an alternative to probation. The judge told Carll that Wally had an alternative to probation.

Wally brought out his box. He smiled at Jeremy. "I have a new product that I want to market. For Jeremy to avoid probation, he must agree to endorse my product. I will call it the Jeremy White Gas Light Bulb."

Wally took out the bulb and the can of chilli. "If a light goes out in a room, all a person has to do is drop his pants and stick this light bulb into his butt. Then he opens the can of chilli with the help of the flashlight and eats three spoons. The chilli has a secret formula to make you fart a lot. The gas from the farting will turn on the light bulb to light up the room. Jeremy's face will be on billboards and television commercials. During the off-season, Jeremy will be required to go door-to-door to sell the Jeremy White Gas Light Bulb. He will receive 20% of the sales. Jeremy can do anything he wants with the money that he earns."

Jeremy got up and started to scream at Wally again. "I will not sell your stupid light bulb. I would become a laughing stock in the entire country if I did!" Wally screamed back at Jeremy.

"If you think that you can get away with trying to rape my wife, who is pregnant. You are crazy!"

Carl waited for Jeremy to calm down. He said, "Jeremy, the only choice you have is to go on probation when you sign your NBA contract and donate the money that you will receive from Nike to the Salvation Army. If you refuse, you will be tried and convicted of attempted rape and will go to prison. I told you that Wally will make your life a living hell."

Wally had all the paperwork ready for Jeremy to sign. Jeremy was livid, but he signed all the paperwork. Wally and Elizabeth thanked Carl and Jeremy and said goodbye. On their way to the Spencers Mill, Elizabeth happily said, "Wally, there is no way that Jeremy is capable of completing his probation." Wally kissed Elizabeth on the cheek and said, "I know." Wally called Uncle Ivan and told him what happened.

Aunt Lydia and Uncle Ivan were waiting for Wally and Elizabeth. They were pleased with what Wally did. For their dinner, Aunt Lydia prepared perogies, breaded chicken breasts, and bean salad, Elizabeth's favourite meal. When Wally and Elizabeth finished their meal, they said goodbye. Cleo and Leo were hungry and waiting.

Wally fed Cleo and Leo and then took them for a walk in the forest trails. Elizabeth went downstairs to see grandmother. She examined Elizabeth. She told Elizabeth that Wally was taking very good care of her. "Elizabeth will give birth to beautiful, healthy babies." The grandmother then prepared tea. Elizabeth sat down, and Purdy jumped on her lap. Elizabeth rubbed Purdy's tummy.

Chapter 52

Aweek before the NBA draft, it was announced that Jeremy White committed suicide. He overdosed on drugs. A note that Jeremy left behind said that he couldn't live with the conditions of his probation. Wally was disappointed. The Salvation Army will not receive any donations from Jeremy White.

Clarence went to pay Wally a visit. Donna led him into Wally's office. Wally saw a worried look on Clarence's face." Clarence, it's nice to see you; what can I do for you?"

Clearance held his head down and mumbled. "Wally, I am very worried. The government just cut off our funding. The Salvation Army is having difficulty helping the homeless. Every year, more people become homeless."

Wally put his hands on Clarence's shoulders. "Don't worry, Clarence, I'll think of something to help you. We'll have breakfast Saturday morning in my office, and I'll let you know what we are going to do". Clarence thanked Wally. He left, still worried.

Lawrence came in to see Wally. He was very happy. "Wally, I want to thank you for bringing Baron to me. My girlfriend, Becky, loves him. She comes to my house to spend time with Baron. That means that I get more time to spend with her." Wally smiled and told Lawrence he was happy to hear he gave Baron a good home.

Lawrence asked Wally. "Where can I get the dog food you brought for Baron? He loves it. Baron doesn't like the dog food that I buy for him." Wally told Lawrence he could get the dog food at the Kozak Naturopathic Clinic. Lawrence thanked Wally and said goodbye.

Elizabeth came barging in. "Wally, we are being sued by Jeremy's mother. She blames us for Jeremy's suicide. I'm worried!"

Wally gave Elizabeth a big hug. "Don't worry, Jeremy's mother has no legal grounds to sue us."

Wally and Elizabeth went to see Samantha to show her the lawsuit. Samantha looked at the lawsuit and said," Wally, you and Elizabeth will not be in court for the lawsuit. Lawrence will represent you and Elizabeth at the trial. He'll take care of the trial. Wally, you take care of Elizabeth."

Wally did get to read Jeremy's mind. He already knew that Jeremy had raped three girls on three different occasions. He was never charged. The college that recruited him paid off all the girls in out-of-court settlements. Jeremy raped three other girls. He was not charged because those girls were too scared to press charges against him. The college never disciplined him for any of his drug violations. Wally typed out this information along with the names of the girls that Jeremy raped for Lawrence.

Wally found Lawrence in his office reading the lawsuit. He showed Lawrence the background information that he typed for him. Lawrence took the information and read it. He smiled." Wally, thank you for providing this information. Jeremy's mother's lawsuit against you and Elizabeth will be dropped before it goes to court."

Lawrence was ready for the pretrial that was scheduled at 1:00 p.m. today. He left for the courthouse at 12:30. Mrs. White and her lawyer, Carl Smith, were already waiting for Lawrence.

Carl shook Lawrence's hand and said, "Good afternoon, Lawrence. Are you ready to negotiate an out-of-court settlement? Wally caused Jeremy to commit suicide. He forced him to go on probation when he was ready to sign an NBA contract. The conditions of the probation were unreasonably strict."

Lawrence smiled and took out his briefcase. He handed Carl the background information that he had received from Wally. As Carl was reading the information, Lawrence said. "Wally never caused Jeremy to commit suicide. He never forced him to go on probation when he was ready to sign an NBA contract. Wally never forced Jeremy to do anything. It was Jeremy's decision to rape Elizabeth

Kozak, a pregnant woman. Wally offered Jeremy an opportunity to be rehabilitated. Jeremy committed suicide before he started his probation. One of the conditions of his probation was to get daily counselling. If Jeremy had gone for counselling, he probably would be alive today. It was the judge who allowed Jeremy the opportunity to go on probation. Mrs. White should sue the judge, not Wally."

Carl finished reading the information on Jeremy. He was very upset." Mrs. White, you must have known what Jeremy did. Why didn't you tell me!" Mrs. White looked bewildered." I don't know. I guess I thought that it was not important to tell you."

Carl got up, shaking his head. "Mrs. White, you have just wasted my time. You have no legal grounds to sue Wally and Elizabeth!" Carl invited Lawrence to lunch. Lawrence left with Carl to have lunch, leaving Mrs. White behind crying.

Lawrence called Wally to tell them the good news. Wally happily said, "Lawrence, dinner is on me at the Spencers Mill. Be there for 7 o'clock tonight. Invite your girlfriend." Wally went to see Elizabeth to tell her the good news. Elizabeth hugged Wally and told him that she wanted to see his grandparents; they should be home by now.

As soon as Elizabeth and Wally arrived home, they ran down to see their grandparents. Purdy was sitting on grandmother's lap, purring. Elizabeth stayed with his grandmother to have tea. Wally went upstairs to take Cleo and Leo for a walk in the trails. When Wally got back from the walk, Cleo and Leo went to sleep.

Wally and Elizabeth walked to the Spencers Mill for dinner with Lawrence and his girlfriend. Lawrence and his girlfriend were waiting for them. Lawrence introduced his girlfriend, Becky. She was Lawrence's age and the same height. Becky had a pleasing smile, a rounded face, and dark short hair. She was pleasantly plumped.

Wally ordered prime rib and scallop potatoes, steamed vegetables, and Caesar salad for everyone. Becky asked Wally and Elizabeth how they stayed so slim. Wally told Becky that she needs self-discipline to exercise and eat properly. If she is serious about losing weight, she should see his grandmother at her naturopath clinic.

Becky told Wally that she and Lawrence would definitely see his grandmother. Lawrence was not happy with Becky's decision to change their lifestyle. He enjoyed overindulging and not exercising. Lawrence thanked Wally and Elizabeth for a wonderful dinner.

Wally and Elizabeth arrived home; Elizabeth went downstairs to see grandmother. Wally went to the kitchen to think of a plan to help Clarence. After meditating for an hour, Wally thought of a plan to help Clarence raise money for the Salvation Army.

Wally took a shelled peanut, stuck a pin, covered it in caramel, and mounted the peanut on a small square piece of Swiss cheese. He then took a fountain pen and managed to somehow draw a face on the peanut. Wally covered the peanut with a glass dome.

Wally woke up early Saturday morning. He let Elizabeth sleep. Wally took the peanut to his office. He also brought muffins and brewed coffee for the meeting with Clarence. When Clarence showed up, he still had that worried look on his face. Wally showed Clarence the peanut. He looked at the peanut and was puzzled. "Wally, how will this peanut make money for the Salvation Army?"

Wally looked at Clarence and smiled. "Clarence, you will sell me this peanut for $1,000,000 and give me a receipt for it. I will then have the peanut insured for $1,000,000. Once the peanut is insured, I will arrange for it to be displayed in museums throughout New York. People will pay five dollars each to see the peanut. The peanut will be promoted by billboards and television commercials. T-shirts showing the peanut will be sold. All the proceeds that the peanut generates will be donated to the Salvation Army."

Clarence looked at Wally. He thought Wally lost his mind. "Wally, are you joking? Who is going to pay money to see a stupid peanut?"

Wally took out his chequebook. "Clarence, the Salvation Army is desperate for money. Therefore, desperate measures must be taken." Wally wrote out a cheque for $1,000,000 to the Salvation Army. Clarence wrote out a receipt for Wally.

Clarence still thought that Wally had actually lost his mind. He asked Wally, "Why are you going to insure the peanut for $1,000,000?"

Wally smiled. "Clarence, people will pay money to see the peanut if they believe it is valuable. They will not pay money to see the peanut if they believe it to be worthless. By insuring the peanut for $1,000,000, people will believe that the peanut is valuable. Don't forget to announce that the Salvation Army sold me the peanut for $1,000,000."

Wally called an insurance company. They thought Wally was crazy but agreed to insure the peanut for $1,000,000. Wally paid $50,000 for the insurance policy. Wally spent another $200,000 on television commercials, billboards and T-shirts. Wally needed tax receipts for income tax. He inherited a fortune from Henry Wilson.

Arrangements were made to exhibit the peanut at museums. Wally had to pay another $20,000 for security in order to get insurance for the peanut. In the first month, the peanut generated over $100,000, and another $25,000 was generated by the sale of the peanut T-shirts. Clarence was amazed at how much money was generated. He apologized to Wally for thinking that he lost his mind. Wally knew that everyone would think that he was crazy. That's why he didn't tell Elizabeth.

Two weeks later, the peanut was stolen from the museum. Wally couldn't believe that anyone would want to steal the peanut. Wally filed an insurance claim to collect $1,000,000. The insurance company started a thorough investigation. They wanted to ensure that Wally didn't hire somebody to steal the peanut.

Sydney Crowe, the person who stole the peanut, had it analyzed in the lab. He wanted to know why the peanut was so valuable. The test results showed that the peanut was an ordinary, worthless peanut. This made Sidney very angry. He took out a hammer and smashed the peanut. Sidney then called his lawyer. He was going to sue Wally for $1,000,000 for tricking him into stealing the worthless peanut.

When Wally received the summons to appear in court, he couldn't believe how stupid people can be. By admitting that he stole the peanut, the insurance company will go after Sydney after they pay Wally $1,000,000. Sydney's lawyer should have told him that, after all, Wally did announce to the public that the peanut was insured for $1,000,000.

Elizabeth was not happy when she found out about the lawsuit. She knew that the lawsuit was stupid. She was amazed at how a worthless peanut could generate so much money. She also knew that the proceeds went to the Salvation Army.

Chapter 53

Elizabeth was tired from being pregnant. She decided to go home early. When she got home, she saw Purdy purring. She picked her up and went downstairs to see Grandmother.

Samantha walked into Wally's office and said, "Where is Elizabeth? I booked a room at the Spencers Mill for her baby shower. Remind Elizabeth that it is this Sunday. Everyone invited will be there."

Elizabeth was not looking forward to her baby shower. Wally was glad that he wasn't invited. Wally walked with Elizabeth to her baby shower. Samantha invited the entire women's staff at her law firm. She also invited Wally's grandmother, Lydia, Joan, Judy, Christine Kelly, and Christine Bell. Everyone who was there gave Elizabeth a big hug. Cindy was the only person invited who didn't show up. Aunt Lydia prepared perogies, lasagna, pizza, and Caesar salad. She baked various pastries for dessert. Uncle Ivan brought wine, coffee, and tea.

Elizabeth enjoyed the food but not her baby shower. When the time came for Elizabeth to open her presents, everyone laughed, watching her react to the presents she received. Elizabeth received a lot of disposable diapers, baby clothes, baby toys, and earplugs. At the end of the shower, Elizabeth was glad to see Wally show up to take her home.

Wally was ready for his pretrial. Elizabeth decided to stay home. When Wally showed up at the interview room, Sydney and his lawyer, Charles Kraft, were waiting for him. Charles asked Wally," Do you want to negotiate a settlement?"

Wally refused to negotiate. He said. "The peanut was only valuable to the Salvation Army. It generated a lot of money for them.

People were willing to pay money to see the peanut because it looked unusual; it was insured for $1,000,000, and it was sold to me for $1,000,000. The minute that Sydney stole the peanut, it became worthless. My intentions were to have the peanut generate as much money as possible for the Salvation Army. I did not want Sydney to steal the peanut or trick him into stealing it."

Charles looked at Sydney, shaking his head. "Do you still want to proceed with the lawsuit? I advise you not to. You better return the peanut as soon as possible. The insurance company will be coming after you if you don't."

Sydney just realized what a stupid fool he was. He couldn't return the peanut because he smashed it with a hammer. The Insurance company eventually paid Wally $1,000,000 and went after Sydney. Clarence happily accepted the $1,000,000 donation from Wally.

Chapter 54

Elizabeth went to see Grandmother for her monthly checkup. She smiled. "Elizabeth, you will give birth to healthy babies. Where do you want to deliver your babies, at home or in a hospital?" Elizabeth chose to deliver in a hospital. Grandmother was disappointed but respected Elizabeth's decision. Elizabeth hugged grandmother goodbye and went home to see Wally.

Elizabeth grabbed a bowl of bean salad from the refrigerator and went to the back patio to enjoy it. She found a skunk sleeping under a chair. She screamed! "Wally, there is a skunk sleeping on our back patio, call animal control!"

Wally opened a can of unsalted peanuts and poured them into a bowl. He then took the bowl of peanuts to the skunk and gently awakened him. The skunk started to eat the peanuts. When he finished eating, Wally scratched his tummy.

Elizabeth started screaming again. "Wally, have you lost your mind? I want you to get rid of the skunk, not keep him as a pet!"

Wally smiled at Elizabeth. "We are going to keep the skunk. He will keep the raccoons and rats away. I'm going to call the skunk Orval."

Elizabeth ran out of the house to see grandmother at her clinic. Grandmother was sitting in her office doing paperwork. Elizabeth barged in and screamed! "Grandmother, Wally, lost his mind. A skunk was sleeping on our back patio. Wally fed it peanuts. Wally wants to keep the skunk for a pet. He's going to call him Orval!"

Grandmother hugged Elizabeth. "Don't worry, Wally knows what he is doing. Orval will keep away the raccoons and rats." Elizabeth was still furious,"

Grandmother I don't care if Orval does keep raccoons and rats away. I won't go near him, and I don't want our children to go near him!" Grandmother gave Elizabeth some hot tea to calm her down. She was not happy having a skunk around the house.

Wally decided to leave the office early to go home to prepare dinner. He wanted to have dinner ready for Elizabeth when she came home. Elizabeth is about to go into labour any day. Uncle Ivan offered to drive Elizabeth home. Elizabeth insisted on going to the office. She was happy to see dinner waiting for her. After dinner, Elizabeth went to feed Cleo and Leo. Wally went to the back patio to feed Orval. Elizabeth didn't want to go near Orval. Wally couldn't understand why she didn't like Orval. Cleo and Leo like him. Orval even showed up for walks with Wally, Cleo and Leo on the trails.

Elizabeth has become very bitchy lately. Wally decided to leave her alone. Wally didn't want to upset her. Wally grabbed a bag of unsalted sunflower seeds for a snack. He went to sit on the back patio. While Wally was eating the sunflower seeds, a chipmunk showed up. He ran up Wally's arm and onto his hand, the one that held the sunflower seeds. Wally cried out. "Elizabeth, come here; we have another visitor." Elizabeth came running and saw the chipmunk.

Wally smiled and said, "Elizabeth, I'm going to call the chipmunk Charlie." Elizabeth ran downstairs to see grandmother. She told her that Wally had lost his mind again. "He is feeding a chipmunk of sunflower seeds. Wally is going to call the chipmunk Charlie!"

Grandmother called Grandfather and said, "Let's go upstairs to see Wally feeding Charlie the chipmunk." They left Elizabeth behind. She had no interest in Charlie, the chipmunk. The grandparents were watching Wally feed Charlie. They both thought it was very sweet of him feeding the chipmunk.

When Charlie finished eating, Wally rubbed Charlie's little head with his finger. He asked his grandmother, "Where is Elizabeth, and what is wrong with her? "

Grandmother was smiling. "Elizabeth is downstairs. She has a big-city attitude towards wild animals. She believes that all wild animals are dangerous, Wally. I'll go get her. Please try not to upset Elizabeth."

Chapter 55

Samantha walked into Wally's office. She was very upset that Elizabeth was still in her office. Samantha insisted that Wally take Elizabeth home. The last thing she wanted was to have Elizabeth give birth in her office. Wally dragged Elizabeth out of her office. Elizabeth didn't want to leave." Elizabeth. You heard Samantha; she says that you have to go home.

Wally called Grandmother. She agreed to stay with Elizabeth until she went into labour. Wally helped his Grandfather at the clinic. Wally was tired and nervous at the end of the day. He left the clinic to go home. Grandmother told Wally to get the car ready. It was time for Elizabeth to go to the hospital. Wally and grandmother led Elizabeth to the car. They drove to the hospital. Elizabeth was placed in a maternity ward. Wally called Joan, Aunt Judy, Aunt Lydia, Uncle Ivan, and Samantha. An hour later, Elizabeth went into labour. Everyone showed up just in time to see Elizabeth give birth to twins, a boy and a girl. They weighed 7 pounds each. Everyone was happy watching Elizabeth holding her babies. Elizabeth will be going home tomorrow afternoon. Everyone congratulated Wally and Elizabeth. They gave Wally a goodbye hug and went home.

Grandmother insisted that Wally go home. "Wally, I will stay with Elizabeth. You will only upset her if you stay. I will call you if anything happens." Wally went home disappointed.

The next morning, Wally got up, said his prayer, did his dance, and meditated. He fed Cleo and Leo. He also placed a dish of peanuts for Orval, a dish of sunflower seeds for Charlie, and a bowl of cat food beside a sleeping Purdy. Wally then took Cleo and Leo for a walk; Orval joined them.

It was 11:30 in the morning when Grandmother called Wally to take Elizabeth and the babies home. Wally drove to the hospital.

Elizabeth was discharged. On their way home, Elizabeth was sleeping while Grandmother was holding the babies. Elizabeth woke up when they arrived home. Grandmother handed the babies to Wally and went downstairs to bed.

Elizabeth was worried. She looked at Wally holding the babies and said, "Wally, I never planned to be a mother. I'm scared. What am I supposed to do?"

Wally gave Elizabeth a kiss. "Don't worry, Elizabeth; you will have plenty of support from family and friends and a whole year of maternity leave to figure out what to do." Wally brought the babies to the bedroom. There were two baby cribs waiting for them. Elizabeth watched Wally place the babies into their cribs. Wally then took several pictures of them. Wally asked Elizabeth if she decided on names for their babies.

Elizabeth smiled at Wally. "I want to call our baby girl Sarah and our baby boy Daniel."

Wally smiled and gave Elizabeth another kiss. "Elizabeth, you have chosen beautiful names for our babies." Wally left Elizabeth alone with Daniel and Sarah. He started to prepare dinner. Wally was expecting a lot of visitors soon. He prepared a huge pot of chili. Wally used organic ground turkey instead of ground beef for his chili. He prepared several baked potatoes, breaded chicken and Caesar salad.

Joan, aunt Judy, Wally's grandparents, aunt Lydia, uncle Ivan and Samantha, showed up for dinner. They wanted to spend some time with Elizabeth and the twins. Uncle Ivan brought wine, and Aunt Lydia brought various pastries. Wally plugged in the coffee percolator and plugged in the kettle for tea. When the guests arrived, they all went to the bedroom to see Elizabeth and the twins. Wally then went to the piano to play and sing some love ballads. The twins fell asleep. Everyone had dinner and listened to Wally sing. Elizabeth had a good time with her visitors.

In the next few days, Elizabeth started to feel like a mother. She didn't mind staying at home with Daniel and Sarah. Every day, she had visitors to keep her from being lonely. In the morning, Wally stayed with the twins, while Elizabeth walked Cleo and Leo. She walked them through the neighbourhood. Elizabeth didn't want to go into the trails because she didn't want Orval to come. When Wally gets home from the office, he takes Cleo, Leo and Orval for a walk in the trails.

Wally drove to the office, a happy father. He bought a box of Cuban cigars on the black market to hand out. Everyone received a cigar, even the non-smokers. Elizabeth called Wally at his office. "Wally, there is an owl lying on the grass near the patio. Looks like the owl is dying. Please come home."

Wally left his office and drove home. He saw the owl lying on the grass. He called grandmother, knowing that she would know what to do. Wally wrapped the owl in a towel and took him to see Grandmother. Fifteen minutes later, Grandmother was examining the owl.

Grandmother said, "Wally, this owl is still alive. We may be able to save him. He was probably poisoned by pesticides. I will prepare a solution to flush out his stomach. Wally, you must use a dropper to force the solution down his throat."

Grandmother gave Wally a basket. He placed the owl in the basket and took the prepared solution that grandmother made. Wally thanked his grandmother and went home.

Elizabeth was furious! She wanted Wally to call animal control. "Wally, how do you know that the owl doesn't have rabies!" Wally was annoyed. "Elizabeth, if the owl had rabies, he would not be lying on the grass dying. Grandmother said that we have a chance to save his life, and that is what I plan to do." Elizabeth was not happy. "Wally, you better keep that owl away from me, Sarah, and Daniel!"

Wally ignored Elizabeth. He put the owl in the den away from Elizabeth. Every day, Wally forced grandmother's solution down the owl's throat. The owl started to get stronger. Wally fed him some doggie food. The owl soon fully recovered. The owl flew away. Wally was pleased, and so was Elizabeth. However, the owl soon returned and landed on Wally's shoulder. Wally was happy to see him. Elizabeth was not. Wally decided to call the owl Howard. He was a large, long-horned owl. His wing span was four feet wide. Since that day, Wally had decided to ensure that Howard would never be hungry when he was near the other pets. Wally didn't want any of his pets to become Howard's dinner. Elizabeth was not happy.

"Wally, you better keep Howard, Orval, and Charlie away from me, Daniel, and Sarah!"

Wally ignored Elizabeth. He took Howard outside on the patio. He had some doggie food for Howard. Wally stayed with Howard until he decided to fly away.

Wally enjoyed watching NFL football. He watched every Sunday afternoon. Howard, Orval, Charlie, Purdy, Cleo and Leo began watching NFL football with Wally. He provided peanuts for Orval, sunflower seeds for Charlie, popcorn for Howard, cat food for Purdy and doggie food for Cleo and Leo. Elizabeth took Daniel and Sarah to see grandmother. She and her grandmother do not like NFL football.

Chapter 56

Wally was sitting at his desk doing paperwork. He received an unexpected visitor. It was Louis holding a chessboard. Louis smiled. "Wally, it's been a long time since we played chess. I came to see you last night. Elizabeth answered the door. She told me to get lost."

Wally saw the sad look on Louis's face. "I'll be having lunch in an hour. Meet me in the office cafeteria. Donna will show you where it is."

Louis left Wally's office with a big smile on his face. It had been a long time since Wally played chess with Louis. Wally knew why he came to see him. Louis got a lot better playing chess by joining a chess club. He thought he could beat Wally. Poor Louis didn't realize that Wally could retrieve any information he wanted at any time, including the chess moves from the chess masters because Wally never forgets.

It was time for Wally to play chess with Louis. He saw him in the cafeteria. "Louis, are you hungry, my treat?" Louis finished setting up his chessboard. "Wally, I didn't come here to eat. I came to kick your butt playing chess."

Wally sat down, ready to play chess with Louis. He said, "Louis, how did you know that Tommy sent goons after Harry, and how did you know that Harry was my friend?"

Louis smiled, "Jason, a friend of mine, belongs to the same chess club that I do. He works for Tommy. Jason told me that Tommy ordered him to send the goons to kill Harry. Tommy knew that Harry was your friend and was pissed off when Harry refused to be his lawyer. That's why I called you to warn him. I play a lot of chess with Jason and win most of the time."

Wally then asked Louis if he had burned down any buildings lately. Louis didn't like the question that Wally just asked. He said, "My father insisted that I learn his trade. He taught me everything there is to know. I torched a few buildings for him. Are you going to report me to the police?"

Wally smiled at him. "Relax, Louis. Your secret is safe with me; concentrate on playing chess; you're about to be checkmated." Wally already knew that Louis had torched some buildings for his father.

Louis was really annoyed. Not because he told Wally that he knew how to burn down buildings, but because he was annoyed because Wally beat him in chess twice quite easily. Louis said to Wally. "God blessed you with the ability to become a great chess master. Don't ignore your calling".

Wally replied, "Louis, God didn't encourage me to play chess; I'm very happy being a successful lawyer." Louis was disappointed with Wally. "Suit yourself, Wally. Can I come back later to play with you? If I can't beat you, I can learn from you."

Wally scheduled to play chess with Louis twice a month. Louis thanked Wally. He was happy to have him as a friend. Louis couldn't figure out why Elizabeth didn't like him.

Elizabeth was waiting for Wally to get home. When Wally arrived, she took him by the hand and led him to the den. There, Wally saw Purdy sleeping in her bed. Underneath her tummy, Charlie was sleeping. Wally took out his phone to take a picture of Purdy and Charlie sleeping together. This picture could win first prize in the amateur photography contest. Clarence would be happy if Wally won the first prize.

Joan came to visit Elizabeth. She wanted to spend time with Elizabeth, Daniel and Sarah. Elizabeth was waiting for Joan in the bedroom. Wally brought perogies and pizza into the bedroom so Joan and Elizabeth could have some privacy. Wally then placed a dish of sunflower seeds for Charlie and a bowl of cat food for Purdy. He grabbed a bag full of peanuts for Orval and fed Cleo and Leo.

When Orval, Cleo, and Leo finished eating, Wally took them for a walk on the trails.

Joan and Elizabeth were enjoying their dinner. Daniel and Sarah were asleep. Joan smiled. "Elizabeth, your babies are beautiful. You must really enjoy motherhood."

Elizabeth laughed. "Mother, I don't think motherhood is so great. All day long, Daniel and Sarah cry, eat, sleep, pee, and poop. That doesn't sound so wonderful to me." Joan smiled and told Elizabeth not to worry. It gets much better as they get older. "How is Wally behaving?"

Elizabeth laughed again. "Wally is acting like a child. He has a skunk called Orval, a chipmunk called Charlie, and an owl called Howard for pets. Wally likes to watch Sunday afternoon football; those three, along with Cleo, Leo, and Purdy, watch football with Wally."

Wally returned from walking Cleo, Leo and Orval. Elizabeth said, "Wally, mother enjoyed dinner very much. She and aunt Judy are coming over Sunday afternoon to watch football with you and your pets. Mother just left; Daniel and Sarah are sleeping I'm going to take a nap." Wally made some tea and went to sit on the patio.

Wally got up very early the next morning. He said his prayer, did his dance and meditated. Elizabeth was sleeping. She had no interest in praying, dancing, or meditating. Grandmother would wake her up. Grandfather would feed Orval, Cleo, and Leo and then take them for a walk in the trails. Wally had court this afternoon. He was preparing for his court.

Samantha walked into his office and asked him how is family life was. Wally smiled, "Samantha, I am happy to be a family man. However, Elizabeth is having some difficulty adjusting. I have to leave for court soon. Could you please visit her during lunch?"

Samantha was happy to visit Elizabeth at lunchtime. She wanted to see Daniel, Sarah, Cleo, and Leo. On her way to see Elizabeth, Samantha brought with her a box of chocolates. Elizabeth was happy to see her. She placed a pizza in the oven.

"Uncle Ivan was just here. He left me a pizza. Daniel and Sarah are asleep. You have to walk on your tippy toes to see them."

Samantha and Elizabeth walked on their tippy toes to the bedroom. Samantha whispered in Elizabeth's ear. "Daniel and Sarah are beautiful. You must be very happy."

A few minutes later, they left for the kitchen. Samantha went looking for Cleo and Leo. Elizabeth took out the pizza from the oven. She said to Samantha, "I don't understand why women think that motherhood is so wonderful. Daniel and Sarah cry, eat, sleep, pee, and poop a lot every day. They keep me awake all night, crying. I don't know how Wally can sleep through all that crying."

Samantha looked at a tired Elizabeth and said, "When I gave birth to my son, I only had him for eight months before he was taken away from me for adoption. Tell me, Elizabeth, how would you feel if you had to give up Daniel and Sarah for adoption?"

Elizabeth put her hands on her cheeks and said, "Oh my gosh! I never realized how much I love Daniel and Sarah. I could never give them up for adoption. Samantha, thank you for asking me that question!"

Samantha and Elizabeth started to eat the pizza. Elizabeth then poured some coffee. Elizabeth told Samantha all about Wally's new pets. "Wally and all the pets show up every Sunday afternoon to watch football."

Samantha started to laugh. "I want to come this Sunday afternoon to watch football with Wally and his pets. I'll bring popcorn and chips." When it was time for Samantha to leave, she gave Elizabeth a big hug. Samantha was looking forward to seeing Wally and his pets watch football this Sunday afternoon. Elizabeth was looking forward to eating the chocolates that Samantha brought her.

Chapter 57

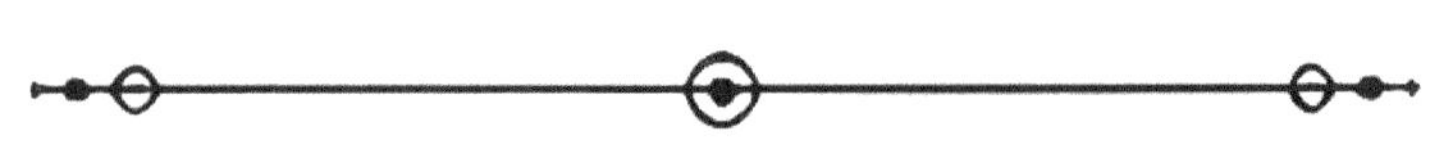

Wally came home from court. He found Elizabeth lying on her stomach, sleeping naked on the bed. This gave Wally an idea. Daniel and Sarah were also asleep. Wally put a handful of sunflower seeds in his mouth and grabbed a straw. Charlie saw Wally blow sunflower seeds into Elizabeth's butt with a straw. Charlie jumped on the bed and shoved his head into Elizabeth's butt to get at the sunflower seeds. Wally took a picture of Charlie's head stuck in Elizabeth's butt. He then gently pulled Charlie out and ran away before Elizabeth could see him. Wally returned to Elizabeth to give her a kiss.

Daniel and Sarah woke up crying. Elizabeth had a big smile on her face. "Wally, it's your turn to change the diapers." Wally took out two disposable diapers from the linen closet and went to the bedroom.

Elizabeth went into the washroom. She had a severe itch in her butt. She stuck her hand in her butt to scratch the itch. When Elizabeth took her hand out, she found sunflower seeds on her fingers. She was puzzled. Elizabeth couldn't figure out how the sunflower seeds got into her butt.

Wally was laughing as he was changing diapers. He entered the picture of Charlie's head stuck in Elizabeth's butt in the amateur photography contest. Wally's hoping that the picture would win first prize. If it did, he would donate the price to the Salvation Army. The picture of Purdy and Charlie sleeping together didn't win first prize. When Wally finished changing the diapers, Daniel and Sarah stopped crying.

Grandmother came upstairs to see Daniel and Sarah. This gave Elizabeth and Wally an opportunity to take Cleo and Leo for a walk. They walked in the neighbourhood. Elizabeth didn't want to go into the trails because she didn't want Orval to come with them. After their walk with Cleo and Leo, Wally had to take an unhappy Orval for a walk in the trails.

Elizabeth went inside the house to see Grandmother. She had tea and hot oatmeal with blueberries and maple syrup waiting for Elizabeth. "Grandmother, I had an itch in my butt. When I stuck my hand to scratch the itch, I found sunflower seeds on my fingers. Do you think Wally is somehow responsible?"

Grandmother laughed. "If Wally is responsible, you'll find out soon enough." Grandmother and Elizabeth drank their tea and finished their oatmeal.

Chapter 58

Patricia and Mike's wedding is in four weeks. Wally had to make an appointment for the ushers to be fitted for tuxedos. Elizabeth wanted the bridesmaids to wear the same dresses that the bridesmaids wore at her wedding. She called Samantha to find out where to get those dresses. Elizabeth still couldn't figure out why Patricia wanted her to be the maid of honour. Elizabeth thought that she and Patricia hated each other. Elizabeth and Patricia were roommates in law school. Patricia was very rude to Elizabeth. She drove Elizabeth with her cleanliness obsession. Elizabeth tolerated Patricia because she was a very good study partner. Elizabeth and Patricia never met Wally at law school because they didn't have any classes with him, and Harvard Law School had over 10,000 law students.

Wally and the ushers were fitted for the tuxedos. He invited the ushers to have dinner at Spencers Mill. Wally called Elizabeth to invite the bridesmaids.

Wally walked out of the tuxedo shop; he saw Gloria sitting on a bench drinking coffee. Wally approached her. He smiled at Gloria and said, "Gloria, you are looking good. I can see that rehab is doing wonders for you. When was the last time you had a drink or drugs?"

Gloria replied, "Wally, I have been clean for the last four months, and it's driving me crazy. I hate going to rehab! The only reason I'm going is to save my job!" Wally told her to start praying and meditating. This will make coping with the rehab a lot easier.

Gloria gave Wally a big hug. "I saw you coming out of the tuxedo shop. What is the occasion?" Wally smiled and said. "I am the best man at a wedding. Michael Cook and Patricia Conrad are getting married. Elizabeth is the maid of honour."

Gloria started to laugh. "Wally, Patricia is a mean bitch that nobody likes. Michael had to be drunk or high on drugs when he proposed to her."

Wally became upset. "Gloria, Patricia, Michael, Elizabeth, and I work for the same law firm. Patricia is a very attractive girl, and I like her. She was a bridesmaid, and Michael was an usher at our wedding."

Glory kept on laughing. "Wally, Elizabeth told me that she hates Patricia. Why did Patricia ask Elizabeth to be her maid of honour, and why did Elizabeth accept? Did Elizabeth and Patricia fight at your wedding?"

Wally was still upset. "Elizabeth told me to choose the wedding party. Elizabeth and Patricia did not fight at our wedding. You were invited to come to our wedding; why didn't you?"

Gloria sadly said, "Oh Wally, I really wanted to come, but I couldn't. One of the conditions of my rehab is that I stay away from places that serve alcohol or drugs." Wally told Gloria that it would be nice to see her at Patricia's and Michael's wedding.

Wally hugged Gloria goodbye and left for the Spencers Mill. Elizabeth, the bridesmaids and ushers, were waiting for him. Uncle Ivan brought a bottle of champagne to celebrate the engagement. Wally was asked to sing and play the piano. He sang some romantic love songs. Patricia and Michael blushed. Aunt Lydia served dinner. She brought perogies, cabbage rolls, head cheese made with turkey, not pork, breaded chicken breast and Caesar salad. Everyone enjoyed dinner. Wally insisted on paying the entire bill.

Chapter 59

On their wedding day, Michael and Patricia were married at the Spencers Mill wedding chapel. Aunt Lydia and Uncle Ivan were getting ready for the guests. Wally was pleasantly surprised to see Gloria. She was not alone. Wally went over to see her. He asked Gloria who her friend was.

Gloria blushed. "Wally, meet Dave Smith. He's my new counselor. He'll make sure that I won't have any alcohol. I took your advice and started to pray and meditate. You're right; it helped me a lot."

Dave was a tall, slender, good-looking man. He had dark hair, brown eyes, and a friendly smile. When Wally shook his hand, he found out that Dave was a vegan and worked out at a gym. He also enjoyed running. He not only came to the wedding to make sure Gloria stayed sober, but he also wanted Gloria to have a good time. Dan wants to have a serious relationship with Gloria if she successfully completes her rehab.

For dinner, Aunt Lydia prepared cabbage rolls, Pierogis, turkey meatballs, lasagna, breaded chicken breasts, bean salad and Caesar salad. Dan only ate several servings of the bean salad and Caesar salad. For dessert there were various pastries served with coffee or tea. Samantha was chosen to be the master of the ceremony. Her speech was short and sweet. When all the speeches were finished, the band started to play. Michael asked Wally to sing some songs with the band. Wally sang songs by Frank Sinatra, Al Martino and Marty Robbins.

When Wally finished singing, it was time for Patricia to throw her bouquet of flowers over her shoulders. Gloria was the lucky girl who caught it. Wally went to congratulate her. "Gloria, you are a beautiful girl. A lot of guys will want to marry you."

Gloria gave Wally a big hug. Dave Smith also congratulated Gloria.

Patricia went to Elizabeth to give her a hug. She thanked her for being her maid of honour. Elizabeth was still puzzled. She couldn't figure out why Patricia wanted her to be her maid of honour. Elizabeth thought that Patricia hated her. Patricia said to Elizabeth, "I know that I was rude to you in law school, but that doesn't mean that I hated you. I don't know why, but I am rude to everyone. I was happy to have you as a roommate because you were such a good study partner.

Near the end of the night, Patricia and Michael left. Early the next morning, they were to leave for Niagara Falls for their honeymoon. Wally and Elizabeth also left to go home. Grandmother was babysitting. When they arrived home, Daniel and Sarah began crying.

Grandmother took Elizabeth by the hand. "Elizabeth, it's feeding time." Wally followed them into the bedroom. Howard was perched on the floor lamp. He was hungry. Wally headed for the kitchen to get some food for Howard. When Howard finished his meal, he flew out of the bedroom window. Wally changed into his pyjamas. He fell asleep before Elizabeth finished feeding Daniel and Sarah.

Wally woke up; Elizabeth, Daniel, and Sarah were still asleep. Wally said his prayer, did his dance and meditated. He fed Cleo and Leo and then took them along with Orval for a walk in the forest trails. When he returned, Wally left a bowl of peanuts for Orval on the patio. He placed some sunflower seeds and cat food beside Purdy's bed. Wally also left the bowl of perogies for Elizabeth before he left for the office.

Donna entered Wally's office to tell him that she and Thomas had a wonderful time at the wedding. Lawrence came in five minutes later. He wanted to thank Wally for inviting him to the wedding. He and his girlfriend Becky had a good time. Lawrence also mentioned that Baron loves his food. "The vet said that Baron is a very healthy dog."

Lawrence and Becky went to see Wally's grandmother at her clinic. Lawrence said, "Wally, I'm glad that you told us to go see your grandmother. Her diet plan is delicious, and I enjoy doing the exercises your grandfather showed me with Becky. I'm starting to feel much better and have more energy."

Wally finished his paperwork; it was still early. He decided to go home to see how Elizabeth was feeling. When Wally arrived home, he didn't expect Elizabeth to be waiting for him. The look on her face told Wally that he should run for his life. Elizabeth threw a magazine at Wally and screamed! "Wally, how could you!" Wally picked up the magazine, and in it was a cheque for $10,000. The cover of the magazine showed a naked girl lying in bed with a chipmunk stuck in her butt. Wally looked at Elizabeth and said to her, "How do you know that the girl in this picture is you? Your face is not shown, and no name has been given."

A red-faced Elizabeth grabbed the magazine from Wally. "I saw you pick up your cheque. I also found sunflower seeds stuck in my butt. You feed Charlie sunflower seeds!" Wally believed that Elizabeth would never find out. He didn't expect Elizabeth to find sunflower seeds stuck in her butt. Before Wally could say another word, Elizabeth ran out of the house to see Grandmother. Luckily, grandmother was alone in her office.

Elizabeth showed his grandmother the magazine cover. Grandmother took a look and said, "Elizabeth, how do you know that the girl on this magazine cover is you?"

Elizabeth was breathing heavily and said, "Grandmother, I found sunflower seeds stuck in my butt, remember. I also saw Wally pick up a cheque and put it in his pocket."

Elizabeth and his grandmother went home to see Wally. Grandmother was holding the magazine. She was angry at Wally and said to him, "Wally, if this is your idea of a joke, it's not funny. Elizabeth has every right to be upset!"

Wally, feeling very embarrassed, said, "Grandmother, I didn't do it for a joke. I did it to help Clarence. The Salvation Army is desperate for donations. I didn't think Elizabeth would ever find out." Grandmother was very disappointed. "Wally, that is no excuse for upsetting Elizabeth. I think it's time for you and Elizabeth to pay another visit to Dr. Reggie. One of his patients called to cancel an appointment for tomorrow at 8 o'clock in the morning. I will call him to let him know that you and Elizabeth will be seeing him tomorrow morning at 8 o'clock. Both of you better show up."

It was 8 o'clock in the morning. Wally and Elizabeth were waiting for Dr. Reggie in his office. He came five minutes later. Dr. Reggie said, "Good morning, Wally; your grandmother told me that Elizabeth gave birth to twins, a boy and a girl; congratulations. Now, what brings you and Elizabeth to see me today?"

Elizabeth elbowed Wally in the ribs and gave the photography magazine to Dr. Reggie. He looked at the front cover. Elizabeth said, "Wally somehow managed to stick sunflower seeds into my butt. Charlie, Wally's pet chipmunk, stuck his head into my butt while I was sleeping. He then took a picture of Charlie's head stuck in my butt. Wally entered the picture in an amateur photography contest and won $10,000 first prize again." Dr. Reggie asked Elizabeth how she knew the girl in this picture was her.

Elizabeth gave Wally a dirty look and said, "Wally feeds Charlie sunflower seeds. I had an itch in my butt. When I went to scratch the itch, I found sunflower seeds stuck to my fingers. I also saw Wally's cheque for winning the contest fall out of the magazine."

Dr. Reggie became upset. "Wally, what you did was despicable. Please explain yourself?" Wally pressed his lips together, took a deep breath, and said, "I know I did a terrible thing to Elizabeth. I did it because I wanted to help Clarence. He works for the Salvation Army. They are desperate for donations because the government cut their funding. Elizabeth wasn't supposed to find out what I did. I was irresponsible for what I did. I just realized if Elizabeth blew a fart when Charlie had his head stuck in her butt, he would have suffocated."

Dr. Reggie began laughing. Elizabeth screamed at Dr. Reggie. "Dr., have you lost your mind? What's the matter with you?"

Dr. Reggie stopped laughing and shook his head. "Elizabeth, I sincerely apologize. I would've been heartbroken if you had blown a fart and suffocated Charlie."

Wally said to Dr. Reggie, "It could have been much worse. I have another pet, a skunk called Orval. I feed him peanuts. If I would have shoved peanuts into Elizabeth's butt, Oral would have stuck his head into her butt."

Dr. Reggie started to laugh again. Elizabeth shouted! "Dr., did you receive your license to practice psychology by sending cereal box tops to Kelloggs!"

Dr. Reggie continued laughing. When he finally stopped, he said to Elizabeth, "I thought what you just said was funny. I better write it down before I forget." Elizabeth managed to control her urge to smack Dr. Reggie in the face.

Wally felt very remorseful. He promised Elizabeth that he would make every effort not to upset her. Wally told Dr. Reggie that a lot of homeless people depended on the Salvation Army. Nobody else knew that the picture on the magazine cover was Elizabeth. Her head is not shown, and no name is given. Dr. Reggie told Wally that it was noble of him to help his friend Clarence, but it shouldn't be at the expense of Elizabeth's feelings.

Elizabeth was still upset. "Dr. Reggie, Wally also asked me a stupid question to get me upset. Some of the girls in our office building wear extremely long fingernails. Wally asked me when the girls need to go for a poop, how do they manage to clean their butt after pooping."

Dr. Reggie started to think about that question and then said, "Hmm, Elizabeth, I would like to know the answer to that question myself."

Elizabeth became very angry at Dr. Reggie. She stood up and looked down at him and shouted. "Dr. Reggie, If I had the authority to send you to the nut house, I would!"

Dr. Reggie stood up. He was much taller than Elizabeth. Dr. Reggie looked down at her and said, "Young lady, the problem with you is that you take life too seriously. You also lack a sense of humour!"

Elizabeth took Wally by the hand. "Wally, it is time to leave. Our session with Dr. Reggie is over." Dr. Reggie walked over to the front door and opened it. He said, "It was a pleasure seeing the both of you again." Wally and Elizabeth left without saying a word.

While driving home, Elizabeth asked, "Wally, do you think I lack a sense of humour?"

Wally was smiling as he was driving. "Elizabeth, you have a wonderful sense of humour. You are just a little stressed out from being a wonderful mother." Neither one of them said another word, driving home.

Chapter 60

Wally was in his office when Michael walked in. He was very worried and wanted to talk to Wally. He sat down and said, "Wally, I have a huge problem with Patricia. She is extremely germophobic. When we are at home, I have to wash my hands whenever I touch my phone. We live in a condo on the 15ᵗʰ floor. Our balcony faces a beautiful forest. We are not allowed to go on the balcony because of the dust and germs. We have an indoor saltwater swimming pool. Patricia refuses to go swimming because of germs. I insist on going swimming. When I get back to the apartment after swimming, Patricia makes me put plastic bags on my feet. She doesn't want me to get salt on the floor. Then I have to wash my hands and take another shower. There is a changing room, shower, and sauna at the pool. Because it is a public place, it has germs, and I must shower again. When we dine at a restaurant, Patricia brings clean plastic knives, forks, and spoons. She doesn't trust the restaurant dishwashers. Patricia believes the restaurant utensils have germs. Wally, I don't know what to do. Patricia is driving me crazy!"

Wally felt sorry for Michael and said, "I don't know what I can do to help you. The only advice that I can give you is to keep praying and meditating every day."

Wally wrote out a prayer that he gave to Michael when they were at law school. "You and Patricia should stand in front of a mirror and say this prayer out loud at least three times a day. Take Patricia and see my grandmother at her clinic. She may be able to help you."

Michael thanked Wally. He definitely has plans to see Wally's grandmother. However, he was not so sure if Patricia was willing to go with him. Michael used to pray and meditate in college, and it helped him a lot. He doesn't know why he stopped, but he will start again right away. He's going to try to convince Patricia to pray and meditate with him.

An hour later, Michael entered Wally's office. "Wally, Patricia agreed to see your grandmother with me if you agree to come with us." Wally didn't want to go but agreed to come with them. He called his grandmother to make an appointment. Elizabeth was not happy that Wally agreed to go with them.

Early the next morning, Wally, Michael, and Patricia were waiting at the Kozak Naturopath Clinic in Wally's grandmother's office. She arrived a few minutes later. Michael explained the problem he had with Patricia being a germaphobe. Grandmother advised Michael and Patricia to make an appointment to see her friend, Dr. Reggie Neale. Patricia was offended by grandmother's advice. She believed that there was nothing wrong with her. Grandmother gently took hold of Patricia's hand and said, "Patricia, there is no need to be ashamed of seeing a psychiatrist. Many high-profile people see a psychiatrist. Some continue seeing them for years. Wally and Elizabeth went to see Dr. Reggie."

Patricia agreed to go with Michael to see Dr. Reggie Neale, provided Wally came with them. Wally was not happy with Patricia's decision, but he agreed to go with them.

Elizabeth was not happy that Wally agreed to go with Michael and Patricia to see Dr. Reggie Neale. "Wally, everyone hates Patricia because of her germophobic antics. You don't have to go with them."

Wally replied, "Elizabeth, I do have to go with them. Patricia would refuse to go unless I agreed to come with them." Elizabeth shook her head and said nothing. She thought it was stupid for Wally to go with Patricia and Michael to see Dr. Reggie Neale.

Wally drove Patricia and Michael to their appointment with Dr. Reggie Neale. They arrived just in time. Dr. Reggie was waiting for them. Dr. Reggie smiled. "Good morning, everyone. Wally, your grandmother explained why you all came to see me. I need to talk to Patricia alone. Patricia, please come with me to the next room." Patricia got up and followed Dr. Reggie. She sat down feeling doom and gloom. Dr. Reggie sat down beside Patricia and took out a pen and writing pad.

He said, "Patricia, your germophobic problem is deeply rooted in your subconscious. Please tell me everything that you can remember about your childhood?"

Patricia looked puzzled. "Dr. Neale, I had a wonderful childhood. My parents were loving and caring people. There's not much that I could tell you about my childhood."

Dr. Reggie sadly said, "Patricia, you have experienced a traumatic event or events during your childhood. The event is hidden deep in your subconscious to protect you from the pain it causes. It also is the cause of your germaphobia. It is very important to find out what happened that gave you the germaphobia. Your germaphobia will get much worse as you get older. Patricia, you need to be hypnotized to find out what happened. If you allow yourself to be hypnotized, I can help you."

Patricia didn't like Dr. Reggie's advice but would allow herself to be hypnotized. She loved Michael and didn't want to lose him. Dr. Reggie told Patricia that she must be patient because it took years to develop germaphobia. It'll take several months or longer to cure her.

Dr. Reggie Neale explained to Michael and Wally why Patricia needed to be hypnotized. He told everyone that he would book an appointment for Patricia to see a hypnotherapist next week. Wally had a big smile on his face. "Dr. Neale, some of the naturopaths are hypnotherapists. I happen to be one of them."

Dr. Reggie smiled. "Wally, let's get Patricia hypnotized. Sorry, Michael, you are not allowed to attend. There are a lot of books and magazines for you to read. I will also have coffee and donuts brought to you while you wait."

Wally followed Dr. Reggie and Patricia into the next room. He put Patricia in a hypnotic trance. She was able to recall her traumatic event. When Patricia was eight years old, she and her parents lived in an apartment behind a Chinese restaurant. The entrance to the apartment was in the back of the restaurant. They had to tolerate the bad smell from the garbage cans. One day, Patricia tripped and knocked over a garbage can. She fell down, and an army of maggots from the garbage can crawled all over her. Patricia started screaming. Her parents came out of the apartment. They rolled Patricia in a rug and carried her inside.

Patricia was placed in a tub. Her parents removed the rug and all her clothes. They turned on the water and scrubbed all of the maggots off her. Patricia came out of the tub crying. Although Patricia had no maggots crawling all over her body, she could still feel them crawling all over her. It took almost two years before Patricia no longer felt the maggots crawling all over her.

Dr. Reggie finished writing his notes. "Wally, thanks to you, we know what caused Patricia's germaphobia. She can be cured, but it will take several months or longer. Dr. Reggie scheduled another appointment next week for Patricia and Michael."

Chapter 61

Elizabeth was at home sitting beside Daniel and Sarah. They were asleep. Elizabeth was happily reading a book. The doorbell rang. Elizabeth received an unexpected visitor. Christine Kelly entered, holding a dozen roses and two cute little teddy bears. Christine looked at Elizabeth and smiled. "Elizabeth, I came here because I wanted to know how Wally is treating you."

Elizabeth took the roses, put them in a vase and filled it with water. "Wally takes really good care of us, but he sometimes does stupid things and asks stupid questions to upset me."

Christine laughed. "Elizabeth, you are the daughter that I wish I had. Let me tell you that all men drive their wives crazy sometimes by doing stupid things or asking stupid questions. Get used to it. Now, please show me your twins." Elizabeth led Christine to the bedroom.

Christine put a teddy bear in each crib for Daniel and Sarah. They were asleep. "Elizabeth, Daniel and Sarah are beautiful. I'm so happy that you didn't marry Jeffrey. He takes after his father. Jeffrey would have made your life very miserable."

Cleo and Leo ran into the bedroom. They were hungry. Elizabeth said, "Christine, meet Cleo and Leo. It's time for their dinner. Would you like to stay for tea?" Christine was rubbing Cleo and Leo's ears. "I would love to." Elizabeth led Christine to the den. Purdy and Charlie were sleeping in Purdy's bed. Christine couldn't believe what she just saw. Purdy was sleeping in her bed. Charlie the chipmunk was sleeping underneath Purdy's tummy.

Elizabeth smiled. "Christine, Charlie the chipmunk and Purdy the cat are Wally's pets. Those two are inseparable. They prowl the neighbourhood together and sleep together. Wally also has a pet skunk called Orval and a pet owl called Howard. All of Wally's pets watch Sunday afternoon football with Wally. Mother and Aunt Judy are coming over to watch Sunday afternoon football with Wally and his pets. You're welcome to come."

Wally arrived home from the office just in time for tea. He decided to take Cleo, Leo and Orval for a walk on the trails. He skipped having tea. When Wally came back from his walk, Christine was gone. Elizabeth gave Wally a kiss. "Wally, Christine is coming this Sunday afternoon to watch football with you and your pets. Better order another pizza."

Chapter 62

Uncle Pavlo and Uncle Gregory reserved a room at the Spencers Mill. They invited Wally and Elizabeth to join them for dinner. Elizabeth refused to go. Wally went by himself. Uncle Ivan led Wally to a private room. Uncle Ivan brought a bottle of wine for them. Wally got a hug from both of his uncles. Uncle Pavlo said. "Wally, your uncle Gregory has colon cancer. He has less than a year to live. We are going back home to our village. Our parents are still living there. The Chinese triad gave us permission to leave. Wally, if you ever need to use my services, get in touch with my son Sergei. He is taking over my business. I'll text you his number later."

Uncle Gregory pulled out a briefcase from under the table. He placed it in front of Wally and said,

"Wally, this briefcase contains far more information about the Chinese triad than I gave to the FBI to be in the witness protection program. I want you to give this briefcase to Don Jordan." Wally took the briefcase. He was puzzled. "Uncle Gregory, why are you giving me this briefcase?"

Uncle Pavlo smiled, "I was devastated when the Chinese triad forced me to kill Danelo and your mother. Consider this briefcase as revenge." Wally was still puzzled. "Why did you both decide to go back home?"

Uncle Pavlo smiled." Besides our parents, I have a daughter. She has two boys and a girl. I want to see them. My wife and Gregory's wife disowned us when we joined the Russian army. They didn't realize that if we didn't join, our families would be sent to Siberia. Your uncle Gregory decided that it was better to die peacefully surrounded by family than me putting a bullet in his head."

Wally was happy for his uncles. He asked them if they had any plans when they got home. Uncle Gregory smiled. "Wally, we will be financing the building of a new school, which will have a gymnasium and a swimming pool. We are also going to finance a new sewage system for the village. Our village will finally have indoor plumbing. The village concert hall will also be renovated."

Wally decided to have a going away party for his uncles at his home. They were happy to have a party because they wanted to meet Elizabeth, Daniel and Sarah. They didn't get a chance to meet Elizabeth during the wedding. Wally said goodbye to his uncles and went to see Uncle Ivan. He wanted to invite him and Aunt Lydia to the going away party. Wally then called Jordan to let him know that he had a briefcase waiting for him, courtesy of his uncles. Don showed up at the Spencers Mill 15 minutes later to pick up the briefcase. He thanked Wally for the briefcase and the invitation to his uncle's going away party.

Wally went home to tell Elizabeth about his plans to have a going away party for his uncles. She was not happy. Grandmother told Elizabeth that Wally's uncles were involved with the triad just like Danelo.

"Wally, your uncles are criminals. Why do you want to throw a going away party for them?" Wally told Elizabeth that they are family. This will be the last time that he'll ever see them again.

Elizabeth unhappily said, "Wally, you can have your go-away party for your uncle's next Saturday afternoon. Howard, Orval and Charlie are not invited." Wally gave Elizabeth a big kiss. She went downstairs to see his grandparents. He was happy to have them live in his house. Grandfather took over from Wally to be Elizabeth's personal trainer and yoga instructor. His grandparents did all the gardening in the backyard because he was too busy to do any gardening himself.

Wally's grandparents were happy to hear that Uncle Pavlo and Uncle Gregory were flying back home. Wally mentioned to them the going away party he planned for his uncles at his house next Saturday afternoon. He also let them know that Uncle Gregory was dying from colon cancer. Wally called Aunt Lydia to let her know about the party.

Chapter 63

Wally was in a happy mood. He fed Cleo, Leo and Orval and then took them for a walk in the forest trails. After the walk, Wally was tired and decided to take a nap. It was hot, so he placed a lounge chair under an oak tree in the backyard. Wally laid down in the lounge chair and soon fell asleep.

Cleo and Leo jumped on Wally's stomach and fell asleep. Purdy jumped on his chest. Charlie nestled under Wally's chin. Orval decided to join them. He jumped on Wally's chest beside Purdy. A few minutes later, Howard landed on Wally's head. Wally and all the pets were sleeping.

Elizabeth was watching. She walked out smiling with her phone. Elizabeth took a picture of them sleeping. She wanted revenge. Elizabeth entered the picture in the amateur photography contest. The caption that she chose was Sleeping Beauties.

Wally woke up, and his pets jumped off and ran away. He went inside the house to take a shower. Elizabeth wanted to go out for dinner at the Spencers Mill. Grandmother came up the stairs to look after Daniel and Sarah. Wally asked Elizabeth why she always chooses to go to the Spencers Mill for dinner. Elizabeth smiled and told Wally that the food served there was so good, the atmosphere was so nice, and it only took a few minutes to walk from home.

Wally said, "Elizabeth, didn't you tell me that Uncle Ivan is a royal pain?" Elizabeth smacked her lips. "Wally, Uncle Ivan doesn't bother me anymore. He grows on you once you get to know him, and I adore Aunt Lydia."

Wally and Elizabeth ordered head cheese, perogies and Caesar salad. They quietly ate their dinner. Elizabeth went back to the kitchen. She wanted to thank Aunt Lydia and Uncle Ivan for a wonderful meal before she and Wally walked home.

Wally decided to drive back to his office to pick up some paperwork to work at home. Elizabeth came along for the ride. The block before he reached his office, Wally noticed a police car flashing its lights. Wally pulled over. Officer Janet Wilson walked over to Wally's car. Wally could tell by the way she walked and the look on her face that she was stressed out. Janet Wilson was 6 feet tall, with blonde hair and blue eyes. Her figure was well-proportioned with muscle. Officer Janet asked Wally for his driver's license and insurance. Wally handed her his license and insurance. He was able to touch her hand.

By reading her mind, Wally found out that three years ago, she applied to the FBI and got accepted. She decided not to become an FBI agent because of pressure from her parents. They wanted her to become a police officer just like her fiancé, John Wilson. John's parents owned a pharmaceutical company and were prominent in the community.

When John and Janet were married, his parents bought them a beautiful house. Shortly after the wedding, John began to drink heavily because of the stress of being a police officer. He became abusive both physically and verbally. Janet's parents told her to tolerate John's abusive behaviour. One day, John became so abusive that Janet ended up in the hospital with a broken collar bone. Her parents discouraged her from pressing charges against him.

Janet decided that she had enough of John's abusive behaviour. When John came home from drinking one night, he attacked Janet. She took out her gun to warn him to stay away. He refused to stay away. Janet shot John in the head. It was reported that a break-and-entry intruder killed John and escaped. John's parents never forgave Janet for killing their son. Janet's parents disowned her. She sold her house and gave the money from the sale of the house back to John's parents. Janet moved into an apartment.

Wally took a good look at Officer Janet Wilson. "Officer, you look very stressed out. If you want to talk about your problems, my wife is a good listener." Wally got out of his car and walked across the street to a coffee shop. Officer Janet got in and started to talk. Elizabeth sat quietly, listening to her. After an hour of talking and Elizabeth quietly listening, Officer Janet felt much better. She thanked Elizabeth for listening to her problems and said goodbye. Wally walked back to his car. He saw Elizabeth looking stressed out. Wally went to his office to get his briefcase. Elizabeth started to cry. She realized how lucky she was to be married to Wally.

When they arrived home, Wally called Don Jordan and told him what happened to Janet Wilson. He wanted Don to help Janet to become an FBI agent. Don said, "Wally, I'll see what I can do for her. Janet's application should still be on file if she is accepted by the FBI. Janet should have no problem getting in as long as she passes the psych evaluation test." Wally told Don that Janet's maiden name was Howard and thanked him.

Don went to the FBI files to look up Janet's application. The application showed that she passed all the required tests and had the potential to be a very good FBI agent. Don Jordan picked up the phone to call Janet Wilson. The telephone number on her application is still the same one that she uses now.

Don introduced himself to Janet. He said, "Wally Kozak, the person you pulled over this afternoon, called me and told me that you wanted to become an FBI agent. I looked up your application. It shows that you have the potential to become a very good agent. If you are still interested, I can arrange for you to have a psych evaluation test tomorrow morning. If you pass it, you begin training right away."

Janet said with tears in her eyes, "Mr. Jordan, thank you so much. You don't know how much this means to me!" Don replied, "We should both thank Wally Kozak. The FBI is always looking for good agents." Don called Wally to let him know about Janet. He thanked Wally for calling him. Wally was happy to hear that Janet Wilson would become an FBI agent. He was very confident that Janet would pass her psych evaluation test.

Chapter 64

It was Saturday morning, and Wally was preparing a buffet for his uncle's going away party. The guest list became larger than expected. That is why he decided on a buffet. Grandmother invited Dr. Reggie. Elizabeth invited her mother, Aunt Judy and Christine Kelly. Wally invited Don Jordan, Donna, Thomas and Samantha. Aunt Lydia and Uncle Ivan showed up early to help Wally. They brought lasagna, pizza and wine. Wally's menu included perogies, cabbage rolls, bean salad, broccoli salad and breaded chicken breasts. The three of them spent all morning preparing the buffet.

Around noon, guests were starting to arrive. Elizabeth was with Daniel and Sarah in the bedroom; they were asleep. Wally quietly led the guests into the bedroom to see Daniel and Sarah. Uncle Gregory smiled. "Wally, I'm so happy that you have such a wonderful family. Daniel and Sarah are beautiful." Uncle Pavlo was also happy to see Wally's family. Elizabeth was very polite when Wally introduced his uncles to her.

Everyone helped themselves to the buffet. Don kept Uncle Pavlo and Uncle Gregory's company. The three of them went outside to the patio to have some privacy. Don thanked Gregory and Pavlo for the briefcase. Cleo, Leo and Orval showed up. The moochers were hungry. Don, Uncle Pavlo and Uncle Gregory were happy to feed them. Purdy and Charlie were asleep downstairs. Wally placed some sunflower seeds and cat food for them.

Elizabeth sat with her mother, Aunt Judy and Christine Kelly. Wally sat with Samantha, Donna and Thomas. Wally's grandparents sat with Aunt Lydia and Uncle Ivan. Dr. Reggie sat by himself, observing everyone and making notes. Dr. Reggie walked over to Wally's grandparents. "What a wonderful family you have. I'm glad to see that everyone is healthy and happy. Thank you for inviting me to the going away party."

Grandmother said to Dr. Reggie, "We are happy to have you at our party. Did you have a chance to meet Pavlo and Gregory, the guests of honour?" Dr. Reggie told her that he didn't. Grandmother led Dr. Reggie to the back patio. She introduced Dr. Reggie to Pavlo, Gregory and Don.

Pavlo told Dr. Reggie that he and Gregory are retired businessmen and Don is a good friend. Gregory mentioned to Dr. Reggie that he had terminal colon cancer and wanted to go back home to die.

Don was happy to meet Dr. Reggie. He didn't tell him that Pavlo and Gregory were involved in the drug trade because he was a psychiatrist and a friend of the family. Dr. Reggie enjoyed their company. Wally came to say hello to his uncles. Don told Wally that Janet had passed her psych evaluation test. Wally was happy that she did.

Dr. Reggie asked Wally where all his pets were. He doesn't see any of them. Wally said. "Elizabeth didn't want to invite them to the party. She believes that all wild animals are dangerous. Let's go look for them." Wally led Dr. Reggie downstairs to the basement where Purdy and Charlie were sleeping. Dr. Reggie laughed. "They look so adorable together. Can I take a picture of them?" Wally told Dr. Reggie that he could take all the pictures he wanted.

Wally led Dr. Reggie out into the trails. "Dr. Reggie, Cleo, Leo and Orval are running around here somewhere; let's look for them." Wally and Dr. Reggie found the three of them sleeping in a hollow trunk of a tree. Howard flew by and landed on Wally's shoulder. Dr. Reggie couldn't believe what he just saw. He took a picture of Howard perched on Wally's shoulder. Then he took another picture of Orval, Cleo and Leo sleeping.

Dr. Reggie was amazed. "Wally, I met a lot of animal lovers. You are the only person that I met that the animals loved you back. I know that dogs and cats are loving animals, but they don't live in the woods. You are a very special person." Dr. Reggie then took a lot more pictures.

Everyone had a good time at the party. They thanked Wally and Elizabeth for inviting them. Uncle Pavlo and Uncle Gregory gave Wally and Elizabeth a goodbye hug. Dr. Reggie stayed behind, making notes. Wally was tired and decided to relax by watching college football on the television. Soon, all his pets showed up. There were plenty of leftovers for them. Dr. Reggie took a picture of Wally and his pets. Elizabeth also decided to take a picture of Wally and his pets watching college football on television. She was going to enter the picture in the amateur photography contest. The title she chose was Sunday Afternoon Football with the Family.

Dr. Reggie asked Wally, "I'm taking notes and pictures. I want to use them for a book that I am writing. Do I have your permission to use them for my book?" Wally gave Dr. Reggie permission. He thanked Wally and said goodbye.

Chapter 65

Elizabeth was excited. She went to get the mail. Today was when she would find out if her picture of Sleeping Beauties won the amateur photography contest. Elizabeth opened the mailbox and found the photography magazine. The cover showed a picture of Wally and his pets sleeping, along with a cheque for $10,000. Elizabeth could hardly wait to see the look on Wally's face when he saw the magazine cover.

Wally was very busy and tired. He called Aunt Lydia to prepare something for him to take home. When Wally arrived at the Spencers Mill, Aunt Lydia had lasagna and bean salad waiting for him. She told Wally that Uncle Gregory had very little time left to live; he was very weak. "Wally, Uncle Gregory wants to see you before he dies. He also wants you to be a pallbearer at his funeral. You should go to see him soon."

Wally told Aunt Lydia that he would be flying to the village to see Uncle Gregory in two weeks. He thanked her for the lasagna and bean salad.

Wally brought dinner into the kitchen. Elizabeth was waiting for him. She was excited. Wally saw Elizabeth holding the photography magazine. Elizabeth smiled and told Wally that she had a surprise for him. She gave Wally the magazine. He looked at the cover of the magazine and smiled. Wally then gave Elizabeth a big hug and a kiss. "Congratulations, sweetheart. I'm proud of you."

Elizabeth was very disappointed. She couldn't believe how Wally reacted. Elizabeth took a good look at Wally and shook her head. "Wally, why aren't you angry at me!" Wally gave Elizabeth a hug. "Elizabeth, why should I be angry at you? I love this picture. I'm going to have this picture enlarged, framed and have it hung up in my office."

Elizabeth grabbed the magazine from Wally and ran downstairs to see Grandmother. She handed her the magazine and said, "Grandmother, Wally is driving me crazy again. He is not angry at me for entering this picture in an amateur photography contest. I won first prize. Wally is proud of me. He wants to enlarge this picture, frame it and hang it up in his office."

Grandmother started to laugh. "I like this picture. Tell Wally that I want a copy of this picture enlarged." Elizabeth couldn't believe what grandmother just said. "Grandmother, I took this picture without Wally's knowledge. He didn't know that I entered it in the amateur photography contest. He should be angry with me!"

Grandmother hugged Elizabeth. "Wally has no reason to be angry with you. You have every right to get your revenge. Take a good look at this picture. Aren't Wally and his pets adorable?"

Elizabeth took a good look at the picture and agreed with his grandmother. She said goodbye and went upstairs to see you, Wally. He was gone with Cleo, Leo and Orval for a walk in the forest trails. When Wally returned from his walk, he sat down and had dinner with Elizabeth.

During dinner, Wally told Elizabeth that Uncle Gregory had very little time to live. "Uncle Gregory wants to see me before he dies. He also wants me to be a pallbearer at his funeral." Elizabeth saw the look on Wally's face to know that he was going to see Uncle Gregory before he died. She knew that there was nothing she could do to stop him from going.

Elizabeth wasn't happy. "Wally, your uncle Gregory is a terrible person. How could you even think of going to see him?" Wally shook his head. "My uncle Gregory is a good man. He just chose the wrong profession and is paying the price. I have already booked a flight to the Ukrainian Village. I leave in two weeks."

Two weeks later, Wally's plane landed in Lviv. Uncle Pavlo was waiting for him. He was happy to see Wally. Uncle Pavlo gave Wally a big hug and drove him back to the village. He told Wally that Uncle Gregory would be very happy to see him. He only has a few days to live.

Uncle Gregory was lying in bed waiting for Wally. He was very weak. When he saw Wally, he managed to smile. "Wally, I'm so happy that you came. Thank you for allowing me to see your wonderful family. You have beautiful children."

Uncle Gregory gave Wally a bank card. It had Wally's name on it. He said to Wally, "Your brother Tommy was a very rich man. He inherited a fortune from Danelo. Tommy kept it in a Swiss bank account. Tommy asked me to give you access to his Swiss bank account if anything happens to him. That bank card will allow you to transfer money from Tommy's bank account to your personal bank account. There is over $100,000,000 in it. Tommy knows that you will use his money wisely. Wally, my advice to you is that you tell no one, not even Elizabeth." Wally was shocked. He couldn't believe that Tommy had so much money. Wally assured Uncle Gregory that he would tell no one.

Wally smiled at Uncle Gregory and said, "Shouldn't this money be used to help finance the new school and village sewage treatment?" Uncle Gregory smiled, "Wally, Uncle Pavlo, and I also have a fortune in a Swiss bank account. We don't need any financial help from you. Wally, I will die in a few days. It would be an honour for me if you would be one of my pallbearers at my funeral."

Wally told Uncle Gregory that the reason he came to see him was to be a pallbearer at his funeral. Uncle Gregory smiled and shook Wally's hand before he fell asleep. Uncle Pavlo showed up with a bottle of brandy to have a toast for Uncle Gregory.

Uncle Pavlo introduced Wally to his daughter Natalie, her husband John and their three children. Wally stayed at cousin Peter's home. Wally saw a new school being built. It was almost completed. The school will have an Olympic-sized swimming pool. He noticed that Peter's home had indoor plumbing. The rest of the village will soon have indoor plumbing. He saw the concert hall being renovated.

Uncle Gregory died four days later. He was 65 years old. Wally, Uncle Pavlo, Peter and John were the pallbearers. Wally didn't expect to see so many people at Uncle Gregory's funeral. Two days later, Wally flew back home. Elizabeth was waiting for him at the airport.

Chapter 66

Wally was busy in his office. Elizabeth paid him a surprise visit. "Aunt Judy is looking after Daniel and Sarah. My friend Katie is a fashion designer. She invited us to go to a fashion show next week. I want to go. I need a break from motherhood." Wally gave Elizabeth a kiss. "I guess you want to buy a new dress and have your hair done." Elizabeth smiled. "Wally, you are always reading my mind. How do you do that?"

Wally laughed, "Elizabeth, I don't have to be a mind reader to know what you are thinking. All women want to get their hair done and buy a new dress when they plan to go out. Now, let's go see Aunt Lydia, it's lunchtime." Elizabeth was excited. "Wally, I already have a luncheon date with Katie. Can we invite her to lunch?"

Elizabeth didn't wait for Wally to answer. She called Katie to meet her and Wally at the Spencers Mill for lunch. Uncle Ivan was happy to see Elizabeth and Wally. He had a table reserved for them. A few minutes later, Katie showed up. She was tall and slim and wore a stunning blue dress and red shoes. She had long, black, wavy hair and brown eyes. Katie looked like a model. Wally thought she was attractive but a little malnourished, just like all models.

Elizabeth introduced Katie to Wally. He shook her hand and found out that she was well respected in the fashion industry. Katie also had her own modelling school and was a fashion designer. Katie was full of energy, and Wally liked her. For lunch, Aunt Lydia served perogies, pizza, bean salad and Caesar salad.

Katie said, "Elizabeth, I have great news. We are going to sit in the front row at the fashion show. That row is reserved for fashion designers. Louis Vintage will be showing off his new collection."

Elizabeth got all excited. Wally was not excited at all. He had no interest in the fashion industry. Katie told Elizabeth and Wally to meet her at her modelling school. She arranged for a limousine to drive them to the fashion show. Katie thanked Elizabeth and Wally for a wonderful lunch.

Elizabeth was disappointed. "Wally, you should be excited; we are going to be driven in a limousine to a fashion show!" Wally grumbled." Limousines and fashion shows don't excite me." Uncle Ivan showed up and asked how lunch was.

Elizabeth pouted. "Lunch was wonderful. The problem is Wally was not so wonderful. We are going to be driven in a limousine to a fashion show, and he is not excited."

Uncle Ivan wasn't excited either. "Wally is not excited because he was helping us at the restaurant and his mother at her clinic while he was growing up." Wally looked at a dejected Elizabeth and said, "Don't worry, sweetheart. I'm sure the both of us will have a great time at the fashion show."

Wally drove Elizabeth to a shopping plaza. He knew that Elizabeth would spend the rest of the day shopping for a new dress. Elizabeth was disappointed because Wally didn't want to help her choose a dress for the fashion show. Wally doesn't like to shop. Whenever Wally needs to buy clothes, he lets Elizabeth choose the clothes for him.

On the day of the fashion show, Elizabeth put on her new dress and drove to her hairdresser. She didn't want to walk. It looked like it might rain. Elizabeth told Sally, her hairdresser, how excited she was to be driven by a limousine to a fashion show.

Sally was envious and said, "Is Wally excited as much as you are about going to a fashion show in a limousine?" Elizabeth laughed. "Wally has no interest in limousines and fashion shows. He's more interested in preparing meals and taking care of our children and pets."

Elizabeth's hair was done. She looked in the mirror. Sally whistled. "Wally will be paying more attention to you than the models at the fashion show." Elizabeth gave Sally a big hug.

Wally showed up to pick up Elizabeth. When he saw her, Wally took out his phone and took a picture of her. Wally gave Sally a hug and a huge tip for making Elizabeth look so beautiful.

Wally and Elizabeth drove off to Katie's modelling school. Katie was waiting for them inside the limousine. She was looking forward to seeing Louis Vintage's new clothing line. The limousine arrived at the fashion show. Katie, Wally and Elizabeth were escorted to their seats by an usher. Wally didn't know that Louis Vintage was seated next to him. The fashion show started. Wally couldn't figure out who would buy the clothes that the models were wearing. Some of the models look good wearing the clothes. However, Wally thought that these clothes were suitable only for malnourished models, not the average full-bodied woman.

Louis Vintage was the last fashion designer to show off his clothing line. Wally laughed when he saw one of the models wearing a hat that looked like a lampshade. Wally laughed at most of Louis Vintage's clothing line. Wally was surprised that the audience applauded the Louis Vintage collection. He said to Elizabeth, "Any woman who buys any of his clothes has to be drunk or high on drugs." Louis heard Wally. He was very upset. Poor Wally didn't know that he insulted Louis Vintage. Louise is going to make Wally pay for insulting him.

At the end of the fashion show, Elizabeth asked Katie what she thought of Louis Vintage's collection. Katie said, "I was very disappointed with his collection. I don't believe that he will have a good year." Elizabeth and Wally thanked Katie for inviting them to the fashion show. The three of them got into the limousine and were driven back to Katie's modelling school. Wally and Elizabeth said good night to Katie and drove home.

On the way home, Wally asked Elizabeth if there were any clothes that she would be interested in buying that she saw at the fashion show. Elizabeth smiled. "Wally, I didn't like any of the clothes that the models wore, but I did enjoy the fashion show."

Wally didn't realize that the clothes at the fashion show are art and used to show off the designer's creativity. The designer then creates a wearable clothing line based on their creation for stores or rich people. The designer who wins the competition receives $1,000,000.

Grandmother was waiting for them at home. She said that Daniel and Sarah were angels. They slept most of the day. Grandfather took care of the pets. "Did you enjoy the fashion show?" Elizabeth told Grandmother that she and Wally had a wonderful time and said good night.

Louis Vintage checked the fashion designer's guest list and found out who Wally was and where he worked. He decided to pay Wally a visit.

Louis showed up at Wally's office and demanded to see him. Donna buzzed Wally to let him know that Louis Vintage was outside, demanding to see him. Wally told Donna to let him in. Louis walked in and immediately said, "I heard what you said about my collection last night. You have no clue what the fashion industry is about. I want you to apologize on social media!"

Wally looked up at Louis and said, "I am not going to apologize. No woman in her right mind would wear any of your clothes!" Louis gave Wally a dopey look. "Do you think you can do better?" Wally replied. "Anyone with any intelligence can do better."

Louis smiled and rubbed his hands together. "Wally, you are going to have an opportunity to do better than me. I entered you into next year's fashion show on your behalf. You have a whole year to prepare. You better show up. If you don't show up, the fashion show organizers will sue you for millions of dollars in damages."

Wally looked puzzled. "I didn't give you permission to enter me in the fashion show. What gives you authority?" Louis started to giggle. "Wally, you sat in the fashion designer's box. Any fashion designer can enter another fashion designer on their behalf if the fashion designer sits in a fashion designer's box at the fashion show. Good luck, sucker." Louis happily waved goodbye to Wally and left.

Wally called Elizabeth and told her what Louis did. He then drove home to pick her up. It was good that Elizabeth's mother came to visit. She will look after Daniel and Sarah. Wally and Elizabeth drove off to see Katie at her modelling school. They found Katie alone in her office.

Elizabeth told Katie what Louis did. Katie couldn't believe that Louis would do such a thing. She looked at Wally and said, "What Louis did has never been done before. Wally, you should have apologized to Louis. Sitting in the designer's box makes you a fashion designer. Louis or any other fashion designer has the authority to enter you in next year's fashion show. Wally you better show up and present a clothing line. If you don't, you will have to deal with a multi-million-dollar lawsuit against you from the fashion show organizers."

Elizabeth fainted. Wally suddenly realized that he should have apologized to Louis on social media. Wally was concerned. He asked Katie what he needed to do to put on a fashion show.

Katie became excited. Wally, first, you need to come up with a unique, unforgettable name for your clothing line. Your name doesn't qualify. The name has to be registered. It will cost you $5,000. Next, you need a theme for your clothing line. Then you have to develop and manufacture your clothing line."

Katie picked up a picture of a pink elephant and said, "Wally, take a good look at this picture and tell me the first word that enters your mind." Wally took a good look at the picture and said, "Smedley." Katie picked up another picture of a kitten wearing huge glasses and said, "Wally, again, look at this picture and tell me the first word that enters your mind." Wally took a good look at the picture and said, "Googlepus."

Katie became very excited. "Wally, your new clothing line will be called the Smedley Googlepus collection. For $5,000, I can register the name for you today."

Wally placed his hand on Katie's forehead. He wanted to make sure that Katie wasn't joking or lost her mind. Wally couldn't believe that Katie was sane and serious. "Katie, that is the stupidest name that I ever heard." Katie smiled. "Wally, trust me. The name is awesome; it's unique and unforgettable."

Wally thought that the name was still very stupid. However, he had no choice but to trust Katie. He took out a cheque book and wrote out a cheque for $5,000 to Katie. She happily took the check. "Wally, we need to come up with a theme for your clothing line. Do you have anything in mine?"

Wally closed his eyes and took a deep breath. A minute later, he said, "How about Clothes for the Common People?" Katy became excited and said, "The other designers created outrageous clothing to show off their creativity. Their theme had nothing to do with the clothing that they designed. No one in the audience would be interested in buying the clothes that they designed. Wally, your theme was perfect for your clothing line. People in the audience would be interested in buying Smedley Googlepus clothes. Your theme will impress the judges. That is why I believe that you will win the competition. What material would you want to use to make your clothes?" Wally closed his eyes and took a deep breath. He took another minute and said, "How about hemp."

Katie was really becoming excited. "Wally hemp is an awesome choice. I know a hemp material manufacturing company in Regina, Canada. You can buy hemp material from them. You're also in luck. My brother and I just bought the old building next to my modelling school. We are going to start a clothing manufacturing company. It'll be ready in time for you to be my first customer."

Wally was overwhelmed. "Katie, how do I go about designing my clothing line?" Katie smiled, "Wally, we need to hire a photographer. He'll take pictures of people every day for a week. We would then look at these pictures to see what people are wearing every day. From these pictures, we can choose a style and decide on the colour of the clothes that we want."

Wally, still bewildered, said, "Katie, is there anything else that I should know?" Katie kept smiling. "Elizabeth told me that you have two little teacup Yorkies. They should be included in the fashion show. It's too bad that your cat, Purdy, doesn't have a sister.

Wally couldn't believe what he was about to say. "Katie, Purdy does have a sister. I know the owner. I'm sure that he would allow his cat to be in the fashion show. She looks just like Purdy".

Katie jumped with excitement. "Wally, that is so awesome. Can you get other animals!" Wally closed his eyes and took a deep breath. "I have a pet skunk called Orval, a pet chipmunk called Charlie and a pet owl called Howard." Katie was getting more excited." Wally, if you can get all your pets in the fashion show, the crowd will go crazy in a nice way!"

Wally placed his hand on Katie's forehead again to make sure that she was still sane and serious. "Katie, I can probably get all the pets to be in the fashion show except Howard. He will only perch on my shoulder."

Katie took a good look at Wally and said, "Wally, you are a tall and very handsome young man. You will make a great-looking model. You will be at the fashion show with Howard perched on your shoulder. "

Wally thanked Katie for her support. He asked her to hire a photographer. Katie said, "The photographer will cost you $5,000. However, there is a huge problem: to buy hemp material, I need $100,000."

Wally was shocked. "Katie, how much material do I need!" Katie smiled. "Wally, relax. You don't need that much material, but that is the hemp company's smallest order that they will accept. Don't worry, Wally, I'll buy the excess material from you. I will also need $50,000 to manufacture your clothing line. You better have deep pockets if you want to showcase a clothing line at the fashion show."

Wally was still shocked. "Katie, why so much? I can get clothes at Walmart for $10." Katie was disgusted. "Wally labour is not cheap. My clothing manufacturing company is not a sweatshop. I will hire legal American citizens. Walmart clothing will fall apart if you sneeze!"

Wally couldn't believe what he was about to do. He wrote out a cheque for $155,000. Katie happily took Wally's cheque." Elizabeth finally recovered from fainting. Katie told her not to worry. "Wally will put on an awesome collection at the fashion show. Wally was born to be a fashion designer."

Elizabeth looked very worried and said, "Wally, are you sure that you want to go through with the fashion show?" Wally shrugged his shoulders. "Elizabeth, you heard Katie. Do you want me to face a multimillion-dollar lawsuit.?" Elizabeth was too worried to say anything on their way home.

Chapter 67

Wally and Elizabeth decided not to tell anyone about the fashion show. When they got home, Cleo and Leo came running. Wally was ready to take them for a walk. He found Orval sleeping under a chair on the patio. Wally asked Elizabeth to go with him for a walk. He told her that Orval won't be coming because he's asleep. Elizabeth was happy to go with Wally, Cleo and Leo. Daniel and Sarah were asleep and Christine was looking after them.

Elizabeth asked Wally, "I never see you take that side of the trail. Why don't you ever go there?" Wally replied. "That trail takes you to a house that is behind the parquet. I took that trail with Cleo and Leo once. When we reached that house, Cleo and Leo started to bark like crazy. Don told me that the house belonged to the military. What they do there is classified."

When Wally and Elizabeth got back from their walk, Elizabeth took Cleo and Leo into the house. Orval was waiting for Wally to take him for a walk. Elizabeth put the kettle on to have tea with Christine.

Wally walked into Lawrence's office. He said, "Lawrence, I want to borrow Purdy's sister. Elizabeth's friend Katie wants her to participate in a fashion show for next year." Lawrence hesitated and then said, "Wally, if you want my Jenny to be in your fashion show, I have to be with her."

Wally replied. "Lawrence, that's okay with me as long as you behave. Just promise me that you won't tell anyone about the fashion show." Lawrence asked Wally who was putting on the show. Wally had to tell Lawrence that he was putting on the fashion show. Wally didn't tell Lawrence why he was putting on the fashion show. Lawrence promised Wally that he would not tell anyone about the fashion show.

Elizabeth forgot about the fashion show. She was excited because it was Daniel's and Sarah's first birthday next week. It will also mean the end of her maternity leave. Elizabeth went to the kitchen where Wally was preparing dinner. She told Wally that Daniel and Sarah have a birthday next week. "What shall we do for them?" Wally told Elizabeth that he asked Aunt Lydia to plan a birthday party for them. "Elizabeth, you can invite whoever you want."

Elizabeth smiled." Wally next week is also the end of my maternity leave. Who is going to look after Daniel and Sarah when I go back to work?" Wally gave Elizabeth a kiss." Don't worry, your mother, aunt Judy and Christine Bell volunteered to take a day off to look after them. Our grandparents, aunt Lydia and uncle Ivan will look after them for the other two days. We will have time to go home for lunch to see them."

Elizabeth was happy. She went to make an invitation list for the party. The grandparents, aunt Lydia and Uncle Ivan, didn't need to be on the list. Elizabeth invited her mother, aunt Judy, Christine Bell, Christine Kelly, Samantha, Donna, Thomas, Patricia, Michael, Katie and Lawrence. Grandmother invited Dr. Reggie to the birthday party.

The birthday party was on a Sunday afternoon. Aunt Lydia and Uncle Ivan spent all morning in Wally's kitchen preparing for the party. They decided on having a buffet. There were perogies, lasagna, cabbage rolls and turkey meatballs. For dessert, there were various nuts and pastries served with coffee or tea. It was 11:30; the guest arrived bearing gifts. Wally had no idea what kind of gifts one-year-olds receive on their birthday. He was glad to see no stuffed animals. They are dust magnets.

Everyone was having a good time. Daniel and Sarah were tired from chasing a ball with Cleo and Leo in the backyard. Elizabeth and Joan took them to the bedroom. They quickly fell asleep. Christine Bell gave Elizabeth a hug. "Your children are beautiful. I'm very happy that you had enough sense to marry Wally. Jeffery would make your life miserable."

Daniel and Sarah somehow managed to sleep throughout their entire birthday party. Elizabeth had to open their presents. Daniel and Sarah received lots of baby clothes and story books. Lawrence's present was a video of his cats playing. Dr. Reggie gave Daniel and Sarah each a music box.

Wally and Elizabeth thanked all the guests for coming. Most of the guests left. Samantha, Donna and Thomas stayed behind. They wanted to watch Sunday afternoon football with Wally and his pets. Wally plugged in the popcorn machine. Howard loves popcorn. He had peanuts for Orval and sunflower seeds for Charlie. There were doggie treats for Cleo and Leo and kitty treats for Purdy.

Wally turned on the television. A few minutes later, all the pets showed up. Howard landed on Wally's shoulder. Charlie jumped on Donna's shoulder. Purdy jumped on Thomas's lap. Samantha didn't expect Orval to jump on her lap. Cleo jumped on Wally's lap, and Leo jumped on Donna's lap. Elizabeth was in the bedroom with Daniel and Sarah. She doesn't like to watch football.

A week later, Wally received a call from Katie. "Wally, the pictures that the photographer took are ready to look at. Can you come to my modelling school to look at them this afternoon?" Wally told Katie that he would be there. When he arrived at Katie's modelling school, Katie had all the pictures spread out on her table. Wally never realized that so many fat people lived in New York.

Over half the pictures were discarded because the people in them were too obese. Fortunately, there were still a lot of pictures left. It took several afternoons of looking at the pictures before Wally, with Katie's help, decided on the style and colour for his clothing line.

Katie told Wally that she ordered a truckload of hemp material to be delivered to her manufacturing company. It'll arrive in two weeks. "Wally, by that time, my clothing manufacturing company will be ready for production. There is plenty of time. Wally, you need to take some modelling lessons. Meet me at my modelling school at lunch for lessons every day." Wally was not happy. He asked Katie if there were any more surprises for him. Katie told

Wally that he needed $10,000 to pay for the fashion judges. There was plenty of time to pay for it.

Katie looked at a sulking Wally. "I have some very good news for you. Wally, my modelling student, agreed to wear your clothes at the fashion show for free. Hiring professional models could cost hundreds of thousands of dollars." Wally thanked Katie and said goodbye.

Wally drove back to his office to tell Elizabeth the good news. Elizabeth got excited when Wally told her that he would be taking modelling lessons from Katie at lunchtime every day. "Wally, I'm coming with you to watch you take modelling lessons every day!" Wally had no interest in taking modelling lessons. He had Elizabeth promise that she wouldn't tell anyone that he was taking modelling lessons.

When Wally and Elizabeth got home, Elizabeth ran to see Grandmother. Wally took Cleo, Leo and Orval for a walk in the trails. Elizabeth blabbed everything to Grandmother. Grandmother laughed. "It sounds like Wally is ready to change careers."

Elizabeth smiled. "Grandmother, there is no chance of that happening. Wally has no interest in becoming a model or in the fashion industry. He will be happy when the fashion show is over. Please don't tell anyone."

Grandmother told Grandfather, Grandfather told uncle Ivan and uncle Ivan told aunt Lydia. They all were excited to hear that Wally was going to take modelling lessons for the fashion show.

Wally and Elizabeth arrived at Katie's modelling school. Elizabeth was looking forward to watching Wally take modelling lessons. Katie was waiting for them. She was smiling. Wally, none of the other fashion designers will be using hemp to make their clothes because they didn't want to spend the money to buy hemp. Hemp will make your collection unique. It'll impress the judges. Having your pets in the fashion show will get you a standing ovation from the audience." Elizabeth sat quietly, watching Wally take the modelling instructions from Katie.

Wally walked into his office with a heavy briefcase. He was falling behind in his paperwork. The fashion show is taking too much of his time. Samantha barged into Wally's office. "Lawrence tells me that you are going to showcase a clothing line at a fashion show." Wally was very upset."

Lawrence promised me that he wouldn't tell anyone about the fashion show. "Yes, I'm going to showcase a clothing line at the fashion show. No, I will not become a fashion designer. I have no interest in the fashion industry. I know nothing about the fashion industry. Elizabeth's friend Katie is helping. She owns a modelling school."

Wally then explained to Samantha what happened. Samantha started to laugh. "Wally, Elizabeth is right. Every time you do or say something stupid, you get into trouble. Good luck with the fashion show, and make sure that I get an invitation."

Wally was really upset; he went to see Lawrence in his office. "Lawrence, you promised me that you would not tell anyone about the fashion show!" Lawrence was holding Jenny in his arms. "Wally, I thought Samantha knew about the fashion show. She is the only person that I told." Wally said nothing. He went back to his office to do his paperwork. Elizabeth walked into Wally's office. "It's time to see Katie, Wally, let's go."

Wally and Elizabeth drove off to see Katie. Elizabeth was enjoying watching Wally taking modelling lessons. She took several pictures of him. Katie was very pleased with Wally's progress. She smiled and said, "Wally, you are a natural-born model. I can make you into a supermodel. Elizabeth, how would you like to be married to a supermodel?"

Elizabeth shook her head. "Katie, there's no way that I would allow Wally to become a supermodel. I would have to fight off all the girls that would come after him." Wally thanked Katie for the lesson and left for home with Elizabeth.

Grandmother was waiting for them. Elizabeth wanted to ask Grandmother how Daniel and Sarah were behaving. Grandmother told Elizabeth that Daniel and Sarah were two little angels. Wally smiled.

"Grandmother, next year, Daniel and Sarah will be two years old. Do you think that they will still be two little angels?"

Grandmother laughed. "Wally, they will still be two little angels with a lot more energy." Elizabeth went to the bedroom to see her little angels. Wally took Cleo, Leo, and Orval for a walk in the trails.

Wally and Elizabeth drove off to see Katie. She told Wally that his clothing line looked awesome. By the end of the week, production of Wally's clothing line will start. At the end of the modelling session, Wally was tired. He let Elizabeth drive. On their way home Elizabeth started to sing children's songs to Wally. He ignored her. Grandmother, Joan and aunt Judy were waiting for Elizabeth. Cleo, Leo and Orval were waiting for Wally.

Grandmother asked Elizabeth how Wally's modelling lessons were going. She also wanted to know when Wally's clothing line would be ready for production. Elizabeth happily said, "Wally was a natural-born model. Katie said that she could make Wally into a supermodel. Wally finished designing his clothing line, and production will start by the end of next week."

Aunt Judy asked Elizabeth, "Why is Wally involved in the fashion show?" Elizabeth told Aunt Judy that it was a long story and that it was better for Wally to tell her. Joan and Aunt Judy said," Elizabeth, make sure we get an invitation to the fashion show."

Katie was very happy. Everything was going along as planned. It was time for Wally's modelling lesson. She told Wally that his clothing line would be ready to market next week. "Wally and the models should decide what to wear for the fashion show." Wally agreed to do whatever Katie said. At the end of his lesson, he thanked Katie and said goodbye.

On their way home, Elizabeth sang children's songs to Wally. He asked her, "Elizabeth, shouldn't you save those songs for Daniel and Sarah?" Elizabeth let Wally know that she has enough songs for everyone.

Next month, Wally will be modelling one of his outfits at the fashion show. Katie told Wally to relax. "Wally, your clothing line is awesome, you look awesome, the models look awesome, and your pets are awesome. Make sure that your pets are ready for the dress rehearsal." Wally thanked Katie. He was very grateful for her help.

On their way home, Elizabeth continued to sing children's songs to Wally. He continued to ignore her. Grandma was at home waiting for Elizabeth. Cleo, Leo and Orval were waiting for Wally.

Elizabeth hugged Grandmother. "In less than a month, Wally will be modelling one of his outfits at the fashion show. I never realized how handsome Wally is." Grandmother looked at Elizabeth and said, "I hope you won't be disappointed when Wally's career as a fashion designer is over at the end of the fashion show?" Elizabeth told Grandmother that she didn't want Wally to be a fashion designer. He wouldn't have enough time to spend with his family, pets and friends.

Two weeks before the fashion show, Katie walked into Wally's office. "Wally, the fashion show is in two weeks. It's time for the dress rehearsal with the other models. Can you have your pets ready to go for a dress rehearsal tomorrow night?"

Wally told Katie that it shouldn't be a problem. He mentioned to Katie that Lawrence, the owner of Purdy's sister, wants to be present at the rehearsals and fashion show. Katie told Wally that as long as Lawrence behaves, he could stay.

Wally went to see Lawrence. He saw him working at his desk. "Lawrence, have Jenny ready for the dress rehearsal tomorrow night." Lawrence replied, "Jenny loves tuna; bring her a large tuna steak." Wally told Lawrence that he'd buy Jenny a tuna steak but that he had to be on his best behaviour if he wanted to stay at the rehearsal. Lawrence told Wally not to worry that he'd behave like an angel.

The next day, Wally went to see Lawrence. He was holding Jenny in his arms. Wally said, "Lawrence, you know where Katie has her modelling school. Meet me there at 6 o'clock tonight. Make sure that you bring Jenny."

Wally and Elizabeth drove home to pick up the pets for the fashion show. All the pets went into the back seat of the car except Howard. He was perched on the roof. Many motorists slowed down to look at Howard. Katie was waiting for Wally and Lawrence. She could hardly wait to meet all the pets. Lawrence with Jenny showed up at the same time as Wally and Elizabeth.

Wally introduced all his pets and Jenny to Katie and the models. Elizabeth was holding onto Wally's arms to keep him away from the models. Each model was assigned a pet to walk down the runway. The model who received Orval to walk down the runway was not very happy. The model that had Charlie sitting on her shoulder was very happy. The models took turns walking down the runway with their assigned pets. Elizabeth and Lawrence sat on the far end of the right side of the runway. Elizabeth saw Lawrence staring at the models with his mouth wide open. She elbowed Lawrence in the arm. "Lawrence, get your mind out of the gutter."

Lawrence, rubbing his arm, said, "Elizabeth, I might be getting old, but I'm not dead yet. The model with Jenny is gorgeous. You should keep your eyes on Wally. The models are eyeing him."

At the end of rehearsal, Katie introduced all the models to Elizabeth. Katie wanted the models to know that Wally is a happily married man. Wally's pets and Jenny were well-behaved. Katie was pleased with the first rehearsal. Wally told Lawrence to bring Jenny to dress rehearsal at the same time tomorrow. Wally then gave Lawrence a huge tuna steak. Wally gathered all his pets into the car. He got into the car with Elizabeth and drove home. Howard was perched on the roof.

Elizabeth was feeling great. She said, "Wally, I have a gut feeling that you'll make Louis Vintage very jealous. He'll regret entering you in the fashion show." Wally said nothing; he didn't feel so great. Elizabeth started to sing children's songs to Wally. He ignored her.

The next day at the rehearsal. Elizabeth stayed with Wally until he had to walk the runway. The models are paying too much attention to Wally. All the models were happy to have a cute little animal to walk down the runway with. The model who had Oral became fond of him. She enjoyed rubbing Orval's tummy.

Lawrence was getting worried. Valerie, the model that had Jenny, became very fond of her. They were bonding. Lawrence didn't want to lose Jenny. He told Wally that Valerie was planning to steal Jenny away from him. Wally told Lawrence to bring another cute little kitten tomorrow for Valerie. "That way, you'll be able to keep Jenny."

On the day of the fashion show, Katie was very excited. All the pets are well-behaved. Wally and the models looked awesome wearing their clothes. Elizabeth and Lawrence were excited. He brought a little white kitten with him. Lawrence has a friend who has a Cat Rescue House. That is where he gets all his cats. Wally took the kitten from Lawrence and gave it to Katie. He told her at the end of the fashion show to give this kitten to Valerie. "Lawrence thinks she wants to steal Jenny away from him."

Samantha, Joan, Judy, Christine Kelly, Aunt Lydia, Uncle Ivan and Wally's grandparents were all anxiously awaiting to see Wally walk down the runway. Dr. Reggie volunteered to be with Daniel and Sarah.

Wally was surprised to see Richard Kiley and Samantha together. There was another gentleman with them who Wally didn't know.

In the models' dressing room, one of the models bent down to put on her shoes. Charlie saw her bend down. He ran up her leg and stuck his head in her butt. The model started to scream. Wally heard the screaming and came running. He noticed Charlie missing and knew what happened. Wally forgot to feed Charlie. Wally took out a handful of sunflower seeds from a bag that was in his pant pocket and called out to Charlie. He ran down the model's leg and onto Wally's handful of sunflower seeds.

Wally said to the model. "I'm very sorry, it is my fault. I forgot to feed Charlie. He was hungry and was looking for food. He'll behave once he's fed. All the models started to laugh. They are waiting for the fashion show."

Lawrence was still worried. Jenny and Valerie were bonding. He didn't want to lose Jenny. When the models and Wally were walking the runway, the audience started to applaud. When they finished the audience gave them a standing ovation, just like Katie said they would.

Louis Vintage, who was in the audience, left in disgust. His revenge for Wally backfired. He knew that Wally's clothing line would win the fashion show competition. At the end of the fashion show, the judges announced Wally as the winner. He was asked to come to the podium to say a few words. Wally humbly said a few words, thanking Katie and Elizabeth for their support. The audience gave Wally a standing ovation. The head judge presented Wally with a cheque for $1,000,000 for winning the competition.

Elizabeth gathered all the pets into the car, and Howard was perched on the roof. She drove home, leaving Wally behind. Lawrence went to look for Jenny. He felt that he was in danger of losing her. Lawrence was relieved to find Katie holding Jenny in her arms for him. Katie told Lawrence that Valerie was very happy to receive the little kitten.

Photographers took several pictures of Wally. He was not happy to have his picture shown in a fashion magazine. There is no way that he'll be in the fashion industry.

Samantha and Richard approached Wally to congratulate him. Richard started to laugh. "Wally, it looks like you are leaving your law firm for the fashion industry." Samantha elbowed Richard in the ribs. "Wally will not be leaving his law practice."

Wally looked confused. "Samantha, I thought you and Richard hated each other. Why did you bring him to the fashion show?" Samantha said, "We still hate each other. I wanted to meet one of Richard's clients. He agreed to make an appointment for me to see him if I invited him to the fashion show. Richard's client's name is Billy Bennett. He owns a chain of clothing stores. Billy was impressed with you. He'll be seeing you in your office tomorrow morning at 8:00 clock." Wally asked Samantha why Billy wanted to see him. Samantha said that he'll find out tomorrow morning.

Samantha told Wally that it was time for Richard to take her home. Wally whispered in Richards' ear. "Remember Richard, Samantha hates you. If she invites you to her home, don't go. Samantha has a large collection of whips and chains." Richard began to laugh out loud. Samantha grabbed his arm and dragged him to his car.

It was well after midnight before Wally could leave. Katie drove Wally home. He reminded her that he has no interest in the fashion industry. Katie was disappointed with Wally's decision. When they arrived, Wally thanked Katie for all that she had done for him and said good-night. Wally was surprised that all his guests from the fashion show were waiting for him at home. They wanted to tell Wally that they were proud of him. Elizabeth ran up to him to give him a big kiss. She said, "Wally, you are awesome. Everyone enjoyed your fashion show."

Wally smiled and headed for the bedroom. He was tired. Grandmother plugged in two kettles for tea. The guests were not tired and were not ready to go home.

Chapter 68

Wally slept in. It was 7:00 o'clock in the morning when he woke up. Elizabeth was still sleeping. Wally took a quick shower, got dressed and drove to his office. He arrived just in time for his meeting with Billy Bennett. Donna led Billy into his office. Billy shook hands with Wally and sat down. Wally immediately knew why Billy came to see him.

Billy took out a contract from his briefcase and said, "Samantha tells me that you have no interest in the fashion industry. She also told me why you put on the fashion show to display Clothes for the Common People. Mr. Kozak, I am offering to buy your Smedley Googlepus clothing line for $5,000,000. I also want to hire you and your wife to promote the clothing line."

Wally was confused. "Mr Bennett, why are you interested in the Smedley Googlepuss clothing line? It's such a stupid name and why are you willing to pay so much money for it?"

Billy replied, "I am not interested in the name. I am interested in your theme, "Clothes for the Common People." The name Smedley Googlepus is very stupid. However, I have met many stupid people in the fashion industry. I also feel that you and your wife are perfect for promoting the clothing line. I offered you $5,000,000 for your clothing line because if I didn't, somebody else would."

Wally asked Billy what was involved in promoting Smedley Googlepus clothes. Billy smiled. "All you need to do is pose for photographers for a few hours once a month. Each of you will be paid $10,000 a month for 12 months. Then, if I want to continue to use both of you, I will negotiate another contract." Wally smiled. "Let me go over the contract. If there is anything that I don't like, the contract will be signed before lunch."

Billy left the contract on Wally's desk. "Mr. Kozak, I'm sure you'll sign the contract. Call me before lunch. We'll celebrate at the Spencers Mill." It took Wally less than five minutes to go over the contract. It was a generous, straightforward contract with no surprises. Billy's phone number was on the contract. He called him and said, "Can I invite Elizabeth, my wife, to lunch?"

Billy replied, "Please do; I'm looking forward to meeting her." Wally called Elizabeth to tell her to get ready for lunch at the Spencers Mill. He didn't tell her the occasion. On the way to lunch, Elizabeth was annoyed because Wally refused to tell her why they were having lunch at the Spencers Mill. It was too early for lunch.

Uncle Ivan led them to their table. Billy was waiting for them. Wally introduced Elizabeth to Billy Bennett. He explained to her why he bought Wally's collection. Elizabeth was speechless when he told her that he bought the Smedley Googlepuss clothing line for $5,000,000. Wally told Elizabeth that Billy wants us to promote the clothing line for a year. "All we have to do is pose once a month while a photographer takes pictures of us. Each of us will get paid $10,000." Elizabeth couldn't believe how much money that they were going to get paid.

Wally asked Billy if he decided on a logo to market the Smedley Googlepuss clothing line. Billy smiled.

"Mr. Kozak, I was hoping that you would choose an appropriate logo since you came up with the name. If I like the logo that you choose, I will pay you $50,000. If I need to hire a graphic designer, it could take months before I see a log that I like. I want to get Smedley Googlepus clothes to market as soon as possible."

Wally's eyes lit up. "Billy, I have the perfect logo for your clothing line: a bug-eyed kitten riding on a pink elephant." Billy was pleased with Wally's suggestion. "Mr. Kozak, you have just earned $50,000." Elizabeth was in shock. She couldn't believe how much money Wally made for being in the fashion industry. Billy got up." I'm sorry that I have to leave now; something came up. Enjoy your lunch; it's on me. Mr. Kozak, you are very lucky to have such a beautiful wife. Take good care of her."

Wally and Elizabeth ordered prime rib, scallop potatoes with steamed vegetables and Caesar salad. Uncle Ivan decided to join them. He brought a bottle of brandy. Aunt Lydia came with cheesecake wafers covered in dark chocolate. Wally told aunt Lydia and uncle Ivan who Billy Bennett was and why he invited them for lunch. Uncle Ivan poured three shots of brandy to celebrate Wally's good fortune.

After lunch, Wally and Elizabeth decided to go home to relax. Elizabeth definitely needed to relax. Aunt Judy was looking after Daniel and Sarah. She was surprised to see them home so early. Aunt Judy plugged in the kettle. Wally took Cleo, Leo and Orval for a walk in the trails.

Chapter 69

Wally was happy to be finally out of the fashion industry. Now, he can concentrate on his law career. Elizabeth walked into his office. She handed Wally a file. "Wally, I have a client that you are more suitable to defend." Elizabeth gave Wally a kiss, put the file on his desk and left. Wally looked at the file.

The client's name was Dr. Ted Conley, a plastic surgeon. He specialized in breast enlargements. Susie Benson, a client of his, was suing him for $5,000,000. Her breast implants leaked and caused a serious infection. Susie was using Dr. Conley's nickname in the lawsuit, Dr. Big Tits. Wally could understand why Elizabeth didn't want to handle this lawsuit.

The next morning, Elizabeth introduced Dr. Ted Conley to Wally. Dr. Conley began to explain. "Susie Benson came to see me. She wanted to have her breasts enlarged. I performed the same surgical procedure on her that I did for all my patients. I bought her implants from the Jerseyville Implant Company, the same company that I have been doing business with for the last 20 years. The implants that I received for Susie were a brand-new model. The company comes out with new models every few years. Jerseyville Implant company is very reputable. I thought this new product was a good quality product. I didn't know that a large conglomerate from Mexico bought the Jerseyville Implant company. The new owners had Jerseyville Implant company produce cheaper and inferior products than the regular good quality products. The large conglomerate from Mexico claims that they are not responsible because they are a legally separate company from a different country. Jerseyville Implant company filed for bankruptcy to avoid lawsuits. Susie claims in her lawsuit that with 20 years of experience, I should be able to tell the difference between a good quality implant and a bad quality implant. Other surgeons use the same implants. The best of my knowledge, none of the other surgeons are being sued."

Wally interrupted. "They are not getting sued because they are waiting for the outcome of your lawsuit. You are setting precedents." Dr. Conley continued. "Not all of the implants were bad. There was no way of telling which implants were good or which implants were bad. The problem with Mexico is that quality control is very poor." Wally said to Dr. Conley, "Based on what you have told me, Susie doesn't have any legal grounds for her lawsuit."

Dr. Conley took a deep breath and said, "I'm so happy that Susie has no legal grounds to sue me. This lawsuit caused me a lot of sleepless nights." Wally told Dr. Conley that he still has to convince Susie and her lawyer not to proceed with the lawsuit. "Her lawyer will definitely ask for an out-of-court settlement. I advise against any settlement. A lot of plastic surgeons will be very unhappy if you decide to settle."

Dr. Conley advised Wally to do whatever he thinks is best as long as he doesn't have to appear in court. Wally assured him that he didn't have to appear in court. Before Dr. Conley left, Wally asked him. "Dr. Conley, your nickname is Dr. Big Tits. That name is on your business card. Don't you find that name offensive and stupid?"

Dr. Conley smiled. "When I started off 20 years ago, I hired a marketing firm to promote my business. They insisted that I use that name. I have had the nickname ever since. I know that it's a stupid name, but I got used to it. That name probably brought me a lot of business."

Richard Kiley was Susie's lawyer. Another reason why Elizabeth didn't want this case. She knew that Wally could handle Richard much better than she could.

Wally called Richard to set up a meeting with him and Susie. During the meeting, Wally was able to convince Richard that Susie had no legal grounds to sue Dr. Conley. Wally suggested that

Richard have Susie start a class-action suit against the conglomerate from Mexico in international court. "They would probably want to settle out of court rather than face a lot of time and money fighting a lawsuit and possibly hurt their reputation." Richard agreed to handle the class action suit. He knew legal international court procedures.

He put an announcement in the newspapers to see how many women would respond to the class action suit. Susie told Richard that she knows at least a dozen girls who would be interested in the class action suit.

Chapter 70

Michael walked into Wally's office. Wally could tell that he was still very worried. Michael sat down and quietly said, "Wally, Patricia is slowly showing progress. I meditate and pray at least three times a day daily. I find it helpful for dealing with stress. Patricia has no interest in praying or meditating. Dr. Reggie did say that it would take a long time to have Patricia cured of her germaphobia. Wally, Patricia is pregnant, and I'm scared."

Wally suggested to Michael to get a pet. Dr. Reggie also suggested to Patricia to get a pet. "Patricia is a dog lover but is not ready to have a pet because of germs. Wally, Dr. Reggie wants to have Patricia hypnotized again. You'll be getting a call from him soon." Wally congratulated Michael and told him not to worry. Everything will work out just fine.

Donna walked in as Michael was leaving. "Wally, Katie, and a friend are waiting outside to see you," Wally told Donna to send them in. Katie introduced Kevin, her brother. He looked malnourished, just like Katie. Kevin looked like Katie's twin. They just sold their clothing manufacturing company for a huge profit and bought a microbrewery.

Katie was smiling. "Wally, we want you to invest in our microbrewery." Wally hummed and said, "Katie, how much money do you want me to invest?" Katie closed her eyes and took a breath. "Wally, we paid $500,000 for the building. It was a great bargain. The building is worth at least twice as much. The original owners filed for bankruptcy, and the bank foreclosed on them. We need another $500,000 for renovations, new equipment and marketing."

Wally decided to see the microbrewery building before he would invest money. The three of them left together. Wally found out by reading Kevin's mind that he is a well-experienced brew master. The building was only 10 years old. Kevin showed Wally the equipment used for brewing beer. "Some of this equipment is old and needs to be replaced. A lot of renovation is needed. However, this is a very good location. The building has a room to be used for a beer store; the second floor could be used for a large warehouse. There is lots of parking for employees and customers.

Wally knew that Kevin was serious. He and Katie invested their life savings in the microbrewery. Katie has full confidence in the microbrewery to be successful. Wally decided to invest in the microbrewery. He owes Katie a favour. He told Katie that he'll invest the $500,000 that they need. Kevin will look after brewing beer, and Katie and Wally will look after marketing. Katie and Kevin were very happy that Wally decided to invest.

Wally, Katie and Kevin drove back to Wally's office. Wally drew up a contract for them to sign. He told them to read the contract very carefully. If there are any questions, please let him know. Katie and Kevin read the contract and signed it without any questions. Wally arranged for a company bank account for the microbrewery business. Kevin required Wally's signature to withdraw funds.

Wally went to see Elizabeth. She was furious with him when he told her that he invested in a microbrewery business. "Wally, why did you invest in the microbrewery? You know nothing about brewing beer!"

Wally told Elizabeth not to worry, "I'm only a silent partner. Katie and Kevin invested their life savings to buy the brewery. I owe Katie a favour for helping me to put on the fashion show. Kevin will be brewing the beer, and Katie and I will do the marketing." Elizabeth was still not happy. She said nothing more.

When they arrived home, Wally went to walk Cleo, Leo and Orval. Elizabeth went inside to see grandmother. She was looking after Daniel and Sarah. Grandmother plugged in the kettle for tea. Elizabeth shook her head, "Grandmother, I'm so upset with Wally. He invested $500,000 in a microbrewery business that he knows nothing about. Katie persuaded him to invest."

Grandmother said to Elizabeth to calm down. "Wally invested in the microbrewery because he owes Katie a favour. Without her help, Wally would not be able to produce a clothing line for the fashion show. I know Katie is confident that the microbrewery will be successful. If it fails, Wally can use the investment for a tax write-off. Remember, you and Wally are multimillionaires."

Elizabeth was no longer upset. "Grandmother, Daniel and Sarah are starting to have a lot of energy. Are you able to keep up with them?" Grandmother laughed. "Elizabeth, don't worry. Grandfather is always with me; both of us can keep up with them. We have more fun with Daniel and Sarah when they are running around the house." Elizabeth smiled and told grandmother that she could hardly wait until they were old enough to go to school.

Elizabeth finished her tea and said goodbye to Grandmother. She went to see what was in the refrigerator. She was happy to see perogies, bean salad and sauerkraut. Wally got back from his walk just in time to see Elizabeth's head in the refrigerator. Wally decided to pan-fry the perogies because they were already cooked. He turned on the stovetop and poured some grape seed oil into a pan. A minute later, Wally threw in the perogies. He added chopped onions, chopped garlic and chopped bacon. Wally kept stirring to prevent the perogies from burning. After five minutes, Wally turned off the oven to let the perogies simmer for a few minutes. Elizabeth took out the bean salad and sauerkraut from the refrigerator. She placed them on the kitchen table while Wally brought over the perogies and some sour cream. They quietly ate their delicious dinner.

Katie called Wally and told him to meet her at her modelling school in an hour; it was time to think of a name for their beer and how to market it. Katie was waiting for Wally with coffee and doughnuts. Wally brought salad and two tea bags. They had salad and tea.

Katie said to Wally, "I want you to close your eyes and imagine being in a bar with a room full of people. Then tell me the first thing that enters your mind." Wally closed his eyes and imagined he was in a bar full of people. After a minute, Wally said, "I see a lot of fat, ugly, lazy slobs."

Katie became really excited. She started to jump up and down." Wally, that is awesome. Our beer will be called Fuls beer. It will stand for fat, ugly, lazy slobs. Wally was not impressed." Katie, that name doesn't excite me. I think that it is a very stupid name. "How are we going to market Fuls beer?"

Katie was annoyed. "Wally, you don't drink beer. I don't care that you don't like the name. It's an awesome name. We'll hire a marketing firm to get a bunch of fat, ugly, lazy people to do a taste test of several beers. Our beer against six other brands. We are going to cheat a little by watering down all the other beers except ours to make sure that our beer wins the taste test."

Wally asked Katie, "What will we do with the results of the taste test?" Katie laughed. "Wally, you will be our spokesperson for Fuls beer in a television commercial. You will be staying at Fuls microbrewery; we invited a lot of fat, ugly, lazy slobs to do a taste test. Fuls beer against six other brands. These people know how a great beer should taste. They chose Fuls beer over 90% of the time. This proves that Fuls beer is a great-tasting beer. The best part is that you don't have to be a fat ugly lazy slob to enjoy Fuls beer." Wally was not happy. He asked Katie why he should be the spokesperson for Fuls beer.

Katie smiled. "Wally, isn't it obvious? You are very handsome and a local celebrity. If we got someone else, we would have to pay that person a lot of money. Instead of paying another person to do the commercial, we can use the money for billboards, newspapers and flyers. Don't worry; everything that we are planning to do is in our budget. I have to go now. Wally, please take the doughnuts before you leave. Oh, Wally, I almost forgot to tell you. We start filming the commercial in two days. Make sure you are nicely groomed."

Wally took the box of doughnuts. He knows someone who would be happy to receive a box of doughnuts. Wally drove over to see Clarence. He was happy to see Wally. He was also happy to see the box of doughnuts. Wally handed the box of doughnuts to Clarence and took out his chequebook. He wrote out a cheque for $1,000,000 to the Salvation Army. He told Clarence to give him a tax receipt and continue to help the homeless. Clarence told Wally that he was a God Send and wrote him a tax receipt.

Chapter 71

It was late when Wally got home. Cleo, Leo and Orval were still waiting for him. Wally kissed Elizabeth good night and took out a flashlight from a desk drawer. He was going to tell Elizabeth everything that happened at the meeting with Katie in the morning.

Wally told Elizabeth that the new name of the beer would be Fuls beer, which stands for fat, ugly, lazy slobs. He also told her of the commercial that Katie arranged to be filmed in two days.

Elizabeth started to laugh. "Wally, that name is just as stupid as Smedley Googlepus. You are going to feel stupid and embarrassed filming that commercial."

Wally agreed with Elizabeth. "Katie thinks the name of our beer is awesome, and I am the perfect person to film the commercial. According to her, the commercial will help sell a lot of Fuls beer." Elizabeth had a hard time believing that Wally would allow Katie to make a fool of him by making him do that stupid commercial.

Early the next morning, Wally and Elizabeth drove off to the office. At the end of the day, they drove home. Wally took Cleo, Leo and Orval for a walk in the trails. Elizabeth went inside to see Christine Kelly. She was looking after Daniel and Sarah. When Wally returned from his walk, he prepared dinner. Wally had lentil soup, perogies and pizza. Elizabeth would be happy to eat perogies and pizza every day. Elizabeth invited Christine to have dinner. After dinner, Christine gave Elizabeth a good-bye hug. Wally decided to grab a book and go to bed early. He was tired.

In the early morning, Cleo and Leo were at Wally's bedside. Elizabeth fed them. They wanted their morning walk. Elizabeth grabbed Wally's toe and twisted it. "Duty calls; you better take them out for a walk before they make a mess in the house. Elizabeth was too busy to take them." Elizabeth wanted to prepare for her court date today.

Joan showed up to look after Daniel and Sarah. Wally and Elizabeth drove off to the office. Elizabeth said to Wally, "I hope that your microbrewery business fails. I have a gut feeling that some stupid person will come along and try to sue you." Wally smiled. "Elizabeth, my gut feeling tells me that the microbrewery will be very successful, and no one will come along to sue me. Katie and Kevin know what they are doing."

Wally received a call from Dr. Reggie. He wanted Wally to hypnotize Patricia again. An appointment was scheduled for next Wednesday morning at 8 o'clock.

Katie called Wally and told him that filming the commercial starts in an hour. Wally told her that he was on his way. Katie introduced Wally to Pierre, the film photographer. "Wally, Pierre will be filming you several times wearing different outfits. I will hold up cue cards for you. Then we'll decide which film we will use for the commercial. The commercial will last 30 seconds." After two hours, Wally and Katie finally found the commercial that they wanted to use.

Katie was really excited. "Wally, I just know that we will sell a lot of Fuls beer. I'm going to the local television networks tomorrow morning. You'll be able to see the commercial sometime next week!" Wally was not excited. He didn't know why he let Katie talk him into doing the television commercial.

Wally drove back to the office to pick up Elizabeth. It was time to go home. While driving home, Elizabeth asked Wally how the filming of the television commercial went. Wally was very tired and mumbled. "It went as well as could be expected. The beer commercial will be shown sometime next week. You're right, Elizabeth; I felt stupid and embarrassed doing the commercial."

When they arrived home, Cleo, Leo and Orval were waiting for Wally. Howard was perched on a branch of a tree. He flew over to Wally and landed on his shoulder. Wally was happy to see Howard.

It had been a while since he saw him. All five of them headed for the trails. Elizabeth went inside the house to have tea with her mother. She asked her mother how Daniel and Sara behaved.

Joan smiled. "Elizabeth, they were angels. I let them run around the backyard chasing a ball with Cleo and Leo. It was so much fun watching them." Joan gave Elizabeth a goodbye hug. Wally came back from his walk. Howard was still perched on Wally's shoulder. Wally placed a bowl of doggie food on the back patio for Howard. Wally was hungry. He went inside for dinner. Elizabeth had lasagna and Caesar salad waiting for him. After dinner, Wally went to bed, he was tired.

Chapter 72

It was early Wednesday morning. Wally left for Dr. Reggie's appointment. Elizabeth stayed home. She waited for Aunt Judy to arrive. Wally, Patricia, and Michael arrived at Dr. Reggie's office. Dr. Reggie was happy to see Wally. Dr. Reggie smiled. "Wally, I want to thank you for coming. Let's get started." Dr. Reggie led Wally and Patricia to the next room. Michael stayed behind. He wasn't allowed to watch.

Wally put Patricia in a hypnotic trance. Dr. Reggie gave Wally some notes to read to Patricia. Wally started to read. "Patricia, you are sitting in a room full of germs. Don't worry; there is a bottle of disincentive sitting on a coffee table next to you. Pick up the bottle and spray the entire room. The germs will die. You'll never have to worry about germs again. The spray bottle will always be with you, and you will give birth to a healthy baby in a germ-free room. Remember, the germs are in your mind. Imagine that you are spraying the germs in your mind." Wally was finished, and he took Patricia out of her hypnotic trance.

Wally asked Dr. Reggie, "Why did you want me to tell Patricia that the germs were in her mind? "Dr. Reggie stopped taking notes. "Wally, because the germs are in Patricia's mind. I don't think we want Patricia spraying her imaginary bottle to kill her imaginary germs in real life for everyone to see."

Wally asked Dr. Reggie if this hypnotic session with Patricia was necessary. Dr. Reggie said. "Wally, it's better for Patricia to imagine the germs in her mind than have her imagine the germs in real life. Recovery is a very slow process." Wally said goodbye to Dr. Reggie. Michael and Patricia stayed behind to talk to him.

Wally drove off to see Katie. She was excited. "Wally's beer commercial will be shown today. She wanted Wally to watch it with her at her modelling school. Katie turned on the television. The commercial was about to start. Katie and Wally watched the commercial together. Katie was very happy with the commercial. She asked Wally if he liked his beer commercial.

Wally shrugged his shoulders. "I don't know; it looks like your ordinary beer commercial to me." Katie was disappointed with Wally's attitude. "Wally, those other beer commercials don't have such a handsome man like you. Remember, you are already a local celebrity. Once women see you in the Fuls beer commercial, they will start drinking more Fuls beer and less wine." Wally asked Katie if Kevin had brewed enough beer. Katie told Wally that Kevin had been working 16 hours a day for the last week. "A lot of local bars and restaurants put in large orders already," Wally asked Katie how often and how long the beer commercial will be shown on television.

Katie smiled. "Wally, we have enough money in our budget right now to show the commercial 12 times a day for six months. Your face will be shown on every case of Fuls beer." Katie gave Wally a box full of pictures of him to sign. "A lot of women will be asking for an autographed picture of you. Keep them in your office."

Elizabeth was eager to see Wally's commercial. Wally led her to the media room. They watched the commercial on a 70-inch television screen. "Elizabeth, now that you have seen my beer commercial, do you have the urge to buy a case of Fuls beer?"

Elizabeth was impressed. "Wally, I'm not a beer drinker, but I'm sure a lot of women would buy a case of Fuls beer after watching your commercial." Wally said, "Elizabeth, it's time to go home. Let's go. I'm looking forward to my walk with Cleo, Leo, and Orval."

When they got home, Cleo, Leo, and Orval were not waiting for Wally. Elizabeth ran into the house to put on the television to watch Wally's commercial with Aunt Judy."

Aunt Judy saw Wally's beer commercial. She laughed. "Elizabeth, do you think there'll be a lot of women asking for Wally's autograph? I want an autographed picture of him."

Elizabeth smiled. "They won't come after Wally for autographs as long as I'm with him. Why do you want an autographed picture of Wally?" Aunt Judy replied. "I want to start a family album." Elizabeth smiled back. "Aunt Judy, you can start your family album with pictures of Daniel and Sarah. You can look at my family album anytime you want. There are lots of pictures of Wally in it."

Wally asked Aunt Judy, "Where are Leo, Cleo, and Orval?" She told Wally that Grandfather was taking them for a walk on the forest trails. Wally was disappointed.

Samantha walked into Wally's office. She was not happy. "Wally, I saw you in a beer commercial; what are you up to?" Wally replied. "Samantha, I invested money in a microbrewery. Katie and her brother bought it. They needed help with financing. I agreed to help them because I owe Katie a big favour for helping me with the fashion show. She somehow talked me into filming that stupid commercial. Except for this commercial, I'm not involved with the microbrewery. I'm just a silent partner."

Samantha was relieved. "Wally, make sure I get an autographed picture of you. I'm going to go and buy a case of Fuls beer today."

Donna, Thomas, Lawrence, Michael and Patricia came to see Wally all at once. They wanted to congratulate him on his beer commercial and get an autographed picture of him. They all said that they were going to buy some Fuls beer today. Wally was overwhelmed by praise. He decided to go home to relax. At home, Wally found a photography magazine on the coffee table. The cover showed a picture of him and his pets watching football. He was pleased to see his picture of himself and his pets on the magazine cover.

One month after Wally filmed his beer commercial, Katie walked into his office with a $20,000 cheque for him. "Wally, this is your share of the profits from the Fuls beer sales. Kevin would like you to reinvest some of your profit in the microbrewery. He says that he will need to expand our facility soon."

Wally happily said, "Katie, I want half of my share of the profits to be reinvested in the microbrewery, and the other half will be donated to the Salvation Army. I want tax receipts from the Salvation Army, and I want a monthly expense account from Kevin."

Katie gave Wally a big hug. "Thank you, Wally; Kevin will be happy to send you monthly statements. He is a very responsible person and will not spend money foolishly." Wally knew that Katie was telling the truth because he read Kevin's mind. Katie happily said goodbye.

It was the end of the day and time to go home. When Wally and Elizabeth arrived home from the office, Wally went off to the trails with Cleo, Leo and Orval. He was happy to see Howard joining them. Elizabeth ran quickly into the house. She found Christine Kelly rubbing Purdy's tummy. Charlie was perched on her shoulder. Elizabeth laughed. "It looks to me like you have found two new friends," Christine told Elizabeth that they are so adorable. Elizabeth went to the kitchen cupboard for some sunflower seeds and cat food. She asked Christine how Daniel and Sara behaved.

Christine said, "Daniel and Sarah were two little angels. I let them run in the backyard chasing a ball with Cleo and Leo. They wore themselves out and slept most of the day. I saw Wally's beer commercial and bought a case of Fuls beer."

Chapter 73

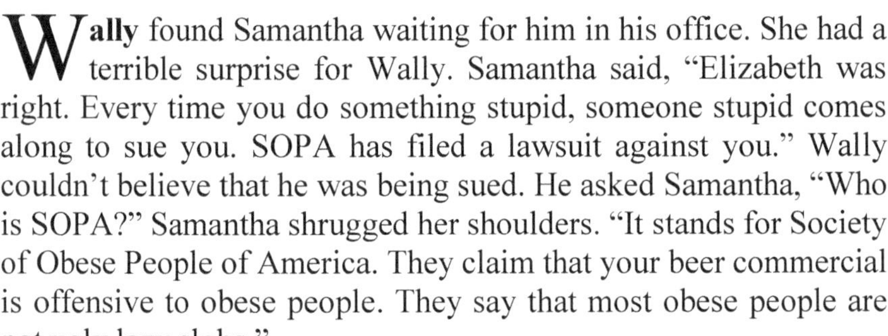

Wally found Samantha waiting for him in his office. She had a terrible surprise for Wally. Samantha said, "Elizabeth was right. Every time you do something stupid, someone stupid comes along to sue you. SOPA has filed a lawsuit against you." Wally couldn't believe that he was being sued. He asked Samantha, "Who is SOPA?" Samantha shrugged her shoulders. "It stands for Society of Obese People of America. They claim that your beer commercial is offensive to obese people. They say that most obese people are not ugly lazy slobs."

Wally couldn't believe that such an organization existed. He received a phone call from Elizabeth. She said Nah! Nah! I told you so and then hung up the phone. Samantha told Wally not to worry. "Lawrence is considered obese, and he loves your beer commercial. He will defend you." Lawrence was still overweight but not considered obese. He and Becky were following Wally's grandparent's diet and exercise program.

Wally invited Lawrence to lunch at the Spencers Mill. He told Wally not to worry. "Lots of people who are obese love your beer commercial. I'm sure SOPA members have bought Fuls beer." Wally thanked Lawrence for his support. They had lunch and then drove back to the office.

Elizabeth was waiting for Wally in his office. She wanted to know how lunch went with Lawrence. Wally told her that Lawrence would take care of the lawsuit and not to worry. At the end of the day, Wally didn't feel like preparing dinner at home and decided to take Elizabeth to the Spencers Mill. Aunt Lydia always had something for them. He called Uncle Ivan to reserve a table for him.

Uncle Ivan was happy to see them. "Wally, thanks to your beer commercial, we are selling a lot of Fuls beer. I ordered 50 cases. We ran out in three days. Aunt Lydia has prepared something special for you and Elizabeth."

Aunt Lydia served dinner. She prepared large potato dumplings, bean salad, broccoli salad, cooked spicy cabbage, and pork back ribs. For dessert, it was cheesecake wafers covered in dark chocolate. Wally laughed. "Just what I wanted, a reminder when Elizabeth almost suffocated me with her dandruff-infested pussy."

Elizabeth said nothing. She was hungry and started to devour her dinner. Just before dessert, Wally and Elizabeth received an ounce of brandy. They enjoyed the brandy and dessert. Wally and Elizabeth thanked Aunt Lydia and Uncle Ivan for a wonderful dinner and drove home. Wally took Cleo, Leo, and Orval for their walk on the forest trails. Elizabeth went inside the house to see her mother.

Joan said to Elizabeth. "I saw Wally's beer commercial. Why didn't you tell me that he was filming a beer commercial?" Elizabeth explained to her mother that Wally was a silent partner in the microbrewery. "One of the partners talked Wally into filming the commercial. Did you buy a case of Fuls beer after you saw Wally's beer commercial.?" Joan said that she did because she wanted to support Wally's microbrewery.

Lawrence and Wally had a pretrial meeting this afternoon. Lawrence told Wally that they were to meet Harriet Babinski, the president of SOPA and her lawyer, Richard Kiley. Wally couldn't believe that Richard would take on such a stupid case.

Richard introduced Harriet to Wally and Lawrence. When Wally shook Harriet's hand, he knew why she filed a lawsuit against him. She and her husband, Harold own several businesses. One of them was Spencer's Brewery. The company has been brewing beer for over 30 years. When Fuls beer came on the market, Spencer's beer started to lose a lot of business. It had to cut back production. He also found out that Harriet organized SOPA two years ago. She put out a monthly newsletter announcing when their monthly buffet meeting will be. For $50, members can pig out on pizza, burgers, sausage, bacon and chicken. She provided Spencer's beer for the buffet. However, some of the members wanted Harriet to provide Fuls beer instead of Spencers beer. That's when Harriet decided to sue Wally.

Richard Kiley smiled. "Wally, ever since you started to air your television beer commercial, everyone started to laugh at Harriet. She felt very humiliated. Harriet is asking for $2,000,000 in punitive damage and wants you to stop airing your beer commercial." Richard knew that Wally would not negotiate a settlement.

Wally asked Richard why he was taking on such a stupid case. Richard shrugged his shoulders. "Harriet and Harold Babinski are long-time clients. Harriet personally asked me to represent her."

Wally then asked Richard how the class-action suit went. Richard told Wally that he was right. "The Mexican conglomerate settled out of court. They didn't want to spend time and money fighting a lawsuit. Each of the 22 women listed in the lawsuit received $2,000,000."

Wally decided to wait a couple of days before he would tell Lawrence what he knew. Wally drove to the Fuls microbrewery. He wanted a tour of the facility. Kevin and Wally toured the building. The expansion to increase production was already starting. New equipment was being installed. Wally was pleased to see that Kevin was spending money wisely.

Wally drove back to his office to see Elizabeth. He explained to her why Harriet Babinski wanted to sue him for $2,000,000 in punitive damages and have him stop airing his beer commercial. Elizabeth was not impressed with Harriet Babinski.

Wally went to see Lawrence the next day. He told Lawrence that he did some research on SOPA. Wally explained everything to Lawrence. He was smiling. "Wally, I bet that Harriet or Harold never told Richard that Spencers beer lost a lot of business when your beer came on the market. I'm sure Richard will want Harriet to drop her lawsuit against you when he finds out."

Wally said goodbye to Lawrence and headed for the lunch room. It was time to play chess with Louis. Wally saw him waiting.

He had the chess board already set up. "Wally, ever since I started to play chess with you, I got better. I started to win more at my chess club. I even won some tournaments, thanks to you."

Wally asked Louis if he had seen his beer commercial. Louis smiled. "I sure did, Wally; you were awesome. I went out and bought a case of Fuls beer as soon as I saw your commercial. I want an autographed picture of you." Wally did notice that Louis was improving his game. It took Wally two minutes longer than usual to beat him.

Lawrence was waiting for Richard and Harriet in court for a meeting. When they showed up, Lawrence started out by saying, "Richard, I know that Harriet and Howard Babinski own Spencers Brewery. Did you know that ever since Wally's beer commercial aired on television, Spencers Brewery lost a considerable amount of business? Harriet is president of SOPA. She organizes a monthly pig-out buffet for her members. She supplies Spencers beer at the buffet. When some of her members saw Wally's beer commercial, they asked Harriet to bring Fuls beer to the buffet instead of Spencers beer."

Richard turned to face Harriet. "Do you still want to proceed with your lawsuit against Wally Kozak? I advise against it. You have a very weak claim." Harriet was not happy. She knew that she had to drop her lawsuit against Wally. Lawrence called Wally to tell him that Harriet dropped her lawsuit against him.

Chapter 74

Wally finished playing chess with Louis. He was not upset that Wally continued to beat him because Louis was becoming a better chess player. Louis received an autograph picture of Wally and happily went home. Wally went back to his office. Elizabeth and Samantha were waiting for him. Wally told them the good news that Harriet dropped her lawsuit against him. Samantha had wonderful news for Wally. She told him that the Harvard Law School chose him to be one of their guest interviewers at their school. He will be interviewing potential students as part of their entrance procedure.

Elizabeth gave Wally a big hug. She called Joan, aunt Judy, Christine Kelly, Grandmother, and Aunt Lydia. Wally and Elizabeth decided to go home early. When they got home, everyone that Elizabeth called was waiting for Wally to congratulate him. Aunt Lydia had tea and pastries ready to celebrate. Wally went to the backyard to look for Cleo, Leo, and Orval; he wanted to take them for a walk in the trails.

The next day, Elizabeth was very excited. She drove Wally to the Harvard Law School. She dropped Wally off and drove to a nearby hotel. Wally was led into an interview room. He meditated while waiting to interview his first potential student.

Jennifer Jones was Wally's first student to be interviewed. He was shocked when he saw her walk in. Jennifer had green spiked hair and three rings stuck in her nose. She wore a sleeveless white blouse showing tattoos all over her arms and wore tight pink leather pants.

Wally cleared his throat and said to her, "Ms. Jones, Harvard Law School has high standards to abide by. The way you look now is unacceptable. My advice to you is to go home, wash out the green dye from your hair, remove the rings from your nose, and buy a longs-sleeve blouse to cover your tattoos. You must also buy a proper dress for business and go to the hairdresser to get your hair done professionally. When you have done all that, then come back tomorrow to see me."

Wally could tell that Jennifer did not like his advice. She got up and, as she was leaving, said, "Mr. Kozak, you are going to hear from my lawyer. I'm going to sue you for discrimination."

Wally was hoping that what Jennifer said was an empty threat. He didn't want to go to court defending himself. The rest of the interviews went by nicely. Wally interviewed six potential students. Four of them will be accepted, but the other two will have difficulty getting in. At the end of the day, Wally called Elizabeth to pick him up. He told Elizabeth how Jennifer looked, and she threatened to sue him for discrimination.

Elizabeth began to worry. "Wally, if she does sue you for discrimination, it will cause you a lot of trouble." Wally shook his head. "Elizabeth there is no way that I would recommend a student that looked like Jennifer to Harvard Law School." Wally spent the rest of the week interviewing potential students. He had no major problems with any of them.

Two weeks later, Wally received a summons to appear in court. Jennifer Jones filed a $2,000,000 lawsuit against him for discrimination. She claimed that Wally didn't like the way she looked and that she was a girl.

Wally and Elizabeth went to see Aunt Judy. She read the summons. She shook her head. "Wally, this is a very serious accusation against you. You should have given her an interview. That way, you would have avoided this lawsuit. Wally, you could have written in your notes how Jennifer looked, and the school would have refused her application."

Wally shook his head. "I know Aunt Judy, but I wanted Jennifer to have another opportunity for an interview. I told you what she looked like. She could have gone home to get properly groomed and come back the next day. There's no way that I'm going to lose if Jennifer shows up in court looking the way she did for the interview." Aunt Judy said to Wally. "You better get a good lawyer yourself. Jennifer's lawyer is Harry O'Reilly. There is no way that he would allow Jennifer to look like a freak in a courtroom. Wally and Elizabeth said goodbye and drove back to the office. Wally went to see Thomas. He wanted him to be his defence lawyer.

Chapter 75

Wally received a call from Kevin. He wanted Wally to meet him at the Spencers Brewery at lunch. They toured the building. Kevin was excited. "Wally, Harold Babinski called me this morning. He offered to sell me Spencers Brewery and the building for $3,000,000. It's worth way more than that. I have a week to decide before he puts it on the market. This building is twice the size of ours. There is a need to replace some of the older equipment. Our brewery could become a restaurant. We still have the beer store and warehouse. I don't have the means to buy this property. I'm hoping that you do. It's a golden opportunity. If you buy the building, Fuls brewery will lease it from you."

Wally saw how serious Kevin was. He knew that Kevin was a responsible person. Wally decided to purchase the brewery. "Kevin, I will finance to buy the building, but I want weekly progress reports. Once all our equipment is removed from our brewery, I'll ask Uncle Ivan for advice on designing a restaurant for us."

Kevin was very happy. 'Wally, I promise you that you will not regret buying the Spencers Brewery." Wally believed him. He went back to his office to make arrangements for the purchase of the brewery and to write a contract for Kevin and Katie to sign. Wally told Elizabeth that he had invested in buying the Spencers Brewery. He didn't tell her that he bought the entire building.

Wally was ready to go to court. Elizabeth decided to stay home with her mother, Daniel, and Sarah. In the courtroom, Wally was surprised to see how Jennifer looked. She washed out the green in her hair and removed the rings from her nose. Her tattoos were covered by a white long-sleeved blouse, and she wore a brown smart-looking skirt. Wally liked what Jennifer's hairdresser did to her hair. It was too bad that Jennifer didn't look like that when she showed up for her interview with Wally. The Court was in session. Harry called Jennifer Jones to the stand. He asked her what happened on the day of her interview with Wally Kozak.

Jennifer testified. "Wally sent me home because I am a girl. It's obvious that Wally doesn't want girls to attend Harvard Law School. He discriminated against me because I'm a girl."

Harry had no other questions for Jennifer. Thomas had no questions for Jennifer. He called Wally to the stand. Thomas asked Wally why he sent Jennifer home.

Wally testified. "I told Jennifer Jones that Harvard Law School has high standards. The way she looked was unacceptable. I told her to go home to get properly groomed and to change her clothes into something that was more professional and then come back tomorrow to have her interview."

Harry got up and approached the bench. "Your Honour, the Charter of Rights allows for freedom of expression. The way Jennifer Jones looks should have no bearing on her qualifications for being a law student at Harvard Law School."

The judge asked Wally to approach the bench. "Mr. Kozak, do you have anything to say on your behalf? The prosecutor raised a very valid point."

Wally took a deep breath and said, "Your Honour, if you were the CEO of a large company that required legal counsel, How would you feel if Jennifer Jones was chosen to represent you? When she walked into the room for her interview with me, she had green spiked hair and three rings stuck in her nose. She wore a sleeveless blouse showing tattoos all over her arms. She wore tight pink leather pants. That's why I sent her home."

The judge banged his gavel on his desk. "All charges against Wally Kozak are dropped. The court is adjourned." Jennifer Jones was shocked. She couldn't believe that she lost. Harry advised her not to waste her time and money on an appeal. He told her the appeals judge was another old fogey. Jennifer ran out of the courthouse crying.

Harry walked over to Wally to congratulate him. He told Wally that he did the right thing when he sent Jennifer home. She should have taken his advice. "Let's have lunch to celebrate. This is the first time that I am happy to lose a case."

Wally called Uncle Ivan to reserve him at a table. Then he called Elizabeth to tell her the good news and have her come to the Spencers Mill for lunch. Wally also called Samantha to invite her for lunch.

Aunt Lydia served lunch. She prepared cabbage rolls, perogies, breaded chicken breasts, and Caesar salad. Uncle Ivan brought a bottle of wine and a bottle of brandy. Wally was asked to go to the piano to play and sing songs. Wally decided to sing songs by the Beatles. Everyone had a good time. When lunch was finished, Harry insisted on paying the entire bill because he had lost it in court today.

Wally and Elizabeth drove home. Wally was looking forward to his walk with Cleo, Leo, and sometimes Orval. Cleo and Leo were waiting for Wally. There was no Orval. Wally was worried; something was not right with him. When Wally came back from his walk, Elizabeth was waiting for him. "Wally, come here quickly." Wally ran up to Elizabeth. He saw Orval, a young skunk was with him.

Elizabeth became worried. "Wally, are you going to take care of two skunks?" Wally replied. "No, just one skunk. Orval is leaving us. He brought the young skunk to take his place."

Elizabeth asked Wally, "Why is Orval leaving us?" Wally told Elizabeth that Orval was old, and he senses that he would die soon. "Orval wants to die alone peacefully." Elizabeth started to cry. She ran downstairs to see Grandmother. Elizabeth blew her nose. "Grandmother, Orval is leaving us. Wally says he is very old and will die soon. Orval wants to die alone peacefully. He brought over a young skunk to take his place. Grandmother, why am I crying?"

Grandmother hugged Elizabeth, "Orval loves you, and you love him. You just didn't realize it. The young skunk that Orval brought will love you, and you will love him back. When you give love, you will receive love. Let's go upstairs to meet the young skunk. Grandfather, are you coming?"

Elizabeth was confused. "Grandmother, how could I love Orval? I ignored him most of the time?" Grandmother smiled. "Elizabeth, you don't have to be near someone you love. When a boy or girl moves far away from home to go to college, do you think their parents stop loving them?"

Elizabeth was beginning to understand what Grandmother said. By the time Elizabeth and the grandparents reached the patio, Orval was gone. Wally decided to call the young skunk Orval. He was feeding him peanuts. Joan was still in the house with Daniel and Sarah. Elizabeth called her to meet the new Orval. Howard flew by to meet the new Orval. So did Cleo, Leo, Charlie, and Purdy. Wally said, "It's time for me to have a walk with Cleo, Leo, and the new Orval."

Chapter 76

Donna told Wally that Kevin and a friend were waiting outside to see him. Kevin introduced his friend Keith Johnson. "Wally, Keith is the coach and owner of the Spencers Marauder Junior hockey team. Keith is looking for people to invest in his team."

Wally shook Keith's hand. He found out that Keith had a gambling problem. He needed investors to pay off his gambling debts. Kevin wanted Wally to invest in the hockey team so he could use it to promote Fuls beer. Wally shook his head. "Kevin, my gut tells me that Keith is hiding something from us. I trust my gut. We are not going to invest in his hockey team." Kevin was disappointed. He told Keith that Wally makes all the investment decisions.

Keith left the office without saying a word. Wally looked at a very disappointed Kevin. He said to him, "I know people who know him. They say that he has a gambling problem. He needs investors to pay off his gambling debts. Any money Keith receives from investors will be used to pay off his gambling debts. No money will be used for running the hockey team. The investors will be responsible for paying the team's expenses." Kevin took a deep breath; he was happy to have Wally as a business partner.

Elizabeth barged into Wally's office. She was excited. "Wally, Billy Bennett called to remind us that we have a photoshoot tomorrow night. His clothing line will be ready to market next week. He asked if we could bring Cleo and Leo."

Wally and Elizabeth showed up with Cleo and Leo at Billy Bennett's studio. Billy introduced them to George, the photographer. He told Wally that the beer commercial that he filmed would help sell Smedley Googlepuss clothes. George told Wally and Elizabeth what he wanted them to do.

George took several pictures of Wally and Elizabeth posing with Cleo and Leo. Elizabeth was happy posing. Wally just wanted the photo session to be over. George picked out a few pictures that he would ask Billy to use for the newspaper ads and flyers. On the way home, Elizabeth was singing children's songs to Wally. He ignored her.

Elizabeth went to her office. She didn't plan on doing much work. She was daydreaming of becoming a model. Wally had no interest in modelling.

Wally saw Keith Johnson coming out of Samantha's office. He was worried. Wally went to ask Samantha if she had invested in his hockey team. Samantha was excited. "Wally, Keith Johnson offered me 40% of his hockey team for only $200,000. That is a generous offer, so I took it."

Wally was really upset. "Samantha, you should have talked to me before you accepted Keith's offer. He has a gambling problem. You just paid off his gambling debt. Let's see the contract that you signed."

Wally read the contract. "Samantha, it says that Keith has complete control of running the hockey team. That means he'll gamble away the profits and not pay any of the expenses. The creditors will come after you since you have a large stake in the hockey team. The Spencers Marauders cannot be sold without Keith's approval."

Samantha fell off her chair. "Keith Johnson played me for a sucker, and I have no legal grounds to sue him!" Wally calmed Samantha down. "Don't worry, I have something planned for Mr. Keith Johnson."

Wally left the office to see Katie at her modelling school. She sold her clothing manufacturing company; however, the new owners hired her to run it. Wally wanted Katie to sew a particular hockey jersey for him. Wally showed Katie a picture of a wingnut and a picture of Keith Johnson's face, which he had gotten from a hockey program.

Wally told Katie that he wanted her to sew him a pink hockey jersey with a large wingnut on the front of it. He also wanted Keith's face shown on the wingnut. Katie looked puzzled. "Wally, why do you want me to sew you such a stupid-looking hockey jersey? If you want just one, I can have it ready for you in about an hour." Katie and Wally went over to the clothing manufacturing company.

In about an hour, Wally was holding a pink hockey jersey with a large wingnut on the front of it. Keith's face was shown on the wingnut. Wally told Katie that this jersey was exactly what he wanted and thanked her.

Wally went to see a sporting goods store. He asked the manager to order him a hockey helmet with two wingnut ears sticking out, one on each side. The manager laughed. "I can do it for you, but it will cost you double the regular price. It'll take three days to get it. I need a $100 deposit."

Wally paid the deposit and left for his office. He called Keith Johnson to make an appointment for next week 's meeting.

Wally picked up his hockey helmet from the sporting goods store. With the hockey jersey and helmet, he was ready to meet Keith Johnson. Donna let Keith into Wally's office. Keith was puzzled; he wondered why Wally called him. Wally hypnotized Keith into putting on the hockey jersey and helmet. He then took a picture of Keith wearing the hockey jersey and helmet with his phone and then unhypnotized him. Keith asked Wally why he called this meeting.

Wally smiled. "Keith, I know that you have control of running the hockey team, and Samantha can't sell it without your approval. I want to help her by purchasing 15% of your share of the hockey team." Keith was surprised that Wally wanted to invest in his hockey team. He thought that Wally had lost his mind. Keith told Wally that if he was serious about investing 15% of the hockey team, it would cost him $75,000.

Wally already had a contract prepared. He took out his chequebook and wrote out a cheque for $75,000 to Keith Johnson.

Keith read the contract and signed it. Keith then made an e-electronic deposit of the cheque into his bank account. Wally was happy to give the cheque to Keith for 15% of his hockey team. Wally told Keith that he and Samantha now have a controlling interest in the hockey team.

Keith was laughing. "Wally, you fool, did you forget that the hockey team cannot be sold without my approval. I have no interest in selling the team!"

Wally smiled, "I know, but we do have the authority to change the name of the team and its jersey." Wally showed Keith the jersey and helmet. Keith, the new name of the team will be called the Spencers Wacky Wing Nuts. The players will be wearing this jersey and this helmet. I checked with the league. They approved the helmet. Here is a picture of you wearing the new uniform."

Keith was in shock. "Wally, you can't be serious. Players will refuse to wear this uniform. Sponsors will pull out. The hockey team will be bankrupt!"

Wally smiled. "If the team goes bankrupt, the bank will go after your house for repayment of the loan. Samantha and I can afford to absorb the loss of our investment in the team; you can't. Are you ready to sell your share in the hockey team? I will pay $150,000 for it. That should pay off the rest of your gambling debt."

Keith started to cry. "Wally, will I still be the coach of the team?" Wally handed Keith a napkin. "You can still be the coach, providing that you agree to go to rehab." Wally had another contract already prepared for Keith to sell 45% of his share of the hockey team for $150,000. Keith signed the contract. Wally called Dr. Reggie to make an appointment to see Keith.

Keith took Wally's cheque. "Wally, I own the hockey arena. I haven't paid any property tax in two years. The arena needs major repairs. I will sell it to you for only $500,000 which I need to pay off the property tax. The arena is worth a lot more. If you don't buy it, the bank will foreclose in two weeks. A developer will buy the arena for $500,000. He wants to tear it down and build a condo on the property. You will then have to move the team." Wally told Keith that if it's worth putting money into the arena, he'll buy it from him.

The next day, Wally had an appraiser look at the arena. He told Wally that the arena was in bad shape. The roof needed to be replaced. The parking lot needed to be paved. A new ice-making machine and Zamboni were needed. The washrooms needed to be gutted and renovated. Same with the concession stands and the ticket box offices. The arena was only worth $1,000,000 as it stands. The repairs will cost $5,000,000.

The appraiser looked at Wally and said, "This building has room to expand seating capacity from 6000 to 8000 with a dozen luxury box seats. I have plans already drawn for the expansion. There will be no problem getting a building permit. If you are willing to spend another $3,000,000 to replace the old seats and expand the seating capacity, then buying the arena for $500,000 is a wise investment. Once the repairs and sitting capacity are complete, the arena will be worth at least $20,000,000. The team sells out every game."

Keith sold the arena to Wally. He had no choice; he couldn't afford to keep the arena, and he didn't want it to be torn down so that a developer could build a condo. Keith told Wally that behind the seats at the far end of the arena was a storage room. It used to be a restaurant.

Wally went to see Samantha to tell her the good news. She was very surprised. "Wally, I don't know how you managed to get Keith to sell his hockey team and arena, and I don't care how you did it. You have a knack for making money. Do whatever you want with the hockey team. I don't need to know."

Wally went to see Elizabeth to tell her that he had bought the Spencers Marauders hockey team. He will tell her that he bought the hockey arena later. Elizabeth screamed. "Wally, you don't know anything about running a hockey team. Why did you buy it!" Wally told Elizabeth to calm down. "I only bought 60% of the team. Samantha bought the other 40%. We have people who know how to run a hockey team. The Spencers Marauders sell out every home game. Didn't you go to the hockey games with Jeffrey? The money from the ticket sales will be more than enough to cover the hockey team's expenses. There is also money from television sponsors. We'll be making a profit."

On their way home, Elizabeth didn't say anything about the hockey team. Cleo, Leo, and Orval were waiting for Wally. Elizabeth ran into the house to see Grandmother. She was waiting for Elizabeth with cookies and tea. "Grandmother, Wally, and Samantha bought the Spencer Marauders hockey team. They don't know anything about running a hockey team."

Grandmother smiled. "Elizabeth, I think Wally and Samantha made a wise investment. Doesn't the team sell out their home games every year? You don't have to worry. Wally knew nothing about the beer brewing business, yet he invested in a brewery and is making money. Wally knew nothing about the fashion industry. He put on a fashion show and became rich."

Elizabeth then asked Grandmother how Daniel and Sarah behaved. She wasn't going to worry about Wally's investments anymore. Grandmother smiled. "Elizabeth, I took your little angels to the park playground this morning. They had a wonderful time on the slides and swings. This afternoon, I played Monopoly with them. They are learning how to play the game quite nicely. In September, Daniel and Sarah will be going to kindergarten. Are you excited?" Elizabeth was looking forward to having Daniel and Sarah start kindergarten. She ate all the cookies before Wally came back from his walk.

Chapter 77

Wally invited Kevin and Katie to lunch at the Spencers Mill. He told them that he and Samantha bought the Spencers Marauders hockey team. Kevin was a little concerned. He asked Wally how much the team cost. Wally looked at Kevin and said, "Don't worry, I didn't use any money from our microbrewery business. Keith sold me 60% of the team for $225,000, and Samantha paid $200,000 for 40%. I bought the arena for $500,000 from Keith. I'll finance the repairs for the arena without using money from the microbrewing business."

Keith became very excited. "Wally, that's great news. We could use the hockey team and arena to promote Fuls beer!" Kevin and Katie thanked Wally for lunch. They were happy that Wally had deep pockets. Kevin recommended that Wally hire Spencers Construction Company for the arena repairs.

George, the owner of the construction company, suggested that Wally include a restaurant in the arena. "There's no need for that huge storage room at the end of the arena. It hasn't been used in years. A restaurant is a good idea if there will be luxury box seats."

The next day, George started to gut out the washrooms. Washroom portables were brought in for the fans. George hired a subcontractor to replace the roof and another one to repave the parking lot.

Wally called Uncle Ivan. He wanted Uncle Ivan's advice of having a restaurant in the arena. Wally met Uncle Ivan at the arena. They looked inside the storage room. It was huge; there was old equipment and dust sitting there for years. It still had a washroom from the previous restaurant.

Uncle Ivan was nodding his head. "Wally, this is a nice size for a restaurant, and it has a washroom. People who buy your luxury boxes don't want to eat burgers, hot dogs, and French fries. I think the restaurant will do well in the business. There is a concert hall and movie theatre across the street.

Wally smiled. "Uncle Ivan, you hire a contractor to do the renovation, and I'll pay the contractor. Design the restaurant anyway you like because I want you to manage it. "Uncle Ivan told Wally that he would own the restaurant and pay rent. Wally was happy with uncle Ivan's decision. The restaurant would be one less headache for him.

Wally wasn't happy with how Keith ran the hockey team. He is a good coach who still has a gambling problem. Dr. Reggie told Wally that it would take several months for Keith to control his gambling addiction. He will never be completely cured. Samantha recommended a managing company to manage the hockey team. He still allowed Keith to coach the team.

Wally got a phone call from Kevin. He wanted to see Wally. Kevin was excited. "Wally, I am happy to tell you that all the brewery equipment has been moved out of our building to the larger Spencers building. All the obsolete equipment was scrapped. We are ready to double our production. Wally, our building is now empty. The extra room can still be used for a beer store but needs to be renovated. I would like you to buy Katie's and my share of the building. We will sell it to you for $500,000. That way, I will have more money for our microbrewery, and you will have your own beer store, warehouse, and restaurant."

Wally knew how serious Kevin was about brewing beer. His weekly progress reports and monthly statements show that he is a responsible person. Wally decided to buy the other half of the building. Uncle Ivan can design and hopefully own the restaurant. He went to see him.

Wally found Uncle Ivan and Aunt Lydia in the kitchen. He said to him, "I bought my partner's share of the Fuls microbrewery building. There'll be no beer production there. Fuls beer will be brewed at a much larger facility, the Spencers Brewery building. I also bought that building. My Fuls building will have a beer store, warehouse, and restaurant. I need your advice again."

Wally and Uncle Ivan said goodbye to Aunt Lydia. Wally gave Uncle Ivan a tour of his building. He saw the potential of having a restaurant there. He told Wally that this is a good place for a restaurant. "The building is in good shape and is in a good location. People will buy beer at the beer store after a meal. There is plenty of parking. The restaurant can use the beer store employee's washroom."

Uncle Ivan was getting a little concerned. He didn't know where Wally was getting all the money to pay for all his investments. "Wally, you have been spending a considerable amount of money lately. Before I help you, I want to know where you are getting all this money?"

Wally smiled. "Uncle Ivan, don't worry. Don't you remember that I inherited Henry Wilson's mansion and sold it for $8,000,000? I sold my clothing line for $5,000,000 and received $1,000,000 for winning the fashion show competition. I received a $2,000,000 settlement from Harvard Law School. Fuls beer is making a good profit, and so is the hockey team."

Uncle Ivan was happy to know that Wally had enough money for all his investments. He agreed to design, renovate, and own the restaurant. Uncle Ivan also agreed to renovate the beer store. There was no need to renovate the warehouse; it just needed a good cleaning.

Wally went to see Samantha. He told her that their leasing agreement for the Spencers Marauders with the arena would end in two years. That is when all the renovations at the arena will be completed. "We will be paying considerably higher rent. Profits will also be considerably higher from increased seating capacity and with the luxury box seats. There have already been inquiries for the luxury box seats. There will be more money from sponsors and higher ticket prices. People will come to see the team as long as they stay competitive." Samantha was very happy.

Chapter 78

Early Saturday morning, Wally decided to take Daniel and Sarah to the farmer's market. He let Elizabeth sleep. Cleo and Leo would soon wake her up. Wally left the bedroom door wide enough for them to get into the bedroom. Daniel and Sarah enjoyed their first trip to the farmer's market. Wally was happy that he brought them. Daniel tugged on Wally's sleeve and said, "Daddy why is that man staring at us?"

Wally looked where Daniel was pointing. He saw a weird looking little man staring at them. Wally took a picture of him. The weird little man disappeared. Wally thought that he better not be another serial killer. Wally then emailed the picture of the weird little man to Don Jordan and called him. "Don, I emailed you a picture of a weird little man. He is following me. I am at the farmer's market with my children. This weird little man gives me the creeps. Can you find out who he is?"

Don looked at the picture of the weird little man that Wally sent him. "Wally, I'll have him checked out right away. I'll let you know soon as I find out." Wally thanked Don and took Daniel and Sarah home. He didn't tell Elizabeth about the weird little man. She would get upset if she knew.

Don Jordan called Wally. "His name is Zach Brown. He works for a classified military agency. That is all that I can tell you. There's nothing I can do unless he breaks the law. He's probably just admiring your children."

Two days later Wally saw Zach Brown outside his home sitting in a car. Wally and Elizabeth were ready to leave for the office. Wally decided to ignore him. A few minutes later Zach Brown disappeared. Wally was sitting in his office. Donna entered Wally's office to tell him that there is a Zach Brown outside waiting to see him.

Zach entered Wally's office, closed the door and approached Wally. He put a business card on Wally's desk and then grabbed him by the throat. "You have an appointment to see Col. Donald Chandler next Wednesday night at 7:30. Don't miss it if you value your life and family."

Zach was incredibly strong. Wally was helpless and for some reason couldn't read his mind. Wally managed to jab him in the ribs with his fingertips. Wally was surprised. Any normal person would have keeled over and possibly died. Wally's grandfather taught him to kill using only his fingertips.

Zac let go of Wally's throat. Without saying a word, he walked out of the office. Wally looked at the business card. He knew where the address on the card was. Wally immediately called Louis. He said. "Louis, are you still going out with that girl who is a computer hacker? I want to hire her."

Louis replied. "Wally, her name is Amy. She belongs to the same chess club that I do. She'll be here tonight if you want to meet her." Wally thanked Louis. He will definitely be there tonight.

That night Wally arrived at Louis's chess club. Louis introduced Wally to Amy. She had short blonde hair. Amy was short and scrawny just like Louis. She could easily pass for Louis's sister. Amy smiled at Wally and said, "Louis says that you are a better chess player than I am. Let's play a game. If you win, you get my services for free, if you lose, I'm not available."

Wally started to play chess with Amy. He found out that Amy was a much better chess player than Louis. It took Wally almost an hour to beat her. Amy was very impressed." She said, "Wally, Louis was right. You could become a chess master if you wanted to be. What can I do for you?"

Wally handed Amy the business card that Zach Brown left for him. He told Amy that he wanted to find out all she could about Col. Donald Chandler and Zach Brown. Amy looked at the business card.

She said, "He works for a classified government agency. This is going to be tough. Let's go to my place."

Amy lived on the ground floor of a dingy apartment. There were wires hanging all over the place. Amy said. "Let's go to my office and get to work." Wally and Louis sat down beside Amy in front of a large computer monitor. Amy needed to get in touch with a computer network of hacking friends. Wally and Louis sat quietly, watching Amy type. The stuff that Amy was typing is gibberish to Wally. After two hours, Amy found out what she was looking for. Amy printed out the information.

Amy was shaking her head and said. "Col. Donald Chandler's agency is part of the military branch. His agency successfully developed drugs to make soldiers 100 times stronger than normal people. They can run 100 times faster than normal people and can heal 100 times faster from injury than normal people. These soldiers can hear and see in the dark much better than any animal. Right now, the Col. has only a handful of super soldiers. He wants to recruit an army of them. Wally, I bet that you are one of the chosen recruits."

Wally's face became pale. "Amy, you are right. I have an appointment to see the Col. next Wednesday night at 7:30. Zach Brown, one of the super soldiers, threatened to harm me and my family if I didn't show up."

Amy looked at Wally and sadly said. "Wally, it's too bad that I won't be able to play chess with you ever again," Wally turned to Louis and told him that he was going to need his services soon. "I need you to torch a building for me," Louis told him that it would be no problem for him to do it. Louis will not ask Wally for any payment because Wally has saved his life.

It was late when he got home. Wally forgot to call Elizabeth. He told her that he was held up helping Uncle Ivan and lost track of time. Elizabeth didn't say a word and headed for the bedroom. Wally followed her.

During dinner, Wally told Elizabeth that he is going to the hockey arena to see how the construction is going. Elizabeth was not happy. She had a gut feeling that Wally was hiding something from her.

Wally drove off to pick up Louis at his home. Louis had everything that he needed ready. When they arrived at their destination. Wally said to Louis. "It is 6:30; the colonel's lab is on the top floor of this deserted building. I want you to start a fire on the floor underneath the lab and a fire on the ground floor. Can you do it?" Louis told Wally that it would be no problem for him to do it.

"Good, get the building ready to be torched and listen for my signal from my phone. When you receive my signal, I will jump out the window and land on the roof of the next building. Louis, did you bring your gun?" Louis had his gun ready. Louis hopes that he doesn't have to use it because he hates guns. "Good, it's very important that you kill anyone who is trying to come out of the building once it is burning," Louis told Wally not to worry, he would be ready and then ran into the building and up the stairwell to get to the floor just below the lab. Twenty minutes later, Louis was ready to receive Wally's signal.

It was now time to meet Col. Donald Chandler. Wally walked into the building. Zach Brown was waiting for him. He frisked Wally for any weapons and then led him to the elevator. Wally set his phone to record video and voice. When Wally got off the elevator, the Col. was standing in front of him. The colonel was a huge muscular man. He reminded Wally of the incredible Hulk. He said, "Good evening Mr. Kozak. I have been expecting you. Thank you for coming. You're very lucky that I have chosen you to recruit. Wally asked the Col. why he chose to recruit him.

Col. Donald Chandler smiled. "We wanted to recruit your brother, Tommy. My sources tell me that you were responsible for having him killed. When we checked your background. We were pleasantly surprised that you are a much better recruit than your brother."

Wally was shaking his head and said, "Col., what if I don't want to be recruited?"

The Col. kept smiling. "Mr. Kozak, you have no choice. You are an American citizen. It is your duty to serve your country."

Wally was getting really upset. "How is becoming a Frankenstein freak serving my country? I had an unpleasant meeting with Zach Brown. He nearly choked me to death!" The Col. told Wally that he wouldn't have to worry about Zach Brown anymore. Once Wally's body is transformed, he will be Zach's superior. "Most of the recruits are not ready. It takes an average of four months for the transformation to be completed. Since you are much bigger than our other recruits, it will take longer for you to be transformed. The government wants to have a super Army to protect our country."

Wally was getting really angry. "Col., it's you who wants to have a super Army. It's you who wants to decide how best to protect our country, not the government!"

The Col. grabbed Wally by the collar. "Mr. Kozak, it doesn't matter what you think. I recruited you, and you will become part of my super Army!"

Wally jabbed the Col. in the ribs; he fell down. Wally then jumped in the air and kicked Zach Brown in the chest. Zach wasn't expecting a kick from Wally and fell down. Wally gave the signal to torch the building and jumped out of the window. He landed on the roof of the next building. Wally ran all the way down using the stairwell. Louis was waiting for him. The both of them watched the building burn. Louis said, "Wally, isn't the fire beautiful?" Wally asked Louis if anyone tried to run out of the building.

Louis told Wally that only one person had run out. He was incredibly fast. He disappeared before Louis could pull the trigger on his gun. Wally heard a voice behind his back. Wally turned around and saw a badly burned little man. He said to Wally. "I'll be back for you. You, your family and friends will die." The burned little man then disappeared. Louis asked Wally who that was. Wally told Louis that he was your worst nightmare. "Pray that you will never meet him." It is a good thing that Wally video-recorded everything that happened.

Wally drove Louis home before the fire trucks showed up. Wally never told Elizabeth that a Frankenstein freak was coming after him. Wally didn't want Elizabeth to have a nervous breakdown. She went to sleep. Wally went outside to call Don Jordan.

Don arrived 15 minutes later. He asked Wally what is so important that he must come to see him right away. Wally gave Don the computer printout that he got from Amy. He then took out his phone and played the video recording that he took. Wally mentioned to Don that Zac Brown came to his office and threatened to kill him and his family if he didn't show up for his appointment with Col. Donald Chandler.

"Don, one of the Frankenstein freaks escaped. He was badly burned. He told me that he'll be back to kill me, my family and friends." Don gave Wally a keychain with the button on it. He said, "Wally, when the Frankenstein freak shows up, press the button on this keychain; within minutes, armed agents will show up." Wally thanked Don and went to bed.

Ted Bradley stopped running. He was weak from his badly burned body. It would take months before his burned skin would dry up and peel off, allowing for new healthy skin to grow back. It was night time and he hid amongst the homeless. Tomorrow, he plans to break into a house to steal some clothes and money. Most of his strength returned to him after a good night's sleep. Ted chose a secluded mansion to break into. He knew that there was no one home. He was able to outrun the guard dogs. Fortunately for him the security system was not turned on. Ted was able to find a safe that he could break into. The safe contained several thousands of dollars. He cleaned out the safe and a closet full of clothes and shoes. Ted also cleaned out the refrigerator, he was hungry. Ted left the mansion and headed for a hotel.

At the hotel, Ted Bradley covered his face. He paid a month in advance with cash. The plan was to stay at the hotel until he was fully healed. Ted was a small man, and the clothes he stole were too big. He would have to break into a clothing store after hours. Ted didn't want people to see his burned body.

Before Ted was recruited by Col. Donald Chandler, he wanted to join his father and become an FBI agent. His father had problems getting him in because he had a criminal record. Ted was charged and convicted of possession of cocaine and driving under the influence when his car ran into a ditch. Ted was honoured to be recruited by the Col. He couldn't understand why Wally Kozak refused to be recruited and why Wally didn't want to have superhuman abilities.

When Ted becomes fully healed, he will go back to his family and apply to the FBI. He will not tell them that he has superhuman abilities. Ted would tell his family that the government shut down the military facility that he worked for. However, he will use his abilities to become an FBI agent. Once he becomes an FBI agent, he'll put his plan for revenge against Wally Kozak into action. He plans to kill Wally, his family and friends. When Wally had the colonel's lab torched, All the super soldiers died. Ted considered them family.

Chapter 79

Elizabeth was excited. It was Daniel and Sarah's first day at kindergarten. She got them cleaned up and dressed. Wally and Elizabeth drove them to kindergarten. They were introduced to the kindergarten teacher. Her name was Mollie Smith. Wally found out that she came from a family of teachers. Wally and Elizabeth liked her. They kissed Daniel and Sarah goodbye.

At the end of kindergarten, Grandmother went to pick up Daniel and Sarah because Elizabeth and Wally were too busy. Elizabeth was anxious to get home. She wanted to know how Daniel and Sarah enjoyed the first day at kindergarten. Elizabeth and Wally ran into the house. Wally's walk with Cleo, Leo and Orval can wait.

Grandmother, Daniel and Sarah were watching television. Elizabeth ran up to them. She asked them how they enjoyed their first day in kindergarten. Sarah smiled, "Mommy, we had lots of fun. We sang songs and drew pictures." Daniel and Sarah handed Elizabeth pictures that they drew. Daniel drew a picture of Wally and Cleo. Sarah drew a picture of Elizabeth and Leo. Wally took those pictures and headed for the back patio.

Elizabeth was annoyed. "Wally, where are you going with those pictures!" Wally replied. "Cleo and Leo will want to see these pictures. Wally showed the pictures to Cleo and Leo. They happily barked at the pictures. A few minutes later Wally brought back the pictures and took Cleo, Leo and Orval for a walk in the trails.

Grandmother poured tea. Daniel and Sarah continued to watch television. Grandmother smiled. "Elizabeth, when Grandfather comes home, could you bring Daniel and Sarah downstairs to visit him. He'll want to hear how Daniel and Sarah's first day at kindergarten went."

Wally came back from his walk. He was glad that Grandmother prepared dinner. She prepared vegetable chili, perogies and Caesar salad. After dinner, Elizabeth Daniel and Sarah went downstairs to visit grandfather. Wally didn't feel like going. He wanted to relax. Wally sat in an easy chair with a newspaper to read.

As Wally was reading, a small newspaper ad caught his attention. An Atlanta radio station was advertising a contest. It is a song writing contest. The writer of the song must sing and record a song. Then the songwriter must send the song to the radio station. An up-and-coming country blues singer, Screaming Mouth Leroy will choose the winner. He will also record the song. The prize is $25,000 plus royalties. The song must be a blues song telling a tragic story. Wally knew that it was not easy to write a song. Wally was in a silly mood and decided to write a song.

Wally recalled the day when Elizabeth jumped on his face and nearly suffocated him with her pussy. Wally thought that it would not be difficult to write a tragic blues song. He headed to the piano with the pen and paper. Wally started to write words to a song. The title he chose was I Got the Blues because…. The words Wally chose were,

I got the blues because my baby wants to sit on my face, repeat twice

when we got married, I weighed 163, and my baby weighed 103

when she sat on my face, it was heavenly.

Today, I weigh 163, and my baby weighs 303

If my baby sat on my face, it would be deadly

I asked my mama what can I do

she said that it was my fault that my baby weighed 303

I told my mama that I had to work long hours

my mama told me that I worked long hours to chase women

and your baby found out that is why she wants to sit on your face

and collect $100,000 from the insurance company

Gifted

oh no, mama, what can I do
she said to me, there's nothing I can do for you
Your wife is cheating, Man
I got the blues because my baby wants to sit on my face. Repeat
twice

Wally had no problem putting music to the words. It took him only two hours to write the entire song. Wally then downloaded a recording app from his phone. He sang and played the piano to his song. When he finished playing, Wally googled the Atlanta radio station's website. He then filled out the entry form and emailed his song to the radio station.

Kevin called Wally to have a meeting. He wanted Wally to make another investment. Wally was not interested in making any more investments, but decided to listen to what Kevin had to say at Spencers Mil for lunch.

The next day Wally was sitting at his usual table at the Spencers Mill. Elizabeth was too busy too have lunch. Katie, Kevin and a friend showed up. Kevin introduced Adolph Gustafson; he looked like a smaller version of Lawrence. "Wally, Adolph worked for a winery in Canada for over 10 years. He specializes in making ice wine. He owns a license to produce the ice wine and gave Niagara Brandt wines permission to produce his ice wine."

"Adolph wants us to produce ice wine and hire him to make the ice wine. Before he left, Adolph had well-trained staff producing the ice wine for Niagara Brandt. The winery will sell us grapes for making ice wine as long as Adolph gives them the license to continue to produce ice wine at their facility. Niagara Brandt Wines won several awards throughout Europe for their ice wine."

Wally asked Kevin where Adolph was supposed to make this iced wine for us. Kevin replied, "Wally, we have enough room at our microbrewery to expand. It's good business to sell both beer and iced wine. Wally, you should become a broker and sell ice wine from your store to restaurants and liquor stores. You have a warehouse to store your ice wine."

331

Wally asked Kevin. "How much will this ice wine operation cost us?" Kevin and Adolph held their breath. Kevin said. "Adolph and I estimated that it would cost us $2,000,000,"

Wally asked them how much money they were willing to invest. Kevin was very nervous and said, "We have no money to invest. All our profits right now are reinvested in our microbrewery. That is why we came to see you."

Wally called his uncle Ivan to the table to ask for advice. Uncle Ivan said. "Wally, we sell a lot of Niagara Brandt ice wine. If your ice winemaker can produce the same quality as Niagara Brandt, I would also carry your brand. Our customers would prefer the iced wine made in America." Uncle Ivan brought a bottle of Niagara Brand ice wine. Adolph took the bottle and told Uncle Ivan that he owned the license to produce the ice wine in this bottle. Adolph said, "Niagara Brant Wines agreed to supply us with grapes to produce the ice wines. I can make the exact same ice wine as the ice wine in this bottle. The only difference is our ice wine will have a different label. The bottom of our labels will say, this ice wine is licensed by the Niagara Brandt Winery Inc. Ontario, Canada. We'll call it Fuls ice wine. We can sell it a lot cheaper than Niagara Brandt ice wine because of our currency exchange rate. That means we'll sell a lot of ice wine." said Adolf holding the bottle."

Uncle Ivan asked Adolph. "Why is Niagara Brandt wine being so generous? Will it not affect their ice wine sales?"

Adolph smiled, "Niagara Brandt has no choice. I own the license for their iced wine. I have the authority to prevent them from producing my ice wine. I left on good terms. Niagara Brand ice wine is only 20% of their business, and only 2% of their ice wine is sold in the United States. The rest stays in Canada or is exported to Europe."

Wally asked Adolph. "Why did you leave Niagara Brandt winery?" He replied. "At Niagara Brandt I was also responsible for harvesting the grapes. During harvest time it takes a lot of hard work and long hours which I didn't enjoy. I came to New York because I have family living here. I also want to make ice wine without the responsibility of harvesting the grapes. I will help supervise the renovation and purchasing equipment without pay. I only get paid when we are ready to make ice wine."

Uncle Ivan looked at Wally and said, "If you can afford to invest, go for it." Kevin told Wally that he didn't have to invest the entire money all at once. "We need $200,000 to start the renovation and expansion. Adolph will know when and where to purchase the ice wine-making equipment. It'll cost $800,000. The rest of the money would be used to buy and transport grapes to our building and to hire employees. Katie and you could market our ice wine. We have enough money in the budget for that. In six months, we could be making ice wine."

Wally looked at Kevin, Adolph and Katie. They were holding their breath, waiting for Wally's decision. Wally agreed to make the investment. Kevin, Adolph and Katie jumped in joy. Uncle Ivan congratulated Wally on his decision. Adolph had some good news for Wally. "Niagara Brandt had to cancel a 500-case order of ice wine. The company that ordered it filed for bankruptcy. The winery decided not to put labels on the bottles to save money. They are willing to sell those cases to us for only $25,000. We can put our Fuls ice wine labels on the bottles. A bottle of Niagara Brandt ice wine sells for $60.00 a bottle. Fuls ice wine will sell for $50.00 a bottle. Wally, you should become a broker. You have a warehouse to store the iced wine to sell to restaurants and through the Beer store." Wally told Kevin to buy those cases of iced wine.

Wally said goodbye and went home. He knows that Elizabeth will freak out when he tells her about his ice wine investment. On his way home, Wally brought a dozen roses and a box of chocolates. Wally knew that the ice wine-making business would take a long time to establish.

When Elizabeth found out about Wally's investment, she freaked out. Grandmother was able to calm her down. "Elizabeth, don't worry; if the ice wine business fails, it will be written off as a business expense. Remember, you and Wally are multi-millionaires." Elizabeth sat down, and Purdy jumped on her lap. Her purring calmed Elizabeth down. Grandmother plugged in the tea kettle.

Wally drove to the office alone. Elizabeth stayed home. One hour later, Wally left his office to see how the renovations at his hockey arena are coming. George, the contractor, told Wally that the roof had been replaced and the parking lot had been paved. The concession stands were also complete, and so were the ticket box offices. The washrooms will be completed before the end of the hockey season. During the off-season, half of the new seats and luxury boxes will be installed. The other half will be installed during the following hockey off-season. The Spencers Marauders will make the playoffs. Their home games continue to sell out despite the construction. The new ice making machine will be installed during the off-season. A new Zamboni was already purchased. When the renovations are complete, the arena will be called The FULS Arena.

Uncle Ivan hired a contractor to start on his restaurant renovations at the arena. The restaurant at the arena will be a smaller version of the Spencers Mill. Uncle Ivan decided to call it Spencers. The restaurant at the Beer store will also be a smaller version of the Spencers Mill. That restaurant will be called Fuls because he knows that Wally wants to promote Fuls beer. Both restaurants will have similar menus.

Chapter 80

U**ncle** Ivan invited Wally to lunch. He wanted him to make another investment. Uncle Ivan had lunch ready for Wally. Aunt Lydia prepared chilli, perogies and Caesar salad. He said to Wally. "Aunt Lydia and I sponsored two families from our village to help with our restaurants. Your grandparents sponsored two families to help out with their clinic. They are getting much older, and business is increasing. The store beside the clinic became available to expand. The Lyschuk daughters are married and pregnant. They want to move out.

All these people need a place to live. My banker tells me of an abandoned row house with six units. Each unit has a garage. It was a casualty of the 2008 real estate crash. It's located just on the outskirts of our neighbourhood. The row house has been empty ever since. A bus stops in front of it daily and it takes only 20 minutes to get to the Spencers Mill. The bank is asking only $200,000 for all six units."

Alex, a friend of Uncle Ivan, was a contractor. "Wally, Alex and I went to look at the rowhouse. After carefully examining all the units, Alex said that he could renovate each unit exactly the same way in order to cut costs. He wants $700,000 to renovate all six units. Each unit is 1,500 square feet with a full-size basement. All the units will have the same appliances and be painted the same colour. Alex wants a $350,000 retainer and the balance when the renovations are completed. That's a $700,000 investment. That will get you a small house in our neighbourhood if you can find one. You get six units for the price of one."

Wally agreed to buy the rowhouse. Uncle Ivan will decide how much rent to charge because he will manage all the six units for Wally. Uncle Ivan gave Wally a big thank you hug. "Wally I almost forgot to tell you that my son Peter and his family are coming to New York this summer. He and his wife will be working in our restaurant and eventually take over running it when Lydia and I decide to retire. The basement at our house is being renovated. We will be living in the basement while Peter and his family will live upstairs."

Wally thanked Ivan for a wonderful lunch. A half hour later Wally drove back to his office. Katie showed up at Wally's office unexpectedly. She was happy. "Wally, you need to film another commercial for Fuls Ice wine. In the commercial you will say Fuls ice wine is licensed by the Niagara Brandt Winery. Their ice wine is world renowned and won many awards throughout Europe. You get the same quality ice wine with Fuls ice wine at a fraction of the cost."

Wally became upset and asked Katie why it was necessary for him to film another commercial. Katie told Wally that his face was synonymous with Fuls beer, so why not make his face synonymous with Fuls ice wine? She also mentioned that he was ready for a local celebrity.

Elizabeth walked into Wally's office. "Wally, congratulations, Screaming Mouth Leroy chose your song to record. You won $25,000 and will receive royalties." Wally looked at an unhappy Elizabeth. He asked her what the problem was. She should be happy that he won.

Elizabeth took a deep breath and said, "Wally how many times that I have to tell you. Every time you do something stupid, someone stupid will come along to sue you." Wally laughed. "Elizabeth, do you honestly believe that someone stupid will come along to sue me?"

Elizabeth told Wally that she honestly believes that somebody stupid will come along to sue him. She placed Wally's cheque on his desk and left shaking her head. Wally picked up the phone to call Clarence. He will be happy to receive another donation from Wally. Katie didn't say a word and waved goodbye.

Two weeks later Wally received a registered letter. Bubba Crawley from Atlanta Georgia wants to sue Wally. Bubba claims that the song Wally wrote was the story of his life. Bubba's lawyer Beaufort Crawley is flying in from Atlanta. He will arrive tomorrow night. Bubba wants the $25,000 that Wally received and all the royalties that he will receive. Beaufort is coming to visit Wally, to collect Bubba's cheque. Wally was really upset. Elizabeth was right. A stupid person did come forward with a lawsuit.

Beaufort met Wally in his office. "Good morning, Mr. Kozak. You can call me Beaufort, and if it's alright with you, I will call you Wally. I hope we can avoid a lawsuit. Bubba claims that he inspired you to write your song about the story of his life."

Wally stared at Beaufort shaking his head. "How did I do that, Beaufort?"

Beaufort smiled. "When Bubba got married, Elmira, his wife, weighed 105 pounds. He weighed160 pounds. Bubba enjoyed having Elmira sit on his face. Elmira now weighs 310 pounds and wants to sit on Bubba's face. Bubba still weighs 160 pounds. She knows that Bubba is cheating on her. That is why she wants to sit on his face so she could collect $500,000 on an insurance policy. You now know why Bubba wants his money?"

Wally couldn't believe what he was hearing. He said. "Beaufort, I have never been to Atlanta and I never knew that Bubba ever existed. My song was just a coincidence!"

Beaufort looked very disappointed. "Wally, we will let the judge decide if your song is a coincidence." Wally was really upset. He knew that Bubba had no chance of winning, but Wally didn't want the hassle of going to court.

Wally looked into Beaufort's eyes and said, "Beaufort, do you honestly believe that Bubba has a chance to win in court!" Beaufort looked back at Wally. "I agree with you Wally. However, Bubba is stubborn and he instructed me to take you to court if you do not cooperate. He honestly believes that you wrote a song about the story of his life."

Wally couldn't believe what he was about to say. "Beaufort, I was inspired to write my song by an incident that happened to me personally."

Beaufort was very interested to know what happened to Wally. He smiled. "Wally, please tell me what happened to you that inspired you to write your song if you want to avoid going to court. Convince me that your incident inspired you to write your song, and Bubba will be very unhappy. We estimate that your royalties will be worth well over $100,000."

Wally decided to tell Beaufort everything that happened on the day that Elizabeth got drunk on brandy. Wally told Beaufort that he thought that if Elizabeth weighed over 300 pounds, he would be dead.

Beaufort laughed. "Wally, Elizabeth did that to you, and you are still married to her. She must be a very beautiful girl. If she admits to me that she did that to you, I will drop Bubba's claim against you."

Wally called Elizabeth to his office to introduce her to Beaufort. He looked at Elizabeth and whistled. "Wally, I can understand why you forgave Elizabeth for almost suffocating you to death with her pussy. She is drop-dead gorgeous!"

Elizabeth screamed at Wally. "Did you tell Beaufort what happened at Aunt Lydia's home that night?"

Wally told Elizabeth that he had no choice. He had to tell Beaufort what happened to avoid a lawsuit. Beaufort laughed, "Elizabeth, I could tell by the look on your face that you did it. There'll be no lawsuit. It's lunchtime now. Will the both of you please join me for lunch, my treat?" Wally called Uncle Ivan to reserve a table for three. Twenty minutes later, Wally, Elizabeth and Beaufort were sitting at Wally's table.

Beaufort was impressed with the Spencers Mill. Everyone had prime rib and scallop potatoes, steamed vegetables with Caesar salad. Beaufort said to Wally. "I like this restaurant a lot. The food is excellent and it has a very nice atmosphere."

Beaufort told Wally that he is happy that he doesn't have to go to court. Bubba is his brother and is glad that Bubba will receive nothing. "It's too bad that I have to leave now. If you ever come to Atlanta, please come see me. Don't worry I won't tell Bubba what Elizabeth did to you." Wally had one more question for Beaufort. He wanted to know whatever happened to Bubba's wife.

Beaufort laughed. "Bubba was ready for her. A friend of his hid in the bedroom closet with a video camera. Bubba was lying naked on his back in bed. Elmira walked in naked and climbed on the bed. When she sat on Bubba's face, his friend was filming and then he came out and managed to pull Elmira off of his face. She is doing time in prison for attempted murder. Bubba filed for divorce."

Elizabeth elbowed Wally. "Why did you have to ask Beaufort such a stupid question?" Beaufort was laughing. He picked up the bill and left.

Chapter 81

It was Saturday morning. Wally woke up Elizabeth. She wanted to go to the farmer's market with him. Wally, Elizabeth, Daniel and Sarah drove off to the farmer's market. At the farmer's market they were enjoying themselves when Wally noticed a man staring at him. He was a creepy little man that had the same look that Zac Brown had on his face. Wally took out his phone and took a picture of him. He emailed the picture to Don Jordan and called him.

"Don, the Frankenstein freak is back. He is watching us at the farmer's market. I just sent you a picture of him." Don looked at the picture that Wally sent him. He said to Wally. "Relax, his name is Ted Bradley. He is a new FBI agent. I know his family; they are good people."

Wally was still worried. "Don, Ted has the same look on his face that Zach Brown had. I'm sure that Ted is one of Col. Chandler's Frankenstein freaks.

Don became annoyed, "Wally, it was six months ago when you had the Col.'s building torched. You said the only person who escaped was badly burned. Burned flesh leaves a lot of burnt scar tissue. Ted has no burn scar tissue on his body. Wally, you are worrying for no reason." Don hung up the phone before Wally could say another word. Wally was convinced that Ted Bradley had superhuman healing powers. Wally saw Ted staring at him.

Wally slowly approached him. He said to Ted. "You're not fooling me. I know exactly who you are." Ted just smiled at Wally. Without saying a word, he disappeared.

Elizabeth asked Wally who was that person watching us. Wally told her that he didn't know. Elizabeth became very nervous.

Ted Bradley was happy that Wally recognized him right away. Ted was ready to put his plan for Wally's revenge into action. He knows Wally's family and his friends. Ted was able to spy on Wally without his knowledge. Wally took his family home from the farmer's market. He knew that Ted had something terrible in store for him, and he would not be receiving any help from Don Jordan.

It was the end of the day and time to go home. Wally and Elizabeth left the office to drive home. Aunt Judy was with Daniel and Sarah, waiting for them. Wally, as usual, took Cleo, Leo and Orval for a walk. Elizabeth ran into the house. It was Daniel and Sarah's first week of kindergarten. Elizabeth wanted to know how they were enjoying school.

Sarah happily said. "Mommy, we like going to kindergarten. We became good friends with Johnny. He moved here from Punky Doodle Corners. That's in Ontario, Canada. Next month they are having their fair. Johnny invited us to the fair. We can stay at their grandparents' dairy farm."

Elizabeth looked at Daniel and Sarah and sadly said. "I'm very sorry, Daddy and Mommy are too busy to go this year." Daniel and Sarah were very unhappy. They ran to Aunt Judy for a hug.

Ted Bradley was watching Wally's home. He was sitting in a school bus parked across the street. Ted brought with him a box of sleeping pellets that he bought on the black market. When Wally returned from his walk, Ted loaded his rifle with sleeping pellets and fired into Wally's front opened window. It only took a few minutes for everyone to fall asleep. Ted went inside the house and picked up Elizabeth and Aunt Judy. He carried them to the school bus. Ted left a note beside a sleeping Wally and drove off. He had no intentions of harming children or elderly seniors.

Ted spent the entire evening abducting Wally's family and friends by using his sleeping pellets. He went after Lydia, Ivan, Joan, Christine Kelly, Samantha, Donna, Thomas, Lawrence, Harry, Richard, Don Jordan and Michael. He didn't take Patricia because she was pregnant.

Ted drove his hostages to an old abandoned building that used to be a gym. It still had exercise equipment and a swimming pool full of water.

Each of Ted's hostages was gagged and tied to a chair while they were still asleep. Ted called Wally. He knew that Wally was awake and had time to read his note that was left for him.

Ted said. "Wally, I know that you had time to read my note. You better come over to the old abandoned gym. The note has directions on how to get there. Wally, you must come alone and unarmed in one hour. If you don't, your family and friends will die."

Wally had no choice. He left Daniel and Sarah with his grandparents. He didn't tell them where he was going. Wally arrived at the gym just in time. When he entered, Wally saw all his family and friends gagged and tied to a chair. Ted was waiting for him.

Ted was happy to see Wally. "Come on in, Wally. You know why I called you. Your family and friends will watch me kill you. Then I will have the gym torched by your friend Louis and kill him. That's what you did to my family and friends."

Wally attacked Ted. He punched and kicked Ted with all his might. Ted stood there laughing. He grabbed Wally by the throat and threw him across the room. Wally landed beside the pool. His head hit the pool ladder.

Ted walked slowly towards Wally. He then bent down to face Wally. He looked straight into Wally's eyes and said to him, "Wally, do you have any last words to say before I kill you?" Wally caught Ted by surprise. He grabbed Ted's throat and rolled into the pool taking Ted with him. Wally used all his strength to keep Ted's head submerged. Wally had both his hands around Ted's throat. It was a good thing that Ted was a small man. When Ted stopped squirming, Wally continued to hold Ted's head under water for a few minutes to make sure that he was dead.

Wally slowly climbed out of the pool. He managed to untie Elizabeth before he fell to the floor and passed out. Elizabeth began untying everyone else. Don was shaking his head. "Elizabeth, I'm very sorry that this happened. This could have been avoided if I listened to Wally." Elizabeth said nothing and walked over to Wally.

Wally opened his eyes and said, "The nightmare is over. Please take me home. Grandma will take care of me."

Don said to everyone. "We need to keep what happened tonight away from the media. It's very important that you don't tell anyone. I will take care of Ted." Don helped Elizabeth to get Wally into his car. Elizabeth drove Wally home. Don drove everyone else home in the school bus and then drove back to see Wally.

Grandmother told Don that Wally just needed rest. No bones were broken. "He has inflamed muscles in his back and a bruise on the back of his head. He can go back to the office in two days. Wally mustn't lift anything heavy. He will be fully recovered in a month."

Elizabeth grabbed Don's arm. "What is going on? I have a right to know!" Don told Elizabeth that what he was about to tell her was strictly confidential. She must not tell anyone. Don began to explain everything to Elizabeth and Grandmother. He mentioned that Col. Chandler recruited Wally to become a superhuman soldier. Wally refused and had someone torch the Col.'s lab with him and all his soldiers. Ted was able to escape. However, his body was badly burned.

When Ted was completely healed, he went after Wally for revenge. "Elizabeth, if I listened to Wally, none of this would not have happened." Don apologized and left. He had a lot of work to do.

Grandmother gave Elizabeth a big hug. "Tomorrow morning, I'm going to call Dr.Reggie to make an appointment for a group counselling session. Make sure that everyone attends. I'll give you a lotion to rub Wally's back every day."

The next day, Elizabeth drove Daniel and Sarah to school. Grandfather took Cleo, Leo and Orval for a walk in the trails. Howard flew through the bedroom window to pay Wally a visit.

At lunchtime Wally received another visitor. It was Dr. Reggie, "Wally, I scheduled a group counseling session for your family and friends for tomorrow morning at 8 o'clock. Your grandmother told me what happened. I want you to attend. Your grandmother said that you can attend if you agree to go in a wheelchair. I think it would be a very good idea if you hypnotized everyone into forgetting that terrible night." Grandmother came into the bedroom with pizza and perogies for Wally and Dr. Reggie. Cleo and Leo came in for a visit.

Early next morning, a wheelchair van showed up to take Wally to Dr. Reggie's group counseling session. Everyone showed up, including Don Jordan. During the session, everyone took turns talking about how they felt on that terrible night. Wally then had everyone form a circle around him. He sat in the middle of the circle and was able to put everyone into a hypnotic state. Wally successfully hypnotized everyone into forgetting that terrible night.

Chapter 82

ally was glad to be back in his office. He received a surprise visit from Katie. She was excited. "Wally, I arranged for you to film a commercial for Fuls ice wine next week. I saw your newspaper ad for Smedley Googlepuss clothes. You and Elizabeth looked awesome. Wally, you are a local celebrity. We will sell a lot of iced wine."

Katie left to see Elizabeth to tell her the news. Elizabeth was excited to hear that Wally will be filming the commercial for ice wine.

On their way home, Wally decided to visit Fuls Brewery. Kevin took Elizabeth on a tour of the facility. Wally went to see Adolph. He asked him how things were going.

Adolph smiled. "Wally, the expansion is complete. I purchased all the equipment that we needed. The equipment will arrive next week. Installation will take about a month. Grapes won't be harvested until late December or early January. I just had your 500 cases of iced wine labeled. It said Fuls Ice Wine was licensed under Niagara Brandt Winery. They are ready to be delivered to your warehouse. It won't take long to sell them. In the meantime, Kevin is teaching me how to brew beer."

Wally was happy that everything was coming along the way it should. Elizabeth was not excited about the brewery. She was excited about the commercial Wally would be filming. She intended to watch him film the commercial. Wally had no interest in filming the commercial. They drove home.

Wally was looking forward to walking Cleo, Leo and Orval. When they arrived home, Wally was disappointed that Cleo, Leo and Orval were not waiting for him. Joan and Grandmother were having tea. Daniel and Sarah were watching television.

Wally asked Grandmother where Cleo, Leo and Orval were. Grandmother told Wally that Grandfather was taking them for a walk in the trails. She asked him how his back was feeling. Wally told Grandmother that his back was just fine. "The ointment that you gave Elizabeth helped to relieve the pain."

Wally said. "What's to eat? I'm hungry?" Grandmother took out a large bowl of perogies. She chopped up some bacon, garlic and onions into a frying pan. Grandmother said to Wally. "There is a pizza in the refrigerator. You better eat it because Elizabeth will hog most of the perogies."

Wally called uncle Ivan to ask him how the renovations are going at the restaurants. Uncle Ivan told Wally not to worry. Everything is under control and on budget. Uncle Ivan visits the restaurants every day. The contractors were doing a good job. The restaurant at the arena should be ready for business in the first week of next month. It will be called Spencers. The restaurant at the beer store should be ready for business in two weeks. It will be called Fuls. The Beer store is already ready for business.

Wally said to Uncle Ivan, "It's the end of the hockey season. I am leaving to see how construction is going on in my arena. You want to come with me?"

Wally met Uncle Ivan at the hockey arena. He saw a brand-new Zamboni parked in the parking lot. The Ice making machine was already installed. The washrooms were completed with state-of-the-art plumbing. The seats on one side of the arena were removed. There'll be 4000 new seats with six luxury box seats installed before the beginning of the hockey season. The other 4000 seats with six luxury box seats will be installed during the following hockey off-season.

Uncle Ivan showed Wally the restaurant. Wally was very impressed. It looked like a smaller version of Spencers Mill. Uncle

Ivan told Wally that this restaurant would be very busy, and so would the other one at the Beer store.

Wally didn't have time to check out the home renovations at his row house. Uncle Ivan told Wally not to worry. "Alex is a very good and responsible contractor. I see him every week. The homes will be completed in time for our friends from our village to arrive. Once they get settled, I will have a large dinner party for you to meet them."

Chapter 83

Jeffrey called his mother to tell her the bad news. "Mother, our family doctor told me that I have terminal colon cancer. It's too late for him to help me." Christine immediately called Wally for help. Wally said, "Christine, I don't know what I can do for Jeffrey. Have him meet me tomorrow afternoon at the Kozak Naturopath Clinic. Tell him to bring his medical files."

Wally called Elizabeth to tell her that Jeffrey has terminal colon cancer. He mentioned that Jeffrey will be going to Grandmother's clinic tomorrow afternoon. Elizabeth felt sorry for Jeffrey, but she would not go to see him at the clinic. She wanted nothing to do with Jeffrey.

Wally went to see Lawrence. He was rubbing Jenny's tummy as Wally walked in. He asked Lawrence if he could get him a kitten for tomorrow afternoon. Lawrence said, "Wally, I'll have a kitten for you tomorrow morning. Make sure that you take good care of him." Wally thanked Lawrence and went to see Patricia.

He asked Patricia if she could bring a cute little puppy to him for tomorrow afternoon. Patricia smiled. "Wally, you are in luck; my friend's dog just gave birth to puppies three weeks ago. I will bring you one tomorrow morning. You better take good care of the puppy."

Patricia groaned; the baby that she was carrying just kicked her. "Wally, Elizabeth told me that motherhood is overrated." Wally smiled, "Patricia, ask Elizabeth now what she thinks about motherhood."

Wally thanked Patricia and went to see Elizabeth. "Aunt Lydia invited us to lunch; do you want to go?" Elizabeth smacked her lips.

"Wally, don't ask stupid questions. Let's go, Aunt Lydia's perogies and pizza are the best."

The next morning Lawrence came into Wally's office carrying in his arms a cute little white kitten. Wally thanked Lawrence for the kitten and assured him that the kitten would be well looked after.

A few minutes later, Patricia came waddling in, carrying in her arms a cute little Beagle puppy. "Wally, this puppy's name is Benny; make sure that he's healthy and happy." Wally thanked Patricia and assured her that Benny would be healthy and happy.

Wally placed the little kitten and Benny in a basket. He went off to see his grandmother at her clinic. Grandmother was happy to see the kitten and Benny. A few minutes later, Jeffrey and his mother showed up. Wally looked at Jeffrey's medical file. Wally couldn't do anything for him.

Wally looked straight into Jeffrey's eyes and said, "I'm sorry Jeffrey but I don't do miracles. Only God can. Let me tell you what my mother taught me."

Jeffery was puzzled. He didn't want a lecture on religion. Christine elbowed him in the ribs and told him to be quiet and listen to Wally.

Wally began saying, "Jeffrey, you and I and everyone else and everything is "the sum of all there is." Some people call the sum of all there is God, consciousness or whatever. I like to call it love. Everything around you that you can see and not see is love. Everything in other galaxies and universes is the sum of all there is, or love. Love has no sense of time, no past or future, just present. Love wanted to create but couldn't because love knows all there is to know. That is why love created us. Love also created ego, to give us individuality. Love gave us a choice to control the ego or let the ego control us.

When you control your ego with your thoughts, beautiful and wonderful things are created. When you let your ego control your thoughts, fear, greed and destruction are created. That is why individuals and groups of individuals cause wars and destruction of our planet. With love, there is always enough. With the ego, there is never enough. How many people who are incredibly wealthy live the life of a pauper? Remember that the body dies, but love never dies. The ego never dies. That is why the ego doesn't care if the body dies. The ego gets a new body every time a baby is born. Without body and ego, love cannot be created. Jeffrey, you are love without body and ego."

Jeffrey had no interest in what Wally was saying. Christine elbowed Jeffrey again and told Wally to continue. "Jeffrey's love can cure or do anything. The problem with you is that you allowed your ego to control you. Ego says there's not enough; therefore, there is a competition to grab as much wealth as possible and indulge the body as much as possible. You have terminal cancer because of your egotistic lifestyle. You have to drive ego out of your body and let love in."

Jeffrey didn't like what Wally was saying. He wanted to leave. Christine told Jeffrey to stay and listen to what Wally had to say. "Jeffrey, to get love, you have to give love. Unfortunately, you are not giving or receiving any love from anyone except your mother."

Wally picked up the kitten and Benny and placed them on Jeffrey's lap. He said, "The puppy's name is Benny; the kitten has no name yet. You can start to give love to them. They give a lot more love than they receive. Spend as much time as you can with them."

Jeffrey was solely confused; Christine was not; she understood exactly what Wally was saying. Wally looked at a confused Jeffrey. "The ego will try to do anything to prevent you from receiving love. It is very important that you start to pray. The more you use foul language and lose your temper, the more the ego has control of you. Wally handed Jeffrey a piece of paper with a prayer written on it.

Jeffrey, my grandmother, taught me this prayer when I was eight years old. I stand in front of a mirror and say this prayer three times daily. I want you to say it 10 times a day in front of the mirror. You also must take care of your health. I will give you a diet plan to follow and show you how to meditate and exercise at your office gym. Do all this, and you will be able to control your foul mouth and bad temper."

Jeffrey was not happy to hear Wally's advice. Christine was very pleased. "Wally, I will personally see that Jeffrey follows your diet plan, exercises, and meditations. He will also say your wonderful prayer 10 times a day."

Wally said. "Jeffrey, there is a war going on inside your body between your white blood cells and the cancerous cells. I want to hypnotize you to convince your immune system to produce white blood cells at a much faster rate. Then, I want you to have chemotherapy treatment. Hopefully, a lot more cancer cells will be killed than white blood cells."

Jeffrey was still confused. "Wally, I don't understand why you're trying to help me. I hate you and try to cause you trouble."

Wally smiled. "Viktor Frankl was a prisoner of war in the Nazi concentration camps. Millions of people died. He survived because he found meaning in life. The more meaning in life you have, the more love you receive. Viktor believed that once you find meaning in your life, you must help other people find meaning in their lives. Jeffrey, do you think that Victor had a better chance of surviving the Nazi concentration camp than you with terminal cancer? Thanks to the trouble you caused me, I am happily married to Elizabeth and have two beautiful children. Thanks to you, I graduated from Harvard Law School at the head of the class. I also received a $2,000,000 out-of-court settlement from them. I just want to return a favour by helping you find meaning in your life. Right now, that means to get enough love in you to cure your cancer."

Jeffrey didn't like Wally's advice. Christine did. She was grateful for Wally's help. Christine will make sure that Jeffrey says his prayer 10 times daily and follows Wally's diet plan, meditations, and exercises. Wally told Jeffrey to stop by Spencers Mill today; Aunt Lydia will have a diet plan ready for him. He also reminded Jeffrey to spend time loving his pets. Jeffrey took home his pets without saying a word. Chrisitine thanked Wally.

Wally will teach Christine how to be Jeffrey's personal trainer and how to meditate. Christine will make sure that Jeffrey says his prayer 10 times daily, meditates, exercises, and follows his diet plan.

Christine dragged Jeffrey out of bed. It was 6 o'clock in the morning. Jeffrey screamed! "What the fuck are you doing!' Christine slapped Jeffrey on the back of his head. She told Jeffrey that every time she heard him use foul language, she was going to smack him on the head. Jeffrey got dressed. He and Christine were going to say Wally's prayer together. Then, they would do the exercises that Wally showed them. When Jeffery finished his exercises, he would meditate for 10 minutes before breakfast. After breakfast, he would spend half an hour loving his pets. Christine will make sure that Jeffrey does this every day.

Two weeks later, Jeffery was ready to have chemotherapy. Wally put Jeffery in a hypnotic trance to get his immune system to produce white cells at a faster rate. Wally then told Jeffrey to meditate, saying his prayer during chemotherapy. This will prevent the ego from controlling him with fear. Wally also asked Jeffrey to bring him his health files after his chemotherapy. There should be a noticeable improvement.

Chapter 84

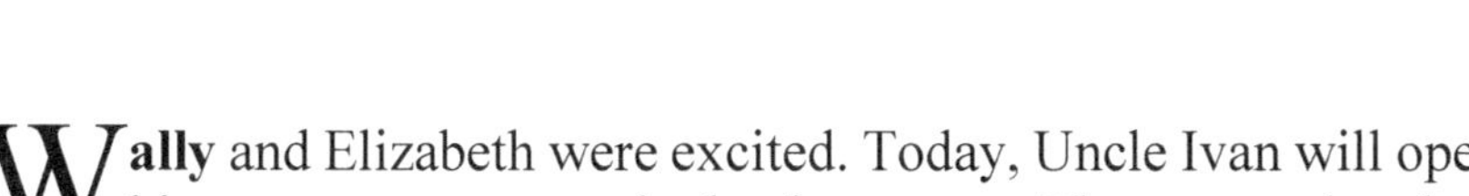

Wally and Elizabeth were excited. Today, Uncle Ivan will open his new restaurant at the hockey arena. There was already a long line of people waiting for the grand opening. Wally and Elizabeth didn't have to wait. They were the first customers. Katie and Kevin showed up a few minutes later to join them. Wally ordered prime rib for everyone.

Katie reminded Wally that he has an appointment at her modelling school to film the commercial for FULS ice wine. "Wally, in two weeks, you will be able to sell our iced wine. Kevin brought you your brokerage license." Elizabeth was also excited. She wanted to watch Wally filming the commercial.

Elizabeth asked Wally if the restaurant would cater to the fans in the luxury box seats. Wally replied. "The restaurant will cater to all our fans. I have already reserved two box seats for us, two box seats for Uncle Ivan and Aunt Lydia, one box seat for Samantha, and one for Richard."

Uncle Ivan was pleased with his grand opening. In two weeks, he will open a restaurant at the Beer store. He wanted Wally to do commercials for his two restaurants. Aunt Lydia will have lots of perogies and pizza delivered to Wally's home. That will get Elizabeth to encourage Wally to film the two commercials for these restaurants.

Wally and Elizabeth picked up Daniel and Samantha from school. They were very excited. Sarah said, "Our friend Johnny invited us to the Punky Doodle Corners fair. We will be staying at his grandparent's dairy farm. Daddy, you promised us that we'll go this year." Wally saw how happy Daniel and Sarah looked. "Thank Johnny for inviting us," said Wally.

Daniel handed Wally a piece of paper. On it was written the name of Johnny's grandparent's farm, telephone number, address, email address, and website.

Wally googled the website. It showed that Punky Doodle Corners was a farming community not far from Toronto. Wally called Johnny's grandparents to thank them for inviting his family to stay at their farm.

It was time to see Jeffrey; he had just finished having chemotherapy. Jeffrey's doctor told Wally that his cancer was spreading at a much slower rate. His doctor also told Jeffrey that he should keep doing what he was doing. Christine was making sure that Jeffrey followed Wally's instructions.

Wally was happy with Jeffrey's progress. He asked him how much weight he lost since starting his diet. Jeffrey told Wally that he lost 20 pounds in four weeks. The food on aunt Lydia's diet plan is delicious.

Wally smiled. "Congratulations, Jeffrey. Keep up the good work. Tomorrow afternoon I want you to come with me to the Children's Hospital. Bring Benny with you. There is an eight-year-old boy who is very lonely. His mother's too busy to see him because she has two jobs. He has no father. His name is Sean. You're going to keep Sean busy with Benny, and then you will read him a story. Remember Jeffrey, with love, there is always hope." With ego, there is no hope.

The next day, Wally drove Jeffrey to the Children's Hospital. Jeffrey brought Benny. Wally brought a storybook. Sean was happy to see Benny. He started to jump all over Sean. A few minutes later, Benny lay quietly beside Sean while Jeffrey was reading a story to him.

After Jeffrey finished the story, Shawn asked him if he would be coming again with Benny to read him another story. Jeffrey told him that he definitely would come to visit him with Benny again. Jeffrey asked Wally why Sean was in the hospital. Wally told him that Sean was born with a defective heart. "He will have surgery tomorrow morning. Jeffrey, you will be seeing Sean next week. How did you feel when you read Sean a story?"

Jeffrey was holding Benny in his arms and said, "I felt so good. I'm looking forward to seeing Sean again." Wally told Jeffrey that he was feeling love.

Chapter 85

Samantha entered Wally's office to tell him some good news. Wally called Elizabeth to come to his office. Samantha told Wally that Harvard Law School chose him to be a guest lecturer. He is to prepare an assignment for the students and then discuss the assignment in class. Elizabeth was excited. Wally asked Samantha, when was the lecture? She told Wally that it was on October 27.

Wally was really disappointed. "Elizabeth, we have to leave for the Punky Doodle Corners fair on October 25. We can't disappoint Daniel and Sarah, we promised to take them. "

Wally called William Khan, the president of Harvard Law School. "Mr. Khan, my name is Wally Kozak. I am honoured that you chose me to be a guest lecturer. Unfortunately, I must decline. I promised my children that I would take them to the Punky Doodle Corners fair on October 25. Last year I couldn't take them. I don't want to disappoint them again this year."

William Khan laughed. "Mr. Kozak, that is the flimsiest excuse that I have ever heard. You better show up for your lecture. If you don't, I will have you in front of the law society tribunal." Wally was really upset.

"Mr. Khan, if you insist that I show up for the lecture, I will find the most stupid and disgusting court case. When the students see it, they will refuse to participate in the assignment." William Khan told Wally if he did that, he would face the consequences. Wally didn't care; he would not break his promise to Daniel and Sarah.

Wally called Jeffrey to remind him that he and Benny have an appointment to see Sean today. He asked Jeffrey if he wanted him to come with him. Jeffrey told Wally that he wanted to see Sean alone. Wally was happy that he didn't have to go with Jeffrey. He spent the rest of the afternoon looking for a stupid and disgusting case to give the students for an assignment.

It didn't take long for Wally to find out what he was looking for. In Franklin, Tennessee, Lucinda Marbles attempted to cut off her husband's penis with a cleaver. Her husband, Judge Joshua Marbles, was asleep. He woke up just in time to stop her. Lucinda Marbles was charged and convicted of assault with intent to cause bodily harm. She was sentenced to three years in prison.

In her defence, Lucinda asked the court to have her husband committed. She told the court that she was in a romantic mood. She offered to give her husband oral sex. He refused her because he wanted to watch American Idol on television. Lucinda claimed that no sane man would turn down oral sex to watch American Idol.

A newspaper headline read: Wicked Weenie Whacker gets three years in the slammer. Another headline read Judge Joshua Marbles Lost His Marbles. Wally sent the case to William Khan. Two days later, he was standing in front of the law society tribunal. Judge Neville White was a huge black man. He could pass for Clarence's twin.

Judge Neville White said, "William Khan brought some serious charges against you, Mr. Kozak. Please explain yourself. I'm not happy with what you did."

Wally explained to Judge Neville that he had promised his children that he would take them to the Punky Doodle Corners fair in Ontario, Canada. He couldn't take them last year and didn't want to disappoint them again this year.

Judge Neville asked Wally if the case that he submitted to William Khan was real or one that he had made up. Wally replied, "The case is real. William Khan said that I had the flimsiest excuse that he had ever heard. I was insulted; that's why I chose that case."

Judge Neville asked Wally how old are his children and why do they want to go to the fair. Wally said. "We have 7-year-old twins, Daniel and Sarah. Your honour, all children would want to go to a fair called the Punky Doodle Corners Fair. The children will have a chance to chase young piglets and chickens, spend time at a petting zoo, go on hayrides, and eat baked goods and chocolates. I'm looking forward to going there myself."

Judge Neville White was smiling. "Mr. Kozak, I understand the importance of a good family life. All charges against you are dropped." Wally thanked the judge and shook his hand. Wally smiled. He found out that Judge Neville White was going to check out the Punky Doodle Corners fair. He was considering taking his children there. Wally called Elizabeth to tell her the good news.

Wally called Jeffrey. He wanted to know how his visit with Sean went. Jeffrey told Wally that he enjoyed his time with Sean. "Wally, the hockey season will start soon. I promised him that I would take him to a game. The problem is that the Spencer Marauder home games sell out. I gave up my season tickets when you married Elizabeth."

Wally told Jeffrey to relax. "I have season tickets; just let me know when you are planning to take Sean. Tomorrow is your second chemotherapy session. I'm very busy, my grandparents will be with you.

Wally and his family took a flight to Toronto, Canada. At the airport, a limousine will take Wally's family to the Punky Doodle Corners fair. Daniel and Sarah were too excited to sleep. They kept Wally and Elizabeth awake all night.

When they arrived at the Toronto airport, a limousine was waiting to drive them to the PunkyDoodles Corners Fair. Johnny and his grandfather were waiting for them. As soon as Wally and Elizabeth were introduced to Johnny and his grandfather, Daniel and Sarah ran off with Johnny. Elizabeth ran after them.

Johnny's grandfather's name was Billy Johnson. He and Wally headed for the cafeteria. Billy owned a dairy farm. He also had some pigs and chickens. He handed Wally some hot apple cider. "Wally, tomorrow morning the children will have fun chasing baby pigs and chickens. I hope you brought extra clean clothes for them. Johnny will also take Daniel and Sarah to the hen house to pick eggs. Then after lunch we will be going back to the fair."

Billy and Wally were drinking hot apple cider waiting for Elizabeth and the children. They were looking at all the exhibits in the cafeteria. Wally said, "Billy, Daniel and Sarah said that there are a lot of weird looking animals at the petting zoo." Billy smiled. "Wally, some of the animals would look weird to city folks, but not to us farmers."

Elizabeth showed up with the children. Their faces were covered with cotton candy. Elizabeth told Wally that she took a lot of pictures of some weird-looking animals at the petting zoo. Both Billy and Wally laughed. It was time to leave the fair. Billy drove everyone back to the farm in his truck.

Early next morning the children were ready to chase baby pigs and chickens. It was a good thing that Wally brought extra clean clothes. The children were covered in mud. A huge tub of water was waiting for them in the barn. Billy's wife was preparing breakfast while the children were having a bath. She prepared eggs, sausages, bacon, pancakes and toast.

After breakfast, Johnny took Daniel and Sarah to the hen house to gather eggs. They were each given a basket. Johnny showed Daniel and Sarah where to look. After an hour they returned, each carrying a basket full of eggs. Wally was surprised to see that no eggs were broken.

Billy said, "It's time to drive the children back to the fair. There will be a hayride going through a cornfield maze for them. Tomorrow morning, I will show Daniel and Sarah how we milked the cows. After breakfast, a limousine will drive you back to the Toronto airport. "

Elizabeth went on the hayride with the children. A farmer was playing the banjo and singing songs to the children. Wally and Billy stayed at the cafeteria drinking apple cider. Wally was surprised to see Judge Neville White and William Khan together with their children. Wally waved to them and they waved back. The children had a wonderful time on the hayride. It was time to leave, Billy drove everyone back to the farm.

It was 4:30 in the morning when Wally woke up Daniel and Sarah. Billy was ready to show them how the cows are milked. He let Daniel and Sarah hook up a milking machine to the cow's udder. Billy's wife had breakfast ready. She prepared eggs, sausage, pancakes, and homemade bread.

Wally and Elizabeth thanked Johnny's grandparents for their hospitality. Daniel and Sarah said goodbye to Johnny. A limousine showed up to take Wally's family to the Toronto airport. Everyone had a wonderful time, but were glad to be going home.

In the morning Wally went to see Grandmother at her clinic. He wanted to find out how Jeffrey was doing after his chemotherapy. Grandmother told Wally that the chemotherapy did slow down the spreading of the cancer but also made Jeffery very weak. She recommended no more chemotherapy for Jeffrey. Wally said goodbye to his grandmother and left to see Jeffrey at his home.

Jeffrey was happy to see Wally. He smiled, "Wally, Sean's mother called me. His surgery went as expected. He will be discharged in two days. I still want to take him to the Spencers Marauders hockey game."

Wally told Jeffrey that he should be strong enough to take Sean to a hockey game when the season starts. Wally had tickets ready for him. Jeffrey thanked Wally and fell asleep. Wally said to Christine, "Jeffrey is very weak. He needs to build up his strength. When he wakes up, get him out of bed. He needs to walk as much as possible. When he gets too tired, have him sit. Do not let him lie down until bedtime. Tomorrow, start off slowly on his exercise routine. Make sure he keeps on praying and meditating. I'll come by tomorrow to see how he is doing.

Chapter 86

Wally drove back to his office. He saw Lawrence in his office reading a newspaper in disgust. Lawrence said to Wally, "The college is about to drop the varsity hockey team due to lack of funding. The college just gave some group $200,000 to study the mating habits of the bumblebee. That money should have been used to save the varsity hockey team. I enjoy going to those games."

Wally totally agreed with Lawrence, but there is nothing that can be done. Wally went back to his office. Wally decided to apply for a college grant to study the mating habits of the Tasmanian Big Foot. Wally did this as a joke to relieve tension.

The next morning Wally went to see Jeffrey. Christine was happy to see him. Christine was worried, "Wally, Jeffrey is too stubborn. He refuses to get out of bed."

Wally walked into Jeffrey's bedroom and whacked him in the head. He said, "Jeffrey, if you don't get out of bed, you will be too weak to take Sean to the hockey game." Wally then grabbed Jeffrey's arm and dragged him out of bed. "Jeffrey, you need to build up your strength. The only way to do that is to keep moving. When you get very tired, sit down, do not lie down until bedtime. Eat as much as you can. Keep saying your prayer 10 times a day, meditate and tomorrow begin your exercise program." Wally told Christine if Jeffrey refuses to cooperate to call him. Christine gave Wally a big hug; Wally left for his office.

At the end of the day, Wally and Elizabeth drove home. Joan picked up Daniel and Sarah from school. Cleo, Leo, and Orval were with Grandfather in the trails. Wally went to get the mail. He was shocked to see a letter from the College. They approved Wally's application to study the mating habits of the Tasmanian Big Foot.

Wally received a $200,000 cheque. He put the cheque in his pocket. Elizabeth would freak out if she found out what he did.

Next day Wally walked into Lawrence's office. He was smiling. "Lawrence, I applied to the College for a grant to study the mating habits of the Tasmanian Big Foot. The college approved my application. They gave me a $200,000 cheque. Is it too late to save the varsity hockey team?"

Lawrence grabbed the cheque from Wally's hand to look at it. He gave Wally a big hug. "Wally, let's go to the college administrator right now. He happens to be the coach of the hockey team. Wally, you don't know how happy you have made me!" The varsity hockey team was saved just in time to start the season.

Lawrence told Wally that he couldn't get tickets to the Spencers Marauders, because they always sell out. Wally told Lawrence that the hockey arena will be expanding seating capacity from 6000 to 8000. He will have plenty of opportunities to buy tickets.

A week later Charles Winchester came to see Wally. He was the president of the college faculty. He said, "Mr. Kozak you applied for a grant that you are not qualified to receive."

Wally smiled, "According to the person who gave me that grant, I am qualified to receive it." Charles told Wally that the person who gave him the grant was no longer employed by the College. "Mr. Kozak, you applied for a grant under false pretense. There's no such thing as a Tasmanian Big Foot. I want you to return the money. If you refuse, the College will sue you."

Wally was annoyed. "Who says that there is no such thing as a Tasmanian Big Foot?"

Charles laughed, "Mr. Kozak, if you can prove to the college faculty that a Tasmanian Big Foot exists, you can keep the money. Call me in two weeks when you have your proof."

Wally went to see Lawrence. He shook his head and said, "I have a big problem. The college wants me to return the grant unless I prove to them that the Tasmanian Big Foot exists. If I refuse to return the money, the college will sue me." Lawrence told Wally to relax. The college will not sue him because they would become a laughing stock if the media found out. The taxpayers will not be happy.

Wally was still worried, "Lawrence, Charles Winchester is the president of the faculty. He fired the person who gave me the grant. I don't think he cares what the media or the taxpayers think. I have to get someone to get into a monkey suit and convince the college faculty that the Tasmanian Big Foot does exist." Lawrence turned away and told Wally that there was no way that he was getting into a monkey suit. He told Wally that it was his problem. Wally knew that it was his problem. He wasn't planning on asking Lawrence to get into a monkey suit.

Wally drove off to see Katie at her modelling school to film the ice wine commercial. He didn't tell Elizabeth because he didn't want her watching him.

Katie was happy to see him. "Wally, I'm glad that you came early. The cameraman and director are here. The suit that you are wearing now is perfect. The director is ready for you." In the commercial, Wally said that Fuls Ice Wine was Licensed under Niagara Brandt Wines. Their ice wine won several awards throughout Europe. You get the same quality of ice wine with Fuls at a fraction of the cost. It took two hours to film the ice wine commercial the way the director wanted. Wally was glad that the filming was over. The director told Wally that this commercial was way better than the one he did for Fuls beer.

Wally was finally able to explain to Katie his problem. When she heard what Wally wanted, she began to laugh. A few minutes later, she was able to say, "Wally, I can borrow a monkey suit for you from someone who works for the film studio. My makeup artist can make the person wearing the monkey suit look real. I could also borrow a cage for the monkey from the film studio. Who is going to wear the monkey suit?" Wally told Katie that he didn't know yet, but he would definitely have somebody wearing a monkey suit for him. Katie gave Wally a hug and wished him well.

Chapter 87

Wally went to see Jeffrey. Christine was happy to see Wally. She told Wally that Jeffrey was beginning to get stronger ever since he started to move. Christine opened the door to Jeffrey's room, and Wally walked in. He saw Jeffrey sitting in a chair reading a magazine. Jeffrey was excited, "Wally, there is a clinic in Mexico that claims to cure 80% of cancer patients. They inject the patient with a mixture of herbs. I'm planning to go there. Will you come with me?"

Wally shook his head. "Jeffrey, I am familiar with that clinic in Mexico. They don't say how many of their patients have terminal cancer. I know which herbs that they use. Some of them are poisonous. They will kill a weak patient with terminal cancer. Jeffrey, you are too weak to take those herbs. My advice is to keep doing what you are doing. If I feel that you are getting strong enough to take those herbs, I will administer them to you myself."

Christine looked at a dejected Jeffrey. She said to him, "Jeffrey, you better listen to Wally. Our doctor believed that you would be dead by now. Remember, he told you to keep doing what you are doing. I'll make sure that you do."

Christine left Jeffrey alone with Wally. Jeffrey was still dejected. Wally smiled, "Jeffrey, I'm going to ask you for a favour. When I do, pretend that you are to play a part in a movie."

Wally explained his problem to Jeffrey and why he wanted him to put on a monkey suit. "Jeffrey, I'm not forcing you to do it. If you feel uncomfortable putting on a monkey suit, say so. I'll get somebody else. However, if you agree, I will set you up with a dinner date with Cindy O'Reilly at the Spencers Mill, my treat.

Jeffrey told Wally that Cindy hates him. She will never go out with him in a million years. "Jeffrey, Cindy owes me a favour. If you refuse to put on the monkey suit, she will. If you agree to put on the monkey suit, she will go out with you, I promise. Jeffrey, if you pretend that you are in a movie playing at Tasmainian Bigfoot, you might have fun doing it. Think of all the actors who put on monkey suits in the Planet of the Ape movies. All you have to do is stand in a cage and growl. If anybody gets too close, bonk them in the head. I will take care of everything else."

Jeffrey agreed to put on the monkey suit because he wanted to have a date with Cindy. Wally thanked Jeffrey and reminded him to love his pets.

Jeffrey did love his pets. He enjoyed throwing a ball in the backyard for Benny to chase. He also enjoyed taking him for a walk. When watching television, Jeffrey had the kitten on his lap. He liked rubbing his tummy. Jeffrey called the kitten Kitty.

Wally needed someone to play the part of an anthropologist. He thought that Dr. Reggie would be perfect for the part. Wally called Dr. Reggie to explain his problem and why he needed his help. Dr. Reggie laughed, "Wally that sounds like fun. I will be happy to play the part of an anthropologist for you."

Dr. Reggie was to pretend to be an anthropologist who represented the Tasmanian government. He would tell the college faculty that the Tasmanian Big Foot was caught illegally, and the Tasmanian government wanted him immediately returned because he was an endangered species.

Wally started to type out some authentic-looking documents from the Tasmanian government to give to Dr. Reggie. He will give the documents to Charles Winchester as proof that the Tasmanian Big Foot does exist.

Wally made arrangements to use a nearby school's gym. He would have the college faculty meet him there. Katie brought Jeffrey a monkey suit. He put it on, and Katie, a makeup artist, started to work on Jeffrey's face and mouth. Three hours later, the makeup artist finished. Jeffrey looked like a real ape.

Wally drove Jeffrey to the school gym. Dr. Reggie was already waiting for them. A truck arrived carrying a cage with wheels. Wally and Dr. Reggie carried the cage off the truck. Jeffrey got in. Wally and Dr. Reggie opened the double doors to the entrance and pushed the cage into the gym. Ten minutes later the college faculty arrived. Charles took a close look at Jeffrey growling. Jeffrey bonked Charles on the head. Charles rubbing his head said, "That is not a Tasmanian Big Foot, that is an ape."

Wally introduced Dr. Reggie to the college faculty. Dr. Reggie said, "A Tasmanian Big Foot is a rare breed of ape that lives only in Tasmania. It is an endangered species and was captured illegally. I'm here as a representative of the Tasmanian government to take possession of the Tasmanian Big Foot immediately and send it back to Tasmania."

Dr. Reggie handed his documents to Charles. As Charles was reading them, Wally and Dr. Reggie pushed the cage out of the gym to the back of the school. The school faculty watched them, they said nothing.

Dr. Reggie was laughing, "Wally, I don't remember the last time that I had so much fun." Jeffery came out of the cage and took off his monkey suit. He told Wally that he had a blast. Wally picked up the monkey suit and placed it in a plastic bag. He told Jeffrey that his dinner date with Cindy will be this Friday night at 7 o'clock at the Spencers Mill. "Jeffrey, make sure you control your foul mouth and bad temper."

Jeffrey laughed, "Wally, every time I swore, my mother would whack me in the head. I no longer have a foul mouth and prayer and meditation helps me control my temper." Wally and Dr. Reggie loaded the cage onto the truck. Wally thanked the driver with a $50 handshake. He told Dr. Reggie and Jeffrey to meet him at the Spencers Mill for lunch in two hours. "I'm going to see what Charles has to say."

Charles was not impressed. "Mr. Kozak, you didn't fool us one bit. Our college anthropologists said that there is no such thing as a Tasmanian Big Foot. However, one of the faculty members told me that you used the money to save our varsity hockey team. If you would have told me what you did with the money, I would not have asked you to return it. The college faculty thanks you for saving our varsity hockey team. "

Wally was annoyed and asked Charles if he wasn't going to ask him to return the money, why did he have to produce proof that the Tasmanian Big Foot exists. Charles smiled, "Mr. Kozak, we just wanted to see what kind of proof you would come up with. The college faculty commends you on your ingenuity. We enjoyed your performance." Wally was not mad. Everyone had a good laugh. He called Lawrence to tell him the good news. He then drove back to the office to see Cindy.

Cindy was not happy to see Wally. She never forgave him for dumping her. Cindy even refused to go to Wally's wedding. Her father was the master of ceremony at his wedding. Without looking at Wally she said, "What do you want?"

Wally told Cindy that Jeffrey Kelly has terminal colon cancer and wants to go out on a dinner date with her. "I reserved a table for Jeffrey and you at the Spencers Mill this Friday night at 7 o'clock." Cindy turned around and told Wally that there was no way that she was going out on a dinner date with that fat, disgusting pig.

Wally told Cindy that Jeffrey lost a lot of weight. He no longer had a foul mouth and a bad temper. Wally took out his phone to show Cindy the video of her and Michael having sex. Cindy was shocked. "Wally, are you going to blackmail me for the rest of my life!"

Wally smiled, "Don't worry, Cindy, I'm not interested in the blackmailing business. I owe Jeffrey a favour. If you agree to go with him on a dinner date, Samantha will never see this video. Cindy was relieved and said, "Tell Jeffrey that I will meet him at the Spencers Mill this Friday night at 7 o'clock."

Wally thanked Cindy and left to meet Jeffery and Dr. Reggie at the Spencers Mill. They were waiting for him. Wally ordered beef stew, perogies, and Caesar salad. Dr. Reggie and Jeffery ordered what Wally ordered. Wally told Jeffrey that Cindy would meet him for dinner this Friday night at 7 o'clock. He reminded Jeffrey to be on his best behaviour. Jeffrey could hardly believe that he was going to have a dinner date with Cindy. Wally told Jeffrey that love was starting to flow into him. "Jeffrey, you have another reason to start living. There is more meaning in your life. Keep up the good work."

Dr. Reggie was pleased to hear that Wally had arranged a dinner date for Jeffrey. He also wanted to know what Charles Winchester had to say. Wally said, "Charles wasn't going to ask me to return the money when he found out that I used it to save the varsity hockey team. However, he still wanted to see the proof that I would produce that the Tasmanian Big Foot existed." Dr. Reggie and Jeffery laughed. They thanked Wally for the wonderful lunch.

Chapter 88

Wally and Elizabeth drove home. Elizabeth continued to sing children's songs to Wally. He continued to ignore her. When they arrived home, Elizabeth went inside to see Aunt Judy, Daniel, and Sarah. Wally went to look for Grandfather, Cleo, Leo, and Orval in the trails. Aunt Judy had cookies and tea waiting for Elizabeth. Daniel and Sarah ate cookies while watching television.

Grandfather Wally and his pets returned just in time to avoid a heavy rain. Aunt Judy had to drive home in the heavy rain. Grandfather and Wally went downstairs to visit Purdy, Charlie, and Grandmother.

It was bedtime for Daniel and Sarah. Elizabeth put Daniel to bed. Sarah refuses to go to bed. Elizabeth called Wally to come and deal with Sarah. Wally went upstairs to see Sarah. He asked her why she didn't want to go to bed.

Sarah said, "Daddy, at school, the teacher said that God gave us the ability to make decisions to choose whatever we want. I decided to choose not to go to bed." Wally took Sarah by the hand and led her to the back door. He opened it and said, "Sarah, you can decide to stay in the house and go to bed, or you can decide to go outside and do whatever your little heart desires; it is your choice."

Sarah looked outside at the pouring rain and then looked up at Wally and began to cry. Elizabeth took Sarah by the hand and led her to the bedroom.

Wally was in his office doing paperwork. Gloria paid him a surprise visit. "Wally, I have been clean for a whole year. To celebrate, Dan Smith, my counselor, quit his job and proposed to me." Gloria showed Wally her beautiful engagement ring. "Our wedding is set for June 21. It will be held at the Spencers Mill. We'll be getting married at their wedding chapel just like you and Elizabeth did. Dan and I decided that we want you to be the best man and Elizabeth, the maid of honour. I did take your advice and started to pray and meditate. Dan started to pray and meditate with me. It helped me a lot with rehab, just like you said."

Wally gave Gloria a big hug. "Congratulations, I'm happy for you. Elizabeth and I will be happy to be the best man and maid of honour." Wally and Gloria went to see Elizabeth in her office. Gloria showed Elizabeth her engagement ring. Elizabeth was surprised.

Wally said, "Elizabeth, Gloria is engaged to Dan, her counselor. They want me to be the best man and you the maid of honour." Elizabeth was speechless. Wally told Gloria that Elizabeth will be happy to be her maid of honour. Gloria gave Elizabeth a big goodbye hug.

Chapter 89

Jeffrey was waiting at his table for Cindy to arrive at the Spencers Mill. Cindy showed up five minutes later. She came from the hairdresser wearing a stunning red dress. Jeffrey took a good look at Cindy and told her that she looked fabulous. Cindy blushed. She thanked Jeffrey and told him that he looked pretty good himself since he lost a lot of weight.

Jeffrey and Cindy ordered dinner. They had prime rib, scallop potatoes, steamed vegetables and Caesar salad. For dessert they had brandy, coffee and cheesecake wafers covered in dark chocolate.

Jeffrey asked Cindy, "Do you like hockey?" Cindy told Jeffrey that she went to see a hockey game with a friend. She enjoyed watching hockey a lot. She used to go to basketball games. Cindy lost interest in basketball, when her team started to suck.

Jeffrey smiled, "Cindy, the hockey season will start soon. I can get tickets to the Spencer Marauder games. There is a new restaurant in the arena. We could have dinner there and then watch the game." Cindy was happy to accept his invitation. "Jeffrey, thank you for a wonderful dinner. I had a good time. My parents are having dinner over there. Call me when you get those hockey tickets."

Jeffrey was really happy. He never dreamed that he would have another date with Cindy. He asked for the bill. Uncle Ivan told him that Wally will take care of it.

Cindy went to her parent's table. Harry was smiling. "Cindy, you never told us that your date was with Jeffrey Kelly. I'm very surprised that the both of you behaved so well. I was expecting to see a big fight. Are you going to see him again?"

Cindy said, "Father, I couldn't believe that Jeffrey behaved like a gentleman. He didn't swear or lose his temper. If he is still alive,

Jeffrey will take me to dinner at the new restaurant at the hockey arena, and then we will watch the hockey game. I only went out with Jeffrey as a favour to Wally and because Jeffrey does have terminal colon cancer."

Wally drove Elizabeth home. He dropped her off and then went to see Jeffrey. Wally was happy that he and Cindy had a good time. Wally was surprised that Cindy had accepted Jeffrey's invitation to dinner and hockey. "Jeffrey, it sounds like Cindy is giving you another reason to live. I brought you tickets for the first Marauders' home game for you to take Shaun. I will get you tickets to the next home game to take Cindy."

Wally could see the happiness in Jeffrey's eyes. "Jeffrey, I believe you are strong enough to consider the herbal cancer cure. However, some of those herbs are poisonous and will kill you if you are too weak. You will experience an incredible amount of pain, and there is no guarantee that you will be cured."

Jeffrey became excited. "Wally, you said with love there is always hope. I feel a lot of love. I want to take herbal cancer remedies. I'm confident that I will survive. There is no way that I'm going to die. Cindy likes hockey." Wally said goodbye to a happy Jeffrey.

When Wally arrived home, Elizabeth handed him a letter. "Screaming Mouth Leroy wants you to write another song for him. If he likes your song, he will pay you $25,000 plus royalties. Wally please don't be stupid. If you write a song for him and he likes it, someone stupid will come along to sue you."

Wally was smiling. "Elizabeth, I know the perfect song to write for Screaming Mouth Leroy."

Elizabeth was shaking her head. "Let me guess. You are going to write a song about Lucinda the Wicked Weenie Whacker."

Wally kept on smiling. "Elizabeth, you got that right. I'm not worried about any stupid idiot wanting to sue me. It won't take me long to write the song."

Chapter 90

Wally was looking forward to having dinner with Elizabeth at Uncle Ivan's new restaurant at the Beer store. They will be the first guests for the grand opening this afternoon. There was a long lineup at Fuls restaurant's grand opening. The menu was very similar to Spencers at the arena. Wally and Elizabeth had prime rib, scallop potatoes, and Caesar salad. The first day of business was a success. It will help increase beer sales at the Beer store.

Uncle Ivan came to Wally's table. He said, "Wally, the renovations to the row house are complete. Alex wants to be paid. Families will be arriving next week. They will start paying rent next month." Wally took out his chequebook and wrote out a cheque for $350,000. He gave the cheque to Uncle Ivan to give to Alex. Wally and Elizabeth thanked Uncle Ivan for a wonderful lunch. Wally believed that both of Uncle Ivan's new restaurants would be successful.

On their way back to the office, Elizabeth asked Wally how Jeffrey was doing. "Elizabeth, Jeffrey is doing as well as expected. I'm going to administer an herbal remedy for him tomorrow morning. The remedy will either cure him or kill him. Jeffrey said that he has a lot to live for. He wants to take herbal remedies. Are you going to come to watch Jeffrey when he takes the herbal remedies?"

Elizabeth told Wally that she feels sorry for Jeffrey and wishes him the best but doesn't want to see him.

Jeffrey was at the Kozak Naturopath Clinic waiting for Wally. He walked in and asked Jeffrey if he still wanted to go through with the herbal remedy. Jeffrey gave Wally a serious look. "You bet; I had a great time with Cindy at dinner. She likes hockey and wants to go to the Spencer Marauders hockey games with me. There's no way that I'm going to die!"

Wally smiled. "Jeffrey, you got the right attitude. I don't believe you are strong enough to have the herbs injected. You will have to ingest the herbs. It will take much longer for the herbs to cure you but it will be much safer. Before I administer the herbal cure, I want you to say your prayer and meditate for five minutes. As soon as you ingest the herbs, I will hypnotize you to fall asleep. Tomorrow morning when you wake up, you will experience incredible pain. To keep you from screaming, I will have you suck on a large piece of hard ginger candy. You should keep your eyes closed. If you can withstand the pain in the next three days, you should be cured."

Jeffrey said his prayer, meditated and five minutes later he ingested the herbs. Wally hypnotized him. "Sweet dreams Jeffrey, I'll see you tomorrow morning. My grandparents will look in on you."

Wally stopped by the Spencers Mill for a takeout lunch on his way back to the office. He had perogies and bean salad for lunch. Elizabeth barged into Wally's office. "Congratulations Wally, Screaming Mouth Leroy loved your song. He sent you a cheque for $25,000, royalties will follow." Elizabeth placed Wally's cheque on his desk, then grabbed Wally's perogies and bean salad and ran out of the office.

Early the next morning, Wally went to see how Jeffrey was doing. Grandmother sadly looked at Wally. "Jeffrey's is very weak. He has to get stronger if he is to survive."

Wally called Sean's mother to ask her if he had time to visit Jeffrey. A half-hour later, she arrived with Sean. Grandmother brought in Jeffrey's pets. Wally placed the hockey tickets on Jeffrey's chest. He gave Sean a storybook to read to Jeffery. Sean asked Wally if Jeffrey was going to die. Wally told Sean, "Jeffrey is very weak, but he is not going to die. He just needs some company. Read him a story to cheer him up. He can't talk, but he will listen."

Sean started to read a story for Jeffrey. When Sean finished reading, he noticed tears running down Jeffrey's cheeks. Sean asked Wally, "Why is Jeffrey crying, I thought you said that the story would make him happy." Wally told Sean that the story did make Jeffrey happy. "Sean, those are happy tears. Jeffrey can't talk so he is smiling with happy tears."

Wally reminded Sean that Jeffrey will be well enough to take him to a hockey game. Sean thanked Wally and his mother drove him home. Grandmother was smiling. "Wally, that was smart thinking. Jeffrey's pulse is much stronger. If his pulse stays at this rate, Jeffrey will have a good chance of being cured. We won't know until the next two days." Grandmother placed Benny and Kitty on Jeffrey's chest. Wally stuck the hockey tickets into Jeffrey's hand. Wally drove back to the office.

Samantha barged into Wally's office. She was furious. "Wally, there are six people filing six separate lawsuits against you for stealing their song. What is this all about!" Wally said in disbelief, "Screaming Mouth Leroy, a southern blues singer, wanted me to write a song for him. He loved the song that I wrote for him and paid me $25,000 plus royalties. The people who want to sue me are gold diggers. They have no grounds for their lawsuit."

Samantha shook her head and told Wally to stick to being a lawyer. "It's going to take money and time to get rid of these people." Wally then got a call from Elizabeth. She said, "Nah! Nah! I told you so."

Wally decided to go to the cafeteria for a pot of tea. He saw Lawrence sitting at a table. He went over to see him. Lawrence looked up at Wally and said, "Priscilla Johnson changed her will. She left her entire fortune to the cat. Priscilla's sister Janice has power of attorney. She has custody of the cat. Jennifer, Priscilla's daughter, hired me. She wants to contest the will. Priscilla's original will left her entire estate to Jennifer. Janice managed to get Priscilla to change the will while she was in a nursing home. She wants Jennifer to move out of the house."

Wally smiled. "Lawrence, I wrote a song for Screaming Mouth Leroy. He loved it and paid me $25,000 plus royalties. Six people are suing me with six lawsuits for stealing their song. I will take on your case if you are willing to take on mine." Lawrence happily accepted Wally's offer. He told Wally not to worry about those gold diggers. He knows how to deal with them.

During lunch Wally brought a cup of tea and a pumpkin spice muffin into Elizabeth's office. He found her head buried in paperwork. He placed the tea and muffin on her desk and gave her a kiss on the back of her neck. Elizabeth looked up at Wally and told him that she hates doing wills and divorces. There is too much paperwork involved.

Wally smiled, "Elizabeth, I have some good news. Lawrence agreed to defend me against the gold diggers if I took a case that he didn't want. You want to take a look?" Elizabeth started to read the file and munched on the muffin that Wally brought. Wally told Elizabeth that if she wants, he'll do her paperwork while she can do Lawrence's kitty case.

Elizabeth jumped up and gave Wally a big kiss. She then grabbed all her papers and stuffed them into a briefcase. "Here you are Wally, my paperwork. It was nice of you to bring me tea and a muffin."

Wally went back to his office with the briefcase to do Elizabeth's paperwork. Wally was able to do all of her paperwork in three hours by using his photographic memory and ability to retrieve any information that he wanted from his memory bank. It would've taken three days for Elizabeth to do her paperwork.

Wally left the office to see Jeffrey at the clinic. Grandmother told Wally that Jeffrey's pulse is stable and if he survives the next 24 hours, he should be cured. Wally told Grandmother that Jeffrey will survive because he is determined to take Cindy to dinner and a hockey game. Wally saw a huge smile on Jeffrey's face as he left.

Wally went to see his Beer store. He was pleased to see it busy. Wally went upstairs to see his warehouse. He saw 500 cases of Fuls ice wine ready for the market. He had a dozen cases brought down to the Beer store. Wally called uncle Ivan to have a dozen more cases of ice wine delivered to the Spencers Mill. Wally decided to have a snack at the Fuls restaurant. He had tea and cheesecake wafers. Wally received a call from Kevin. He wanted to meet with Wally.

Several minutes later, Kevin and Katie showed up. Kevin was smiling. "Wally, I sent out a survey to see how we can improve business. A huge response suggested that we should also brew a cream ale. I know how to brew a very good cream ale. We still have enough room to expand. There is enough profit to pay for the expansion. I just need your approval." Wally gave his approval, and Kevin happily thanked him.

Katie was smiling. "Wally, since you gave us your approval. We need you to make another commercial for Fuls cream ale. I booked an appointment to film the commercial at my modelling school for next Wednesday." Wally was not happy. He told Katie not to tell Elizabeth.

Chapter 91

Elizabeth sat down with Jennifer Johnson. She asked her who owned the cat. Jennifer told Elizabeth that the cat belonged to her. "Elizabeth, I brought my cat with me to live with my mother because I left an abusive husband."

Elizabeth told Jennifer that since she owned the cat, the court should not have given custody of the cat to her aunt, Janice. Jennifer told Elizabeth that her aunt was a very demanding and controlling person. "Elizabeth, she persuaded my mother to change her will when she was in a nursing home."

Elizabeth smiled. "Jennifer, your aunt probably didn't realize that you owned the cat. That is why she wanted to get custody of the cat. We will motion the court to have you receive custody of the cat because you own the cat. There is no reason for the court not to give you custody of your own cat. Since the cat owns the house, your aunt has no authority to force you to move out. You will be inheriting the cat's estate. You will also be the cat's power of attorney." Jennifer was very pleased with what Elizabeth proposed.

On their way home, Wally asked Elizabeth if she had a chance to meet with Jennifer Johnson. Elizabeth told Wally that she met her an hour ago. "I told Jennifer that the best thing for her to do is to get custody of the cat, since the cat belongs to her. That would allow her to inherit the cat's estate."

Christine was waiting for Elizabeth. Daniel and Sarah were watching television. Wally went back to the backyard to sit on the patio. He was going to wait for Grandfather, Cleo, Leo and Orval. Howard flew by. He landed on Wally's shoulders. Grandfather, Cleo, Leo and Orval showed up a few minutes later. Cleo and Leo ran up to Wally and jumped on his lap. Wally scratched their tummy.

He also scratched Orval's tummy. Wally and Grandfather then went inside the house to have dinner.

Chapter 92

Wally went to see Jeffrey at the clinic. Grandmother said to Wally, "Jeffrey is very weak but he is alive. Jeffrey has no cancer and will live." Wally hugged grandmother. He called Christine to tell her the good news. Wally went back home to pick up Elizabeth, to drive back to the office. Wally had Elizabeth's briefcase full of paperwork completed. Elizabeth couldn't believe that Wally managed to complete her paperwork in such a short time. "Wally, how did you get everything done so quickly? It would've taken me three days to do it?"

Wally laughed, "Elizabeth, while you were sleeping, I hired a bunch of elves to do your paperwork." Elizabeth was not laughing.

Lawrence came to see Wally. He had good news for him. "Wally, I wrote letters to each of the people who want to sue you. The letter said that you would file a million-dollar counter lawsuit if they proceeded with their lawsuits. All six of the people dropped their lawsuit against you." Wally thanked Lawrence and told him that Elizabeth would be taking his kitty case.

Elizabeth was ready to go home. She asked Wally how Jeffrey was doing. "Elizabeth, Jeffrey is very weak but still alive. It will take some time to get all his strength back. I'm going to go and see him on our way home, you want to come with me?" Elizabeth had no intentions of seeing Jeffrey.

Wally and Elizabeth drove home. For dinner, there was pizza, perogies and bean salad. Wally kissed Elizabeth goodbye and left to see Jeffrey at the clinic.

Grandmother told Wally that Jeffrey was still very weak and it would take some time to get all his strength back. All he needed was plenty of food, sleep, and exercise. "Wally, since Jeffrey no longer has colon cancer, you can take him home today," Wally called Christine to tell her the good news.

Wally looked at Jeffrey and smiled. "Jeffrey, you heard what Grandmother said. It's time for you to go home. Soon, you'll be able to take Cindy to dinner and a hockey game. " Jeffery also had to take Sean to a hockey game.

Wally helped Jeffrey to put on his clothes. Christine called Wally. She asked him to bring Jeffrey to the hospital. "Dr. Craig, our family doctor, wants to examine him."

Wally drove Jeffrey to the hospital. Dr. Craig was waiting for Jeffrey in the examination room. Christine and Wally brought Jeffery into the examination room. They waited outside. One hour later, Dr. Craig came out of the examination room. He was shaking his head in disbelief. "Wally, you performed a miracle. I was certain that Jeffrey's colon cancer was terminal and he would die soon. I know that Jeffrey is very weak, but he is still alive and cancer free!" Christine started to cry and gave Wally a big hug.

A week later, Jeffrey was starting to feel like himself. Today, he will be taking Sean to see the Spencer Marauders. Next week he will be taking Cindy to dinner at the arena's restaurant and the Spencer Marauders game. Jeffrey was surprised that Wally gave him tickets for the luxury box seats. Jeffrey and Sean had a very good time at the game. Sean told Jeffery that his mother had a new boyfriend. He has season tickets to the Spencer Marauders hockey games. Jeffrey drove Sean home.

Jeffery was excited. Tonight, he was going to take Cindy to dinner and a hockey game. He called Cindy. She was at home with her parents. Jeffery told her that the hockey game started at 8 o'clock. Dinner will be at the hockey arena's restaurant at 6:30. Cindy was very surprised to hear from Jeffrey. She thought that he would be too weak or dead to take her. Cindy told Jeffrey to pick her up for dinner at 6 o'clock tonight.

Harry asked Cindy, who was on the phone. Cindy looked puzzled. "Believe it or not, it was Jeffrey Kelly. He is still alive.

Jeffrey invited me for dinner and to watch the Spencer Marauders." Harry asked Cindy if she was going to go. Cindy smiled, "Why not? Jeffrey behaved himself on our last date. I promised him that I would go to the hockey game if he could get tickets. He is taking me to dinner at the hockey arena before the game."

Jeffrey showed up at Cindy's home at 6 o'clock. Cindy was very surprised at how good Jeffrey looked. He lost more weight and gained muscle. "Jeffrey, I see that you lost more weight; you are looking good." Jeffrey took a good look at Cindy, "You look pretty good yourself." Jeffrey and Cindy drove off to have dinner at Spencer's. Jeffrey asked Cindy if she would like to have prime rib for dinner again.

Cindy was shocked. The Jeffrey that she knew was fat, cheap, had a foul mouth and a bad temper. This Jeffrey was not fat, not cheap, and was a complete gentleman. Cindy didn't know that Jeffrey saved a lot of money by not going to the massage parlour every Friday afternoon to pay for sex.

Jeffrey and Cindy didn't say much during dinner. Jeffrey didn't care, he just enjoyed being with Cindy. During the hockey game, Cindy was screaming in delight. Spencer Marauders won the game. Jeffery invited Cindy to dinner and the next home game. Cindy could hardly wait for the next home game. She was looking forward to sitting in the luxury box seat again.

Jeffrey was counting on Wally to get him tickets to the next home game. He could tell that Cindy was a huge hockey fan.

When Jeffrey arrived at Cindy's home, he had the urge to kiss her, but decided not to. Jeffrey would not know how Cindy would react. Cindy went inside the house. Harry asked her how the date was. "Father, I can't believe it. I really had a good time. The Spencers Marauders won the game easily. We sat in luxury box seats. We had prime rib for dinner. Jeffrey wanted to kiss me goodnight but chickened out."

Harry asked Cindy if she wanted Jeffrey to kiss her good night. "Father, I don't know. I'm glad that he didn't kiss me, because I wouldn't know how to react."

Harry asked Cindy if she was going to go out with Jeffrey again. "Father, Jeffrey has asked me to go out to the next home game and dinner. Good food and hockey, how could I refuse. Good night."

When Jeffrey got home, he called Wally. It was late, and Wally was sleeping. When Wally answered his phone, Jeffrey said, "Wally, Cindy, and I had a great time tonight. I promised her that I would take her to the next home game. Can you get me tickets? "Wally said that he will have tickets for him.

Jeffrey asked Wally how he had gotten luxury box seats. Wally told Jeffrey that he and Samantha bought the hockey team. Next hockey season, six more luxury box seats will be available. There'll be two reserved for him.

Jeffrey said, "Wally, you are right; with love, there is always hope. I almost kissed Cindy tonight. Do you think I should have?" Wally told Jeffrey that he would know when it was time to kiss Cindy good night. "Jeffrey, just keep on saying your prayer, eat right, meditate, and exercise. Good night."

Mary, Harry's wife, asked him. "Do you think Cindy is getting serious about having a relationship with Jeffrey?" Harry shook his head and told Mary that when the hockey season was over, Cindy would probably dump him. Harry didn't think that Cindy would ever get married.

Chapter 93

Elizabeth was excited. Today was her court date with Jennifer Johnson. Wally went with her to court. He helped Elizabeth to prepare for court. Just before court was to proceed, Elizabeth received a phone call. It made her very upset. "Wally, Sarah punched a boy in school. He went home with a bleeding nose. Sarah's in the principal's office. He wants me to pick her up and take her home."

Elizabeth begged Wally to pick up Sarah. He refused to go. Elizabeth punched Wally in the arm and ran out of the courtroom.

Wally approached the bench. He cleared his throat. "Your Honour, we seem to have a family crisis. Our eight-year-old daughter is a bully. She punched a boy in the nose at school. My wife had to go to the principal's office to take her home. An adjournment is not necessary. I am ready to proceed."

Everyone in court laughed. Court proceeded. Wally approached the bench to make a motion. Wally said, "Your Honour, the cat belongs to Jennifer Jones, not her mother. She left her abusive husband to live with her mother. She brought her cat with her. Janice, her aunt, had Priscilla, Jennifer's mother, change her will while she was in a nursing home. The original will leave her entire estate to Jennifer. Since Jennifer owns the cat, I motion that she gets custody of her cat."

The Court granted Wally's motion. Jennifer was very happy. She was going to inherit the cat's estate. Jennifer will also be the cat's power of attorney. Janice was not very happy. She knew that there was no way that she could get custody of the cat. She prayed that Jennifer would not ask her to move out of her sister's house.

Elizabeth arrived at the school. The principal was waiting for her. He was not happy. "Mrs. Kozak, we don't allow bullies at our school. You better have a long talk with Sarah."

Elizabeth took Sarah by her hand and drove home. Sarah refused to talk. Elizabeth was very upset.

"Sarah, wait till your father gets home. He'll teach you a lesson. Sarah still refused to talk."

Wally arrived home; Sarah was sitting on a chair in a corner. Elizabeth was still upset. "Wally, Sarah is all yours. You deal with her." Wally walked over to Sarah and asked her what happened at school. Sarah looked up at Wally. "Daddy, I just wanted to be friends with Billy. When I talk to him, he keeps ignoring me, he doesn't say a word, he doesn't even look at me. I got mad and punched him in the nose."

Wally smiled, "Sweetheart, some boys are very shy. They are afraid of girls. Next time you see Billy, talk to him. Be patient if he doesn't talk to you. Just smile and keep talking to him. Billy will get used to seeing you and will eventually start talking to you." Sarah jumped up and gave Wally a hug. "Elizabeth, you won't have to worry about Sarah behaving badly at school. You will also be happy to hear that the court awarded custody of Jennifer's cat to her. She will inherit the cat's estate.

Chapter 94

Jeffrey picked up Cindy at her home. They drove to Spencers for dinner. Cindy wanted to have fish. Jeffrey ordered halibut and scallop potatoes. They quietly enjoyed their dinner. Cindy thanked Jeffrey for a delicious dinner. They were ready to watch the hockey game. Cindy was happily screaming every time the Spencer Marauders scored a goal. The Spencers Marauders won again. She thanked him for dinner and hockey. Jeffery drove Cindy home.

During the drive to Cindy's home, Jeffrey smiled and said, "Cindy, if I could get hockey tickets for the rest of the season, would you go with me.?" Cindy told Jeffrey that she would be happy to go with him to watch hockey.

When they arrived, Jeffrey was so happy, that he kissed Cindy and ran to his car. Cindy was laughing when she went inside the house. Her parents were waiting for her. Cindy told Harry that she enjoyed dinner and watching the hockey game. "Jeffrey told me that he could get tickets to the hockey games for the rest of the season and invited me to go with him. He was so happy that he kissed me when I said that I would love to watch the hockey games with him."

Harry said, "Cindy, it sounds like Jeffrey wants to have a serious relationship with you. Do you have any interest?" Cindy looked confused. "I don't know. All I know is that I enjoy having dinner and watching hockey games. Good night."

Mary asked Harry, "Do you think Cindy has any interest in having a relationship with Jeffrey?" Harry shook his head and said, "I doubt it. As soon as the hockey season is over, Cindy will probably dump Jeffrey.

Jeffrey called Wally. It was late, and Wally was sleeping. Jeffrey said to a sleepy Wally. "I had a great time tonight. I asked

Cindy if I could get tickets for the rest of the hockey season will she would go with me. She said yes. Can I buy your luxury box seats from you?"

A sleepy Wally said, "Jeffrey that won't be necessary. I'm too busy to go to the games this year. I have two luxury box seats reserved for you for next hockey season. Did you see Samantha, Richard Kiley or my aunt and uncle at the game? They own the other box seats."

Jeffrey told Wally that he didn't see them at the game, their seats were empty. If they do show up, he will say hello. Wally hung up the phone and went back to sleep.

Jeffrey arrived home. Christine was waiting for him. "Mother, we had a great time. Cindy loves hockey and Wally gave me his season tickets. I'm taking Cindy to the next home game next week."

Christine was smiling. "Jeffrey, why don't you ask Cindy out this week? I can get you tickets to the ballet this Friday." Jeffrey told his mother that Cindy loves hockey. He didn't think that she would be interested in going to the ballet.

Christine was still smiling. "Jeffrey, why don't you call Cindy. You never know. She might surprise you and want to see the ballet with you. Please call her tomorrow."

The next day Jeffrey was sitting in his office. He was nervous. Jeffery called Cindy. He asked Cindy if she wanted to go to the ballet this Friday night with him. His mother has tickets. He also mentioned that they could have dinner. Jeffrey couldn't believe that Cindy accepted his invitation to go to the ballet. He ran out of his office to see Christine. "Mother, I can't believe it, Cindy accepted my invitation to go to the ballet!"

Christine gave Jeffrey a hug. "I think it's time for you to get a new suit. You lost a lot of weight and your clothes are getting too big for you. We will go shopping this afternoon for a new suit. You want to impress Cindy, don't you?"

Cindy called Harry. "Father, I can't believe it. Jeffrey just called me. He invited me to go to the ballet with him this Friday night. His mother has tickets but can't go." Harry asked Cindy if she was going to go to the ballet with him.

Cindy said, "I thought about it and decided why not. Jeffrey is taking me out to dinner before the ballet. This gives me a good excuse to get my hair done and buy a new dress."

Harry called Mary to let her know that Cindy was going to the ballet with Jeffrey. Mary was confused, "Harry, I've been trying to get Cindy to go to the ballet with me for years. She has no interest in ballet. Do you think Cindy will have a serious relationship with Jeffrey?" Harry told Mary that it was quite possible. "Cindy is getting her hair done and will buy a new dress."

Mary was still confused. "Harry, I thought that you said that Cindy hated Jeffrey." Harry smiled. "That was before Jeffrey had terminal colon cancer. Somehow, Wally cured him. Jeffrey lost a lot of weight. I don't hear him using foul language or losing his temper anymore. He stays away from his father and gets along with everyone in the office."

Friday night Jeffrey picked up Cindy at her home. He was surprised to see that Cindy had her hair done and wore a beautiful dress. "Cindy, you look fabulous."

Cindy smiled, "Jeffrey, ever since you lost weight, you became a handsome looking man. You look smashing in your new suit."

Jeffrey drove Cindy to the Spencers Mill. Jeffrey looked at the menu. "They have potato dumplings, spicy cabbage and pork back ribs. That's my mother's favourite. She orders that a lot. Do you want to try it?" Cindy wanted to try it. Jeffrey ordered it.

Cindy was puzzled and said, "The Jeffrey that I know is fat, cheap and has a foul mouth and a bad temper. The Jeffrey that I'm looking at now is slim, handsome, not cheap and is a perfect gentleman. Did you die and get reincarnated?"

Jeffrey laughed. "Not quite. When I was diagnosed with terminal colon cancer, my mother took me to see Wally. It was a good thing that she did. Wally taught me how to pray, meditate, eat properly and exercise. Mother made sure that I did everything that Wally instructed me to do."

Cindy asked Jeffrey if that was all that Wally did to cure him of colon cancer. Jeffery laughed again, "No, but it did help. Wally offered me to take an herbal remedy. Some of the herbs are poisonous. He said that these herbs will either cure me or kill me. I decided to take the herbal remedy. For three days I was in incredible pain. I kept thinking of you all that time. That thought saved my life."

Cindy smiled. "Jeffrey, that was so sweet of you for thinking of me. I'm very happy that you survived." Jeffrey and Cindy enjoyed their dinner and left for the ballet. During the ballet Jeffrey held Cindy's hand. He didn't say a word while watching the ballet. Cindy told Jeffrey that she enjoyed watching the ballet. She thanked him for taking her. Jeffrey told Cindy that anytime that she wants to go to the ballet, let him know. His mother can always get tickets.

Jeffrey drove Cindy home. Her parents were waiting for her. Cindy told them that she enjoyed dinner and the ballet. She also mentioned that Jeffrey was a perfect gentleman. Christine was waiting for Jeffrey to get home. He told her that the both of them enjoyed dinner and the ballet.

Chapter 95

Wally and Elizabeth drove to the Fuls brewery to see how the expansion for the cream ale was coming. Kevin told Wally that construction started and it wouldn't take long. The equipment will arrive in two weeks. By the time the construction will be finished, Fuls cream ale will be ready for the market. Wally was pleased that everything was going as planned. Wally and Elizabeth decided that it was time to drive home.

Wally and Elizabeth arrived home. Elizabeth went to see Grandmother, Daniel, and Sarah. Grandfather was walking Cleo, Leo, and Orval into the trails. Wally went to get the mail. A letter from the United States military was addressed to him. It said that Col. Samuel Bung requested his services. He was to report to an address that Wally was very familiar with. The letter said that criminal charges would be brought against him if he failed to show up.

Wally was to report to a government owned house located in the forest behind the parquet. The house that Cleo and Leo barked like crazy every time they went near it. He was supposed to report next Tuesday night at 7 o'clock. Sounded like another one of the Government human experiments that Wally had to attend. Wally didn't tell Elizabeth. He didn't want to upset her.

Wally called Louis to ask him if Amy was available to play chess with him tonight. Louis told Wally that Amy was always available to play chess with him at any time. She was anxious for a rematch. Wally told Louis to tell Amy that he will be seeing her tonight.

Louis told Wally that he would be cheering him on. He hopes that he beats Amy. She improved a lot. Amy is the only other person that Louis can never beat. No one else in the chess club could beat her. Wally told Louis that he would not disappoint him. He needed Amy's services again.

Wally hated to lie to Elizabeth. He told her that Uncle Ivan needed help right away. Wally drove off to the chess club. Amy was anxiously waiting for him. Louis led Wally to Amy's table. Everyone in the club stood around to watch. Amy was ready for Wally. He found out that Amy had improved her chess game a lot. It took almost two hours to beat her.

Amy was very upset. "Wally, Louis tells me that you never practice and only play chess when he comes over. How is it possible that you can beat me?" Wally told Amy that he remembered a few good moves and the rest was luck. Amy didn't believe Wally and knew that he would not show her his few good moves. "Wally, what do you want hacked?"

Wally showed Amy the letter from the military. She read it. "Wally, this is another government agency. I bet they do human experiments. Let's go to my place. This will be tough to hack; there was no name of the government agency in the letter. It took Amy just over two hours to find out what Wally wanted to know. She printed out the information.

Amy looked at Wally, shaking her head. "Col. Samuel Bung is in charge of a military mind control agency. They use experiments that the Nazis developed before World War II. A person is exposed to massive psychological and physical trauma, which causes their minds to be shattered into hundreds of personalities, which can be separately programmed to perform any job or function that the programmer wishes. Each altered personality can be brought to the surface using special codes by the programmer with a laptop."

Wally couldn't believe what the government was doing. First, they wanted him to become a Frankenstein freak. Now, they want him to become a zombie slave.

Louis saw Wally looking at him. "I guess you want me to torch the house without starting a forest fire. I can do that. Just show me where the house is. Wally, you don't have to pay me. Watching you beat Amy is payment enough."

Wally was happy to have Louis as a friend. His appointment with the Col. was in three days. Wally will be showing the house to Louis tomorrow night.

When Louis saw the house, he said. "Wally, torching this house will be a piece of cake. I'll be ready for your signal just like before."

Tuesday night, Wally drove Louis to the house a half hour before his appointment. Wally took out a pair of wire cutters to cut a hole in the fence so Louis could get near the house. Wally watched Louis as he prepared to torch a house. Louis will be ready to receive Wally's signal. Wally set his phone to video record.

Wally knocked on the front gate. It opened, and Wally drove in. The front door of the house opened. He was greeted by a huge gorilla-faced man and a scrawny little man. The scrawny little man said, "Good evening, Mr. Kozak. I'm very pleased that you decided to come. We waited a very long time to recruit you. My name is Sidney Dinkeldorf, and this is my assistant Clyde. He'll make sure that you won't run away." Wally shook Sydney's hand to get as much information as he could.

Wally asked Sydney "Where is Colonel?" He smiled. "The Col. was detained. He is not coming tonight. It's only the three of us tonight. He doesn't need to be here." Wally was not smiling and asked Sydney what he was going to do with him.

Sydney was still smiling. "Mr. Kozak, I will slowly transform you into a highly skilled special soldier," Wally asked Sydney, "What if he didn't want to become a highly skilled special soldier?

Sydney kept on smiling. "Mr. Kozak, you have no choice. Since we recruited you, it's your duty as an American citizen to serve your country." Wally shouted. "I don't need to become a zombie slave to serve my country!" Wally jumped up and gave Clyde a kick in the chest. He fell down. Wally ran out the front door, giving Louis the signal to torch the house. Louis set the house on fire. Sydney and Clyde were trapped inside.

Wally and Louis watched the burning house. Louis said, "Wally, isn't the fire beautiful? Not a single tree is burning." When they heard the fire trucks, Wally drove Louis home. After Wally dropped Louis off, he called his cousin Sergei to hire an assassin and a safecracker. All the files on Col. Bung's mind control program were in a safe at his home. Wally found this out by reading Sydney's mind.

Sergei was pleasantly surprised to hear from Wally. "It's nice to hear from you, cousin Wally. What can I do for you?" Wally told Sergei that he wanted to hire an assassin and a safecracker. He told him that he had enough funds available. Sergei told Wally that the safecracker would cost him as much as an assassin. Wally told Sergei that he could afford to hire both.

Sergei said, "Wally, you know what to do. Make the e-money transfer and give me all the information." Wally made the e-money transfer and gave Sergei Col. Samuel Bung's home address. Wally said, "The safecracker needs to gain access to a safe hidden in a wall. He is to destroy all documents that are in it. Any money or jewellery that he finds, he can keep. Can you make the Col.'s death look like an accident?"

Sergei said to Wally, "No problem, it was nice doing business with you. I hope we can meet under different circumstances." Wally thanked Sergei. He will sleep well tonight.

Two days later, Wally read in the newspaper that Col. Samuel Bung was found dead on his living room floor. An autopsy revealed that he died of a heart attack. When Wally arrived at his office, he found Don Jordan waiting for him.

Don Jordan was very upset. "Wally, Col. Samuel Bung was a friend of mine. There's no way that he died of a heart attack. He was a health nut. I also found out that the Col.'s safe had all the contents removed. My gut tells me that you were responsible. Wally, don't lie to me; please tell me the truth!"

Wally told Don all about Col. Samuel Bung's government mind control program. He showed Don Amy's printout and the video that he had taken before the house was burned down. Wally then showed Don the letter he received saying that he must report to Col. Samuel Bung's agency. "All the files on Col. Bung's mind control program were in his safe. I have a list of all the people that the colonel recruited." Don took the list from Wally. He didn't ask Wally how he got the list.

After Don saw the video and read the letter, he took a deep breath and said, "Wally, you deserve a medal. I can't believe that our government is forcing innocent civilians to endure such hideous experiments. The FBI will keep an eye on the recruits. Let's have lunch. I'm buying it."

Chapter 96

Jeffrey was seeing Cindy after the hockey season. He took her to dinner and a movie or dinner and a concert every week. Jeffrey was in love with Cindy and wanted to marry her. He went to see his mother to ask for advice. Christine said, "Jeffrey, keep on doing what Wally told you to do. Keep saying your prayers, meditate, eat right, and exercise. You said that you are taking Cindy to dinner on her birthday next week. Go buy her an engagement ring and propose to her."

Jeffrey shook his head. "Mother, I don't know. What if she turns me down? She may not want to go out with me anymore?" Christine was getting annoyed. Jeffrey, you lost a lot of weight and gained a lot of muscle. You are a very handsome young man. Tomorrow we will go to the jewellers. I'll help you pick out a ring." The next day Jefrey and his mother rent to the jewellers.

Jeffrey was nervous. He was glad that his mother came to the jewellers with him. He told his mother that he was too nervous to choose a ring. Christine chose a very expensive, beautiful ring for Jeffrey. He was shocked to see such a ring.

Saturday night, Jeffery was having dinner at the Spencers Mill. It was Cindy's birthday. Jeffrey ordered prime rib and lobster. During dinner, Jeffrey started to sweat. Cindy looked at him and said, "Jeffrey, is something wrong?" Jeffrey closed his eyes, held his breath, and slowly said, "Cindy, I have a special birthday gift for you. I'm afraid that you might not like it."

Cindy was getting anxious. "Jeffrey, don't just sit there; show me the gift that you have for me." Jeffrey slowly took a very small box out of his pocket and gave it to Cindy. When Cindy opened it, she was shocked. "Jeffrey, this is such a beautiful diamond ring. You caught me by surprise; I don't know what to say."

Uncle Ivan was watching Jeffrey propose to Cindy. He walked over to their table and bent down to whisper into Cindy's ear. "Cindy, don't be a fool. Jeffrey loves you. This could be your last chance for happiness." Cindy put the ring on her finger and said, "Yes, Jeffrey, I will marry you." Everyone in the restaurant gave them a standing ovation.

Jeffrey and Cindy were blushing. Jeffrey paid for dinner and quickly left with Cindy. On their way home, neither one of them said anything. Cindy didn't bother kissing Jeffrey good night. She just walked inside the house without saying a word. Her parents were watching. They noticed that something was bothering Cindy. Harry asked her what happened. Cindy held up her hand to show her parents the engagement ring.

Cindy said, "Jeffrey surprised me on my birthday. He proposed marriage. I was shocked and ready to turn him down. Ivan saw Jeffrey proposing to me. He whispered in my ear and said that I would be a fool to turn Jeffrey down. I don't know why, but I did say yes."

Harry and Mary jumped in joy. Cindy was overwhelmed and told Harry that she changed her mind. She doesn't want to marry Jeffrey. Harry put his hands on Cindy's shoulder. "Honey, if you don't marry Jeffrey, you will end up as an old maid. You said that you enjoy his company and find him attractive. Tell me, why don't you want to marry him?"

Cindy started to cry. "I don't know." Harry gave Cindy a hug. "It seems to me that you love Jeffrey but are afraid to admit it. Don't worry; lots of people are afraid to admit that they're in love, and you will have plenty of emotional support. Wally transformed Jeffrey from an overbearing foul-mouth slob to a handsome, loving person. All the wedding arrangements will be taken care of by us and Christine."

Jeffrey walked into the house. Christine saw Jeffrey sweating. She said, "Jeffrey, did Cindy turn you down? She would be a fool if she did." Jeffrey was still sweating. "Mother, when I proposed to

Cindy, I wanted her to say no. Ivan whispered something in her ear, and she said yes."

Christine jumped for joy. She hugged Jeffrey and said, "Jeffrey, you don't know how happy you made me. Who is going to be your best man? I think Wally is the obvious choice. Elizabeth should be the maid of honour. You better call Wally tomorrow morning!"

Jeffrey said, "Mother, don't you think we should tell Father, do you know where he is?" Christine pressed her lips together. "Jeffrey, I don't know where he is, and I don't care. He's probably somewhere in bed with some young floozy. I don't want him to be at your wedding. I don't think that he cares if you ever get married. You need a cup of chamomile tea to calm you down before you go to bed."

Early the next morning, Jeffrey showered and got dressed. Christine called Wally and handed the phone to Jeffrey. Wally answered, "Good morning, Jeffrey; what can I do for you?"

Jeffrey took a deep breath and said, "Wally, last night was Cindy's birthday. I proposed to her, and she said yes. I want you to be the best man."

Wally was very surprised. "Congratulations, Jeffrey. I am happy for you, and it will be a pleasure to be your best man. Who will be Cindy's maid of honour, when is the wedding, and where will it be held?"

Jeffrey said, "Wally, I don't know who the maid of honour will be, but I hope Cindy chooses Elizabeth. My mother and Cindy's parents are making their wedding arrangements. A date hasn't been set yet. I would like to get married at Spencers Mill just like you and Elizabeth did. Do you think Elizabeth would want to be Cindy's maid of honour?" Wally told Jeffrey that if he was going to be his best man, Elizabeth would definitely want to be the maid of honour. "Jeffrey, I will tell Elizabeth the good news."

Wally received another call. It was Katie calling to remind him of his appointment to film a Fuls beer commercial for cream ale tonight at 8 o'clock at her modelling school. Wally thanked Katie for the reminder and went to see Elizabeth. Wally walked into her office and said, "Elizabeth, guess what? Jeffrey and Cindy are getting married. He wants me to be the best man, and Cindy wants you to be the maid of honour."

Elizabeth was annoyed. "Wally, that is a very stupid joke. Cindy hates Jeffrey!"

Wally smiled. "Elizabeth, the Jeffrey that you know is not the same Jeffrey that will marry Cindy. You haven't seen him since we got married. Jeffrey has lost a lot of weight and gained muscle. He prays and meditates every day, eating right and exercising. Jeffrey can control his foul mouth and bad temper. He loves Cindy."

Elizabeth ran out of her office to see Cindy. She said, "Cindy, Wally tells me that you are engaged to Jeffrey. Are you out of your mind!"

Cindy smiled. "Elizabeth, it must have been a long time since you saw Jeffrey. He lost a lot of weight; he is handsome and is a gentleman. Jeffrey loves me." Elizabeth couldn't believe what she was about to say. "Wally tells me that Jeffrey wants him to be his best man, and you want me to be your maid of honour."

Cindy took a deep breath and said, "Elizabeth, I know that we are not the best of friends, but I do want you to be my maid of honour." Elizabeth gave Cindy a big hug and told her that she would be happy to be her maid of honour.

Elizabeth went back to Wally's office. She told Wally that she gave Cindy a big hug and told her that she would be happy to be her maid of honour. Wally told Elizabeth that Katie called to remind him that he had an appointment tonight at her modelling school to film a Fuls cream ale commercial. "Are you coming to watch?" Elizabeth gave Wally a kiss and said, "You bet I am."

Wally was very happy. His mother was right. ***"Good health, Good friends = Good life"***

www.ingramcontent.com/pod-product-compliance
Lightning Source LLC
Chambersburg PA
CBHW062112290726
48975CB00001B/200